Also by Paula Dáil

Uneasy States of Grace

A Widow of the Roman Church

Memories of You

Women and Poverty in 21st Century America

Hard Living in America's Heartland:
21st Century Rural Poverty

Mother Nature's Daughters:
21st Century Women Farmers

We Rise to Resist:
Voices from a New Era in Women's Political Action

*Fearless

* Republished as *Outrage: Sister Molly Cleary vs. The Catholic Church*
under the pen name Avery Michael

Praise for Paula Dáil's Other Books

Fearless is an emotional roller coaster that contains an amazing message: no matter the circumstances, if someone is dedicated and courageous enough, they can use their voice to stand up for their rights and succeed. *Literary Titan Gold Star Winner Book Review*

Inspired by the collective stories of real women, *Fearless* is an insightful, captivating, and sometimes harrowing novel about the pursuit of greater equality, justice, and reproductive rights for women. *Readers' Choice Silver Star Award Book Review.*

I cannot express how much I loved *Fearless*. Kudos to Paula Dail for weaving research so beautifully into an engaging and unique plot. This novel proved to be far from just an interesting story with an unforgettable protagonist. This is a thinker's book and for those with inquiring minds, a "must read." *Readers' Favorite five-star review by Viga Boland*

Released at a time when women in the United States are fighting for their reproductive rights and their rights as humans, *Fearless* is the perfect story to remind people some things are worth fighting for… and how deep this issue is in society. The message to fight until your last breath will live on forever. *Readers' Favorite five-star review by Rabia Tanveer*

Fearless is an astute and heartfelt examination of the role of women in society and the Catholic Church. Books with these kinds of empowering, realistic messages are much needed in the oppressive world of fake news and false rhetoric we live in. The development of the dialogue and the emotional portrayal of the characters through their words and actions was superbly well done. *Readers' Favorite five-star review by K.C. Finn*

Dáil creates a story unlike anything you'd expect. I opened *Fearless* expecting a soft launch of a slightly feminist nun, but Dail creates something much bigger that inspires serious reflection. *Five-star Independent Book Review by Jaylynn Korrell*

Fearless will inspire serious reflection in readers and push them to question what they believe. You will be entertained, inspired, and then you will think, realistically, about one of the most controversial topics that is the highlight of discussion in American politics. *The Book Commentary five-star review by: Romuald Dzemo*

—

Paula Dáil has written an incredible masterpiece… an empowering book that is guaranteed to wake the feminist inside you. *Goodreads five-star review*

—

For every person who railed in private or public protest against assaults on our nation's cherished institutions, Dáil *[We Rise to Resist: Voices from a New Era in Women's Political Action]* provides essential validation, affirming that dissent eventually works and that one's outrage need not be in vain. *Booklist starred review by Carol Haggas*

—

Paula Dáil's riveting descriptions and accounts of the lives of women living in poverty in America will cause everyone who reads *Women and Poverty in 21st Century America* to rethink our social policies and priorities. C*ouncil for Wisconsin Writers 2012 August Derleth-Kenneth Kingery Non-Fiction Book of the Year Award review*

—

Mother Nature's Daughters: 21st Century Women Farmers is such an enticing read it made me want to become one. C*ouncil for Wisconsin Writers 2016 August Derleth-Norbert Bly Non-Fiction Book of the Year Award review*

—

Outrage (written under pen name Avery Michael) We need more books like this! *BookFest Second Place Award,* October, 2024

RED ANEMONES
כלניות אדומות

A Story of Struggle, Resilience, and Hope

Paula Dáil

HISTORIUM PRESS

Copyright © 2025 by Paula Dáil

All rights reserved. No part of this book may be reproduced or transmitted in any form or by any means, electronic or mechanical, including photocopying, recording, or by any information storage and retrieval system, without written permission from the publisher.

This is a work of fiction. All characters, locations and events in the narrative – other than those based on actual people – are products of the author's imagination and are used fictitiously. Any resemblance to real persons, living or dead, is entirely coincidental and not intended by the author. Where real historical figures, locations and events appear, these have been depicted in a fictional context.

No Generative AI Training Use.

For avoidance of doubt, Author reserves the rights, and **NO outside source (online or in print)** has rights to, can reproduce and/or otherwise use the Work in any manner for purposes of training artificial intelligence technologies to generate text, including without limitation, technologies that are capable of generating works in the same style or genre as the Work, unless outside source (online or in print) obtains Author's specific and express permission to do so. Nor does any outside source (online or in print) have the right to sublicense others to reproduce and/or otherwise use the Work in any manner for purposes of training artificial intelligence technologies to generate text without Author's specific and express permission.

Visit Historium Press at
www.historiumpress.com

Library of Congress Cataloging-in-Publication Data on file
Copyright Registration on file

Paperback ISBN: 978-1-964700-37-3
E-Book ISBN: 978-1-964700-38-0

I am a Jew. Hath not a Jew eyes? Hath not a Jew hands, organs, dimensions, senses, affections, passions; fed with the same food, hurt with the same weapons, subject to the same diseases, healed by the same means, warmed and cooled by the same winter and summer as a Christian is? If you prick us, do we not bleed? If you tickle us, do we not laugh? If you poison us, do we not die? And if you wrong us, shall we not revenge?
William Shakespeare
The Merchant of Venice (3.1.49-61)

The Priestly Benediction over the Jewish People

!עליך וישמור יברכך הנצח
!ובחן בחביבות עמך ינהג הנצח
!שלום לך ויעניק אלוהי חן לך יעניק הנצחי

The Eternal bless you and protect you!
The Eternal deal kindly and graciously with you!
The Eternal bestow [divine] favor upon you and grant you peace!

–Numbers 6: 24-26; Book Four of the Torah

Dedication
הַקְדָשָׁה

To my courageous maternal great-grandmother, Bertha Michael. She had no way to know her decision to leave Germany for America as a young woman, traveling alone into an unknowable future, preserved an ancestral bloodline and heritage that eventually passed to me. All indications are that those of her family who remained behind in Germany perished either during or in the aftermath of World War I, or in the Holocaust. If Bertha had not undertaken her brave winter journey across the treacherous Atlantic, I wouldn't be writing this story.

And to Bertha's granddaughter, Gladys Bertha Wende, my caring, dedicated maternal aunt. She taught me how to knit when I was five years old, giving me both enduring love and a skill that guaranteed my sanity for the rest of my life.

May their memories be for a blessing.

Author's Preface
הקדמת המחבר

I come from a small family. As a result, I have never been particularly interested in genealogy or learning more about my ancestors because, as far as I know, there aren't many of them. Then, one rainy Sunday afternoon during the COVID-19 crisis, for reasons that remain a mystery, I decided to do a little ancestral internet sleuthing.

Working backward from what little I knew about my mother's family, I was astonished to discover that my maternal great-grandmother, Bertha Michael, had immigrated to America from Germany early in the last century, passing through Ellis Island ten days after leaving Bremerhaven, Germany. According to the ship's manifest, she traveled second class rather than steerage, which suggests she was not a poor immigrant escaping a pogrom to seek a better life in America; instead, she came for some other reason, perhaps one involving a man and love.

I never knew Bertha and have never seen a picture of her or her only child, a daughter who was my grandmother. I never heard either of them mentioned by name, yet what I discovered about Bertha was so captivating it compelled me to keep going.

Ultimately, I learned that Michael is a Hebrew name, and that four hundred forty-six records containing information about individuals bearing this surname end in the Holocaust death records. After further investigation, I determined it was likely that forty-nine of these individuals, including Minna Michael, who was euthanized in a home for the disabled operated by the Catholic Church, were possibly either directly or distantly related to my great-grandmother and, by extension, to me.

I sat with the emotional chaos this horrifying realization induced for more than a month, allowing it free rein to sort itself out. Depending on the moment, I was smiling proudly at my newly discovered heritage, overwhelmed with questions about why neither my mother or her sister ever admitted to a Jewish lineage, outraged at the suffering Jews have endured across the centuries, or generally upset about being thrown into a life-changing orbit I had no idea how to navigate. I was flooded with gratitude, drained by anger, and grieving the likelihood of a family that, if Hitler hadn't had his way, I could've known. Sometimes, the staggering impact of the new reality that had descended upon my life left me feeling dizzy and disoriented – like I was riding a tilt-a-whirl on the midway at the county fair.

A cloud of melancholy settled over me. I became profoundly lonely for a great-grandmother I never knew, an ancestral story I would never hear, and a family Bertha left behind when she came to America, whose descendants, as far as I could tell, no longer existed. Most of all, I will never know how much of her lives on in me.

Despite all this, learning I was a matrilineal Jew confirmed something I'd suspected for a long time and had hard evidence to support, but had never taken the time to explore. I've always been deeply drawn to the Jewish culture, traditions, and beliefs about G-d, and in many ways finding out there was a reason for this strong attraction released a deep exhale. Finally, I understood why, each year, without knowing why, I felt compelled to drive thirty-five miles to the nearest synagogue to observe Yom HaShoah, Holocaust Remembrance Day. I had a better grasp on my chronic thirst for knowledge about Jewish history, faith, and culture that, for years, I'd been quenching with books, lectures, movies, and sometimes instructional classes. I was coming home to myself in a way that finally made sense. Ever so slowly, the heavy burden of unknowing began lifting from my shoulders.

Becoming even slightly acquainted with my great-grandmother also propelled me into an entirely different way of being in the world. Despite the sparse details of her life available to me, there was no way I could just write her off as some obscure relative I'd never known. Without sounding too dramatic, I felt like I had been presented with a sacred challenge to configure a story about Bertha's life, and the complicated legacy she bestowed upon her daughters and granddaughters, with reverence and care. From that moment forward, this story owned me.

Fortunately, I already had something to work with. I'd spent a lot of time in Germany, even in the town Bertha identified as home, although I did not know that at the time. I'd paid my respects at Auschwitz and spent time in Israel at a time when Syria was routinely bombing the Golan Heights. I remained at the Holocaust Museum until my stomach demanded I leave and spent an entire day at Ellis Island. Being a native Californian, I also knew a lot about that location as the setting for the story.

Normally writing, while not without its struggles, comes naturally to me. But not this time. The challenges I faced as I began putting Bertha's story into words blindsided me. I struggled with the thought that I was too emotionally involved to write a story like this one. I wondered if my inherited German-Welsh tendency to not express every emotion I feel, in as many words as possible, was the barrier I was unable to overcome. Maybe my commitment to the story was interfering with my ability to be the instrument through which the story could tell itself and I was trying to control it too much. Maybe non-fiction writers can't transform themselves into novelists.

Eventually, I decided the most authentic way to write my great-grandmother's story was to not overthink it and, instead, be faithful to who I am as her great-granddaughter. She would want me to chronicle how I imagined her life in ways that convey what she experienced but not emotionalize her suffering too much. She was a Jew; she accepted suffering as her inherited destiny and endeavored to make the best of her life anyway. She resolved to endure whatever came her way with dignity and as little wallowing as possible – a legacy I am deeply grateful for. She would not want her life portrayed as an emotional quagmire; she would want it to be a clear statement of strength, determination, and forbearance in a world that did not value or respect her as a child of G-d, a daughter of Avraham and Sarah, or as the human being she was.

Some would say that this story should be labeled a fictionalized memoir, or a fictionalized autobiography, but I've never understood what those terms mean. It is a novel inspired by a true story about a very courageous woman who left the home and family she loved dearly to embark upon a journey into the unknown. She landed in America unable to speak the language or understand the customs yet willingly faced whatever challenges awaited her in what, for Jews, proved to be one of the darkest eras in both American and world history.

As I am completing this book, written a century after Bertha lived, the current American president has been in office for six months. His administrative style favors loyalty over competence, lying over truth attacking the judiciary and ignoring the rule of law, military dominance, and silencing anyone who disagrees with him by whatever means possible. He mobilized the military against American citizens exercising their constitutional right to protest in Los Angeles, America's second largest city, and is using gestapo techniques to rid the nation everyone who is not a white nationalist.

To this end, he is rounding up immigrants and other non-citizens, even those who are in the country legally, and deporting them, without due process, to nations known for their torture techniques and human rights violations. Neither the Congress nor the Supreme Court of the United States, as co-equal branches of our democratic form of government, have mounted a serious effort to stop him.

There are many who want to deny the genocide of six million Jews in Fascist Germany nearly a century ago and turn a blind eye to the pervasive antisemitism that surrounded those who survived. History denied is destined to become history repeated. If what is happening in America today reminds readers of Fascist Germany in the 1930's and 1940's, you would not be wrong. If you are deeply frightened by what is happening in America today, you are not alone. Your concerns are valid.

Meanwhile, half a world away, Israeli Prime Minister Benjamin Netanyahu's response to the 7 October 2023 Hamas attack against Israel has resulted in over 55,000 civilian deaths in Gaza.

While nearly all Jews support Israel's right to exist and to defend itself, most strongly oppose Netanyahu's protracted "killing ants with a steamroller" war policy and deeply grieve the carnage he has wrought. On 21 November 2024, the International Criminal Court issued an arrest warrant for Netanyahu, accusing him of war crimes and crimes against humanity. While I firmly believe in and fully support the State of Israel, I also firmly believe this action against its current leader is justified. Netanyahu's war tactics are morally wrong and have resulted in far, far too many innocent civilian casualties.

I eagerly join with Jews worldwide who are honoring the Talmud mandate to not ignore the wrongs they see around them and are demanding this war end. Massive humanitarian aid to Gaza must begin immediately and, like many other Jews, I have personally taken action to support this effort.

The title of this story is taken from Israel's national flower, the red anemone. This small blossom is laden with spiritual meaning for the people of the five-thousand-year Diaspora: protection from harm; resiliency and embracing the changes that lead to new beginnings; anticipation and hope; and life's fleeting nature. Some say the red anemone also symbolizes love and passion. In my mind, all of these embody the Jewish story across history, and I hope the tiny piece of Jewish experience this story reveals honors that history and inspires a heart-felt, passionate commitment to work tirelessly to bend the long, slow arc of justice further toward empathy, compassion, equality and freedom not just for Jews, but for all people.

Prologue
פרולוג

Hildesheim, Germany
Summer, 1910

Gain and loss are the two sides of the same coin.

"Nathalie, my beloved daughter... by G-d's blessing, you are beginning the third decade of life, and your brother, Levi, is well into his fourth. I am becoming an old man fortunate enough to see his dear children into adulthood, and now, the time has come to be thinking of grandchildren," Papa tells me, fingering his tzitzit, which he wears only when he is praying or distressed. This father-daughter conversation, which we have repeated many times over the last months, always distresses him.

The sweet smell of blooming summer in the sprawling riverside gardens wrap around us as we sit side-by-side, quiet and still, staring straight ahead. From a distance, we are two solitary figures resting on a wooden bench near a small pond, no more than a shallow widening along the gently flowing Innerste River. Papa throws breadcrumbs to the ducks patrolling the riverbank, and I attempt to hold onto the hat shading my face despite the breeze off the water. The occasional fluffy white cloud passing overhead offers a brief respite from the summer sun. Minutes go by without a word from either of us, until finally, I respond.

"Don't worry so much, Papa. Levi is now married and living in a nice apartment on Lindenstrasse. He and Irina will be giving you grandchildren soon," I remind him again, as I have done every time my future comes up for discussion, which is too often.

"It is not the same. Our Jewish bloodline passes through the mother. This is not your brother's responsibility. You bear the special obligation bestowed only upon daughters. You cannot ignore this destiny." I remain silent, watching the ducks tease each other, then my father, as they beg for more crumbs.

"You are too much your mother's daughter – in looks and skill in the art of communication through silence," Papa simultaneously frowns and chuckles, pushing upward on his wire-rimmed glasses, resting so far down his nose they are in danger of falling all the way off his face. He often compares me to my mother, claiming my structured features, hazel-blue eyes and thick chestnut hair, easily streaked gold by the summer sun, offers what he lovingly describes as "a breathless image of your mother's graceful beauty" that caused him, as a young civil engineering student, to immediately fall in love for the first and only time in his life.

It is my good fortune that this vision, wrapped in treasured memory, opens his heart to forgiving what he calls "the modern ideas of my willful daughter," who, he is forced to admit, is on the brink of full womanhood. He insists I joyfully cultivate ideas intentionally conceived to upset him, because I know he will automatically resist. He is not wrong.

The humid summer heat soaks into his black suit, one of the two he wears year-round that are too warm in the summer and not warm enough in the winter. No matter the season, a broad-brimmed black hat futilely attempts to restrain his wildly unkempt hair. Neither the day, the weather, nor the occasion cause my father to vary his dress.

"Not having to decide what to wear each day simplifies life. It frees the mind to meditate on G-d... cultivating new ideas and attending to my music," he insists.

In addition to praying, my father teaches young men the engineering skills required to build roads and bridges and plays first violin in Hildesheim's symphony orchestra. He rises at five each morning to practice, which isn't an altogether bad way to wake up our household.

My mother, Sarah, and I see the clothing issue differently and enjoy dressing for the seasons. Tall and stately, with tastefully French sensibilities I am grateful I inherited, she brags that when my father proposed marriage, she insisted on certain conditions, one of them being that she would not be forced to give up the stylish dress she enjoys in favor of German practicality and the drab, poorly fitting garments expected of an observant Jewish wife.

"Mikael offered no disagreement on this issue," she proudly proclaims. Knowing that my father believes what he believes, and rarely entertains alternatives, I'm not sure this is an entirely true statement, but regardless, she prevailed.

Some weeks back, allowing my father's encouragement to override her daughter's objections, my mother called the matchmaker. After a lengthy discussion with my parents, the wizened old busybody, a self-appointed marriage expert despite never having been married herself, announced she was "fully prepared to find a match for Sarah and Mikael Weiss's lovely daughter, Nathalie." Later, after meeting with me alone, she reported to my parents that I am "a little strong-willed, with my own mind, so a match may be difficult".

"You think I do not know this?" my father replied, throwing his hands in the air. This was the only thing I found amusing about the entire plan my parents and the matchmaker conspired to set into motion.

"I told Maman I'm not interested in marriage," I remind my father again, using the French familiar form of mother, in deference to her origins near Strasbourg, on the French-German border.

"I said, don't bother with the matchmaker. Does she listen? No, Papa, she doesn't listen. Every time I say this, she says G-d only saw fit to give her one daughter, so of course she will bother. Why is no one listening to what I want?" I ask. In response, three ducks quack, begging from my father, who brought a bag of stale bread he pilfered from my mother's kitchen, hoping the ducks would distract him from what he knew would be a difficult conversation.

"Your mother wants you to have a husband and children... be happy like she is. And what message does it send when a devout Jew's daughter refuses marriage?" my father sighs, repeating a theme that has dominated our conversations for over a year.

"I don't want a husband and children – at least not yet. There are many ways to be happy, Papa, and I want to think about all of them. Maman's happiness is not necessarily my happiness," I answer, avoiding his concern about the entrenched social and religious expectations imposed upon a Jewish daughter.

"Every young woman wants children to mother and a husband to take care of – and to take care of her, Nathalie. This is a universal truth. Even if you think you are different, you are not. You don't want to die alone."

"Do I look like I am about to die? If so, it is a surprise to me," I point out, raising my voice a little higher than I intend. My father mindlessly throws more breadcrumbs to the ducks, who continue quacking.

"See the hem of my dress, Papa – how straight it is, how perfect the stitches. Women pay me money to make them clothes like this," I say, fingering the fine gauze skirt of the dress I made for myself over the previous months, purposely ignoring my father's mandate to find a husband and begin producing children.

"A husband is not necessary to my future – I can take care of myself." I point out.

"The mother creates the Jewish home and raises the children. Preserving this five-thousand-year-old tradition that keeps our culture and religion alive in this family falls to you, Nathalie. Put your strong head on the shelf because your mother is right – it is time for a husband. By your age, nearly all women are years married and already rearing children. You wait too long, and no one will be left to make a match – then what?" my father exasperates, throwing his hands in the air.

"You are telling me what is expected of me, not listening to what I want… what will make me happy with my life. You sound just like Maman… and I'm tired of hearing it," I say, making no attempt to mask my frustration with my father, whom I love so dearly. No matter how often this conversation occurs, as soon as I speak my own mind, he suddenly falls deaf as a rock and the only voice he hears is his own.

"Chasing happiness is chasing an illusion, dear daughter. Doing what is expected of you becomes your happiness. Anything else is frivolous fantasy that brings a lifetime of heartache. A good Jewish home is all that matters. Our people's survival depends upon this commitment. Nothing else is as important." Reaching for my father's hand, I assure him I love him very much, but just like his ears are deaf to my desires, my ears are deaf to his outdated ideas. Finding a husband and giving my parents grandchildren is very far from my twenty-year-old mind.

"You are just like your mother – a will of your own. This the burden G-d has given me to carry – two women who think for themselves… and G-d help me, I love them both," my gentle-natured father laments, while watching a hummingbird dart among bright red blossoms on the bush beside the bench.

"It falls to me to tell you the matchmaker has selected Eitan Rosenblum for you," my father continues, taking a very deep breath.

"And why didn't Maman tell me about this? Isn't it the mother's responsibility to prepare her daughter for marriage?" I ask, slightly insulted.

"She claimed you are less likely to overreact if you hear the words from me. I told her this was a false assumption, but she disagreed." I don't respond.

"She also said you already know him. Is this true?"

"I know who he is, which isn't the same as knowing him," I point out.

"And is he someone you can live with?"

"How can I know this when we are barely acquainted? I like him… and he is very handsome. But this doesn't mean I want to marry him," I reply, struggling to contain my frustration. My impression is that twenty-nine-year-old Eitan Rosenblum is strong, fit, learned, full of enthusiasm for life, and in need of a wife, which he has postponed taking on while he quenches his thirst for adventure. He recently returned from six months in Zurich where he studied in the mornings, skied in the afternoons, and still managed to earn a full certificate as a civil engineer. Before that, he studied first with my father at the polytechnic, then in Paris, then traveled around Italy, from the Mediterranean to the Adriatic, as a crew member on a sailing boat. Papa says all this running around means he is now ready to finally settle down and become serious about life.

"Such a speedy decision is a good sign," my father insists.

Later, when discussing Eitan's potential as a husband with Maman, I point out that I've never traveled any further than Berlin and suffer from wanderlust of my own. She dismisses me, saying this does not matter, because girls are not afflicted with the same desires as boys.

"The matchmaker says he became smitten with you immediately upon laying his eyes, deep brown and gentle like a milk cow, upon you," Maman tells me, ignoring my retort that eyes like a milk cow are not necessarily a positive trait.

Sooner than I wish, the matchmaker formally declares that Nathalie Rachael Weiss, daughter of Mikael Issac Weiss and Sarah Rebekkah Michel Weiss, and Eitan Noem Rosenblum, son of Naomi Miriam Singer Rosenblum and Sh'mul Avid Rosenblum, are a good match.

"Eitan is the last of Naomi and Sh'mul's sons without a wife to look after him. They are anxious to work something out, and your mother and I are agreeable to the marriage," my father declares.

"But I am not agreeable, Papa – at least not yet. I like Eitan, but he wants a marriage soon, and I am not ready. This is a problem – a very big, very serious problem."

"It is not an impossible problem to solve. A shtar tna'im…"

"Is a contract that makes it very difficult for me to change my mind," I interrupt.

"Difficult for either of you to change your mind, although I feel sure you are the only one thinking this way," my father says.

"Eitan has already agreed to the details Sh'mul and I have put into the shtar tn'am for the marriage, which you both can sign at the formal celebration."

"But I don't know that I am agreeable Papa, and I should not sign anything until I am ready. Love and marriage are a big responsibility. They cannot be taken lightly."

"Love? Who knows what love is, Nathalie? It is different for everyone. The most important thing is Eitan loves you. In the beginning, it is better when the man loves more than the woman. It means he will work hard to make her happy. You will not do better than Eitan, no matter how long you wait… and I don't want to die with my beloved daughter unmarried."

"You're not dying, Papa, and the possibility that you will die some day in the far future is no reason to rush me into a betrothal. I agree to this now, and Maman will go crazy planning a wedding. Next thing I know, I'm standing under the chuppah, even if I'm not ready to be there."

"Your brother and Irina have already made a baby. Planning for this will distract her while you get used to the idea of marriage."

"Already a baby? They only married a month, maybe two months ago. Now you have no worries about grandchildren, Papa. One is coming," I smile, recalling how my tall, dark-haired brother and his reed-slender, lively-eyed bride, with flowing black hair all the way down her back, turned heads at their wedding. Irina has never struck me as someone who would enthusiastically embrace motherhood, so this news surprises me.

"My son and his bride take marriage and making a family seriously. This is good, but the child is not of my daughter," my father exclaims, again referring to an obscure Jewish law to support his insistence that continuance of the family bloodline flows through his daughter, not his son.

Always welcoming an excuse to celebrate, my mother takes time out from her preparations for impending grandmotherhood to collaborate with Eitan's mother in planning an extravagant betrothal celebration for their children. They rent the spacious Burgerstrasse Halle near the city centre, and after inviting everyone they can possibly think of to join the celebration, enlist the help of the temple sisterhood to decorate and cook mountains of food. I do my best to ignore this chaos and avoid Maman's questions about the dress I will wear, how I will fix my hair, or other adornments I will choose. If I don't offer a satisfactory answer quickly enough, she reminds me that she will only be the mother of the bride once in her life, and she intends to make the most of the experience. I don't doubt this for a moment.

When the day of celebration finally arrives, I am surprisingly calm – a result of reminding myself at least a thousand times that this is not a marriage celebration – it is only celebrating an agreement to marry at a future time and does not require selecting an exact date, even though this is the first question every guest will ask me.

Following the blessings, Eitan, every inch a nervous bridegroom-to-be, stumbles through random, disconnected thoughts on the Torah, alarming my father, a prominent leader in Hildesheim's modest Jewish community. After five painful minutes listening to my future husband, who is also his future son-in-law, brutalize Hebrew as he quotes Torah, Papa interrupts to assure everyone present that he will tutor Eitan in both Torah and Hebrew, beginning at once.

This outburst is met with silence on Eitan's part, and coughs from everyone else, until our two mothers each break a plate, signaling the start of the celebration. My father picks up his violin and the music begins, followed by singing, dancing hora, and many l'chaim proclamations. The evening is, to my introverted way of thinking, too loud, lasts too long, and involves too many people eating too much food.

Early the next morning, I hear my father on the phone telling Eitan to meet him at Café Berliner on Friederichstrasse in one hour to begin Hebrew instructions. Apparently, Eitan objects until my father points out they serve the best jelly-filled donuts in Hildesheim. After he hangs up the phone and finds me standing in the doorway overhearing the conversation, my father frowns.

"Eitan could be a better Jew. So what if I have to bribe him with rich, delicious sufganiyah? At least he agrees to show up," Eitan's future father-in-law mumbles, reaching for his hat.

Further distressing my uncertain mind as I think about my future, Eitan begins speaking about going to America within days after our betrothal is made official. When Maman overhears this, she concludes the matchmaker betrayed her by giving her only daughter to the red-headed son of Vikings, the first inhabitants of the Jutland Peninsula where his family originates and only changed from Danish to German rule late in the last century. She takes to her bed, sobbing and refusing to speak. I don't like the idea of going to America either, but I find my mother's reaction overly dramatic, even for her.

"Not to worry, liebling; enjoy the silence. She will start speaking again soon enough," my father assures me, while waiting for me to make him a morning meal because he is too helpless to do it himself.

"Men can only eat, not cook," he proclaims when I suggest he make his own breakfast.

As the weeks pass, Eitan never misses an opportunity to remind me of the promises a future in America offers, which I don't necessarily believe are as exciting or as rewarding as he makes them out to be. I can't help recalling my mother's repeated warning, early in my teenage years, that when a man wants something from a woman, he says what he thinks the woman wants to hear so she will give in to him.

"Your Papa said a lot of things I knew weren't true… made promises I knew he'd never keep just to convince me to marry him, but I didn't care, because I loved him and wanted to marry him," my mother told me, wistfully remembering her earlier life as a young bride. Meanwhile, Eitan never misses an opportunity to tell me how much we have to look forward to in America, insisting that it will be a much better life than we enjoy now.

"Life is fine here, Eitan. Our families and lifelong friends surround us, no one goes hungry, we go to shul, and we enjoy connections with the wider community. This is as good as life gets," I counter.

"Political storm clouds are forming across Germany, Nathalie. Sooner or later, someone will get angry about something, start trouble, and blame the Jews... maybe not tomorrow, but something will happen eventually, and we will be forced to move on and start all over again. Waiting for this is no way to live. In America, it will be different... better," Eitan claims, as we walk along the path above the river. He stops to pick a stray flower, offering it to me along with his beautiful smile.

"Running away from something that could happen, but might not happen at all, doesn't make sense to me, Eitan. It is like moving away from a perfectly nice apartment because it might burn down, even though the building is solid stone and fireproof. Living life involves risk; we can't always be controlled by fear," I argue, sighing deeply. Eitan again recites his litany of reasons why America will be free of this worry. While I am growing more and more fond of my betrothed each day, I cannot agree with him that going to America is a good idea.

"If what you say is true and political problems are on Germany's horizon, I don't think abandoning our families to face these threats alone while we are far away in America frees us from anything. This is our home... our hearts will always be here, no matter if we are here or somewhere else," I counter, with growing suspicion that I will never win this argument.

"The Kaiser is power-hungry and will start a war just to show how big his muscles are. Pogroms are happening in Russia now, and the Kaiser and the Czar are in each other's pockets. Who knows what that means or how it will affect us as Jews?" Eitan continues. I remind him that Jews are deeply woven into the wider German community, so the Kaiser is unlikely to single them out and instead, will probably ignore us.

"No one here thinks of us as Jews, Eitan. We are ordinary people leading ordinary lives just like everyone else. No one will bother us."

"Maybe people here don't think of us as Jews, but they know we are Jews, Nathalie, and it's naïve to believe otherwise. The Catholics are starting the blood libel rumors again, and the Kaiser won't ignore this. He's look for any excuse to cause us trouble just to show the Czar they are on the same side... join forces and build a military. It's going to happen." With each word, Eitan becomes more animated.

"No one believes the myths about the blood rituals anymore, Eitan."

"Catholics believe what the priest says, and this always brings trouble for us," Eitan insists. Equally insistent, I disagree with him.

"You are unrealistic, Nathalie. You believe only the good in people, and people aren't always good. More often than not, they are bad toward others, especially if they see an advantage in it. This is right in front of you, and you refuse to look."

"Maybe you're right, Eitan, but what harm is there in believing people are basically good?"

"The harm is you can be hurt, because you aren't prepared to defend yourself… or you put yourself in harm's way without realizing it. Refusing to believe evil exists is an invitation for it to slap you in the face." Knowing history proves his point, I don't have a comeback.

"All you know is a loving family who lives a typical Jewish life. You observe the rituals and celebrate the holidays, listen to your father read Torah, and live in a world where everything is questioned… All Jews do is think and question, argue about whatever we are thinking and questioning, then eat and start all over again. It is a harmless life, and everyone enjoys themselves… but it never goes anywhere and can't last forever. Trouble always finds us," Eitan declares, running his hand through his curly hair.

"Everything you say about what might happen here is rumor, Eitan. It's better to ignore the gossip and pay attention to all we have to celebrate."

"We can't ignore the rumors, Nathalie. There is a reason they start. The Kaiser can't be trusted; both Jewish and non-Jewish Germans must live with whatever he does… and when it all goes wrong, Jews will be the favorite target for blame. It's always been that way, and nothing has happened to change it," he says, frowning as his eyes grow dark with worry.

"And still we survive. What you fear happening here is not a reason to disappear to America. Maybe it will happen someday, but that won't be for a long time, and what's to say America will be any better… any safer for us?"

"Jews have mitzvah obligations that include Tikkun Olam. We want to make the world better… make each day a push into a better future, and America needs that attitude as it grows. We will be welcome – you'll see."

"For someone who stumbled through Torah at our engagement, suddenly you are an observant Jew?" I say with a slightly sarcastic half-smile.

"America is expanding. It needs good labor to construct railroads, buildings, and streets. I don't think anyone cares where the men come from, what they believe about G-d, or what traditions they practice, as long as they work hard," Eitan answers, his exasperation with me leaking through his words. We stroll in sober silence, until I ask Eitan what his parents think about him going to America.

"My oldest brother is there now and earning so much money he sends some back. My parents believe all their sons will eventually travel to America."

"They're not upset?"

"If they are, they don't say anything to me about it. Maybe they will follow us – maybe not. Perhaps they can convince your parents to come with them. Who knows?"

"Maman will never leave her mother and her sisters… and my father will never leave the Jewish community here – they need him, and he needs them. If I go to America, I go alone, leaving behind any hope of ever seeing them again. It is a one-way journey into a vast unknown, Eitan and you must understand what you are asking of me. I am becoming very warm to a marriage with you, but it is very hard to say yes to the idea of America." When minutes go by and Eitan doesn't offer any more assurances, we say no more, leaving the issue to slowly fester between us.

Less than a week after the end of the High Holy Days, I accept Eitan's invitation to take a Sunday stroll on what may be one of the last pleasant afternoons before the icy fall rains begin. The city centre is busy with others enjoying the warm afternoon, and we are lucky to find an empty sidewalk table at Café Berliner. Eitan orders us coffee with fresh cream and two fat, rich sufganiyah bulging with sweet cherry filling.

We sit quietly, watching the people wander across the Kirchplatz, whose most impressive features are the large Lutheran church on one side, facing the even larger, more majestic Catholic church directly opposite. In between are shoppes and cafes, with apartments above. Occasionally, someone stops to feed the pigeons that scavenge among the cobblestones. Eventually, Eitan breaks our easy silence.

"I have been thinking about how difficult it is for you to go to American and think it will be easier if I go first, get a job, save money, find a good place to live, and then send for you. I can write letters about what life is like, so you'll know what to expect when you arrive. This is a good plan, Nathalie – it gives you and your parents more time to get used to the idea," he says, waiting for me to take the first bite of our sugar-encrusted donuts.

"I am their only daughter, Eitan. If I leave, who will look after them in their old age? Not my brother, who has a wife with a baby coming and a mind of her own that doesn't include worrying over my parents. Irina focuses only on herself." Taking a deep breath, I declare that the repeated America conversation is giving me a never-ending headache. Eitan groans in frustration. Again, he assures me he will do everything possible to make me a happy wife, and that he understands how difficult the decision to leave Germany is for me, but eventually I must choose between staying here or following him, because he is out of arguments trying to convince me that we can have a good life together in America.

"I am leaving the week following Passover. By then, I will have saved enough money for both of us to sail to America. I want you to come with me, but if you want me to go first, I will. All you have to agree to is coming later." This is the moment when Eitan's words penetrate my reluctance and sink into my heart, making me realize how much he loves me. I know there is no shortage of young women eager to marry who would never hesitate to say yes to going to America with Eitan, yet he is willing to accommodate my reluctance by going first and waiting for me to come later.

"I love you, Eitan, but I do not know if love is enough to sustain the life you seek and want me to join. Today, all I can promise you is that I will not stop thinking about it." I speak honestly, knowing what I say offers only weak hope that what he envisions will ever come true.

"For today, this is enough," Eitan replies after a moment, taking my hand and smiling. His whole face lights up with the loving expression that always melts my heart. We finish our coffee and then stroll through Kirchplatz, illuminated in shades of bright orange and gold from the setting sun. In this light, even the dull, gray pigeons are beautiful.

The next time they ask, I reassure my parents that Eitan has agreed to wait for an answer about America. Maman is not consoled and continues to pout, speaking only what is necessary to keep our household functioning. Papa is growing impatient with her theatrics and insists his wife snap out of it long enough to prepare a Shabbat celebration each week that includes Eitan and his parents, as soon-to-be family members. When Eitan's mother offers Shabbat at their home, my father instructs his wife to bake the challah, make a kuchen, and act like we are a happy family. Maman does as he asks, but as soon as the Sabbath ends, she again falls mute.

"What does Maman hope to accomplish with her silent treatment?" I ask my father as we walk home from shul on a Saturday morning, more than a month into my mother's word strike.

"She wants you not to go to America, liebling. But, if this is your wish, you must honor it, because your life is yours. Just because she birthed you doesn't mean she owns you. All mothers wish their daughters to repeat their lives and take it very personally when this does not occur, especially when the reason is because the daughter wants something different and makes different choices. Surrendering a daughter is a mother's greatest pain. A son she knows she can never keep – a daughter she hopes to keep until she dies," my father says, exhibiting a rare and surprising willingness to let me think for myself. We continue in comfortable silence, enjoying brief glimpses of sun through northern Germany's chronically overcast winter skies.

"Eitan could be a better Jew, but he is a good man and will be a good husband. And he is right that life in America will be better than it is destined to be here. Right now, there is a break in the clouds hovering over our lives as Jews, allowing us some warmth and light, but it won't last forever. Soon enough life will grow dark and heavy for us once again. It pains me greatly to say this, my daughter, but if you want to be Eitan's wife, you should go with him," my father says, choking back tears. He assures me that, with G-d's help, he and my mother will survive my absence, and who knows – maybe someday I will return to Germany to visit them, bringing the grandchildren with me.

Despite his reassurances, Papa refuses to entertain the possibility of crossing the ocean himself, saying that if he was meant to travel across water, G-d would've given him fins. Maman disagrees but refuses to argue with him when he gets into these moods. He reminds me I can send letters and pictures… maybe talk to each other on a telephone because eventually the contraption he cannot bring himself to trust and rarely speaks into might reach all the way across the Atlantic Ocean.

Meanwhile, each day as I sew for women who come to me because they admire my skill with a needle and thread, I think about Eitan's claims about a better life in America and what that really means. Even with all its constraints and expectations, being an observant Jew is important to me, and I understand that a good Jewish wife is expected to surrender her life to keeping a traditional Jewish home and dedicate herself to meeting her husband's needs while raising a large family of observant children. I fret endlessly over how I can possibly accomplish all this without being surrounded by my extended family and a familiar, tightly knit community that is so central to a fully lived Jewish life. I can't envision how our treasured traditions can possibly be maintained in isolation, which is how I think of life in America. These questions poke at me as I am taking small, precise stitches, meticulously sewing finely crafted, handmade Belgian lace onto exquisite silk fabric in a soothing, meditative rhythm. *On the other hand, if even half of what Eitan says about America as a place of endless opportunity is true, maybe going there means I can be a wife, a mother, and a dressmaker,* I tell myself, smiling as I allow a small sliver of optimism about my future to sneak into my thoughts.

On the last day of Passover, Irina gives birth to big, healthy twin boys, Avram and Isaac, who have not stopped screaming since the moment they entered the world. Just as Papa predicted, these fat, red-faced babies cause Maman to suddenly find her voice again. When she isn't cooing over her new grandsons, she is bragging about them to anyone who will listen, and many who would rather not. I overhear her tell her sister, Ermalein, that unlike the women in their family, her daughter-in-law is very fertile, producing two babies exactly one week less than nine months after her marriage to my brother. Ermalein's response is that Irina is either very fertile or very affectionate. Maman dismisses her sister's comment as rude, insisting that either way brought babies.

Because Irina's mother is fully occupied consoling her wildly overwrought daughter, who has never shown any interest in children of any age and now has two screaming infants to deal with, it falls to Maman to prepare for the b'rit milah. Hildesheim's only mohel is already booked on the day he is needed, creating a crisis so monumental it pushes my mother's upset with me far out of her mind.

"Now that Maman has grandchildren within her reach, I no longer exist," I inform my father while heating water for morning coffee.

"You should leave now – she'll never notice," my father chuckles as his wife rushes out the door at the same time she is, again, instructing me to make my father's breakfast and, if she has not returned in time, also his noon and evening meals.

"I have not yet promised Eitan I will come to America. I told him I think I want to come eventually, but I am not yet ready to leave here," I continue, carefully watching my father's reaction. Without looking at me, he adjusts his yarmulke, wraps himself in his prayer shawl, says his morning prayers, removes the shawl and carefully folds it before finally asking about Eitan's response.

"He says he understands. We will write to each other often, and our letters will help us to build our dreams and plan for our children. Then he flashes the big smile that makes me want to follow him anywhere… even to America," I confess, slicing off a generous section of rye bread Maman somehow found time to bake yesterday.

"Ah – young love… a distant memory," my father sighs, nodding his thanks as I hand him a cup of strong coffee and ask what, besides bread, he wants for breakfast.

Two days later, Eitan leaves for America. In pouring rain, we say goodbye at the Adlerplatz station, where he will take the train to Hamburg, arriving with little time to spare before boarding the SS Deutschlander to cross the Atlantic Ocean to America.

"In good weather, the trip takes about a week; in bad weather, it is sometimes longer, but don't worry... storms should not be a big problem this time of year," Eitan reassures me.

"I want to be excited for your adventure, Eitan, but I am too sad you are leaving. I can't sleep and my stomach refuses to hold food. Every time I try to eat, I burst into tears. Everything is so complicated, and you are taking so much of me with you... all that is left is a lonely, empty person who is too weak to tear herself away from home," I sob into his shoulder, hoping others on the platform are too busy with their own goodbyes to notice the daughter of Hildesheim's most prominent Jew engaged in an overt, unembarrassed, and very public display of affection.

"Keep this with you for now and bring it when you come," Eitan says, reaching into his pocket and bringing forth a clenched fist holding a piece of material, which he places into my hand, closing my fingers tightly over it. As the train pulls away, I discover he has left me with his yarmulke. Holding it close to my heart and wishing him a safe journey, I leave the station and begin walking home, not looking back as the train pulls away.

Later, when I show what Eitan has entrusted me with to my father, who sleeps in his yarmulke rather than risk being found without it, he frowns deeply, accuses Eitan of going to America to forget he is a Jew, then takes up his violin and plays mournfully for over an hour.

Nearly two months pass before Eitan's first letter arrives. The long, disconnected silence encourages my mind to sink deeply into questions about whether he still loves me, has changed his mind about having me as his wife, fell overboard and drowned before reaching America, had another kind of accident, or has met someone else and his guilt over this betrayal has stolen his words from him. I convince myself he left Hildesheim believing I will never follow him to America, and is trying to forget about me. When a letter, mailed six weeks earlier, finally arrives, I am so afraid of what it says that I carry it with me, unopened, for many hours before finding the courage to read it.

Dear Nathalie –
I hope you and everyone are well and happy. I am now in a city called Cleveland, next to Lake Erie, one of what

America calls its great lakes. There are five of them and this is not the biggest one, but it is almost like the ocean, because you cannot see from one shore to the other.

I have a job with the Baltimore and Ohio railroad planning rail lines. Learning English is not hard, and because I can already read and write, I will be promoted as soon as I am better with the new language. I am also learning how to send messages by tapping my finger on a machine. This is an important job that will be easier when my English is better, but it is very interesting now. Saving money is easy, and soon I will have plenty for you to come and we can marry, find a house, and make a family immediately. In the meantime, I will write to you every day.

Please write to me soon at this address. The railroad office where I come for my paycheck each week is also where I can receive mail.

I miss you very much. Long may we live...

Your loving Eitan.

As I read Eitan's letter, my face expands into a broad smile. Then, I notice he signed the letter long may we live, making it seem like America is so far away we could die before we see each other again, I burst into tears.

Despite being overjoyed to finally hear from him, Eitan's words also remind me of how much I miss him, deepening the raw emotional conflict about leaving my family hovering just beneath the surface of my daily life. Surrendering to an unknown future in a place I have no connection to, and even less interest in, asks a lot of me... maybe more than I have to give. Yet I love him and want to be with him.

I don't believe Eitan will write every day, but his promise to do so lightens my heart. Later that day, I write to him that I am also saving money, miss him, and will write again soon. It is a brief letter, but I don't know what else to say since I am still unwilling to make a commitment I'm not sure I can keep.

As the days pass, Maman's pouting slowly lessens because she is busy helping Irina, who, two months past the twins' arrival, is already expecting another baby. When she isn't throwing up, she is either crying or otherwise bemoaning how her life is turning out. My mother repeatedly tells her daughter-in-law that she should be grateful that babies come so easily because it took her over ten years to have two children, and she would have joyfully welcomed more, but G-d disagreed.

Observing Irina with her babies makes me unable to share my mother's positive view of motherhood. My constantly screaming nephews scrape at my eardrums, and my formerly pleasant, very attractive sister-in-law has been transformed from a lovely, graceful woman with an enviable wardrobe and a generally happy disposition into a heavy, irritable, exhausted one. Now weighing nearly twice as much as she did when she married my brother, Irina's hips have spread wide and her breasts are huge, causing her to complain that they ache constantly, which her mother explains is what happens when you must produce enough milk to feed two big, hungry babies.

The changes in Irina, who continually wails, with good reason, that she will never fit into her elegant dresses with their slender, buttoned bodices, and flowing skirts again, have seeded my mind with even deeper uncertainties about being a wife and mother. I want to confide my doubts about the heavy, dependent relationships between a man and a woman and between a mother and her child to Maman, but my mother does not have a sympathetic ear for such a conversation. Instead, I write to Eitan that sewing keeps me too busy to help with the twins, who never stop fussing and throw up almost as much as their mother, leaving Irina little time for anything other than washing mountains of sour laundry and sobbing into a pillow. I've never known anyone who looks so exhausted or so unhappy as my formerly elegant sister-in-law does now.

After mailing this letter, I begin worrying that when he reads it, Eitan will decide I am not a suitable wife after all, and I will never hear from him again. I wonder about writing another letter, but don't know how to back away from what I said previously, because it was true.

Meanwhile, Irina, in a rare moment of calm, suggests I should start sewing marriage clothes to take to America. She begs me to remake her dresses, saying she knows they will never fit her again, and she doesn't want them around to remind her of life before having babies turned her into a dairy cow. I explain I already have enough good clothes, causing Irina, who is very moody, to burst into tears yet again. To comfort her, I agree to think about altering her dresses to fit me, after I finish knitting Eitan's sweater. The repetitive motion of long, slender wooden needles pulling fine wool yarn through loops again and again calms my mind and, as the garment takes shape, I slowly begin to think about the future as something I might be able to, little by little, create for myself, rather than having it imposed upon me.

Eitan's next letter arrives on Rosh Hashanah, and I wait until after Yom Kippur, when the High Holy Days are over, before opening it. He says he has been looking at places to live and finds we can afford something he promises I will like. He doesn't mention a synagogue or being friendly with other Jews, which, recalling what Papa said about Eitan going to America to forget he is a Jew, gives me pause. I don't understand how someone can forget who they are, but maybe in America, that is possible. *I don't want to forget about being Jewish, so if that is Eitan's plan, I will disappoint him*, I admit to myself, wondering whether I should say this in my next letter.

Meanwhile, Irina, about to explode, says she hopes the next baby is a girl because now that her brother is living with her, Levi, and the twins, she can't stand the idea of another penis in the house. I find this very funny, but she does not, moaning that she can't remember the last time she laughed at anything.

"I will write this to Eitan, and give him a good chuckle," I tell my sister-in-law, who sends me a look intended to strike me dead.

At the beginning of Hanukkah, another letter from America arrives. This one is very short and includes a book about learning English. Eitan explains that it isn't so different from German and is easy to figure out. He says I can practice by talking to the twins, which isn't a helpful suggestion because I talk to the twins as little as possible. He says I should start planning my trip to America soon because a good passage must be arranged far in advance. Reading this, I realize I can't wait any longer to give him an answer.

Meanwhile, Irina gives birth to another set of twins – a boy and a girl. Everyone is in an uproar – even Papa, who accuses Levi and Irina of reproducing like rabbits. Maman insists on bringing Irina and the new babies to our apartment to give Irina peace away from the other twins, who never sleep, hang on her like curtains on a rod, and are always demanding something. Irina's mother comes every day to offer solace to her hysterical daughter, now faced with caring for two more babies, who scream even louder than the first ones, which both Papa and I find incomprehensible.

"This is too many people and too much noise. Three people living in our apartment are very comfortable; adding four more is insanity. Irina, her mother, and the babies take up all the space in the sitting room. I have no place to sit quietly and think," my normally calm father tells his wife. He threatens to start sleeping on a bench in the railway station because even with so many people coming and going, it is calmer than his own home.

"I need peace and solitude… and here I have neither of those things," he shouts in an unusual outburst of frustration. My mother tells him to stop bleating like a goat then, as an afterthought, instructs him to stop playing his violin in the mornings because it wakes the babies. Gesturing wildly, he points out that the babies never sleep anyway, then takes his violin outside and sits in the courtyard, playing as fast and as loud as he can. The sun is not yet up, several nearby windows forcefully slam down, and my father plays on.

Four months later, Irina and the new twins are still living with us. One twin sleeps all day and screams all night, while the other one screams all day and sleeps all night. Irina's mother spends part of each day helping with the first twins, then comes to us to help with the newer ones, constantly complaining that she is too old for all this responsibility. Levi brings the other twins every evening, hoping to cheer Irina up, but instead has the opposite effect. She continues refusing to go home to her own apartment because she is afraid that if she shares a bed with Levi again, he will give her even more babies. Based upon what has occurred so far, no one disagrees with her.

"Who knows how many the next time?" Irina shouts whenever Levi suggests that his wife leave his parents' home and return to their life together. Maman ignores the tension by spending most of the day cooking because, according to her, people need to eat no matter what is happening. Watching this daily chaos for more than a year causes me to conclude that babies are demanding and marriage is a very big responsibility, further fueling my doubts about whether I am able to be a good wife or mother.

One warm afternoon, when Irina, her mother, and the younger twins are on a walk, offering a rare moment of peace in the household, Papa sits at the table drinking his afternoon coffee and reading his newspaper. A few minutes later, he says he has heard a rumor about America not being as welcoming as everyone claims.

"Protestant men who hate Jews and Catholics are in charge of everything," he exclaims. When I ask how he knows this, he says men at Hannover yeshiva know men who have gone and come back, and this is what they report. He points to an article in the newspaper confirming this.

"Er farfiert die ganze welt," he rants in Danish, German, and even in Yiddish, which he rarely speaks and only under extreme duress. Maman asks him to explain, and he says Jesus was a renegade Jew who seduced the whole world into following him, which caused great unhealed divisions lasting almost two thousand years, and there is nothing the Jews can do about it.

"Christians, they are taite Hasidim," he laments. When I ask what he means, he says they follow a dead rebbe instead of thinking for themselves. "They never reassess and update…"

"Jews have been believing the same thing and doing the same thing for five thousand years, Papa. We aren't exactly experts on modernization."

"Maybe not, my daughter, but at least Jews are discussing. We ask questions and do mitzvot… we don't believe a dead rebbe supposedly coming back to life proves anything. People who die stay dead, Nathalie… it's a scientific fact that includes Jesus," he repeats again and again, with an occasional fist on the table for emphasis.

Maman reminds me Eitan is saying America is a place where honey flows into the milk and gold falls out of rainbows, so I won't change my mind about following him.

"He wants what he wants; he won't tell you the bad things," she stresses again and again. Elbows on the tiny kitchen table and head in my hands, I admit I don't know who or what to believe, then break into tears. Maman says this is reality with men, and I better get used to it, which I do not find comforting.

Two days later, a letter arrives with the money for a ticket to America. Eitan writes that he is sending enough for a second-class travel ticket in a room with only five others, instead of in steerage crowded in among hundreds of strangers, with no privacy or place to rest.

There is a wash basin, and you have your own bed. This is better than the places in the bottom of the ship where everyone is pushed together in one big place and there is no privacy and a lot of noise, he writes, adding that I must reserve a crossing soon. It is clear he has run out of patience with me, and I must either return the money and tell him I am not coming or reserve passage.

The twins have begun teething, causing them to cry night and day. Irina, cursing Levi for turning her into a barnyard animal nursing a litter, shows no sign of returning to her own apartment. Unable to remember the last time I had a quiet meal or enjoyed a peaceful evening, I conclude America can't be any worse than this.

I book passage to America the next day, leaving on November 25th. When I tell Maman and Papa of my decision, my father blames Irina for disrupting their home so much it has forced his daughter out. While continuing to wash the supper dishes, Maman responds by straightening her slender back to its full height and telling her husband to shut up. Her tone of voice, which I have never heard my mother use before, surprises me, and shocks my father into silence.

That evening, while Maman is busy with her nightly ritual quieting Irina and the twins, Papa invites me to sit with him in the small garden in back of our apartment building, where he goes to smoke, which Maman does not allow in the house and believes he has stopped doing.

"Your mother doesn't need to know," he cautions, bringing forth a cigarette.

"Hearing Moishe sing the Kol Nidre on Yom Kippur for the last time will break my heart," I tell him, ignoring the cigarette smoke wafting toward me. Moishe is Eitan's younger brother, with the voice of an angel and studying to be a cantor.

"I will mourn you, Maman and shul, where I grew up, for the rest of my life. Nothing and no place will ever warm my heart in all the ways my home here warms me…" I sob through free-flowing tears running down my face. Papa pulls a cloth package, wrapped with a ribbon, from under the bench and hands it to me.

"It is a tapestry from the synagogue for you to take to America," he says, struggling to hold back tears of his own as he unties the ribbon.

"This is beautiful, but I can't take something so sacred away from our synagogue, Papa," I exclaim, fingering the delicate red, gold, and bronze silk threads.

"There are others, so no one will miss it. Besides, I am the president of the congregation – I decide who gets what." He takes a deep draw from his cigarette before continuing.

"I haven't changed my mind that Eitan is a good man, Nathalie, but he is not a devout Jew. It will be up to you to make a good Jewish home and keep our rituals and traditions alive in America. Eitan will go along with it but won't do it himself."

Minutes later, Maman comes outside, causing my father to hastily drop his cigarette behind him. Holding two packages, she sits down next to me.

"This is from Irina. It is a small notebook," she says. Opening it, I see that Irina has written a message on the front page: *Write your life in this book to help you remember what to write to us. Love, Irina.*

"I have never written about my life before," I say, after reading the inscription out loud.

"Then maybe this is a good time to start," Maman says, handing me the other package. Unwrapping it, I discover she has crocheted a white table covering.

"For your Shabbat table," she says.

"You didn't know I was going until yesterday. When did you have time to make this?"

"I always knew you were going, so I made time," she smiles softly, choking on her words. We sit quietly together until Maman pats my hand and returns to the apartment without saying more.

"I've said all I have to say, liebling. G-d has taken care of us for five thousand years… he will accompany you to America and take care of you there," Papa says, wiping his eyes. He stands up to walk behind the bench and stomp out his cigarette before opening the gate and proceeding down the street on his nightly walk.

Chapter One
פרק ראשון

Elyria, Ohio
January 1971

If you aren't who I think you are, then who are you?

"Dad – what are we doing here?" I ask my father, while shivering in a bitter wind, insistently spitting snow at us. We are standing side by side in a place neither of us has ever heard of, can't pronounce, and never expected to find ourselves. As I speak, I stare at a pile of partially hidden, freshly dug dirt. Fifty yards away, gigantic chunks of frozen water crashing onto Lake Erie's shore sound like ice cubes stuck in a meat grinder.

"I told you – we're here to bury your mother," my father answers through chattering teeth. He moves closer, linking his arm through mine, seeking to share each other's warmth as we move toward a synthetic grass tarp, obscenely green against the dormant ground beneath it. A slowly moving hearse becomes visible from the left.

"I think we're in the wrong place. This headstone says Rachael Rebekkah Rosenblum Barlow, and my mother's name was Charlotte," I point out.

"Until forty-eight hours ago, I thought her name was Charlotte, too. Apparently, we were both wrong," my father replies in a barely audible whisper punctuated by a deep sigh.

"Look at the headstones next to hers. Mikael Jacob Weiss and Sarah Rebekkah Michal Weiss, with no dates and an inscription, 'May their memories be for a blessing.' Another says Nathalie Avigail Weiss Rosenblum d.1934 and Eitan Noem Rosenblum d.1938. Do you know who any of these people are?"

"No idea." The two-word answer rides on a deep exhale and a slight shake of my father's head. We pass the time waiting for the hearse by staring out across the partially frozen lake, mesmerized by the icebergs floating rhythmically back and forth, until a wave hurls them toward the shore. An idling backhoe, partially hidden behind a large, dormant tree down slope from the hill where we stand, hums a steady dirge.

"According to her lawyer, your mother, Charlotte Rose Barlow's legal name was Rachael Rebekkah Rosenblum Barlow. These others must be related to her somehow; otherwise, there's no reason for her to want to be buried in this godforsaken place, and she was very insistent about it," my dad explains as the hearse pulls up. He takes my hand, and together we walk closer to the tarp. The driver and another solemn-faced man get out and walk toward us, putting on gloves. They peel back the artificial turf, exposing the hole underneath, then walk back to the hearse, where two men wearing black overcoats and fedoras are extracting a wooden, sarcophagus-shaped coffin. A small nameplate is affixed to the flat top.

"That can't have been easy to find," I remark, referring to the European-style box containing my mother's remains.

"Your mother was very specific about what she wanted. I think the funeral director pulled in a favor from some cloistered French nuns up near Santa Rosa, then had to put handles on the sides so we could maneuver it," my father explains. Hatless and gloveless, because these are unnecessary wardrobe items in the mild San Francisco climate he enjoys, he releases my hand and walks toward the hearse.

"I'm Paul Barlow," he says, shaking hands with the man who steps forward. "I'll help you carry her."

My father and four strangers arrange themselves around the awkwardly-shaped container, then proceed unsteadily across rough, semi-frozen slush leading up the hill toward the open grave. Unbidden tears form as I watch my dad carry the woman who abandoned us both within weeks of my birth to her final resting place. They carefully set the coffin down onto a canvas-strapped rack. One of the men turns a crank, committing the remains of the mother I never knew, and the wife my father freely admits he never understood, yet profoundly loved, deep into the earth. *Ashes to ashes and dust to dust,* I think as my father shovels dirt off the nearby pile, tossing it into the hole. He hands the shovel to me, dropping clods of wet dirt along the hem of his lightweight, navy-blue cashmere overcoat onto his once polished shoes. Not knowing what else to do, I follow his dirt-throwing lead, and my shovelful lands directly on my mother's coffin with a disrespectful thud.

"Oops, sorry," I murmur.

"I hope you can rest more peacefully in death than you did in life,

Charlotte – or whoever you were," my dad whispers, walking away while reaching for his handkerchief. I search my memory for another time I've ever heard his voice shake and come up empty.

Instead of following him, I remain beside the grave, trying to think of something to say. After several minutes, my mind remains blank and the cold is chilling me to the bone, so I turn my back on my mother's still open grave and walk toward the rental car my dad and I picked up at Cleveland International Airport, where, from across the two thousand miles separating us, we'd flown into each other's arms earlier this afternoon.

Less than forty-eight hours ago, my dad was in his San Francisco penthouse, where normally he would be sitting in his den, shoes off, tie loosened, preparing to watch the evening news while the dinner his housekeeper left for him earlier in the day reheated in the oven. Two thousand miles east, I was in my top floor apartment in a charmingly renovated old Victorian house in one of Chicago's more appealing North Shore communities, wrapped in a warm bathrobe and drinking exotic chai tea while listening to a classical guitar version of Beethoven's M*oonlight Sonata* on my new stereo. Instead of preparing the next day's lecture which, as a university professor is what I should have been doing, I was devouring a gripping WWII romance novel my research colleague, Elena Horowitz, had placed in my office mail slot earlier in the day, along with a note saying she pulled an all-niter to finish it. The wind off Lake Michigan, twenty yards out my window, was howling and my fireplace was pouring heat into my high-ceiling sitting room. Life was good. Then the telephone rang. Without his usual preliminaries, my father told me my mother had died earlier that day.

"From what I understand, she hemorrhaged during routine surgery, and they couldn't control the bleeding quickly enough," he explained, pausing for a deep breath.

"We have to deal with this, Natalie. Can you meet me in Cleveland the day after tomorrow?"

"Of course I can, but why is burying my mother our responsibility, and why do we have to do it in Ohio? I can't remember the last time I saw her, and I assume you can't either…"

"Your mother left instructions to be buried in Agudath Achim Cemetery in Elyria, Ohio," my dad continued, ignoring my question.

"Where?"

"Elyria, Ohio… in the general vicinity of Cleveland, according to the funeral director handling things on that end. She wanted to be buried as soon as possible after her death, without ceremony. The plot and headstone were paid for several years ago, so all the cemetery needs to do is dig the grave. They can bury her at three-thirty in the afternoon, day after tomorrow."

"I think you misunderstood, Dad – the ground's too frozen to bury anyone this time of year."

"I'm told it has been a mild winter and they're still able to dig," he answers, with less emotion than he generally expressed when reminding me to file my income tax.

"Do you have any idea why she wanted to be buried in a weirdly named cemetery in Elyria, Ohio? Have you even heard of the place?"

"No to both questions, but I might have a better idea after I meet with my lawyer tomorrow."

"What does your lawyer have to do with this?"

"Several years ago, she sent a letter telling me I was the contact person in case something happened to her. She said her attorney in Santa Barbara had supplied my attorney with all the necessary information, including a key to a safety deposit box in the downtown San Francisco branch of the Bank of California. Right now, all I know is what he told me when I called to let him know she had died and that my understanding was he had information regarding her final instructions, which he read to me over the telephone. He asked me to come to his office as soon as possible, because he has several things to give me."

"Like what?" My father claimed he had no idea.

"Do you have any idea how to find a cemetery in Elyria, Ohio?" I asked.

"We'll figure it out. There can't be that many Agudath Achim cemeteries in the greater Cleveland area."

"I suppose it won't matter if we get lost and are a few minutes late. It's not like she has any place else to be," I commented. Hearing my flippant tone, my father cleared his throat, obviously holding back a response.

"Dad – why do we have to be there when she's buried? I'm sure it's not required"

"Not required, but the right thing to do, Natalie. Regardless of everything that happened over the years, she was my wife and your mother, and we owe her that respect."

"Actually, we don't owe her anything, Dad. She left us – remember?"

"Of course I remember, but none of that matters now... she still deserves a respectful burial, not the convenient disposal of a body."

"How does it work – they fly the body to Cleveland, and we pick it up at the baggage claim?" I wondered aloud, unable to curtail my lack of reverence.

"I'm bringing her in my plane." This plan silenced me, confirming my long-held suspicion that, despite everything, my father remains deeply committed to the "until death do us part" promise he made in the marriage vows he took more than thirty years ago.

"How's the weather there?" my dad asked, shifting to a less volatile subject.

"Barely above zero. I have a warm coat, but you better bring every sweater you own."

"Right…" More silence.

"I've always wished you could've known your mother more, Natalie… and now that will never happen," my father remarked, clearing his throat.

"Knowing her more, or even at all, has never been a wish of mine, Dad."

"I suppose not… but I promise you that someday it will be." An involuntary sob escapes him as he says he'll be in touch with the details about meeting in Cleveland the day after tomorrow, then hung up the phone.

I stared at the fire crackling in my fireplace for the next hour, moving only when necessary to add another log. As the flames danced, I ruminated over the woman who gave birth to me but was never my mother. Depending on who was doing the describing, Charlotte Barlow was a unique combination of brilliant, beautiful, complicated, selfish, and emotionally disturbed. What I have known since I was old enough to understand such things is that my mother, for whatever reason, was never going to allow me, her daughter, to know her. It wasn't difficult to figure out that wishing for something I was never going to get was futile. Our encounters were brief, awkward, devoid of emotion, and never left me longing for more. I didn't care whether I ever saw her again and dreaded the possibility I might. The woman who gave birth to me was unpredictable, prone to unprovoked outbursts, and obviously uneasy about relationships that involved any expectation of emotional connection. Growing up, my way of coping with this was to either ignore her or pretend she didn't exist. Over time, I became quite accomplished at both.

"It's very hard to spend time with someone who, no matter how hard you try, you just don't like," I told my father after refusing my mother's invitation to have lunch and spend an afternoon shopping. I was fifteen years old at the time, and nothing in the world was more important to me than shopping. Later, as an adult, I began to grasp the two opposing truths that defined my mother – she was desperate for love yet feared it so much she pushed back as hard as she could against anyone who tried to give it to her. As a child, my mother's conflicted personality and unpredictability confused me, destroying my ability to trust her. I trusted nearly everyone, including my nippy cocker spaniel, Dominic, who occasionally bit people for no other reason than he felt like it, more than I trusted my own mother.

"Even though she was my mother, and as her daughter I was supposed to love her, eventually I gave up trying," I told my Aunt Sally, my mother's sister, one warm afternoon when we were sitting on Sally's back porch knitting. It was the summer before I was leaving for college and my aunt had just taught me how to use a cable hook to twist stitches. In recent months, Charlotte had become a more frequent topic of conversation between us because we both struggled to understand her, and I was finally old enough to talk about it.

Over the years, my failure to unconditionally love my mother morphed into burdensome guilt over my inability to achieve the impossible. I was angry at her for who she wasn't, not for who she was, and whatever emotional currency I spent on her had been invested in learning to live with her failures, and with my own, I told my aunt. She patted my hand, reassuring me that she understood exactly what I was saying, except the part about my own failures.

"Children don't fail their parents, Natalie. If Charlotte made you feel you had somehow failed her, it was because she was failing you – badly," Sally said, pouring us more lemonade, then changing the subject by exclaiming that the lavender yarn I was knitting was the exact color as the blooming wisteria growing over the arched entrance to her garden, which desperately needed weeding.

"Good choice, Natalie. Natural fiber yarns in nature's colors always turn out best," she advised.

"Let's sit here until my hands thaw out and the car warms up. Then we'll find a coffee shop somewhere," my dad suggests as I settle into the passenger seat just as the backhoe grinds to life. Out of the corner of my eye, I see my father watching the shovel pivot back and forth, scooping dirt off the loose dirt pile, then dropping it into the recently dug hole. After the backhoe presses the dirt down, the cemetery workers stomp down on the grave, breaking up the larger dirt clods. They replace the dormant sod, then move the equipment away, which is the signal for the funeral home staffers to begin driving toward the cemetery entrance. Moments later, my dad shivers slightly, puts our car in gear and follows the hearse down the winding road, where the it stops, waiting for us to exit so the driver can latch the cemetery gate, locking the estranged wife my father never stopped loving and the estranged mother I couldn't love, inside where she will remain for eternity. Snow has begun sticking to the car's windshield.

Forty-five minutes later, my weary father and I are sitting across from each other on cracked plastic seats in a booth beside a window in a small diner filled with the comforting aroma of freshly-brewed coffee. As I take off my coat and beret, shaking out my thick, shoulder-length hair, my dad requests one large piece of apple pie with cheddar cheese, warmed, and accompanied by two plates and two forks. Still shivering, he leaves his coat on. Condensation drips lines down the window, and the snow showers of an hour ago have become a near white-out. A smiling older waitress brings two mugs of steaming coffee we did not order.

"The weather forecast said something about lake effect snow showers, whatever those are," my dad frowns, looking out the window.

"They're locally heavy snow squalls that blow off the lake and usually don't last long or amount to much. Hopefully, this one isn't an exception," I explain, rubbing my hands together and watching fluffy snow accumulate on the sidewalk.

"I don't know about you, but I'm exhausted. Our flight plan out of San Francisco International had us leaving at three o'clock this morning to get us a landing slot between the commercial flights into Cleveland. Hopefully a good jolt of caffeine and copious amounts of sugar will perk me up," my father says, smiling weakly and suddenly looking remarkably older than he did when I saw him a few weeks ago.

"Where's Raynor?" I ask, referring to my dad's pilot. Due to his wide smile and the slightly cocky good looks his surfboarding hobby bestowed on him in his younger days, I've had a crush on Ray since I was a teenager and became aware of my sucker tendencies when it comes to good looking men, even ones at least fifteen years older than I am.

"He's back with the plane, hopefully sleeping. We'll drop you back in Chicago and then go on to San Francisco, so it'll be a long day."

It might be my imagination, but my dad's eyes, darker blue than my own hazel blue, look sadder than I've ever seen them, and his dark, wavy hair seems slightly more threaded with gray. Despite this, he still looks younger than his fifty-eight years imply, and his tall, solidly-built body projects a confident demeanor common among professional athletes and powerful political figures. By any measure, he is an exceptionally handsome man any woman would easily fall in love with, and I've sometimes wondered why this never occurred, at least as far as I know. More importantly, resembling my dad more than Charlotte rescued me from the teenage horror of being reminded, every time I looked in a mirror, which was a lot in those days, of a mother I seriously disliked, even if she was, by any standard, beautiful. Any hint of a resemblance would've caused me to spend a great deal of money on colored contact lenses and permanent hair dye.

"You're pretty upset about all this," I offer, reaching out to grasp my dad's hand.

"More confused than upset... I stopped allowing your mother to upset me a long time ago."

"Why didn't Aunt Sally come with you?" I ask, referring to my mother's sister.

"She said she couldn't remember the last time she heard from Charlotte. Evidently Mick had a serious heart attack a month ago and she didn't want to leave him."

"She should've left him a long time ago," I opine about the irritable, scrappy drunk of a husband my long-suffering aunt does not deserve to be burdened with.

"Some people say the same thing about your mother and me... that I should've divorced her a long time ago."

"She left you with a six-week-old baby... you had to be really pissed off about that. Why didn't you divorce her?"

"Because I knew I'd never love anyone as much as I loved her, and I suppose I hoped everything would eventually work itself out. The fact is, hope springs eternal in the human heart, which has a tendency to ignore reality, even when it's staring you in the face, which is something you're still too young to understand," he sighs.

"She left thirty years ago, Dad..."

"Actually, it was twenty-nine years ago last month."

"Regardless, you had to know things were never going to work out," I say, tucking my hair behind my ear and rolling my eyes. Clearly, my father is in a great deal more emotional pain than I am, which, given the circumstances of the last thirty years, is hard for me to get my head around. Our waitress rescues me with refills on our coffee and a generous slice of pie topped with melting cheddar cheese.

"Rationally, I knew that, but you can't help who you love, Natalie, even when it's complicated. Love is like a second skin – you don't need it, but you want it, even though you know it could eventually peel off, leaving you raw and exposed. Someday, if you're lucky, you'll love someone so much you'll understand what I'm saying." My response to my father's sudden attack of poetic consciousness, revealing a side of him I've never seen before, is jaw-dropping silence, which he takes as an invitation to continue.

"I could never imagine bringing anyone else into our lives... and I was never unhappy enough about the situation between your mother and me to completely sever my ties to her, which I would've been obligated to do if I became seriously involved with someone else. She was a truly exceptional woman, Natalie, which I know is difficult for you to understand or accept. But for me, loving her was a great privilege... a rare gift I was fully aware few others receive – from anyone." Never having heard my father speak like this before leaves me speechless – or maybe slightly in shock. Thinking he's either lost his mind or about to break into a Hollywood love song, either of which I would find acutely embarrassing, my only response is to stare at him.

"Did you ever hear from her? She wasn't that far away... did she keep in touch or visit occasionally?"

"Not really. I used to send her a Christmas card, but she was never one to celebrate the holidays, so she never reciprocated. I was surprised to learn I was the person she chose to be notified in case of her death. I always assumed it would be Sally. But since we never divorced, legally I'm her next of kin, which I'm sure she was aware of, and means it's up to me to settle her estate."

"She left an estate?"

"Apparently. I don't know the details yet."

"I wish you'd find someone decent and settle down," my father says, suddenly shifting the conversation in a direction we rarely go, especially after my very expensive wedding resulted in an extremely brief marriage. When it ended, he made me promise to never upset him like that again.

"That entire ordeal was very stressful for me," he pointed out every chance he got for months afterwards, claiming that it aged him ten years in a matter of days.

"I'm doing fine – better than fine. I'm a PhD from the University of Chicago and now a tenured professor of sociology at Northwestern, which isn't a bad gig for someone my age. I'm very happy with my life."

"So, you're over Liam?"

"I'm so far over Liam Cafferty I can't even remember what he looked like."

"Sally and I both knew marrying him was a mistake. But you wouldn't listen…"

"Aunt Sally was apoplectic – said something about Irish men being great to look at and hell to live with. I suppose she was referring to Mick, although nothing about him is great to look at. He's short, bald, built like a brick outhouse, and his face cultivates a loose relationship with a razor." Wincing at my description of my aunt's husband, my dad asks me how it's possible I know anything about brick outhouses?

"I don't. It was a character description in a novel I read that stuck with me because the guy reminded me of Mick." This prompts his first, albeit suppressed, grin of the day.

"It takes a strong, self-assured man to live with someone as smart and self-confident as you are, Natalie, and unfortunately, Liam was neither of those. Sally and I knew you wouldn't tolerate his insecurities for long, but there was no joy in being right – believe me. The marriage lasted what – six weeks? All I remember is that the wedding wasn't fully paid for when you announced it was over."

"About that. You never told me how much the annulment cost you."

"Surprisingly little, considering the archbishop himself had married you and there were no grounds under canon law for granting one. He settled for a generous contribution to the cathedral restoration that included repairing the bell tower plus paying his annual dues at the Pebble Beach Golf course for a couple of years. I thought getting you out of that marriage and away from the family from hell was worth every nickel, so I appreciated his cooperation."

"Liam's family was a piece of work – they thought a woman's sole purpose was producing babies for the pope and his father thrived on creating conflict and picked drunken fights for sport. Jack Cafferty was a mean bastard with an opinion on everything and just couldn't shut up. Poor Maureen – I can't imagine any wife or mother crying as much as she did, even when she was sober."

"Jack was a crude blow-hard… a small man whose entire ego was tied to his son's success. Liam never had a chance just to be himself, and I felt sorry for him in that regard, but not sorry enough to think he'd make a good son-in-law."

"Jack was jealous of you, Dad. You represent the success he couldn't even dream about. That made him hypercritical of me, especially after I rejected the baby machine idea in favor of finishing graduate school. I admit I should've listened to you."

"Why didn't you? You're a smart girl, Natalie, and I still can't figure out how you got into that mess."

"I'm a very poor judge of character when good looks are involved. Liam was very handsome, which blinded me to everything else."

"Well, I hope by now you have solved that problem and learned something in the process."

"Now that Charlotte is gone, you have the perfect opportunity to rethink your life – find someone to share it with…" I say, shifting the conversation away from failed marriages, a topic my father can hardly claim to be an expert on.

"Maybe… but it's not something I can consider right now. Too many questions… Like you, I'm content with my life, and at my age, I don't like change," my father teases, putting a generous helping of rapidly cooling pie onto a plate and pushing it across the table in my direction.

"What did the lawyer say yesterday?"

"Not a lot. He gave me the letter outlining your mother's final wishes that he'd already read to me on the phone, the key to the safety deposit box, and the name of her lawyer in Santa Barbara, who has the details regarding her estate and what's involved in settling it."

"That's it?"

"Basically."

"Did she explain why she wanted to be buried here?"

"She said there was a family plot that had space for her. She was adamant about a quick burial and no memorial or graveside service."

"So, she was related to those other people."

"That's as good a guess as any. I don't recall ever hearing her mention any of them, but conversations like that would've occurred over thirty years ago, and those days are mostly a distant memory."

"Did she say anything about her name?"

"No, but it's pretty obvious it wasn't Charlotte Rose."

"So, you don't really know who she was?"

"I thought I did. Obviously, I'm not so sure now…" My father pauses to take a bite of his pie before continuing. So far, mine remains untouched.

"The lawyer did ask me to tell you that you need to make an appointment with her lawyer in Santa Barbara, as there are a few things that directly concern you."

"Like what?"

"I don't know. Something about a letter for you, which the other lawyer mentioned to him when informed of Charlotte's death."

"I'm in no hurry to read a letter from my mother. Actually, I'd rather not read it at all."

"Are you sure?" my dad asks, signaling the waitress for more coffee.

"Very sure. I wouldn't believe anything she told me anyway, so no point."

"I can understand why you feel that way, Natalie, but you might change your mind later. She was your mother, and in her own way, she loved you. In spite of her faults, she was a remarkable, gracefully beautiful woman. Sometimes you remind me of her…"

"Please don't say that, Dad." I interrupt.

"You inherited your height and eyes from me, but like it or not, you also have her genes, and some of them are pretty good – a flawless complexion, a noble face, and exceptional intelligence… although I've often thought she might've been much happier if she wasn't quite so smart."

"I don't want to talk about this right now," I say, suddenly diving into my pie as if I care how it tastes.

"What was in the safety deposit box?" I ask, three bites of pie and two gulps of coffee later.

"What looks like a tapestry of some kind, a yarmulke, a hand crocheted white something that might be a tablecloth, and this letter." He reaches into the breast pocket of his suit jacket and pulls out an overseas airmail letter, written on tissue-thin paper with a foreign postmark and addressed to Mrs. Paul Barlow. When he opens it, a threadbare yellow cloth star falls out. He hands me the letter, written in German, dated the day I was born.

"Do you know anything about this?" I ask, pointing to the star which seems almost sacred. I'm afraid to touch it.

"I don't read German, so no, I don't."

"You do know what it means, though, right?"

"I know it's the identification symbol the Nazis forced Jews to wear, if that's what you're asking."

"That's exactly what I'm asking. You don't know why my mother had it, or kept it in a safety deposit box?"

"I have no idea, but it's safe to assume it was very important to her."

"Do you think Aunt Sally knows anything about it?"

"She might, but even if she does, I doubt she'll tell us."

"Why not?"

"Just a feeling. There wasn't much question that your mother and Sally were hiding something. Your mother occasionally spoke German on the telephone, which she denied, even when she knew I overheard her. Occasionally, I would come home to find her sobbing into the phone; other times, she'd be screaming in anger. The worst arguments we ever had were when she clammed up, refused to answer my questions, and disappeared for hours." As he tells me this, my dad carefully places the star on a paper napkin to protect it from who knows what kind of contamination resting on the bare tabletop.

"Who was she talking to?"

"She wouldn't tell me. When she and Sally argued, they'd slip into German, then head out to the garage. A while later, they'd both end up in tears, and months would go by before they would speak to each other again. In the meantime, your mother continued refusing to discuss it, and I was reluctant to keep asking her. I figured she'd tell me when she was ready, which turned out to be never."

"You have the patience of a saint, putting up with all that crap," I tell my father.

"I was sure things would settle down after you were born, and they did, just not in the way I expected. Charlotte left within weeks to join the International Red Cross as a nurse. It happened so fast I was too flabbergasted to respond."

"She didn't explain herself?"

"Not really. She just took all her upset with her and left. The world was at war, and she knew nurses were desperately needed to support the war effort... and she was convinced Sally could care for you better than she could."

"Did Aunt Sally agree?"

"Whether she agreed or not was irrelevant – she did it. It meant quitting her teaching job, which broke her heart, but you were the only reason for me to come home at night and she knew I'd never agree to sending you to her, so she felt she didn't have a choice."

"What was Mick doing all this time?"

"Working the docks at the port of Los Angeles. Back then, he had a volatile temper and a tendency to drink his paycheck on Friday nights, usually winding up in a bar fight it took him all weekend to recover from. It was up to Sally to hold things together, which she did a damned good job of doing."

"Why didn't Mick get called up?"

"He wasn't an American citizen... probably still isn't. But after Pearl Harbor, fighting an actual enemy instead of taking a few swings at some loud mouth drunk in a bar became too tempting. He volunteered and ended up somewhere in Europe. When Charlotte left, Sally brought Emily and moved in with me to take care of you. A few months later, just after Tommy was born, the army sent my sister Jane's husband, Charlie, to North Africa. She didn't want to stay at Fort Bragg, where he'd been stationed, so asked to come back to California and move in with us. I left the decision up to Sally, and even though she and Jane didn't know each other, Sally thought they'd both appreciate the company.

"So, the household was you, Sally, Emily, Jane, and two babies – Tommy and me."

"Charlotte and I had the biggest house, and there was enough room for everyone. But you already know all this."

"What were you doing all this time?"

I'd received a draft deferment so my construction company could build military installations on the west coast as fast as possible, trying to stay ahead of the Japanese invasion of California everybody was expecting. I helped the Navy set up anti-aircraft guns on the coast to shoot the Japanese down if they got that far, then was asked to take on a project in New Mexico."

"New Mexico? Where they developed the atomic bomb?"

"Yes."

"Please don't tell me you were involved with that, Dad…"

"Not directly, no."

"What, exactly, does 'not directly' mean?"

"I was designing and building the facilities that housed the labs at Los Alamos."

"Did you build the test towers?"

"Yes."

"Were you there when they tested it?" My dad nods.

"How about when they dropped the bombs on Japan?"

"I was back in California by then."

"And you're just telling me this now?"

"There was no reason to tell you, Natalie. It isn't something I like talking about. I didn't disagree with Truman dropping the bomb because the Japanese were never going to surrender, and it was the only way to end the war. But a lot of innocent people died as a result, and whatever part I played in that outcome – and I can't deny that I did play some part – is very difficult to live with. I was sick to my stomach for weeks after Hiroshima and then Nagasaki, and still get nauseated when I think about it," my father explains, looking up from the marred red Formica table separating us for the first time since our conversation turned in this direction. His eyes beg for understanding.

"Did Charlotte know?" I finally ask, crossing over the dead space that has opened between us.

"If she did, she didn't hear it from me. It's possible she figured it out at some point, but we never discussed it. We never discussed the war years at all."

"Does Aunt Sally know?"

"She knew I was going to Los Alamos and eventually found out what went on there. I'm sure she assumes I was involved somehow, but she never asked any questions, and was just as relieved as everyone else when the war in the Pacific finally ended."

"Do you regret it?"

"I deeply regret that the bomb wasn't developed in time to use it to stop Hitler, and I profoundly regret that an atomic bomb exists at all as a threat to human civilization. I was just doing what my country and its government asked me to do, which was no different from what any soldier carrying a gun, or any pilot dropping a bomb, was being asked to do. My job was to build a bunch of buildings in the middle of a desert as fast as possible. Security around the entire project was extremely tight, and it was a while before I began suspecting what was going on." My dad pauses to take a deep breath.

"The bottom line is I helped end a war that needed to end, and there wasn't any other way to do it, which is what I remind myself of when I think about Los Alamos. It was a horrible ending, but it was the only sure option we had, and it ultimately saved American lives. I certainly don't feel proud of my role in it. Mostly, I try not to feel anything at all about it, which is probably how everyone who was involved copes with participating in the development of a project with the potential to wipe out the entire human race and end life as we know it. There's a lot of truth in Einstein's observation that he doesn't know how World War III will be fought, but World War IV will be fought with sticks and stones."

"What about Mick?" I ask.

"He ended up someplace in Belgium, if I recall, then took extended duty to help liberate Dachau and Buchenwald. He returned with an even worse drinking problem and a deep hatred of the Germans I expect he still harbors. In his defense, I'd hate people and drink too much too, if I'd seen some of the things he saw. You need to cut him a little slack; he came back pretty messed up, with good reason. I don't much like him, but when he realized he was needed, he stepped up, even though he didn't have to, and I've always respected him for that."

"I've never heard him say anything about the war."

"Some things are unspeakable; the only way to live with them is to never talk about them. A lot of soldiers who fought in the war and lived through it can't talk about it… It's not unusual."

"I still don't see why Aunt Sally stays with him."

"She loved him once, and now she views him as just as much of a war casualty as any soldier who took a bullet and was maimed for life. She knows he needs her, and for that reason alone, she'll never turn her back on him, regardless of how bad it gets – and there have been times when it's gotten pretty bad, particularly in the years right after he returned. She's had plenty of reason to take a hike on the whole deal, and nobody would've blamed her if she did, but she didn't."

"So, I come from a family who remains faithful to each other, no matter what," I whisper.

"I guess you could say that…" my dad answers, suddenly seeming to relax slightly, as if a question that has been bothering him for a long time has suddenly been answered.

"Which means bailing out on my marriage violated this unwritten family rule."

"Your situation wasn't a marriage. It was an unfortunate error in judgment about something that seemed like a good idea at the time."

"Do you think Charlotte was a war casualty?" I ask, moving the conversation away from the biggest mistake in my life to date."

"In her own way. That war wasn't just some minor skirmish. One way or another, it messed everybody up. After Pearl Harbor, we realized the entire west coast was a direct target and the Japanese could bomb the hell out of us whenever they wanted to do it – next week, next month, or in five minutes – and we'd all be dead. We lived in constant fear, waiting for the next shoe to drop… didn't know if we'd still be alive in twenty-four hours or what kind of country we'd be living in if we did survive the war. Life was lived moment-by-moment, with no sense of a future." His words rivet me to a reality that, until this moment, I never knew existed.

"You were born during a time when survival was everything. The Great Depression and the Dust Bowl had exhausted the country, and most people were not emotionally equipped to take on another life-or-death challenge. Bad things just kept piling on, and there wasn't a damned thing anyone could do about any of it. No one knew what would happen next, and in many ways the uncertainty was the hardest of all. The only choice was to get out of bed every morning, put on your clothes, and hope for the best. Terror filled every minute of every day – there was no getting away from it."

This conversation is the most I can ever remember my father saying about the war that stole my mother from him. My response is to wipe away enough condensation from the window to watch snowflakes swirl while he takes another bite of pie.

"I had no idea…" I finally whisper.

"Of course you didn't, and Sally and I are very grateful for that. We did everything we could to give you as normal a life as possible. I doubt Emily, who was six years old when it started, understood much about what was happening either. But that doesn't mean you both – maybe especially you – weren't affected by it, because we all were. The war changed everything about life as we knew it. Your mother would've been an entirely different person – a different wife and a different mother – if the war hadn't happened, and you're going to have to find some way to forgive her for what the war did to her… for who she became as a result, and for how that affected you. Even if you don't understand why she was who she was, you still should respect her as the imperfect human being she was, because she couldn't help any of it."

"That's not true, Dad – she had choices. Everybody has choices."

"Sorry, Natalie, but I don't agree. Sometimes life takes those choices away. Men get drafted, go off to war and die; Jews get murdered by an evil political regime; an earthquake levels a city… the list is endless."

"Did you forgive her?"

"It never occurred to me not to. But that didn't mean I could trust her or live with her emotional volatility and the constant chaos it wrought. The war profoundly changed her and she returned as an unpredictable, deeply troubled stranger I had to protect you from. Sally agreed with me but had a much harder time… said forgiving someone who couldn't apologize for what they had done was impossible, and Charlotte never acknowledged how her actions affected anyone else or indicated she had any regrets about anything. While I didn't feel as strongly about all this as Sally did, I could see her point."

"What do you mean by emotional volatility?"

"Charlotte returned a lost soul. She was completely hollowed out and couldn't handle ordinary life. She was prone to unprovoked rage and in no shape to care for herself, much less a four-year-old. She didn't want to face the reality that everything here at home had changed while she was gone. There was no place for her in the tightly knit family Sally, Jane, and I cobbled together in her absence. Sally was spitting mad at her for leaving, Jane was suspicious of her, and I felt my primary responsibility was to you, not her. She had nothing to come back to…" I wait for more.

"In your happy four-year-old mind, Sally was your mother, and Emily was your big sister. Nobody wanted to disrupt that bond in any way, for you or for Emily. Charlotte was an intruder you were afraid of and didn't want anything to do with. I didn't want the marriage to end, but I didn't know how to be a husband to a woman I no longer recognized." As he tells me this, my dad stares over my head into the distance.

"At first, she was surprised that we weren't enthusiastically embracing her return with open arms, but eventually she realized she had to live with the consequences of her decision to leave, and how it had affected the rest of us. She was forced to accept that the Bible might argue for welcoming the prodigal son back, but things don't play out that way in real life, and she couldn't just suddenly walk out of our lives without explanation and expect to return to a warm welcome, no questions asked, whenever she decided to show up again."

"Did you know where she'd been or what she'd been doing?"

"I knew she'd volunteered with the Red Cross nursing corps, and their mission was treating the war wounded, which was most likely what she was doing. She spoke German, which the Allies might've found useful, so it's possible she didn't just do nursing. There was an occasional letter, but no details or return address."

"What did Aunt Sally think?"

"Neither of us was especially interested in discussing it. My wife, who was also her sister, had suddenly walked out on us both, with little explanation, to go fight a war in Europe. We had responsibilities to you and Emily, plus a war in the Pacific to worry about, and both she and Jane had husbands fighting in Europe to be constantly concerned about. That was as much as we could manage; nobody had a lot of energy left over to think about Charlotte or try to figure out why she did what she did."

"What if I don't know how to forgive her?"

"Then you'll have to figure it out, because you can't spend the rest of your life angry at your mother. She harbored deep distress about something that held sway over her entire life, and you can't let the same thing happen to you."

"I've managed fine so far."

"Of course you have, but that doesn't mean this hasn't affected you."

"I don't know what you mean…"

"You prefer the safety of your own company over the company of others. You're too content being alone."

"I don't see anything wrong with that, Dad."

"Right now, there's nothing wrong with it, because you have me and Sally to rely on. But we won't always be here, and eventually you'll have to navigate the world entirely on your own, without us as backup." I don't have an answer for my father, because I know he's right. I'm generally quite content in my own company. I don't need a lot of friends to distract me from the rich inner life I've cultivated over the years.

"You have to come to terms with all this, Natalie, and you have to do it yourself, because nobody can do it for you."

"Even if I agreed with you, which I'm not sure I do, I wouldn't know where to start…"

"Read the letter your mother left for you and find someone to translate this one." He gently pushes the thin airmail envelope resting on the table toward me.

"Why not ask Aunt Sally to translate it?"

"I'm not sure she'd want to be asked."

"Because of the star?"

"That's one reason," my dad says, as the waitress refills our coffee yet again. Nodding our thanks, both of us retreat into our own thoughts.

"Why would explaining the star be a problem? We all know what it means," I finally say.

"Mick Mulligan has an opinion on everything and evidence of a family connection with Germany would hand him an opportunity to express his hateful feelings about 'the goddamned krauts'. Sally won't want to invite that conversation."

"He must know Aunt Sally is German."

"Not necessarily. He's not the curious type, so it's possible the issue never came up. Regardless, there's no point in giving him a reason to ask the question now."

"Not all Germans were Nazis, and the war ended a long time ago. Can't he just let it go?"

"Mick's the Guinness Book of World Records champion grudge holder and proud of it. He's not a complex thinker. For him, the world is black and white, and there's nothing in between, particularly as concerns the Germans, and I don't see that ever changing. Just get the letter translated, and then we can decide whether it's worth mentioning to Sally. The star might not be significant at all."

"There's no way it's not significant, Dad."

"I know, but let's not jump to conclusions…"

"You really don't know what my mother was distressed and upset about because of the phone calls or when she and Sally argued?"

"It's not like I haven't tried to figure it out, but there's only so much time a person can spend trying to understand someone who doesn't want to be understood. They'll outwit you every time," my dad answers, staring at his well-groomed fingernails.

"One more thing before I forget…" he finally continues, shifting the conversation into safer territory as he reaches into his suit coat pocket again.

"Your mother's doctor said after the hemorrhage they discovered she had a blood clotting disorder she'd failed to mention prior to surgery and may not have known about – although he doubted that, since she'd had a hysterectomy before she was forty, and bleeding issues are generally the only reason to remove the uterus of a younger woman. He said that this problem is often inherited and Charlotte's daughter and nieces, if she had any, should be made aware of this possibility… said it's a manageable problem as long as the person knows about it. Here's his name and phone number; he's expecting to hear from you."

"I suppose you didn't know anything about this either?"

"No, I didn't. But you need to follow up on it, Natalie."

"Apparently, there's a lot I need to follow up on.

Chapter Two
פרק שני

Hildesheim, Germany
November 1912

*America is the land of the free and the home of the brave,
yet I am already as free and as brave as I want to be.
Perhaps there is no place for me there.*

The morning I leave Hildesheim for America dawns cold and rainy, perfectly matching my mood. I am grateful for the heavy, dark gray skies; a bright, sunny morning would be unbearable.

"Even the heavens are sad about your leaving and cannot hold back their tears," Irina says, surprising me in the kitchen at first light. Wearing a loose, milk-stained nightgown, dark shadows circle her sad, puffy eyes, and the light that radiated from her once beautiful face has gone dim. I've often wondered whether my brother notices that the vibrant beauty he married three years ago has disappeared and a stranger, exhausted and old before her time, has taken her place.

"I awoke early to say my own goodbye to you, Nathalie. You are my only sister – I have none of my own, and I will miss you too much for words to say," she gasps, opening her arms and heart to me, her husband's younger sister, for the first time. I never sought closeness with Irina nor considered her the sister I never had, and her confession surprises me.

"I'll miss you, too, Irina… and I promise to write."

"You must do more than that, Nathalie. You must promise to tell me everything about your life – every detail. If bad times come, as everyone predicts they will, we may be the only family left to each other. We must keep close… not drift apart." Puzzled by her outburst, which has echoes of the dire warnings Eitan has put forth about the future of Germany, and my father has not refuted, I assure her we will never lose each other. Then, wanting to end this sad, frightening conversation that has erased my already weak appetite, I excuse myself to finish packing.

Back in my sleeping room, folding the last of my clothes into my suitcase, it suddenly occurs to me that saying goodbye to Papa and Maman truly is the end of a life I have loved, and for the first time, I am meeting death face to face. We'll promise to see each other again, knowing we are lying to make ourselves feel better. Choking back sobs, I realize the time to change my mind is less than one hour; either I go bravely into a new life or stay here, happy and comfortable in this one. Hearing my father's footsteps in the hallway shocks me back to the present moment.

"Nathalie, my liebling… you are thinking about not leaving," he says quietly. Staring at the floor, I nod, frustrated with myself for not showing greater resolve.

"Listen to me as I say again that black clouds are on the horizon, darkening the future. My only comfort is knowing you are safe in America, where our bloodline will be preserved as it should be, through my daughter. Leaving Germany promises our future for generations – remaining here guarantees nothing. You must go. There is no other choice." With the decision about whether to stay or go having been made for me, I put on my hat, buckle my suitcase, then walk toward down the stairs for the last time. My father follows behind me, while my mother waits at the outside door.

We travel to Adlerplatz station in heavy silence. Our goodbye, larger than life itself, is a battle between unspeakable sadness and a deep desire for the last words we say to each other to be comforting, reassuring, and unforgettable ones. This fragile internal chaos is held captive by my own verbal and emotional inadequacies, sitting in my chest like rocks that are one deep breath away from dislodging, crushing me speechless. Papa and Maman, both looking unnaturally pale in recent days, are doing no better. Yesterday, I pushed back at their idea to travel all the way to Hamburg with me, just to steal a few more moments together. Dragging out out the longest goodbye I will ever utter would only make it worse.

On this weekday morning, the train platform is crowded with passengers going to Hannover to work or to shop. I am the only one carrying a suitcase, meaning everyone else, unlike me, will be returning home in the evening. The moment I step on the train I will become homeless, with no guarantee that I will ever return. Handing me a first-class ticket, Papa says I might as well be as comfortable as possible for as long as possible, because G-d only knows what discomforts await on the ship. Smiling through tears, I reach out to hug him goodbye. Maman hands me a basket, then unwraps the woolen shawl she is wearing and places it around my shoulders.

RED ANEMONES

"Maman, you will need this against the winter chill... please keep it. Otherwise, I will worry about you catching your death," I insist, frowning.

"It is cold in the middle of the ocean. You will need it more... as a hug from me to keep you warm. Besides, I am almost finished knitting another one," Maman smiles weakly. Then, without another word, my mother turns and begins walking away, accompanied by the constricted sound of muffled wailing.

"She does not want you to see her cry," Papa tells me, wiping his eyes. Wordlessly, he nods goodbye as the waiting passengers begin to board. Leaving the only home I have ever known, and will never see again, I board the train without looking back or, once finding my seat, staring out the window for one last glimpse of the place where I have lived all my life. Alone in my compartment with no one to notice me, I collapse in grief as the train pulls away from the station platform.

Why am I doing this? I want to go back home and speak German for the rest of my life. I will tell Eitan that I love him, but one wife is as good as any other, and he should forget me and find someone else... someone more adventurous and willing to sacrifice everything familiar and beloved to face the unknown, I torture myself, overwhelmed by the temptation to get off the train at Hannover and catch the next train back to Hildesheim.

My sobbing continues erupting and exhausting itself until I finally doze off. Awaking with a start sometime later, I realize I slept through the stop at Hannover and estimate we are not far from Hamburg... my last chance to turn back. To distract myself from this thought I peek into the basket my mother sent with me. I discover fruit, cheese, bread, nuts, and her famously delicious honey lemon cake no one else can bake like she can, and is requested for every Shabbat, Shiva, wedding feast, and other occasion involving Jews and food, which is all of them. Carefully folded in the bottom of the basket is Maman's recipe, which she has always refused to share, no matter who asks. Suddenly, my heart knows the ties to the home I am leaving are unbreakable... that I will always have Maman's uniquely sweet honey lemon cake like no other to comfort me. A melancholy relief settles over me.

Just over an hour later, grateful for Maman's woolen shawl around me, I walk out of Hamburg's gigantic, glass-domed Hauptbahnhof into a fine, cold mist. Moments later, coming around a corner near the docks, the foul smells of rotting fish and slick sea gull excrement smack me in the face, creating more havoc in my already unstable stomach. Straight ahead, a large combination freighter and passenger ship, black on the bottom and white on top, with gigantic smoke stacks, comes into view. Never having been on a ship and having no idea what to expect, the image is surprisingly reassuring. *It looks seaworthy,* I think, not really knowing what seaworthy looks like.

The trip west across the north Atlantic, against the prevailing winds, depends upon the weather. Although the massive ocean can be treacherous any time of year, the chances of encountering extreme weather are less in November than later in winter, and I expect to be on dry land again within ten days at the most. I'm counting on a calm sea to help me digest the fears lumped in my stomach like cold, day-old porridge. *The coming days will move my mind from sadness at leaving to anticipation of what awaits me*, I convince myself. Despite all that fastened me firmly to the love that is my family and the little town as familiar to me as my own fingers, I can't help feeling a glimmer of hopeful excitement as I think about forging ahead into a new life. A courage that, until now, I never knew I possessed is quietly pushing me forward.

Signs telling the first and second-class passengers to bear left are posted just before reaching the main gangplank. A large crowd of wide-eyed people is standing in the steerage line off to the right. Held together by hope, faith, and each other, their vacant faces reveal neither fear nor courage as they desperately cling to their meager possessions, preparing to file into the cargo hold. Unlike them, a room with a bed awaits me, which is reassuring, but as soon as I pass into the transit hall, where my documents are stamped, my brief moment of relief vanishes like the smoke billowing from the stacks on the ship to which I am about to surrender my life.

An hour later, as the last one to arrive, I greet each of the other five occupants of the room we are all sharing in German. It turns out that only one is a native German speaker; two others are Yiddish-speaking Polish sisters who look no older than fifteen or sixteen; another is a French speaker from a village on the French-German border, and the other is a Dane. The Polish sisters, occupying two of the three beds across from me are chatty and excited to explain that they are mail-order brides on their way to Aberdeen, South Dakota, where their soon-to-be husbands have staked claims to land the United States government is, according to them, giving away for free, to anyone who asks.

"We will have land to grow food – it will be the same life as the shtetl, but no threats of pogroms hanging on us," the older of the two sisters enthusiastically explains… at least this is what I think she is saying, given my limited ability to understand rapid-fire Yiddish punctuated with enthusiasm and excitement. When I don't respond, she slows down to offer me a broad, optimistic smile, awaiting some indication that I understand what she is saying. I nod to indicate a grasp some of what she has told me, without revealing that I don't believe a word of it. No country would give away free land, and I am sure the sisters misunderstand. On the other hand, I have almost no idea about what awaits me either, so I can't fault their hopes and dreams any more than I fault my own.

The French speaker occupies the bunk above me. She mumbles a greeting in response to mine, so she must understand at least some German, but she quickly turns toward the wall without saying more. The other German, who introduces herself as Malka Faber, has claimed the bunk below me, while the Dane, so blond she could be almost any age, silently acknowledges me. Soon, the ship's horn blasts twice, and the engines groan to life.

"We have begun our journey down the Elbe to the North Sea. Maybe we should explore now, while the boat is still steady under our feet – find the toilet and the place to get food," Malka suggests, refastening her abundant hair beneath her hat, and straightening her long skirt. Her dark eyes look older than the rest of her slightly rounded face, and her self-confidence suggests this is not her first crossing.

"We can lock our room?" I ask, as the only one responding to her suggestion. Malka nods but warns us to keep our, passports, transit visas and money with us regardless.

"The locks are flimsy and there are more than two hundred passengers in second class – it would be foolish to assume all of them are trustworthy," she cautions

"You have made the trip before?" I ask.

"First was ten years past. Six months ago, I came back to care for my sick mother until her death. Now I am returning to my own family in Detroit. You?" she gestures.

"I am on my way to Cleveland... to someone I promised myself to in Hildesheim more than a year ago. He came to America first to give my family and me time to get used to the idea. I'm not sure any of us ever got used to it, but eventually it was time to either follow him to America or tell him goodbye and remain in Germany, and I chose to follow him."

"And you are not sure how you feel about it?"

"Sometimes I am sad about leaving, other times excited to be with Eitan, and still other times worried I will hate America and want to return to Germany. Most of the time, I avoid feeling anything because I don't want to give in to my doubts. I was happy with my life in Germany and not eager to abandon it."

"Bringing such heavy thoughts along with you tells me you don't travel with a light heart. Perhaps you should have stayed."

"I made my decision, and it's too late to change my mind. The ship has set sail, and I am not a swimmer who could make it back to shore." I say this last with a slight smile since I can't swim at all.

"We have about five hours until we enter the open sea, so let's look around while we can," Malka says, cautioning the others to lock the door if they leave the room unattended.

"You sound as though things will change when we are in the ocean. I thought this time of year almost certainly guaranteed a smooth crossing," I remark, beginning to worry.

"It is impossible to know, and foolish to assume," Malka answers, motioning me to follow her down a narrow hallway toward the canteen. We obtain two cups of tea and move to the small adjacent room with tables along each wall. Other passengers also drink tea or eat something, and one man reads a newspaper. No one seems interested in carrying on a conversation.

"Tell me about America," I ask, while straining for a glance out the window at the passing riverbank.

"It's a strange place – a collection of people with almost nothing in common struggling to figure out how to live together. It's not old and comfortably settled into itself. Americans don't know who they are, because there is no shared history or treasured traditions carried from past generations holding them together. Mostly, it is every person for himself, which is no way to build a country. There is no national pride because there is no unity to encourage it… no concern for the common good. If someone takes time just to enjoy life, they are called lazy. But my husband has a good job, we have a nice home, and plenty of food to eat. I have a housekeeper, and my children are learning well in school, so I shouldn't complain. What I miss most is that there isn't the same sense of connection to each other… no mother, father, sisters or brothers to lean into, argue with, and share everyday life with."

"This is what keeps me awake at night. A family is not replaceable, Malka. I only have one family – one Maman, one Papa, and one brother, even if I don't like him so much. They are never coming to America, and I can't just replace them with strangers I don't know. I hope to make friends, but friends are not family… they don't have to take you in when trouble comes."

"This is what I find difficult to understand. In America, a woman is supposed to leave her home and family and bind herself only to her husband. In our tradition, two families marry, adding to both. We don't leave our families; we just expand them to make room for more people," Malka remarks. Frowning at her casual analysis of American life as I tell her about Irina, her mother, and the twins coming to our apartment so Irina would have all the support she needed, which was, for her, a lot, as she adjusted to motherhood.

"We complained a lot, but we never thought to have it any other way," I add, surprised I now cherish something that irritated me so much at the time. Just recalling this brings forth unbidden tears.

"America has too much freedom. Many, perhaps most Americans think only of themselves and carry no concern for others. The fledgling country is like a child just starting school – there is so much to figure out and no one knows how to play well with others. There are no common values, like simple good manners, to hold different kinds of people together in a shared purpose," Malka continues, staring out the window. Her words are disturbing, making it difficult to respond.

"I don't mean to put you off, Nathalie, but it is better that your expectations are realistic, and realistically, America is far from as perfect as it thinks it is. It is a strange mixture of people still trying to figure out how to get along with each other, and the richer, more powerful ones have some very strange, not very nice ideas about how to do that, and don't hesitate to exploit others for their own gain." When I remain silent, Malka apologizes for being so negative about the place where I am destined to spend the rest of my life and advises me to ignore her.

"I'm just sad about my mother's death and leaving Germany. My world seems very dark right now, but everything will feel much lighter by the time we arrive in New York. In the meantime, let's talk about happy things. I'll get us more tea, then you can tell me about your fiancé and your hopes for your new life," Malka says, forcing a smile.

"Eitan is an engineer. He works for the railroad, helping figure out routes, design bridges, and put tunnels through mountains. It is a good job, but it sounds like he will be gone a lot," I say a few minutes later, still staring out the window while holding my teacup steady.

"He describes a very nice house for us just outside Cleveland, and I am hoping for a Jewish community nearby that will feel familiar. Living among other Jews and keeping a Jewish home is very important to me. Eitan believes being Jewish in America is easier than in many other places but isn't especially interested for himself, which is the only complaint my Papa has about him."

"I wouldn't count on being Jewish in America being easy, Nathalie.

It's true there are no pogroms, but that doesn't mean Jews are totally accepted. My husband's name is Abraham Faberstein, which he changed to Albert Faber as soon as he got to Detroit and discovered the largest employer and most important person in the city, Henry Ford, is a rabid antisemite. My husband wanted a job designing cars, and knew Ford would never hire a Jew, so he did everything he could think of to not be one and got the job, which he is very good at. He knows that as long as no one is aware he is Jewish, his future at the company is secure."

"You don't have any connection to the Jewish community?"

"Only in the privacy of our home. No shul, and we certainly don't encourage the children to become too familiar with our traditions. We don't even encourage them to speak German. This is for their safety, not because it is our choice. America expects assimilation and blending in, so we try to do that, even though it means giving up much of ourselves to be like everyone else. But it is still better than worrying about the Czar's next pogrom, and that is a very big concern for Jews in Kattowitz, where our families remain. The western border of the Russian Empire is a two-minute bicycle ride; any Russian could shoot us without ever setting foot in Germany. Both our families wanted us to leave for America, so our lineage continues despite the Czar's unpredictability."

"My Papa told me the same thing about preserving our lineage. He also said he has heard Anglo-Saxon, protestant Christian men run America. Is this true?"

"For the most part. There are a lot of immigrants, yet America doesn't really embrace differences. It claims to welcome everyone, but you are only welcomed for what you can do for the country, not for who you are… certainly not for your traditions, your religion, or how you want to live. Who America claims to be and who it really is are as different as night is from day. What politicians promise and what they eventually provide are as wide apart as this ocean we are about to cross. It's best not to take them seriously." I remain silent so long Malka finally asks whether she has upset me.

"Yes and no. My Maman warned me Eitan would say things in America are much rosier than they really are, just to convince me to come… and Papa spoke briefly of there being problems for the Jews in America. Yet, he insisted things were soon to be bad for Jews in Germany and wanted me to leave. You only confirm what I've already been told and didn't want to believe was true."

"I don't think America will ever treat the Jews as badly as they have been treated in other places, but they won't necessarily be welcomed with enthusiasm either." Malka continues, until I interrupt her.

"And we will keep surviving just as we always have. What I don't understand is the need to hate someone, or how it happened that all this hatred fell upon the Jews? Why us and not someone else?"

"It isn't just us, Nathalie. You will soon learn how badly America treats Irish Catholics, Negros, sometimes Germans, and even Italians. Many ignorant people think all Germans are Jews, which makes no sense, yet gets very ugly. Americans are like the Bolsheviks in their ability to murder and maim others, for whatever reason – or for no reason at all. They're just not quite as well organized about it, and the government doesn't officially back it." Hearing Malka say these things, I feel my eyes go wide and my mouth drop.

"But these are not problems we can fix, so better we don't think about them... just try to live as good people and hope for the best," Malka says, patting my hand while offering a reassuring smile.

"Now what I would like to do is go out onto the deck and take one last look at Germany before we enter open water; you should come with me and do the same. We don't know what the future holds. It may be a long time before either of us sees our homeland again," my new friend reflects, taking a deep breath.

Late the next afternoon, having passed through the English Channel into the open Atlantic, the ship begins rolling from side to side and heaving forward and backwards with such force that I fear there is no controlling this gigantic wooden crate as it battles choppy water washing over its bow. Passengers are told to stay away from the outside decks and, as much as possible, avoid walking around. The unrelenting movement ruins my stomach, especially if I open my eyes or try sitting up. I am so sick Malka has traded bunks with me, making it easier for me to hang over the edge of the bed and reach the bucket she found under the sink. When I try to get up to the basin and splash cool water on my sweating, clammy face, the room spins like a dreidel, and I nearly pass out. The two sisters are also seasick. One is managing not to vomit as long as she doesn't move; the other one alternates between moaning and crying. I am feverish from my inability to swallow even water. Malka becomes our self-appointed nurse, and after a loud, angry argument, convinces the French woman to aid her in caring for me, the sisters, and the Dane, who groans constantly. They coax us to drink sips of water and, in my case, bathe me to cool my body. In a moment of relief from my fevered delirium, I wonder aloud about what will happen to me if I die before arriving in America.

"They throw you overboard and you become dinner for the sharks, Nathalie… disappear into nothingness. It is not a good ending. Better to hang on and push against the nausea. It will stop soon," Malka answers. I desperately want to believe I can do that.

I use a hairpin to scratch lines on the wall, next to other lines. There is comfort in knowing earlier passengers counted the days until this misery ends in the same way, adding a line each time a sliver of morning light penetrates the black darkness of night at sea to show itself through the tiny window. In between, to calm myself, I repeat the first words of the Shema again and again, thanking G-d for sending Malka to save me.

On a day when the sea is temporarily calm, the prayer, as much of it as I can remember, becomes the first entry I write in the notebook Irina gave me, written by my weak, shaky hand, first in Hebrew, then in phonetic Hebrew. Perhaps by remembering who I am will draw strength from my ancestors who have endured an eternal diaspora, facing an unknown future again and again. This has been my people's destiny for thousands of years and is the inheritance bestowed upon me. This awareness comforts me and I feel less alone. When Malka finds me writing, she cautions me to keep the diary where it will not be easily discovered, proving I am a Jew.

Sh'ma Yisra'eil Adonai Eloheinu Adonai echad.
[Hear, Israel, the Lord is our God, the Lord is One]

בָּרוּךְ שֵׁם כְּבוֹד מַלְכוּתוֹ

Barukh sheim k'vod malkhuto.
[Blessed be the Name of His glorious kingdom]

לְעוֹלָם וָעֶד

l'olam va'ed.
[for ever and ever]

וְאָהַבְתָּ אֵת יְיָ אֱלֹהֶיךָ

V'ahavta eit Adonai Elohekha.
[And you shall love the Lord your God]

בְּכָל לְבָבְךָ וּבְכָל נַפְשְׁךָ

b'khol l'vavkha uv'khol nafsh'kha.
[with all your heart and with all your soul]

וּבְכָל מְאֹדֶךָ

uv'khol m'odekha
[and with all your might]

וְהָיוּ הַדְּבָרִים הָאֵל

V'hayu had'varim ha'eileh
[And it shall be that these words]

RED ANEMONES

אֲשֶׁר אָנֹכִי מְצַוְּךָ הַיּוֹם

asher anokhi m'tzavkha hayom
[that I command you today]

עַל לְבָבֶךָ

al l'vavekha
[shall be in your heart]

וְשִׁנַּנְתָּם לְבָנֶיךָ

V'shinantam l'vanekha
[And you shall teach them diligently to your children]

וְדִבַּרְתָּ בָּם

v'dibarta bam
[and you shall speak of them]

בְּשִׁבְתְּךָ בְּבֵיתֶךָ

b'shivt'kha b'veitekha
[when you sit at home]

וּבְלֶכְתְּךָ בַדֶּרֶךְ

uv'lekht'kha vaderekh
[and when you walk along the way]

וּבְשָׁכְבְּךָ וּבְקוּמֶךָ

uv'shakhb'kha uv'kumekha
[and when you lie down and when you rise up.]

וּקְשַׁרְתָּם לְאוֹת עַל יָדֶךָ

Uk'shartam l'ot al yadekha.
[And you shall bind them as a sign on your hand]

וְהָיוּ לְטֹטָפֹת בֵּין עֵינֶיךָ

v'hayu l'totafot bein einekha.
[and they shall be for <u>totafot</u> between your eyes]

וּכְתַבְתָּם

Ukhtavtam
[And you shall write them]

עַל מְזֻזוֹת בֵּיתֶךָ וּבִשְׁעָרֶיךָ

al m'zuzot beitekha uvish'arekha
[on the doorposts of your house and on your gates]

    Although there are moments when I think I feel better, Malka cautions against moving more than necessary and continues keeping me alive with bits of bread dipped in broth she brings from the canteen. Without her, I would be dead by now... thrown overboard into the ocean, disappearing into the deep as if I never existed at all. The others are feeling better than I am and are taking turns caring for each other in a room that smells of vomit, unclean bodies, and clothing bearing evidence of all that has befallen us. Hourly, tempers flare, igniting the misery. The Polish sisters fret that anyone suffering seasickness will be judged too weak for America and turned back, which never occurred to me until they mention it, and is now one more thing to worry about. Catching a glimpse of my sunken gray face, hollow eyes, and ratty, sweat-soaked hair in the reflection of the small window forces me to seriously doubt any country, even my own, would want me.

"If I am refused entry, I will die right where I am standing," I tell Malka, tearfully, meaning every word, without exaggeration. The thought of another sea voyage brings forth sobbing so intense it triggers more vomiting, which by now has been going on so long my stomach has forgotten how to settle itself. Malka admits this is a rough crossing that is taking longer than usual, which the captain affirmed when he announced that everyone was to stay in their rooms and not walk the decks until further notice, and further notice never came.

By the time we enter New York harbor, my clothes are stiff and filthy, hanging on me like rags on a clothesline. So weak I'm barely able to walk, Malka and Inga, the Danish girl, help me down the ship's gangplank, holding firmly as I take my first step into my new life in America. The air smells of sea water, which induces a queasiness different from the seasickness I suffered, and the famous statue standing in the harbor holding a torch welcoming the tired and poor to their new home is shrouded in fog held in place by freezing temperatures and ice pellets falling from the dark sky.

"She holds all this promised freedom very close to her… maybe it's just for some, and not for everyone," I whisper to Malka as we stand in the misty fog, staring at Lady Liberty while waiting to enter the building where an immigration officer will decide whether I will remain in America or be sent back to Germany.

"You have finally arrived on solid ground again. Be glad about that and stop fretting," Malka scolds as I struggle to put one foot in front of another.

"It is impossible to feel greater misery and still be alive. If they refuse me entry, I'll kill myself before I'll get back on another ship. My stomach has given away half my body; there is nothing left of me to make another crossing," I complain, nearly falling over each step forward. Someone checks my eyes, which, still able to open and close, are the only things about me that function properly. Someone else writes my name on a list, tells me I am granted admittance into the United States of America on December 6, 1912, and points me to a line on my left, where I will pay the entry fee. This is where Malka and Inga, as re-entrants, are directed to a different line, leaving me on my own. Malka says she will return for me as soon as she can and to wait for her in the transit hall.

After being processed, I sit on a bench in a big room with hundreds of other new immigrants. We look at each other, but no one speaks. When Malka finally returns, we walk outdoors, which, despite the freezing rain, is a welcome relief after a transit hall filled with people who smell as bad as I know I do. She shows me to a small boat that takes us across the harbor to the mainland, depositing us at the end of a wooden dock. Soon we are standing on a patch of dirt staring at crowds of people, greeted by blowing trash, stinking garbage, and tall buildings obscuring the daylight. My first impression is that America is a loud, dirty place that smells bad, and people are so crowded together all they do is yell at each other. There are no trees, flowers, singing birds, squirrels, ducks, or gardens... nothing to make people want to be alive.

"If this is America, I am walking with one foot in an ugly life and one foot in the comfort of death," I tell Malka, struggling to hold back tears.

"Loneliness will make me sicker than the heaving ship. I don't like it here, and the only reason not to die is if you promise me Cleveland will be better," I wail. Patting my hand, Malka promises me Cleveland will be much better. I want to believe her too much to wonder whether she is telling me the truth.

Chapter Three
פרק שלישי

Chicago
Early Spring, 1973

Do all questions deserve an answer? It depends...

"How soon do you think you can come home?" My dad asks, sounding even more weary than when we last spoke on the phone less than forty-eight hours ago. I don't bother reminding him that being in Chicago rather than San Francisco doesn't mean I'm not home, or that ten o'clock on the West Coast is midnight in the Midwest and I'm already in bed. Normally we talk once or twice a week, but in the two months since we buried his mysterious wife, also known as my mysterious mother, we have needed each other more as we've tried to piece together her fragmented, incoherent and complex life. Attacking a fifteen-hundred-piece puzzle having lots of tiny parts with no obvious clues about how they fit together to form a whole picture would be easier.

"The quarter ends in three weeks, then we break for two. I can come then," I answer, putting on my ancient flannel bathrobe, which would be much warmer if it wasn't nearly threadbare. Carrying the phone into the sitting room of my quirky apartment, I settle in for what could be a long conversation.

"You can't come sooner?"

"What's so pressing it can't wait?"

"Your mother's living situation, for one thing. I managed to vacate the occupancy contract, which doesn't expire until September, but in return I agreed to clear out her casita as soon as possible. We settled on April first."

"You were paying her rent?"

"It wasn't rent exactly. The details aren't important."

"But you were paying for it?"

"That's not the point, Natalie. We need to figure this out, and I don't think your mother would want me sorting through her things, deciding what to keep and what to throw away."

"I can't imagine she'd want me doing it either, Dad. Can't Aunt Sally do it?"

"I doubt it. When I called to ask her about the things in Charlotte's safety deposit box, she begged off like the kitchen was on fire and hung up on me. When I called again a few days later, Mick said he'd give her the message to call me, but she never has."

"Maybe he didn't tell her."

"Or maybe she doesn't want to talk about this right now. Regardless, her place needs to be emptied out by April first at the latest, and the lawyer said he had the distinct impression your mother wanted you to do it."

"What gave him that idea?" I ask.

"You might know the answer to that question if you'd read the letter she left you."

"Fair point. Do you want to get the letter from the lawyer and read it to me?"

"She addressed it to you, Natalie, not to both of us. Ask the lawyer to send it to you."

"Hopefully it's in English," I grouse, taking a deep breath and looking out my large window into the expansive black hole that is Lake Michigan on a moonless night.

"Speaking of letters, did you get the other one translated?" my dad asks hesitantly.

"Not yet. The handwriting's legible, so I might get a German-English dictionary and try translating it myself. I should be able to get a general notion of what it says." I hadn't thought of this until now, but it suddenly seems like a good idea.

"I guess that could work. I keep forgetting to ask whether you've spoken to your mother's doctor?" my dad continues, dragging out the conversation.

"I spoke with him earlier today. He said there isn't anything to be acutely concerned about, and any doctor can run the test and explain results… offered to be in touch with my local doctor to discuss this and share Charlotte's results. He also said even if I don't have a clotting disorder, if I ever have a daughter, she could have it, and repeated that if my mother had sisters or nieces, they need to know, so I have to get in touch with Emily and Aunt Sally. He cautioned that if something should happen in the meantime, just mention this possibility to the doctor treating me."

"You don't sound frightened by all this."

"I'm not... at least not yet."

"Since you don't have your mother's letter, I take it you haven't been in touch with her Santa Barbara lawyer."

"I'll do it when I'm back in California. I don't see any rush."

"There are some things that need taking care of... something about you being a beneficiary on an insurance policy, and some other details."

"What details are we talking about?"

"The lawyer didn't elaborate. When do you think you'll have the letter translated?"

"I'll stop at the bookstore tomorrow and pick up a dictionary."

"Will you let me know what it says?"

"It hadn't occurred to me not to, Dad. Now, unless we need to talk about something else, I'd like to go to sleep... it's past midnight here."

"Sorry – I forgot. Good night, sweetheart." With that, we end the conversation, and I return to bed. After endless tossing and turning, I get up and make a cup of tea, which I drink while staring out the window into Lake Michigan's dark abyss. When I've finally had enough of gazing into nothingness, I take the German letter from my desk drawer, make another cup of tea, and sit down in the chair nearest the window.

The airmail paper, so thin the ink bleeds through in places, is folded into an envelope postmarked Hildesheim, DE, which I assume is Germany. I very carefully place the star on my desk, then rummage through my bookcase for my world atlas. A few minutes later, I'm able to determine Hildesheim is in Lower Saxony, about thirty-two kilometers southeast of Hanover. The letter is dated October 21, 1942 – the day I was born. It is impossible to know when my mother received it, but she was gone by Christmas. If the letter came before she left, it might help explain what compelled her to abandon her husband and infant daughter to disappear into the dangers of a war in Europe, with no guarantees of survival. Being neither a wife nor a mother myself, I have no clue about what my mother might've been thinking, or what internal battle she was fighting, but there obviously was one.

Holding the fragile letter in my hand, which begins by addressing my mother by the name chiseled on her tombstone, I wonder whether it is from a member of her family in Germany I could be related to and about whom I know nothing. Other than Aunt Sally, my mother's family is a deep mystery that envelopes my grandparents and other blood relatives. I don't know their names and I've never seen pictures of them. Suddenly this feels like a terrible loss – a void in my life that, with my mother's death, can never be filled... unless Aunt Sally is willing to talk, and that doesn't sound likely.

The next morning, icy drizzle blankets the sidewalks, and me, as I walk over to the Northwestern University campus bookstore, hoping to find a German-English dictionary, which takes a harried clerk nearly fifteen minutes to locate.

"We only stock French and German dictionaries fall term, for beginning foreign language classes. I had to do some digging," she apologizes, ringing up the sale. I wasn't intending to work on the letter right away, but now that I have the means to do it, curiosity is eating away at me, so instead of going to my campus office, I slip and slide my way back to my apartment.

An hour later, after exchanging my wet clothes for dry ones, I notice that the sun has broken through the heavy overcast and is shining directly onto my desk, inviting me to sit down and begin the laborious, one word at a time task of translating a letter, written in the tiniest possible handwriting by someone named Irina.

> *Our Dearest Rachael,*
> *I am sorrowfully writing with sad news. Your mother's brother, who is also my husband and your Uncle Levi, and your cousin, my dear son Avram, have been taken by Hitler's Gestapo. They came in the night, but we had been expecting this, so were not sleeping soundly. Levi told them he is an old man so they could have him and did not put up a fight. Avram fought back and was beaten without mercy. Washing his blood from our rug is impossible. Still, some remains.*
>
> *Since Kristallnacht, which I have already written you about in the best details I can offer, more and more Jews are being shot in the streets or put on trains to what they call work camps. Many more are starving. No one who has been taken away has ever returned, and the rumors about what happens to them all end in death. Isaac says now his brother is taken, he is fighting back, says not to worry, then kisses me goodbye and leaves. I hear nothing from him since... and expect to know nothing of Levi or Avram for a long time.*
>
> *They will come for our Lazar soon, and then Jacob, as he is now old enough to cause trouble. When he goes, all*

my beloved sons are gone from me.

Your cousin Minna, born to me when I was too old, is slow and clumsy, yet a loving comfort to me. There are rumors the Reich is making lists of those who are in some way afflicted, both Jews and non-Jews, and will take them away to what they call rehabilitation camps. If this is true, Minna will certainly be on that list. There is a convent of Catholic nuns near Hannover willing to take in children, and am sending her there, hoping money you have sent is enough they will not refuse her because she is a Jew. Otherwise, I am unable to protect her, and she cannot survive on her own like the rest of us might be able to do, if G-d wills it be so.

I give to you the yellow star from Levi's coat because I have other things to remember him by. I keep my son's star for myself. If we never see them again, which Lazar thinks we won't, or if we all perish, which is more likely each day, you must bear witness that we once lived and were faithful Jews brave in the face of hatred we don't understand. If it is the Jewish destiny to suffer, we have no choice but to accept this life sentence.

I stop translating as the reality of my relationship to the letter's writer vice-grips my stomach and I can barely breathe. I put on my winter coat and wrap my longest wool scarf around myself, then leave my apartment in the direction of the lake shore. After nearly an hour of wandering aimlessly along the waterline, the biting wind begins forcing clarity into the foreign words I never thought I would be reading, much less hold such profound personal meaning to me. Obviously, my mother was the product of a German-Jewish heritage that barely survived its face-to-face encounter with evil in an era I am vaguely aware of but also apparently deeply connected to and, from this moment forward, will be impossible to dismiss, bury, or ignore. I have no idea how to think about this, or how what I have just learned will change my life, but have no doubt that it will.

I never saw this coming... I tell myself as I turn back toward the stately old house I love.

Once resettled in my apartment, I return to the letter, which has now, in my mind, become a sacred scripture. I go back to the beginning and copy each German word in my own hand, and then write the English word next to it, trying to bring Irina closet – to connect more deeply with her and what her words were saying to my mother, and now to me. Bringing my mother's native German language to life in English becomes a profoundly holy experience I imagine ancient monks felt when transcribing the Bible, joining themselves with each word, knowing they are part of each letter they write and ultimately inhabiting the world of whoever reads what they have so carefully written. My effort to copy the German word, then recopy the word in English is my way of bringing Irina into my life.

> *Herr Rhodes at the bank where you have been sending our money has been arrested as a sympathizer with the Jews. Minna and I are with Mayim and the children. Mayim is a loving daughter, but her husband, Fischel, has also been arrested, and we are two more mouths to feed without enough food. Both Levi and Fischel said if they were arrested, not to wait for them, but to leave Germany by whatever means possible. Mayim and I were planning to use the money you sent to purchase transit papers to escape through Lithuania to Japan and then to America, but that chance is now disappeared. Still, we are desperately seeking somewhere to go because the Gestapo will be back to take more of us. The only certainty is it will get worse, and we don't understand. We are good Germans, and still the vaterland hates us. The Reichsvertretung der Deutchen Juden is the only hope of all German Jews but is unable to save us all.*
>
> *We no longer walk in the streets, so our downstairs friend will mail this letter, and I hope it comes to you. We believe in trusting her because otherwise she would have by now turned us in. Daily, when saying Mourner's Kaddish, I remember to thank G-d Mikael and Sarah and your beloved parents Nathalie and Eitan – of blessed memory all – did not live to see this horror. And I am thankful for you being safe in America, which guarantees my children's bloodline continues no matter what evil befalls us here. I know your mutter did not want to leave Deutschland, but if you had not left, it could've been the end of us. G-d willing, I will write again. Long may we all live… Your loving Aunt Irina.*

Wiping away tears, I am surprised to discover it is nearly dark by the time I finish translating the final word. For hours, I've been riveted to a letter, written by a woman with whom I am bonded through family, yet until today, had no idea ever existed in the world. As my pencil moved across the paper, translating the words of my great aunt, whom I was meeting for the very first time as a woman desperate to survive unspeakable horrors she never saw coming and didn't understand, the text became a prayer of desperation.

As I finally write Irina's name, I am fully aware that the robust strands of my own life are carefully weaving themselves into the fragile threads of the life of a woman I will never know but have had the privilege to briefly encounter through the fears she confessed to her niece, and now to me, as my mother's daughter and her great niece. Tears drop off my face onto the translation, and rather than wipe them away, I let them soak into the paper, telling her that I love her too.

I make another cup of tea and eat an apple while pondering the eventual conversation about the letter with my father that I'm not quite ready to have. Instead, I put a Chopin nocturne on my stereo, then sit by my window meditating on the infinitely dark space in the far distance for a very long time before reaching for the phone. Just as I begin to dial, a groaning foghorn blows far out across the lake. I stop, wondering if this agonized warning predicts my father's reaction to the words of my mother's aunt to her niece, who was also his wife.

"You need to sit down for this," I tell my dad a few minutes later, when he answers the phone in a panicked voice.

"How about lying down. It's ten o'clock out here – I was already in bed, dozing off listening to Johnny Carson," he replies.

"Sorry. I lost track of time. I didn't mean to scare you. I've just finished translating the letter and I want to read it to you," I tell him, not giving him a chance to beg off. He tells me to wait while he turns down the TV, then says he's listening. Very slowly, I begin. Silence follows the final words.

"Say something, Dad." More silence, until I ask if he's still there.

"I don't know what to say," my father whispers. These are words I've never heard come out of his mouth before. A steady, mild-mannered man, he is not given to emotional outbursts, but he's never rendered speechless either.

"Who were these people?" I ask.

"I have no idea, but obviously they were related to your mother – and to you... and this letter was important enough to her to save it, so they must've people she cared deeply about."

"Do you think it had anything to do with her joining the war effort?" I ask.

"Frankly, I don't know what to think, but based upon what you've just read, she probably joined the goddamned German underground resistance movement." The whooshing sound of my father releasing a deep breath I didn't realize he was holding passes through the phone line directly into my ear.

"Would she have done something like that... signed up with the resistance?"

"I'm sure if that's what she wanted to do, she would have done it. It's not something she'd necessarily admit – at least not to me."

"Aunt Sally's obviously the one with the answers, but from what you've said, she's not forthcoming."

"And I don't think she will be, Natalie. I urge you not to try to force her."

"Why not?"

"She loves you deeply and pressuring her into revealing things she'd rather not reveal puts her in the very difficult position of having to refuse you. That would hurt her far more than you can imagine. Just let it rest, at least for now... please."

"If you say so... but postponing only makes me more curious. It's not like this is going to go away, Dad."

"I know that. But you can live with a little unsatisfied curiosity for the time being," my father declares.

"Do you think Charlotte ever heard from them again?"

"There's no way to know. But my guess is probably not. I would remember if any letters came after she left, and none did... at least none that Sally ever mentioned, and I don't think she'd have kept something like that from me."

"Maybe the Red Cross was a cover, and Charlotte was going to Germany to try to rescue them."

"That's as good a guess as any. But keep in mind it's only a guess."

"So, what do we do next?" I ask, unsure I really want the answer.

"There's nothing to do until you come home and deal with the immediate issues, and until you read the letter your mother left you."

"Are you getting the feeling there were things she wanted me – us – to know, but just couldn't bring herself to tell us?"

"I've always thought that. One of my great failures as a husband is that no matter how hard I tried, your mother never trusted me enough to stop hiding from herself and just talk to me... fear or anger, or both, made it impossible to get close to her."

"Her inability to trust was her problem, Dad. There wasn't anything you could do about it. She either had enough self-confidence to trust others, or she didn't."

"She had plenty of self-confidence, Natalie. Otherwise, she never would've done what she did. What she lacked was any ability to trust people. A lot of things would have been very different had I been able to break through the wall she hid behind."

"Not letting people get close to her was a way to control them., and maybe she liked it that way. But apparently she wasn't the only one with secrets. From what you say, Aunt Sally hasn't been an open book either. I don't see what she has to lose now – the war's over, her sister is dead, and there's nothing left for her to get all upset about. Even if they were a family of axe murderers, which we'd probably have figured out before now, it's all old history. None of this has anything to do with our current lives, so there's no reason for her not to at least answer any questions that arise."

"Obviously there's something Sally doesn't want known, Natalie, or we wouldn't be having this conversation."

"You didn't have any idea Charlotte was sending money to Germany?"

"Marriage to your mother was like riding a thoroughbred horse – they both needed a loose rein. My choices were to either stay out of her way or risk suffocating her. She had a well-paying job, and I earned more than enough to support us, and I figured if she wanted me to know what she was doing with her money, she'd tell me. It never occurred to me to make an issue of it."

"Aren't you wondering now?"

"Not as much as you are. Those years flowed downriver a very long time ago. Nothing is going to bring them back for a do-over, so I don't waste a lot of time pondering questions I'll never have answers to."

"What if she was an assassin for the German resistance?"

"You're letting your imagination run away with you, Natalie. I'd be shocked if your mother even knew what a gun was, much less owned one. Even if she did, I can't imagine her ever shooting someone."

"There are lots of ways to assassinate people, Dad. They don't all involve a gun."

"Your mother may have been a lot of things, but an assassin wasn't one of them. Your best bet is to just drop it."

"Aunt Sally's always trusted you. Maybe when you tell her about the letter, she'll talk to you," I explore, returning to my quest for answers.

"I need to think more about this. I'm very fond of Sally, and I have a soft spot for Emily. I don't want any efforts to satisfy a lingering curiosity about Charlotte to cause either of them unnecessary grief."

"It seems to me that this is moving pretty far beyond satisfying curiosity, Dad. For one thing, there's apparently a potentially inherited blood disease nobody thought to mention, and for another, there are relatives who, at one time, depended on Charlotte's financial help to survive Hitler's Germany. These aren't merely interesting but insignificant facts of a family's history."

"I still want to think about it, Natalie. Opening a Pandora's box before you're reasonably sure you're able to deal with whatever escapes is never a good idea, and I'm not convinced either of us is prepared to do that just yet."

"Not allowing the facts to lead us wherever they go isn't an option, either…"

"That's always an option. Sometimes just putting something aside and keeping your mouth shut is a very good option."

"And then we end up right back where we started, with a lot of questions nagging at us like kids on a car trip who can't stop asking 'how much longer till we get there?' We'll only find peace in the answers, whatever they are. Alternatively, we'll end up like my mother did – angry and hiding from her life – and hurting a lot of people in the process. I really don't think that's what either of us wants, Dad."

"No, probably not…"

"I have another question…" I say, just this moment thinking of it.

"I'm listening," my dad replies.

"When I got old enough to realize I didn't have a mother, how did you and Aunt Sally handle that?"

"I mostly left it up to Sally and followed her lead. My recollection is she told you something to the effect that your mother loved you but had gone away for a while, so she and Jane were your mothers… made a big deal about how lucky you were to have three mothers to love you when most children only have one, which seemed to satisfy you. Sally knew not to throw more at you than you could understand at any given time, and it seemed to work out OK – at least I think it did. Am I wrong?"

"Not wrong at all. I was just wondering. I don't recall ever giving it much thought, which is a little weird, now that I am thinking about it."

"That was our goal – as little trauma as possible for you. We answered your questions when you asked them, which wasn't often; otherwise, we were focused on providing you and Emily with as normal a life as possible under the circumstances."

My dad and I end the call with a promise to talk again in a day or two. Minutes later, I call him back. When he answers, the TV is back on and he's obviously still awake, suggesting this whole scenario is probably causing him to lose sleep, too.

"Sorry, Dad, but I've been meaning to ask whether Charlotte left you a letter, too – other than the one with all the instructions?" He takes a long time to answer.

"By the time Charlotte died, we'd exhausted the topic of us. Everything that needed saying to each other had already been said. So, the answer is no, she did not leave me a letter."

"Do you know if she left one for Aunt Sally?"

"Not that I'm aware of, but unless Sally mentions it, which she hasn't, I wouldn't have any way of knowing. I could be wrong, but I doubt there was any letter."

"I wonder why not?"

"At one time, Sally and your mother were very close, but Charlotte's leaving drove a wedge between them. Any mention of Charlotte allowed a large elephant into the room, and neither of us was that fond of gigantic wild animals."

"I guess that's all I wanted to know," I tell him, having run out of things to say.

"Then go to sleep, Natalie. Endless ruminating over all this is useless. Whatever you are meant to know will reveal itself in its own good time, and not a moment sooner. In the meantime, there's no point in overthinking everything; it's exhausting and won't accomplish anything."

"Right..." I say, too surprised at my normally pragmatic father's near collapse into philosophic discourse to say anything more. Returning to my favorite overstuffed chair, with its spectacular view of the cavernous lake, I catch an occasional glimpse of lights from a freighter on the distant horizon. Instead of feeling sleepy, I am longing for the time, a few short weeks ago, when my life made sense, and I wasn't Alice in Wonderland walking through the looking glass to face into world that I never knew existed, and makes no sense to me.

Late the following morning, before going to my office, I call my mother's Santa Barbara lawyer, John Evans, Esq., introduce myself and ask him to send the letter from my mother that I understand he has for me.

"I can certainly do that; I'll take care of it today. But we'll still need a face-to-face meeting."

"Forgive me, Mr. Evans, but I have no idea why a meeting is necessary."

"Your mother left you the contents of a safety deposit box, and a very substantial life insurance policy she paid in full shortly after you were born. It has been accumulating interest since then... nearly thirty years, if I'm not mistaken. You are also a co-beneficiary on another policy taken out about five years later, also involving a substantial amount of money."

"Who's the other beneficiary?"

"A trust managed by the Bank of Geneva."

"Geneva in Switzerland?"

"That is correct."

"Why would a trust in a Swiss bank be a beneficiary on my mother's life insurance policy?"

"She never shared the details with me, but there are several possibilities."

"Such as?"

"A trust manages money. The trust beneficiary, or beneficiaries, receive money according to the conditions set forth by the trust. For example, a trust can be set up to support a child, and a certain amount is paid out each month until the child is a certain age. The money could also be intended for a charity or other institutional use. It could provide for someone who is disabled, to be used for their care needs. It could pay for someone's education, or disperse a large amount of money to an entity or person over a certain period of time rather than all at once. The possibilities are endless, really."

"You don't know what kind of trust this one is?"

"I do not. Your mother only made me aware of it because she needed someone to inform the trust of her death and oversee the pending distribution of funds, and wanted to designate those responsibilities to me."

"Does my father, as her executor, know about the trust?"

"Only if she told him. I certainly never mentioned it."

"How can I find out more about this trust?"

"I'm not sure you can, to be perfectly honest. I'm just a small-town lawyer dealing with probates, estate planning, divorces, property disputes, dog bites, traffic tickets, and so on. I've never been involved in anything to do with a trust in a foreign bank. My impression, however, is that foreign banks are notoriously secretive. Any information about an account, including verification of its existence, would be extremely difficult to obtain. There are no laws that I know of that can force foreign banks not doing business in the United States to reveal any information. I can investigate further, if you wish, but I'm not hopeful of success."

"So, with no explanation, and no way to find out why she did it, my mother was funding a trust in a foreign bank. Am I understanding this correctly?"

"Yes," Mr. Evans acknowledges, clearing his throat.

"What's next?" I ask, stunned by what I've just learned.

"Before signing over your portion of the money, your mother instructed me to discuss your options with you."

"How much money are we talking about, Mr. Evans?"

"I've not asked for a final calculation, but it's safe to assume it's substantial."

"I don't need it," I blurt out as it dawns on me that included in inheriting a significant amount of money is the responsibility for managing it – something I personally know nothing about nor, at this time in my life, do I want to. I live comfortably on the salary I earn, and both my father and I want it this way. I ignore the "in case something comes up – no questions asked" account my father regularly deposits money into to cover unforeseen emergencies, such as paying a Mexican lawyer a large wad of cash to arrange a quick divorce mere weeks after a costly wedding that, according to my father, dwarfed the national debt.

"I'm merely pointing out that you will have choices you haven't had previously."

"I already have all the choices I could possibly want, Mr. Evans. Believe me when I say I don't want more."

"We can discuss all this when we meet. In the meantime, don't fret. This is a very nice problem to have."

"Right now, I don't see it that way. Frankly, none of this makes any sense to me, which is very unsettling."

"I can understand that and wish I could help you solve this mystery. Let me think more about it, and we can talk further when you come into the office."

"I'm coming to California in a few weeks. I'll be in touch."

"Then I'll expect to hear from you again shortly, Natalie – or perhaps I should address you as Doctor Barlow?" Without telling him I don't care how he addresses me, I thank him and hang up.

My next call is to my local physician, Doctor Sam Cohen, at the university hospital. I ask his answering service to have him call me.

"I got your message, Natalie... what's going on?" the jovial doctor asks an hour later, when he returns the call. I explain about my mother's death and the need for a follow-up blood test and give him the name of the doctor to contact in Santa Barbara to find out what tests he wants run.

"I know what he's referring to, and we test for that in-house. I'll send the order to the lab today. Stop in whenever it is convenient. I'll have the results a few days afterwards and will let you know."

"I'm not sure what to think about all this... Do I want to know?"

"If I'm right about what he suspects, I'm familiar with the problem, and in my opinion it's unlikely you have it... not out of the question, but unlikely."

"He said it was inheritable."

"That's true, but it's most often seen in Jewish women of northern European extraction, and unless I've missed something, those characteristics don't apply to you."

"My mother was German, at least as far as I know. I don't know about any Jewish connection, but based upon what I've discovered in the last month, I can't dismiss the possibility."

"In that case, the probability needle drifts a little further in your direction. Regardless, it's only a life-threatening condition when you don't know about it. This turned up in my own mother, but we weren't surprised. She's a Polish Jew – Korblinski was her original surname. She won't admit how old she is, but the bloom of youth is a distant memory, and hers isn't the best. She has season tickets to the Chicago Lyric Opera, does her own grocery shopping, keeps kosher, and calls me five times a day, so this blood problem is not a death sentence. But let's not put the cart before the horse. Get the test and I'll be back in touch with the results. No need to worry in the meantime..." I thank him, then decide I've had enough new information for one day and will wait a while before going to the lab. Discussing this with Emily can wait until after I have my own results, which won't be difficult, since Emily hasn't been calling that often recently.

The envelope from Mr. Evans is in my mailbox when I arrive home three days later. Earlier in the day, I'd stopped off at the hospital lab, then checked in with my best friend and deeply valued research colleague, Elena Horowitz. With an undergraduate degree from Hofstra, a PhD from Cornell, and an impressive publication record before she finished graduate school, we met when she was interviewing for a suddenly vacated sociology position created when the previous holder drowned while surfing in Hawaii over Christmas vacation. We hit it off instantly, and I pushed hard for the department to offer her the position over the lesser qualified, yet preferred candidate, a recently married young man from the University of Illinois with a thin publication record and an incomplete dissertation. His new wife's unplanned pregnancy forced him to temporarily forgo his research in favor of searching for a paying job before he finished his degree. He assured the committee he would complete his dissertation within a year of being hired.

"Maybe it was because I am a woman and a Jew," Elena remarked, when I recounted this a year or so after she accepted the position and happened to ask why it took so long for the department to make up its mind.

"Actually, the discussion was more along the lines of 'she's married, and her husband has a good job so he can support her' versus 'he's recently married and will have to support a family soon, so he needs a job more than she does'. Qualifications didn't enter the conversation until I brought them up," I explained.

"Potential pregnancy and the demands of motherhood weren't issues?" she asked, her deep brown eyes focused directly on mine.

"Yes and no. I pointed to recent research suggesting that within ten years, both men and women will be able to get pregnant, so the 'biology is destiny' argument was moot in terms of employment qualifications."

"Seriously, Natalie? I'd remember if I'd come across that research, and I'm sure I haven't," Elena smiled.

"Neither have I, but they didn't know that, and the possibility of sex having personal, real-life consequences for them scared the men enough to drop the possible pregnancy–motherhood issue pronto."

"There ought to be laws against that kind of discrimination," Elena frowned, pulling her thick, curly black hair back into the bun it insisted on escaping from every chance it got.

"I agree, Elena, but there aren't – yet. Meanwhile, all we have to do is keep being better than they are, and that's easy," I smiled.

After five years of solid work, Elena's and my very enjoyable collaboration has made widely recognized contributions to sociology. Her tenure application, which is due in about six weeks, is more formidable than the United States Constitution. Still, she is very nervous about it, which she expresses again when I call her to check in.

"I'm smart, female, and Jewish, Natalie. That's three strikes against me. You only had two – smart and female, plus you're beautiful and no one has ever applied that adjective to me," Elena groans, referring to my own tenure battle last year, which was unnecessarily difficult due to the assaults insecure, male academic egos suffer as they are forced to compete with more women entering their fields. I was ultimately successful, but it wasn't the smooth ride into a secure future my lesser-qualified male colleagues routinely enjoy.

"You have a loving, devoted husband, two great kids, a gigantic extended family that stretches from coast to coast and celebrates everything, including a baby's first burp and the day your son finally peed standing up. They show up with gallons of chicken soup and a month's worth of noodle casseroles every time somebody sneezes. I have none of those…"

"You have the entire Christian world on your side, Natalie. We're Jews… there aren't nearly as many of us, and all we have is each other," my friend, confidant, and colleague points out, saying she can only talk another minute or two before rushing out the door to meet Adva, her elderly mother-in-law who is arriving on the EL, Chicago's unique, notoriously rickety elevated commuter train, in twelve minutes. Invited or not, Adva comes every Friday to prepare a weekly Shabbat meal then stays until after bagels and lox on Sunday morning. Elena routinely complains that she and her husband, David, an investment analyst for Chicago Bank and Trust, haven't had an entire weekend alone with just the boys since returning to David's native Chicago, where Adva's wide open, welcoming arms eagerly awaited them.

"We're fine with Shabbat once a month, but every Friday is too much," she moans, then shifts to observing that I'm too thin and too exhausted, and she's worried about me.

"The circles under your eyes are bigger than Adva's when she gets on one of her 'life is short – sleep is a waste of time' kicks. You've got to get a grip."

"I'm having a personal crisis – I'm entitled to be thin and exhausted," I quip, not bothering to disagree with her assessment of my personal well-being, which is dangerously close to running on empty.

"How often does someone get handed a crisis that invites them to reinvent themselves? You should be enjoying this," she scolds, echoing her earlier reaction when I filled her in on burying my mother and the mysteries that have surfaced since. She insists on dropping off Adva's Shabbat leftovers Saturday morning and before I can protest, she shifts gears to yell at one of her kids, who just threw a baseball through the kitchen window, then hangs up the phone without saying goodbye.

Looking at the envelope, I conclude that, although I don't routinely drink, reading the letter it contains is a wine-worthy occasion and scrounge around my kitchen looking for some. Finding none, I put my coat back on, fold the letter into my pocket, then walk three long blocks to Enzo's, a little Italian restaurant I discovered the first week I was in Evanston. With no Mexican family restaurant in the vicinity, Enzo's quickly became my go-to place when I'm either really hungry or, as it has evolved over the last three or four years, in need of a dose of local familial nurturing.

Enzo and Marie, his highly emotional, barely English-speaking wife, view me as their adopted daughter sent by God, who never saw fit to grace them with a real one – or with any children. They aren't shy about reminding me how anxious they are for me to marry and produce grandchildren, especially a grandson, for them to enjoy before they die, which, although both are in robust good health, they insist can happen at any time.

Enzo greets me with the overabundant show of enthusiasm generally reserved for long-lost relatives, or armed mob bosses, then complains that he hasn't seen me since the last pope died. Leading me to a small table next to the window, he brags that Marie's special powers told her I was coming so she made fresh cannoli this afternoon which is waiting for me along with his secret recipe Italian coffee. Enzo's special coffee is a hand-crafted invitation for the soothing effects of alcohol and the stimulating effects of caffeine to do battle first in a cup and later in the brain. When I ask for a short glass of Chianti instead, his bushy eyebrows shoot straight up.

"You no ever drink wine – what happened… your boyfriend jilt you? Stupid ragazzo – he'll never find another one like you. But no matter – I never liked him anyway," Enzo proclaims. I laughingly remind him he's never met my boyfriend because I don't have one, so he must be confusing me with someone else – and by the way, the bread smells wonderful.

"Forget the bread. Beautiful girl like you have your choice of men. Maybe you too picky. I introduce you to my nephew Berto – so handsome he make you cry. The only problem is my sister – she's like the Blessed Mother – thinks her son is Jesus Christ and does no wrong… wrecks him for any other woman because she wants to be the only woman in his life. But no worries – I fix that."

"I don't want to meet anyone right now, Enzo, but thanks anyway."

"OK – your choice, but life is short – don't make us wait for grandchildren forever. I bring you white wine – better with the cannoli.

You can't be troubled and eat Marie's cannoli at the same time. Later, we talk more about Berto... I fix things so he perfect for you."

Enzo's assessment of the cannoli is severely understated, and the wine is pretty good, too. After the second glass, I'm feeling much better. I tell Enzo I have a letter to read and after the wine would like a cup of plain coffee to finish off the cannoli, then will leave to make room for the late-arriving dinner crowd.

"If it is a love letter you read, then I tell Berto sorry, it is too late for him. Break his heart, but it can't be helped," Enzo says, unwilling to drop the conversation about my love life and angling to see the paper I'm holding.

"It's not that kind of letter, Enzo."

"Then what upsetting you? Tell me and I make OK. Break somebody's kneecaps? No problem, I know people." Clearly, not telling Enzo about my mother's passing risks hurting his feelings because I didn't confide in him, so I briefly explain her recent, unexpected death.

"So sorry, Natalie. When this happen?"

"A few days ago," I answer, thinking it better to fudge on the timing rather than making up an excuse for not telling him sooner.

"We do the wake here. Plenty to drink – everybody be comforted very good. Marie prepare the lunch after the Mass. I tell her to start planning right now," Enzo says, wiping his hands on the towel around his waist and turning toward the kitchen. I thank him for his offer, then explain that my mother was buried in Ohio, without a funeral.

"What kind of mother no give her daughter a chance to be with a funeral? You need the ritual for comfort... to cope with her going off dead. You hafta remind God your mama gone from this life and might need a little help adjusting… requires a lot of food and stories – telling God about her so he make her happy in heaven. Funerals make you laugh and cry to feel better – they an important part of life. Everybody know this," he explains, adding broad hand gestures to punctuate his distress. Smiling, I admit this is a perspective on death I'd not previously thought about, mostly because death is not a topic that interests me very much.

"You too young to think about death. You get to be my age – it's all you think about," he moans, wiping his forehead.

"As mothers go, she was a little different," I say, hoping not to be pressed for details.

"No problem. I tell Marie – she be your mother now," he promises, rushing toward the back of the restaurant. Within seconds, Marie comes flying through the swinging kitchen doors, arms wide and headscarf askew, and wraps me in a tight, garlic-soaked hug. It takes fifteen minutes to reassure them both that, despite no funeral to plan, I'm fine. Then Marie spots the letter and questions me with her eyes. I assure them the letter is from someone I used to know and does not involve a romantic relationship. Looking doubtful, Marie nods and retreats to her kitchen. Enzo pours my wine, then is distracted by Marie hollering at him. Surrounded by the aroma of lovingly prepared Italian pasta, freshly baked bread, and rich olive oil permeating the entire café, I finally turn my attention to the letter and see that it is dated just over ten years ago.

> *Dearest Natalie,*
> *I know you may never bother with this letter, but if you do decide to read it, I am grateful to you for hearing me out. I know you are very angry with me, and you have every right to be. A good mother would not have left you. A greater force – one that I could neither explain nor resist, no matter how much I wanted to resist it – pulled me away from you and your father, into a life I never imagined living. It overtook me, leaving me no choice except to succumb to its power.*
> *It wasn't that I didn't love you both, because no mother loved a child and no wife ever loved a husband more. But love wasn't enough. I was still failing at being a mother and a wife, and I knew it was only going to get worse. I also knew that Paul was a wonderful father who would always take care of you, and that Sally was the natural mother I was not. My sister had so much more to give you than I did and would step in to be the mother I could never be. The only thing that made sense to me was to get out of the way and let her care for you as you deserved, as she naturally knew how to do, and I was incapable of doing.*
> *Unfortunately, you were born at an ugly time, when unspeakable things were happening in the world that no one saw coming. I knew I was failing as a mother, but I also knew I was a very good nurse and that caring for wounded soldiers fighting against the evil overtaking the world was something I could do that would mean something. I believed that if I didn't step up, I'd be failing you even more, and failing family members suffering much*

more than we were here in America. This left me with no choice except to answer the call I was hearing, even though it meant leaving you.

There was never any question in my mind that I was doing what I was being called to do. It was out of my control, and I believed that whatever happened as a result would take care of itself. It was not unlike caring for a very sick or gravely wounded patient – I do the best I can, but ultimately their survival and healing are out of my hands.

I had been called to give birth to you, and then I was called away from motherhood. I had to accept this and turn the ultimate outcome over to the will of G-d. I accepted that others would strongly disagree with what I was doing and judge me harshly, but I hoped they would forgive me. I severely underestimated how difficult that would be.

By the time the war ended, I was a different person. I had to choose between remaining in Germany, where I was needed and had formed attachments, or returning to my family in America. I chose to return to you and found you deeply attached to Emily, Sally, and Jane. You didn't know me, or want anything to do with me, which surprised and deeply hurt me. At first, I failed to understand. I was ready to be your mother and Paul's wife, and because I knew he loved me, I expected to be welcomed home. Instead, I was greeted by an entirely different reality.

Eventually I realized that my attempt at being a wife or mother was destined to be a painful failure. I had no choice other than to accept that too much had been lost, and that my relationships with my husband, sister, and daughter had passed a point of no return.

It was a bitter pill to swallow, and perhaps it was the one I deserved, given the choices I made, and the emotional instability I suffered as a result.

I realize my death will leave you with many questions and no obvious answers, which is something you may have to just live with, unless Sally is still alive. She has answers but may not be willing to reveal them. The important thing to know, and never forget, is that I loved you and Paul and

RED ANEMONES

I will go to my grave with that love in my heart. I wish I could've been a better wife and mother, and I hope you and Paul can accept that I did the very best I could. I know it wasn't good enough and you both deserved more. I beg your forgiveness for all the hurt I caused. That was never my intention. Love, Mother.

It doesn't escape my notice that my mother spells God the same way Irina did, and assume it's some German, or Jewish shorthand. Otherwise, to me, this letter is a collection of words lacking sincerity but intended to say the right things in hopes of being forgiven. Perhaps it is a heartfelt plea for understanding that might pry open a door she hoped I would be tempted to walk through, leading me to eventually loving her as my mother, which I can't imagine ever doing. More likely, she wrote it to feel better about herself at a time when she was questioning her life decisions. On the other hand, she didn't leave a letter for my dad, or her sister, as far as I know, so she can't have felt too badly about how her actions affected them or how her life turned out.

I continue to hold the letter in my hand, trying to convince myself that I should at least appreciate that my mother tried to explain why she did what she did. As far as I know, she never apologized for anything, so writing it could not have been easy for her. But words are cheap – it's behavior that counts, and her behavior told an entirely different story... one that created a lot of hurt.

Sitting with what I have read for a few minutes, I realize my mother's failure to express much concern for how her actions affected me is deeply disappointing. I see no reason to believe anything she wrote when it's obvious she wasn't sorry for what she did or for the pain she caused others. That she expressed no regrets surprises me and is a little hard to grasp. Either she had no capacity for self-understanding whatsoever – and perhaps she didn't – or ordinary self-examination of the sort everyone occasionally undertakes was just too frightening for her.

Most bothersome of all is that she dumped the whole sorry mess into my aunt's lap, and she doesn't deserve the burden of having to answer questions about her sister's life that her sister, my mother, should've been willing to answer herself. Charlotte must've realized I wouldn't be able to let the questions rest until I had some answers, and that by not answering them herself, she was once again burdening her sister with responsibilities that were not rightly hers. I don't blame her for being resentful and wanting to forget everything, but I still want to talk to her about it.

Twirling the stem of my wine glass between both hands, I reflect on the tension between believing you deserve to know something and realizing the person who has the answers you seek has a perfect right not to give them to you. How disrespectful is it to insist someone reveal things they don't want to reveal, failing to honor their right to remain silent? Does the truth really set you free or just put you in a different kind of prison? These questions are exploding deep in my mind when Enzo brings two large paper bags, which he places on the table.

"Marie says take this home – you need to eat more. Invite your friends and bury yourself in spaghetti and fat, juicy meatballs. Good food fix everything," he says. With nothing to be gained by pointing out that I don't eat meat and can never eat this much regardless, I thank Enzo, tell him I love him, and then put two twenty-dollar bills on the table.

"Why you insult me with money?" he groans, putting the bills into my coat pocket. I shrug, then explain I can't carry these heavy bags all the way home. Having an answer for everything, he says he already thought of that and called a taxi.

"He on his way now. I load everything up when he get here... all you hafta do is wait. I put in extra garlic bread you give to Franco. He work for me, no charge to you. He ask for money – you tell me. I deal with him good."

"Wow, lady – I ain't smelled food like that since my nonna died," the beefy taxi driver I strongly suspect is related to Enzo, tells me moments later, as the exotic aromas of fresh tomatoes, garlic, oregano, olive oil, and Parmesan cheese fill his back seat. In addition to a tip, I hand him the quart of meatballs along with the loaf of cheesy garlic bread.

Back in my apartment, after eating a small plate of rich spaghetti, I divide the rest of the food into containers for the freezer, then reread my mother's letter. Just before going to bed, which is nine p.m. California time, I call Emily. My cousin answers on the first ring.

"Natalie – I've been meaning to call you," Emily says after we get past a lengthy exchange of effusive greetings.

"You go first," I insist.

"Mom says Uncle Paul has been calling about some Aunt Charlotte issues. She's not saying much, but she's upset and doesn't want to talk to him. She and Uncle Paul have always been able to talk to each other, and I don't know why she's suddenly clammed up? It makes no sense. Do you know what's going on?"

"Not really, but I might have some clues. For starters, my mother's name wasn't Charlotte, and Aunt Sally probably knows why she changed it, but doesn't want to explain it."

"What do you mean her name wasn't Charlotte? I always liked that name – named my own daughter Charlotte."

"I always thought that was nice of you, Emily."

"Then canonize me a saint – after you tell me who my daughter is really named for."

"Apparently Charlotte's name was Rachael Rebekkah."

"How'd you find that out?"

"It was on her headstone."

"Maybe you buried her in the wrong place. I read someplace that cemeteries screw that up all the time."

"Dad was sure it was the right place. He didn't know anything about the name, though."

"Well, my husband will be glad his daughter isn't named after Charlotte. The Arabs and Jews get along better than Joe and Aunt Charlotte did, and he only went along with the name because he didn't know her that well at the time." I blanch at the Jew-Arab analogy and try to recall where Emily's husband is from. I'm pretty sure it's someplace in the Middle East, but this is probably not the time to ask.

"Since she lived fairly close, did you see Charlotte very often?" I ask, wondering whether to tell Emily about Charlotte's letter to me.

"I used to invite her for holidays. I felt like I should, but thankfully, she generally declined... said she preferred to work those days, so staff with families could have the time off. Truthfully, it was a lot less stressful when she wasn't there. She had this weird, angry streak a yard wide and a mile long, and it was too easy to set her off without meaning to or understanding why. A family meal with Aunt Charlotte was like trying to negotiate a United Nations ceasefire between warring countries hell-bent on destroying each other... extremely stressful. Holidays went much better when it was just us, mom, daddy, and Joe's mother, who doesn't say much because she barely understands English and doesn't understand Christian holidays anyway," Emily continues, sounding delighted to finally unload all this frustration.

"Guess who I'm named after?" I ask.

"Have no idea, sweetie. I just remember there being an argument about it when you were born. The hospital wouldn't discharge you without a name, and finally, Mom told Uncle Paul to name you Natalie, and he did."

"What were the other options?"

"I don't remember. Mary something... but who are you named for?"

"Our grandmother, apparently. She spelled it N-a-t-h-a-l-i-e... Nathalie

Avigail. They dropped the h for me but kept the Avigail instead of Abigail. I always thought it was just a misspelling, but dad said my mother wanted it that way, and he never asked her why."

"Who knows?" Emily responds, then returns to the question of what my father might want to talk with her mother about?"

"Some things in a safety deposit box, plus cleaning out Charlotte's apartment."

"Yea – I was wondering about that. Who's going to do it?" Emily asks.

"Looks like I am. I'm coming to San Francisco shortly."

"Let me know when you'll be in Santa Barbara. I can drive over and help you go through stuff, if you want me to."

"I know you're busy and didn't want to ask, but I'd love your help... though I have no idea what it will involve or what we'll find."

"I visited Aunt Charlotte once, and it's an elegant complex. You're not looking at cleaning out one room with a corner kitchen. I'd plan on at least three days. Let me know as soon as you can, and I'll ask Joe's mother to look after the kids."

"Thanks, Em – you're great. I really do love you!"

"What did you want to call me about?"

"No reason. It's been a while and I just wanted to talk to you…"

"So, talk…" my cousin commands. I describe the letter from my mother, and my reaction to it.

"Frankly, Natalie – from what I knew of Charlotte, it sounds pretty much like what I would expect from her. I'm not that surprised."

"You said Charlotte always worked holidays…what kind of work did she do?"

"Jesus, Natalie – don't you know anything about your mother? When was the last time you were in touch with her?"

"I can't remember."

"She was a nurse anesthesiologist at the county hospital and, according to her holidays were always busy for the surgeons because people get tanked up and wreck cars, get into knife fights, shoot each other, and so on. My impression was her job was the most important thing in her life, because she was always busy with work whenever I suggested getting together. I loved Aunt Charlotte and it hurt my feelings that she never had time for me one-on-one. Whenever we made plans, she'd cancel at the last minute, claiming a work emergency, and it happened too many times to be coincidental. It seemed like she wanted us to be close but was afraid to get too close. The only thing we seemed to manage regularly was a chatty phone call – mostly if I called her, although every so often, she would call me. Once she invited me over to her place. She had some jewelry she thought I might like and wanted to give me, but the visit couldn't have lasted much more than half an hour."

"Aunt Sally said she hadn't seen or been in touch with her in years."

"Mom feels guilty about not trying harder to get along with Aunt Charlotte but claims that she always felt like Charlotte really got off on picking arguments and seeing how much upset she could cause, and didn't care how much she hurt other people's feelings. Mom probably could've tried harder, but in fairness to her, a person can only take so much, and living with Daddy is no picnic, plus Aunt Charlotte didn't make any secret of not having much use for him, either. Let's face it, Natalie – we aren't exactly poster kids for one big happy family. Without Uncle Paul and Jane, God only knows what would've happened to us, but it wouldn't have been good."

"You need to cut Aunt Sally a little slack, Emily. She was a good mother to us, and a great support to Dad over the years we were growing up. I can't begin to imagine what my life would've been like without her."

"That's because she's not your mother."

"That's not quite true, Emily. She's my only mother and she's always had both our best interests at heart. It's not been a typical family situation, but it works, so it's not really fair to make comparisons."

A few minutes later, we end our conversation by promising to talk again within a week. Ninety seconds later, Emily calls back.

"Do you think I should tell Joe that his daughter, Charlotte, isn't really named for Aunt Charlotte?"

"Up to you, Emily, but he might have a lot of questions we don't have answers for."

"That's true. But since Aunt Charlotte died, I've just been thinking about stuff... all the times daddy got drunk and said he didn't see how Sally ended up raising Charlotte's kids, meaning both of us."

"We were kind of a package deal, Emily. First you, then me, and the next thing he knew, the family had entirely rearranged itself while he was off fighting a war. I'm sure that's all he meant."

"It just seems like all of a sudden everything is getting weird... like we're about to make discoveries we never even thought about before."

"I know, and it might get worse before it gets better."

"God, I hope not. I'm not good with stuff like this." Emily exclaims. I don't admit I'm not so sure I'll be great with what might be unfolding either.

"Why do you think that it's going to get worse?" she asks a second later.

"No reason… it's just a feeling I have. But no point worrying about it. We have each other and we'll deal with whatever it is together, like we always have."

Chapter Four
פרק ארבע

Santa Barbara, California
Early Spring, 1971

Oh, what a tangled web we weave when first we practice to deceive...

"Mr. Evans is expecting you, Miss Barlow. Please, take a seat and I'll tell him you're here," an impeccably groomed receptionist flashing a fake smile instructs after I introduce myself and explain I have an appointment.

The law offices of Evans, Evans, Peterson, and Benson suggest they are a group of city lawyer wannabes on tight budgets. Still, I'm wishing I'd tied my hair back and worn something other than khaki trousers, a wrinkled linen shirt, and loafers without socks. While I'm pondering this, a short, bald man with thick glasses and a broad torso stuffed into a suit that might've fit well when he was twenty years younger and twenty-five lbs. lighter walks up to me, extending his hand.

"Miss Barlow, I'm John Evans," he says, offering a flimsy handshake.

"Technically, it's Doctor Barlow, which is a designation I generally reserve for academic settings only, but if we are doing legal business, I probably should mention it," I reluctantly point out. All too often, someone hearing the title "doctor" automatically assumes I'm willing to offer free advice on jock itch, foot fungus, irregular menstrual cycles, bowel problems easily solved by eating more, or less, fiber, and a litany of other private concerns a trip to any local pharmacy could resolve. The list of intimate problems people are willing to share with someone they just met who happens to bear the title doctor is endless, boring, and an excellent reason to avoid the designation in public settings. The last thing I want to do is encourage Mr. Evans to open such a conversation.

"Of course – please forgive my slip-up. I recall your mother mentioning something about your being a university research professor.

That's quite an accomplishment for someone your age! But she did say you were a very precocious child," he remarks. *I don't know how she'd know that when she was never around,* I think as we walk down a wide hallway toward his office. My impression of John Evans in person is the same one I had when we spoke on the telephone: an unattractive mixture of pretentious and condescending old fart that I'm not going to find particularly palatable.

"I guess we have a lot to talk about," I say, taking the chair in front of his desk. He nods, shuffling papers as he sits down, peering at me across a writing surface so large he could sleep on it.

"First, I need to explain that your mother made very specific arrangements for disposing of her financial assets but did not leave a will, per se. Under California law, absent a will, everything else goes to her next of kin, which is technically your father, but he is declining inheritance and signed everything over to you, to do with as you wish. My understanding is this mostly consists of personal property, and there is no real estate involved."

"Later today, my cousin and I will begin clearing out her belongings. I don't plan on keeping anything… it's all going to be donated or dumped somewhere."

"That is entirely up to you. Legally speaking, the only other issue is the two insurance policies. Your mother arranged for the proceeds from the one that is entirely yours, as well as your half of the other one, to be placed in a trust account at Santa Barbara Community Bank for you until you reach thirty-one years of age. At that point, you will have several decisions to make. Basically, you can withdraw up to one-fifth in cash each year until your thirty-fifth birthday, leave it alone to continue drawing interest indefinitely, or make other investment and withdrawal arrangements."

"You indicated this involves a substantial amount of money."

"Approximately $500,000 from the policy of which you are the sole beneficiary. Invested wisely, you could live quite comfortably on that sum."

"I live quite comfortably on the salary I earn now. I love my job and have no intention of quitting, so have no need for extra money," I point out. Ignoring my comment, Mr. Evans hands me a form and says as soon as I sign it, he will instruct the insurance company to cut the check for the exact amount and deposit it in the trust account he just mentioned.

"And the other policy?"

"That one is a little more complicated. Those proceeds are being divided, and the part that isn't going to you will be deposited in the foreign trust managed by the Bank of Geneva. It's a one–third–two–thirds split. Your amount is in the neighborhood of three-quarters of a million dollars, give or take."

"My mother had a good job, and my father covered her basic living expenses. This must be where her money went," I offer, mostly to myself.

"Perhaps. I don't know how often your mother put money into that trust account, and exactly how much is in it at the moment is only a guess," the small-town lawyer replies.

"Going forward, I assume nothing about the foreign account concerns me?"

"That is correct. It's all confidential, and unfortunately, I was unable to learn anything more. I'm sorry I can't be more helpful. However, upon your mother's death, there is another American trustee named. It's possible, although highly unlikely, this person would contact you about this trust."

"Can you tell me who this person is?"

"Your mother wanted that information kept confidential."

"Is he, or she, aware my mother has died?"

"The proper notifications have been made. I apprized Geneva of your mother's death and sent the required documentation. I assume the trust officer at that bank notified the other trustee."

"Can you at least tell me when this trust was established?"

"If memory serves, it was around twenty-five years ago."

"My mother's death has unleashed a thousand questions about who she really was and what she did with her life. Any information about her finances would be very helpful and deeply appreciated by a lot of people." Perhaps it is just the light in the office, but I think I see a thin film of perspiration breaking out on the lawyer's forehead as I am speaking.

"I discussed this with the trust officer at the local bank who negotiates the transfers to Geneva, and hit a brick wall, Dr. Barlow. Neither of us could think of any possible scenario that would force the Bank of Geneva to reveal the details of the trust or the identity of the beneficiary, or beneficiaries, as the case might be. I can try again, but I'm not hopeful."

"Please keep trying, Mr. Evans. Any information you can uncover will be very helpful."

"There is one other thing, Miss – Dr. Barlow. I have two safety deposit box keys I've been instructed to turn over to you. They are in the bank where the trust accounts are managed, so you can open them when you are there, if you wish. They have already received a copy of your mother's death certificate and are aware that you now own the contents of the boxes.

You should have no problem accessing them."

"I don't suppose you have any idea what's in them?"

"None whatsoever. But suffice to say, whatever you find was very important to your mother and she wanted it all kept in a safe place."

"My mother's death has sent me on a journey to an unknown destination. I never saw this coming and am still trying to get my head around it... but this isn't your problem. Is there anything else I need to know?" I ask, very slowly releasing a deep breath.

"You need to sign some documents," Mr. Evans answers, handing me several sheets of paper and a pen. Five minutes later, he walks to the front office door and points me in the direction of the bank.

"Ask for Mr. Newsome, the bank president, who will be expecting you. Don't be put off by Henry being up in years. It's a family-owned enterprise, and his sons don't want to force him to retire before he's ready, but he no longer makes major decisions," Mr. Evans reassures me. After shaking hands and agreeing to be in touch, I begin walking toward the bank, bemoaning my lack of answers and burdened with a hundred more questions.

My first glimpse of Henry D. Newsome, President of Santa Barbara Community Bank, reveals him to be older than California statehood. Parked at an empty desk in the middle of the bank lobby, insofar as I can determine, Henry's work life consists of either sleeping or occasionally glancing over at the bank tellers as they dispense various amounts of cash, which given his age, tendency to doze, and the thickness of his glasses, serves no useful purpose. I seriously doubt Mr. Newsome has any earthly idea where Switzerland is located or even knows what a foreign trust is, so if he is the bank official Mr. Evans consulted about my mother's trust, it's not surprising that no information was forthcoming.

Uncertain of his level of consciousness, I approach Mr. Newsome cautiously. Upon introducing myself, it's obviously he's never heard of me, even after I remind him that Mr. Evans called ahead to say I was coming. Giving no sign he remembers any phone calls, he invites me to help myself to a bowl of jellybeans he produces from one of the desk drawers and instructs me to sit down for a chat while we wait for his associate, whose name escapes him at the moment but will be with us shortly. Keeping up a conversation with Mr. Newsome, who has the attention span of a gnat and forgets what he is saying before he finishes his sentences is like trying to teach pigs to fly – it's not going to happen.

Giving up on further conversation, the challenge of getting both trusts transferred out of Mr. Newsome's family bank is foremost in my thoughts when Mr. Newsome's associate finally arrives. Overflowing with apologies for being late, she smooths her tight black skirt, which cups her butt, fails to reach her knees and is not an attractive look on someone of her generous proportions. Introducing herself as Missy Newsome, she is, most likely Henry's great granddaughter. *She's little too perky for a person whose job is to handle other people's money, but at least she's awake and alert*, I think, handing her the papers Mr. Evans gave me, adding that I'd like to discuss the trust.

"Everything is in place. There's really nothing to discuss..." Missy replies dismissively.

"How many large trusts do you oversee?" I ask.

"That depends upon what you mean by large?" she smiles, standing beside her great-grandfather's empty desk, perusing the forms I've just handed her.

"For discussion purposes, let's say half a million dollars..."

"Not a lot of our trusts are that large..."

"Approximately how many are?"

"Actually, at the moment, yours is the only one, Doctor Barlow," she says, looking at the name on the documentation I just handed her.

"What do you know about the foreign trust in Geneva, Switzerland?" I ask, thinking maybe she'll slip up and tell me something.

"Nothing. It's all confidential. I can't even tell you the name of the bank or trust officer on that end. Our responsibility is to arrange for the money deposited here to be transferred from our account to theirs, per the terms of the trust, nothing more. It's a very straightforward, account-to-account transfer."

"Is this the only foreign trust this bank is involved with?"

"Off hand, I can't answer that. Mr. Newsome might know." I look to Mr. Newsome to supply that information, but he is sound asleep, head back and drooling slightly.

"Forgive me, Miss Newsome, but it doesn't look to me like Mr. Newsome can find his way to the men's room, so I doubt he has up-to-date information on the bank's recent financial transactions at his fingertips. Regardless, my primary concern is that, since I don't live in California, it would be much more convenient for me to have everything transferred to a bank in Chicago, where I do live. Can you help me facilitate that?" Moments ago, I decided the ideal landing spot would be the Chicago Bank and Trust, under Elena's husband's watchful eye. He would gladly rescue me from future dealings with Miss Newsome, whose artificially cheery demeanor isn't inspiring confidence in her ability to manage large sums of money. I make a mental note to have David arrange the transfer as soon as possible.

"Obviously, we'd far prefer you remain with us, Doctor Barlow, and are certainly willing to do all we can to accommodate you. I'll have to get back to you on the mechanics of a trust transfer, but I can say it's complicated and not something that can be handled today."

"Then I'll have my people get in touch with your people. Expect to hear from David Horowitz at Chicago Bank and Trust very soon," I say, smiling my least friendly smile.

"Is there anything else?" Miss Newsome asks, not nearly as upbeat as she was five minutes ago.

"I need to get into two safety deposit boxes."

"Of course. If you'll give me the keys, I'll sign you in and show you to the vault," she answers, standing up and swinging her hips in the general direction of a gigantic steel door. Mr. Newsome is peacefully snoring, so I don't bother waking him up to thank him for his assistance and assure him it's been a pleasure meeting him.

As we are walking toward the vault, the inevitable "what kind of doctor are you?" question arises.

"Not one you've ever heard of," I answer.

"Oh–because I have this..." Miss Newsome whispers conspiratorially.

"Sorry, but I don't make diagnoses in public places," I cut her off, increasing my stride to discourage further conversation.

After being escorted into a private room inside an imposing steel vault housing the safety deposit boxes, I take a deep breath and cautiously open the first one, half expecting something to jump out at me. Inside, I find two packets of letters, three diaries, none of which are written in English, a small, well-used book written in both Hebrew in German that looks similar to the book Adva Horowitz once showed me. Calling it a Siddur, she described it as a Jewish prayer book. There are also what look like several official documents, although I'm not sure exactly what they represent, since all are in German. The only thing in English appears to be a registration card for individuals identified as potential enemies of the state, whatever that means. The date is April 1942, which was six months before I was born; the name on the document is Rachael Rosenblum. At the very bottom of the box is my mother's expired American passport in the name of Charlotte Rose Barlow, an International Red Cross identity card, and Nathalie Weiss's immigration card, issued when she passed through Ellis Island on her journey to America.

The second box holds two well-worn, frayed garments, faded to an aged, yellow-white with patterns of horizontal black stripes and fringe. Each is carefully wrapped in tissue paper. Resting against the metal bottom of the box is a gun.

"Jesus," I exclaim louder than I intended. Never having laid eyes on a gun before, I am afraid to touch it, and stand very still, staring at it. I assume it isn't loaded because I'm sure banks have rules about storing loaded guns. On the other hand, safety deposit boxes are secret, so how would they know?

I finger the garments for several minutes, wondering who, before me, has also touched them, and whether they relate to the gun, resting next to a half-empty box of ammunition, labeled in German. Eventually, I decide to leave everything where it is until I can figure out what to do about the gun. I close the boxes and signal the bank clerk to return them to their locked slots. After she returns the keys to me, I slip quietly out of the bank.

Emily is waiting for me when I arrive at the gated entrance to my mother's complex half an hour later. Constructed to allow a perfect view of the sunsets over the mighty Pacific Ocean to the west and glimpses of the morning sun rising above the scruffy San Ynez Mountain range to the east, she occupied a piece of prime real estate that was not, by any measure, cheap living.

Wearing Levi's and a tight t-shirt, with her hair in a ponytail, my cousin comes running as soon as I pull up. Looking younger than her thirty-seven years, we're frequently taken for sisters.

"How much lemon juice are you putting in your hair?" she asks me, referring to my having succumbed to enhancing my chestnut color with a few artificially induced sun streaks. I shrug.

"Just wondering, because yours looks better than mine," she smiles, adding a tight hug and then a question about the security code to open the gate.

"I'll ring the manager. Dad called him, and he's supposedly expecting us."

After introducing myself through the speaker, the voice on the other end says he has a master key and will meet us at Charlotte Barlow's casita. The gate opens and we drive my rental car into a wide circular area with a large fountain in the center of a courtyard surrounded by generous displays of carefully manicured, blooming plants. Various-sized white stucco casitas with red tile roofs are scattered unevenly around the perimeter.

"Wow, this is even nicer than I remember it," Emily exclaims.

"Yea, it's great, but do you know which one was hers?"

"Don't you?"

"I thought you did. I've never been here before – remember?"

"Then I guess we just drive around until we see someone we can ask," Emily suggests. The first person we meet is a gardener who has no idea which casita belongs to Signora Charlotte Barlow.

"Your Spanish isn't great, Nat – he probably didn't know what you were asking." Emily mumbles as we keep driving. Around the next curve we see an older man wearing Bermuda shorts, a bright orange, Hawaiian flower print shirt that barely buttons around his substantial belly, and a red, sweat-stained Los Angeles Dodgers baseball cap. He is standing in front of one of the units waving his fat arm at us.

"Miss Barlow?" he asks as I drive up and roll down the window. I nod.

"Mr. Oliver, the property manager, had to be away this morning and asked me to take care of letting you in. I'm Buster Jones, in charge of maintenance. Please put the car in the driveway. We prefer to keep street parking to a minimum." I do as Buster instructs while he follows behind on foot, strategically placing himself between the car and the lawn, apparently concerned that I might decide to drive across the grass and park directly in front of the door, which would be more convenient.

"This is your mother's unit. I understand you are planning on staying two or three days, so I'm giving you a key and a code for the gate, which expires in seventy-two hours," he says, as I am getting out of the car.

"Please arrange to have the telephone disconnected and return the key when you leave. The utilities stay on until any needed renovations are completed in preparation for the next occupant. Your only responsibility is disposing of the personal property. Mr. Barlow's security deposit will pay for any damage, but one woman living alone is unlikely to cause much wear and tear, so we don't expect any issues. My phone number is on the back of the code card, in case something comes up," Buster says, handing me the card and appearing to smile, but his mustache covers his entire mouth, so it's hard to be sure.

"Where's the dumpster?" Emily asks.

"Behind the maintenance shed, but trash is picked up from the curb on Tuesday, which is tomorrow, and Friday, if you're still here. Don't put anything out the night before. You'll be tempting the wildlife and greeted with a mess you're responsible for cleaning up in the morning." We nod as he turns to walk away, then stops.

"Is one set of keys enough, or do you need another for your sister?" he calls out. I say one set will be fine.

"By the way, call me Buster. If you need anything, just call the number on the card. If I'm not there, the secretary will know how to find me," he repeats, again offering what might be a smile.

"Let's do this," Emily says, linking arms with me and turning toward the entrance. Opening the door, we stand on the porch, staring into a wide hallway leading toward a large open room.

"I feel like I'm trespassing," I whisper.

"Me too, but we can't just stand here," Emily answers, then remembers the lunch she brought, which is sitting in her car. Asking me to drive her back out the gate to get it offers us the perfect excuse to delay entering Charlotte's home, which neither of us seems anxious to do.

After rescuing a sun-warmed lunch from Emily's hot car and re-entering the complex, we are right back where we started, standing on the casita's front porch, staring at the door. Emily holds lunch in one hand and a box of trash bags in the other.

"Daylight's burning, Natalie, and this stuff needs to go into the refrigerator, so open the damned door," my cousin instructs in her bossy "I'm older than you, so you have to do what I say" voice I've heard all my life.

Moments later, we begin exploring the tastefully furnished casita, equipped with an elaborate stereo system but no television set. There are two large bedrooms, two bathrooms, an eat-in kitchen, and a large living room opening onto a covered patio. Three comfortable-looking chairs, a small picnic table, and five large pots of pitifully brown flowers obviously expired from thirsty neglect occupy the space. We sit down on the patio to figure out the next steps.

"Aunt Charlotte had great taste – this place is really nice," my cousin comments, walking around. I don't volunteer that my dad was paying for it. It now appears that, unknown to him, my father was also indirectly funding a secret trust with an unknown beneficiary that Charlotte set up in a Swiss bank some twenty-five years ago. *Finding this out is sure to raise serious doubts about whether the woman he thought he loved so much was as wonderful as he believed she was*, I think. Eventually, I'll have to decide whether to tell him about the mysterious trust and risk destroying the illusions regarding my mother he has carefully guarded over the years. Emily distracts me from this dilemma by again pointing out we have a job to do and need to get busy.

"I contacted a friend of mine at a charity store that resells nicer furniture, clothing, and other household items to raise money for pediatric cancer, or something – I can't remember exactly. This is nice stuff, and I'm sure they'll want it, plus they'll pick up. If you're not interested in keeping it, they might be a good way to go," Emily suggests.

"Unless you want something for yourself, which you're welcome to take, you've just solved one big problem, because I don't want anything," I answer, rolling up my sleeves. In response, my cousin shoots me a puzzled look.

"I wouldn't know what to do with it," I add as we walk into the main bedroom closet.

"These are very nice clothes… not too surprising, knowing Aunt Charlotte," Emily notes, scooting hangers holding silk blouses across the rod, then fingering a stack of sweaters on an adjacent shelf.

"Take whatever you like," I repeat.

"Are you sure? Some of this stuff will probably fit us both," my cousin answers.

"They're not my taste," I mumble, staring at the silk blouses, which, in fact, are something I might buy for myself, but wearing second-hand clothes belonging to some stranger, and my mother definitely falls into that category, is not particularly appealing.

A small jewelry box sits on the shelf below the sweaters. Inside are two rings, three necklaces with matching bracelets, along with a collection of tasteful accent jewelry. All of it is elegantly understated and expensive.

"What do you think I should do with the jewelry?" I ask, pointing to the case.

"Keep it. It's not cheap stuff kids wear for Halloween or to play dress-up. Despite how you feel now, someday you might wish you had something to remember your mother by."

"I don't see that ever happening, Emily. Take whatever you want, maybe set aside something for little Charlotte, and give the rest to Aunt Sally. She might appreciate it."

"The last time you saw Mom wear jewelry was when?" Emily chuckles.

"I still think you should choose what you want and leave disposing of the rest to Aunt Sally. There might be something she'd like to have."

"About that, Natalie… she knows we're cleaning the place out, and when I asked her if she wanted to be here with us, she took my head off. I'm not bringing it up again, but if you want to approach her, go ahead – she always liked you best," Emily half-teases.

We move on to the closet in the second bedroom, which is empty except for several sealed, tightly stacked cardboard boxes. Staring at them and not moving, Emily points out the boxes won't open themselves and goes into the kitchen to look for something sharp enough to cut through the thick tape.

"This is really heavy. I'll drop it if I pull it down," she says a few minutes later, standing on a kitchen step stool trying to dislodge the box on the top of the pile.

"We need to figure out a Plan B because we can't lift them. Let's break for lunch and discuss," she suggests, stretching out her back while commenting that my mother must've been very serious about no one opening the boxes, because they're sealed tighter than top-secret government documents.

"Maybe Charlotte was a foreign spy," my cousin giggles. *Given how the facts surrounding her life are unfolding, that possibility seems more and more likely,* I think, but am not yet willing to express it out loud.

The Plan B we eventually decide upon is to call Buster. He answers on the first ring, and after identifying myself, sounds a little too happy to hear from me. I explain that the furniture and household goods are being donated to a charity shop but want to offer anyone on the housekeeping or grounds-keeping staff first choice before it's picked up, then ask whether he knows of anyone who would be interested in earning some extra money boxing up the kitchen and the clothes. He says he'll put the word out and get back to me on both questions. Then I describe the stacked boxes problem and he quickly volunteers to help. As soon as I end the call, the phone rings and I'm surprised to hear my dad's voice.

"I'm checking on how it's going?" he says. I give him a quick summary, and he instructs me to tell Buster to pay the packers out of the security deposit and reminds me to check the garage for a car, which I hadn't thought of. Then he asks to say hello to Emily. I give my cousin the phone, explaining that my father wants to talk to his oldest daughter, then head for the garage, where I find what appears to be a new, dark silver BMW. I'm still staring at it when Emily comes out a few minutes later, carrying on about how great talking to Uncle Paul was. I point to the car.

"That's a really nice car, Natalie. Keep it for a while."

"I have no use for it. Can't I donate it to somebody?"

"How about I keep it until you decide? Assuming we can find the keys, Joe and I can pick it up this coming weekend and park it back at our place."

"I have a better idea. Sell it and keep the money to use however you want to... as thanks for helping me out here."

"This is Emily you're talking to, Natalie. Helping each other out is what we do. We don't expect to be paid for it. I'm actually a little insulted."

"Just take the damned car, Emily. Pretend Charlotte left it to you. I'll have the lawyer get the title signed over to you." My cousin stands looking at the car, then shrugs. As she starts to leave, I throw out the question of how my father happened to have my mother's phone number.

"Ever heard of dialing zero and asking for information, Natalie? You'd be surprised what you can find out."

"I think he had the phone number because he and my mother were in contact more often than he's willing to admit."

"Mom said they never got divorced. Is that true?"

"Yes…"

"Then they probably loved each other very much but just couldn't live together, which is something you should find comforting."

"I don't see how?" I snap, eyeing what I hope are the car keys hanging by the door from the garage into the casita.

"Mom and daddy can't look at each other without going at it like sworn enemies. Remember the notorious South Los Angeles oatmeal wars? Who the hell argues over too many lumps in a bowl of oatmeal?" Emily asks, recalling the times a fight over insufficiently smooth hot breakfast cereal resulted in someone eventually slinging the entire amount against the kitchen wall, where it stayed because both her parents were too stubborn to clean it up.

"They'd be much better off divorced but hate each other too much to do the other one that favor. I can't tell you how many times I wished they'd go their separate ways because anything would be better than what they're doing to each other by staying together."

"Dad says Mick is a war casualty, and because of that, Aunt Sally will never leave him. He implied we should respect her decision and not question it."

"That's easy for Uncle Paul to say – he never had to scrape gooey cereal off the wall. That stuff stuck like glue and our kitchen always looked like the entire box of oatmeal exploded in there."

"Who finally cleaned it up?"

"Me—who else? Don't you remember the times you helped?" I don't recall ever scraping oatmeal off my aunt's kitchen wall, and jokingly suggest the experience is probably buried deep in my psyche among other repressed memories.

"I wish I had more of those and fewer of the real ones," Emily says, bursting into tears. I give my cousin a long hug, then remind her Buster is coming any minute, so we need to stop this trip down memory lane and focus.

"Do you know how to dismantle a stereo?" I ask, walking into the sitting room.

"I doubt it's that difficult. Between the two of us, we can probably figure it out."

"Good. That'll save us from having to spend any more time than absolutely necessary with Buster," I remark just as the front doorbell rings.

After Buster removes the boxes from the closet, putting four in the bedroom and the rest in the living room, he asks whether there's anything else. I assure him we can manage the rest but will call if something else comes up. Ignoring the hint to leave, he remains in the living room, not moving. I explain that our time is limited, and we need to get busy, then remember to mention paying the staff for packing up. Smacking his head, he apologizes and says he'll get right on that, then asks if I'm sure there's nothing more he can do while he's here. Holding the front door open, I shake my head toward the driveway more vigorously than necessary, hoping he gets the message that he needs to leave.

"That guy's a creep. If you stay here tonight, you need to remember to lock the patio," Emily remarks.

"Won't matter – he has a master key, remember?"

"Then sleep with a hammer or a baseball bat or something. He's slow and mushy – you could take him out no problem," she instructs as she moves toward the boxes. I can't tell how serious she is.

The first box contains carefully wrapped small items: silverware, an odd assortment of dishes, and what look like small silver wine glasses. Another box holds two hand-knit woolen sweaters packed in mothballs that have been replaced fairly recently. A menorah is hidden among what look like hand-embroidered table linens, faded with age.

"This is all old stuff... probably in the family for a long time. I don't think we should just get rid of it without talking to Aunt Sally," I remark loud enough to be heard in the other room. When Emily doesn't respond, I repeat myself, still getting no response. Finally, I holler at my cousin.

"You better come in here and look at these, Natalie," Emily answers from the bedroom, where she is sitting cross-legged on the floor holding a notebook. As soon as I sit down beside her, she hands it to me, and I see pages of very precise script. Turning to the first page, I find the date 1912 and a phrase written in what looks like Hebrew.

"What are all the hieroglyphics?" Emily asks?

"I think it might be Hebrew..."

"Are you sure? Why would Aunt Charlotte have old notebooks written in Hebrew?"

"I don't know, but that's what this looks like to me... not one hundred percent sure."

"I don't suppose you can read any of this?" Emily finally asks, after thumbing through the pages, which look to be written in German.

"I can read enough to know what isn't Hebrew is German, but otherwise, no."

"That's unfortunate, because there are more just like it, and a couple bundles of letters in envelopes with weird stamps." Captivated, we can't resist looking through the notebooks. The sporadic entries end part way through 1946. In among the pages are photos, yellowed newspaper clippings in German and English, and other scribbled notes. It doesn't appear they were all written by the same person, and the later ones are partly in English.

"My impression is most people who keep diaries are consistent about it, so there must be more of these somewhere," I tell Emily.

"Not necessarily. I only keep a journal when something's bothering me, and I need to work it out. When things are good, I don't bother," she giggles.

"Who do you suppose the letters are from? They're all in something that's not English and aren't all in the same hand." I don't attempt to answer my cousin's question.

"The postmarks are odd," Emily continues, staring at an envelope.

"They're from Germany. They date things differently," I explain.

"Since neither of us can read German, do we keep them or throw them out?"

"Definitely keep them."

"Why? They're private and we can't read them anyway. Even if we could, it would be like opening someone else's mail or eavesdropping on conversations that are none of our business."

"I'm pretty sure I can find someone to translate them, and I'm curious about what they say."

"Seems like a lot of bother when you don't know who wrote them," my cousin grumbles, opening another box and discovering more letters and two German cookbooks, using metric measurements.

"It might be fun to try some of these recipes if we can figure out what they are, and how to follow them," Emily suggests, adding that, on the other hand, nobody in our family's going to get any cook of the year awards.

"I can't imagine what Aunt Charlotte's doing with cookbooks, anyway. Her stove looks like it's never been used – ever!"

"Neither has the one in my apartment in Chicago," I admit. Emily stares at me like she's misunderstood what I've just confessed.

"Seriously, Natalie?"

"Dead serious, and seriously dead is what I would be if I tried cooking anything." Hearing this, my cousin, who has, on occasion, claimed to actually enjoy cooking, looks at me like I'm a vaguely familiar stranger.

The miscellaneous books include nursing journals, medical texts, Winston Churchill's five-volume history of World War II, three biographies of President Roosevelt, one of his equally impressive wife Eleanor, and several Hemingway novels. *A Farewell to Arms* is dog-eared and smudged, suggesting it has traveled far and been read several times.

Other boxes hold loose pictures of unidentified individuals, including two of a solemn, aristocratic-appearing man. None have names, dates, or other identifying information written on the back. The faded photos rest in the folds of a hand-knit baby blanket and a sweater, hat, and booties, all made from neutral yarn and appearing to have been worn.

"Was this you as a baby?" Emily asks, holding the picture of a man smiling at an infant.

"I doubt it – my hair was never that light…"

"Who do you think the handsome guy is?"

"No idea…" I answer, not sure I want to know. We find early pictures of Emily and one of me as a newborn pasted in a scrapbook that includes my baptismal certificates, revealing that, within a week, I was baptized both Roman Catholic and Episcopalian.

"Hopefully this is something Dad can explain, because it appears that, for some mysterious reason, my parents felt my immortal soul was in extreme danger and wanted all the bases covered," I comment, puzzling over the officially signed and stamped documents.

"It's an ugly world out there, Natalie. They probably wanted to be sure the devil never got his hands on you," Emily quips. Speculating about the possible reasons behind this decision to secure my spiritual salvation in a totally non-religious family gives us both our first good laugh of the day.

"Okay – none of this gets thrown away until I talk to Aunt Sally," I say, heading for the kitchen telephone.

"Good luck," Emily calls. The phone rings a long time before my aunt finally answers.

"Natalie, sweetheart, I knew you'd be calling today."

"How'd you know it was me?"

"This is your Aunt Sally you're talking to. I have ESP where you're concerned… and I know you want to come to see me. I've already told Emily I'm not up to discussing Charlotte. I'm sure more questions are surfacing as you go through everything, and I just can't answer them, Natalie. I'm terribly sorry…" I hear a slight quiver in her voice.

"Can I at least show you my latest knitting project? I need help with the pattern," I ask, knowing that excuse is likely to work, since she taught me to knit when I was five years old, and we've shared hundreds of patterns and various yarns in the years since. Waiting for her answer, I suddenly remember that I don't have a project to show her.

"Mick plays cards at the dockworker's union hall tomorrow from one until three. Get here around one and we'll visit for a little while," my aunt finally says.

"Thanks, Aunt Sally… can't wait to see you."

"Me either," she sniffles before hanging up. When I turn around Emily is staring at me.

"That was truly remarkable! I beg her to be here with us, and she hangs up on me – you call, and she can't wait to see you. Just proves what I've always said, she likes you best!" my cousin exclaims, with a smile. It's true that my aunt and I have always enjoyed a deep emotional bond, while Emily's clashes with her mother are legendary. Growing up, we used to joke that we were traded at birth – Emily belonged to Charlotte, and I was Sally's daughter, which, for all practical purposes, is true.

"How about we call it a day and go into town? I need to find a yarn store and am craving a large plate of spicy, greasy Mexican food," I suggest, changing the subject.

"Good idea, Natalie. I could use a great big, ice-cold, salty margarita," Emily declares.

"I thought you didn't drink."

"Only on the sly. Joe's a Muslim, so no alcohol in the house. It's the one thing mom likes about him, probably because daddy can drink five men under the table in a California minute, which she does not view as one of his more positive traits – if he has any."

After finding a yarn store and loading up on yarn to knit Aunt Sally a shawl from the most complicated pattern the store has available, Emily and I are finally settled across from each other in the front-facing window of a dark, cozy Mexican restaurant in west Santa Barbara. Over one gigantic margarita, a bottle of Dos Equis beer, a large pile of salty tortilla chips, and heaping plates of guacamole made fresh table-side, my cousin and I rehash the day and make plans for tomorrow. Munching on a chip, Emily says she'll call the charity shop first thing in the morning to arrange for them to pick up everything that's left after the casita staff have made their choices, then get packing boxes from a local moving company and be back at Charlotte's before noon.

"You okay staying by yourself tonight?" Emily asks, adding that I could come home with her.

"I appreciate the offer, but I have a new knitting project to distract me from strange noises and deep thoughts. It'll be fine. I'll probably sleep on the couch, though," I add quietly, finding that the idea of sleeping in a bed my mother once slept in too much for me.

After finishing our meal, Emily leaves for home, and I return to the casita. Hoping to never return to Santa Barbara again, I need to deal with the safety deposit boxes before leaving, which means calling my dad to ask his advice about the gun. I hear a baseball game on the television in the background when he picks up the phone. I fill him in on seeing Sally tomorrow and my plan to have everything wrapped up so I can leave late Thursday afternoon. He says he'll send Raynor to pick me up, which he knows will cheer me up.

"Can't you come along? There's something I need you to do."

"something you can't handle?" he asks, distracted by the ball game.

"I got into both the safety deposit boxes, and one of them contains a gun," I stammer.

"A gun? What the hell was Charlotte doing with a gun, for Christ's sake?" he sputters.

"I don't know, Dad. I don't even know whether it's loaded. I assume it isn't, but there was a box of ammunition with it. I want to empty the safety deposit boxes and bring everything back, but I'm afraid to touch the gun."

"I have an important meetings Thursday, Natalie. If the gun's all you're worried about, Raynor can help you figure it out. Pick him up at the airport around two and take him to the bank. He'll know how to deal with it."

"I can do that," I smile, thinking about how great some time with my lifelong crush, who views me as nothing more than a cute younger sister, will be.

"I'll tell him to plan on it," my dad says, sounding distracted. In the background, I hear a crowd cheer, meaning somebody probably hit a home run.

"Dammit, he could've caught that," my dad shouts.

"Thanks, Dad. I'll see you soon," I say, realizing any further conversation about what to do with my mother's gun can't compete with a San Francisco Giants baseball game.

Sally and Mick's small, white stucco house in a blue-collar neighborhood about twenty miles inland from the port of Los Angeles is unique only in that it sits on a larger lot than the others on the block and allows Mick to keep an eclectic collection of animals that, at one time or another, included rabbits, chickens, ducks, a stray dog or two, a couple parrots and at least one cat that just had, or was about to have kittens. They bought it before the war and held onto it because my aunt hoped that when the war ended, she could eventually return to teaching the children in the barrios. She dearly loved the job no one else wanted, and was delighted to finally call it her own again a few years later.

My aunt is out the door before I'm all the way up the walk and pulls me into a vice-grip so tight I can barely breathe. Older than her sister, she still stands straight and is as tall as I am. Having magic fingers when it comes to anything having to do with yarn, thread, or cloth, she is wearing a carefully stitched periwinkle blue dress with a creamy white collar she undoubtedly made herself. Seeing it reminds me that I still treasure the belted, navy-blue Irish wool coat she made me when I left Berkeley for graduate school at the University of Chicago. I joked that it weighed more than the sheep the wool came from.

"Honey – Chicago's on Lake Michigan... an iceberg in Antarctica is warmer than the wind off the Great Lakes in the wintertime," she smiled, handing me the matching cashmere scarf and beret she knit to complete the outfit. At the time, I didn't think to ask her how she happened to know anything about the Great Lakes climate.

"I made your favorite honey lemon cake," my aunt smiles as we walk into the house. Her dark red hair is going gray, and more lines than I remember crisscross her face. There's no hiding the deep worry in her eyes as she guides me into the eating area at one end of the L-shaped living room, pulling out a chair facing away from the kitchen, which I secretly appreciate, not wanting to come face to face with any lingering evidence of recent oatmeal events. I love my aunt very much and don't like painful reminders of the terror Mick periodically imposes on her life and no one has ever heard her complain about.

As she brings the fragrant cake out of the kitchen and sets it on the table, I request a generous slice. She smiles and says she'll send the leftover home with me.

"Won't you want to save some for Mick?"

"If he doesn't know I baked it, he won't know he's not getting any," Sally answers, revealing that she stayed up late last night to make it after he fell asleep. *As husbands go, she really could've done better,* I think for the hundredth time in recent weeks.

Over the first slice of sweet cake like no other, my aunt presses for details about my life, carefully avoiding any opportunity for me to inquire about hers. Then she pours more iced tea and offers to look at the knitting project.

"This pattern isn't too complicated for you, Natalie."

"It's my excuse to come see you."

"You never need an excuse to come see me." she whispers.

"I know, and I also know you don't want to talk about Charlotte, so I'm not going to ask, even though I have a zillion questions. I just thought if I came over, you might feel comfortable enough to volunteer something, plus I need to be sure you're doing okay, given all that's been happening."

"I appreciate your concern, sweetheart, and love you even more because of it, but it's not your job to look after me. You deserve answers, Natalie, and with all my heart I wish I could give them to you – but Charlotte's story is not mine to tell."

"Actually, according to the letter she left me, you have her permission to reveal her story, whatever that means…" Hearing this, my aunt frowns and vigorously shakes her head while studying the dining room carpet with an intensity that suggests she believes the meaning of life is buried somewhere in the faded yellow shag that once, in a drunken fury, Mick mowed over with a newly acquired, gas-powered lawn mower. Her bottom lip is quivering.

"Did you know about Charlotte's blood clotting problem?" I ask, finally breaking the long silence that follows my aunt's refusal to reveal my mother's secrets, even though she has her sister's permission to do it.

"Yes."

"Do you have it too?"

"Yes."

"No one ever mentioned it was inheritable?"

"Not that I recall. It probably explains why most of the women in the family had so few children."

"So, you do know something about other family members?"

"I can hardly deny that, can I?"

"They're all dead, Aunt Sally. What's the harm in talking about them?"

"More harm than you can possibly imagine…"

"We found notebooks, mostly in German and some in both German and English, and one with what looks like Hebrew writing."

"What are you going to do with them?" my aunt interrupts, sounding slightly panicky.

"Hopefully find someone to translate them."

"Please don't do that, Natalie. There's nothing in them anyone needs to know, and it'll just cause a lot of unnecessary upset… open deep wounds that will never, ever heal over."

"Since I have no idea what you're referring to, I honestly don't see how that can happen, Aunt Sally. There's no scenario that ends with our family falling apart. Nothing can ever interfere with us being a family who loves each other very much."

"You just have to trust me that no good will come of diving any deeper into Charlotte's life."

"These might not be all the diaries, but they're all we found. Do you know if there are others?" My aunt nods, this time looking into the distance, suddenly lost in thought. Minutes go by without a response.

"Do you have them?" I finally ask.

"Not any more."

"Why not? They were obviously important to somebody. Why destroy them?"

"You won't understand this, but I believed it was safer that way. Charlotte and I discussed this… argued about it. I thought we finally agreed that they all should be gotten rid of, and she was going to do that. Apparently, I was wrong, but I was wrong about a lot of things where she was concerned."

"Safer how? For whom?"

"Safer for everyone – especially you and Emily, but for Charlotte and me, too."

"What were you afraid of?" Sighing deeply, my aunt looks at me but doesn't answer.

"There are also letters."

"I know. I told her to get rid of those, too, but was never sure she would. Obviously, I was right not to trust her."

"I translated a letter with a yellow Star of David included. It mentions…" Before I finish the sentence, my aunt's face flames and she bursts into gut-wrenching sobs, then grabs my hand into a vice grip.

"Does Paul know about it?" she asks, after she catches her breath.

"He found it in a safety deposit box in San Francisco Charlotte left him the key to. He gave it to me when we were in Elyria."

"Does he know what it says?" I nod.

"He wasn't upset by it, if that's what you're wondering."

"Very little upsets you father. He's the most even-tempered man I've ever known. Charlotte was a goddamned fool to treat him the way she did."

"I really want to translate these notebooks, or diaries, or whatever they are." I tell my aunt, looking directly into her light brown eyes to keep her on topic.

"I can understand that, Natalie, but it doesn't mean I think it's a good idea."

"What if we agree that whatever they say will be our secret – yours and mine – until you decide otherwise. Is that fair enough?" I plead. My aunt stops crying long enough to blow her nose and take a deep breath while I walk into the kitchen to get her a drink of water.

"Listen to me, Aunt Sally, please. You have to believe me when I say no secret, whatever it might be, is too awful to change how much I love you. We aren't just glued together – we're cemented into the same brick wall – and too much alike to ever pull apart. Even if you robbed banks for extra cash, had a secret life as a lady of the night, were an arsonist, or were part of an espionage ring selling nuclear secrets to Soviet Russia, you'd still be my favorite aunt, and I'd still love you."

"Your imagination is running away with you, and you only have two aunts, anyway, so it's not much of a competition," my aunt smiles slightly.

"If I stopped loving you, I'd have to stop loving myself… and I like myself too much to do that, so let's not worry about anything between us changing – OK?"

"When Charlotte left you with me, I promised myself that, no matter what, you would grow up happy being who you are. I cannot risk allowing anything to change that."

"Then when I say nothing can ever affect how much I love you, you have to trust that this is my truth. If you don't trust me, Aunt Sally, then how can I honestly trust myself, or anybody else? How can I know I am a trustworthy person others can be honest with?" My arm has begun to ache from holding on to my aunt's hand in the same unyielding grip she holds mine, but I dare not let go.

"I guess nothing guarantees you will remain as happy as you are now," my aunt laments.

"Of course not, but you equipped me well to cope with whatever comes my way, including a Mexican divorce, which I managed fine, if you recall."

"That divorce was a huge positive in your life, but let's stick to the point, which is what you're going to do about these letters and diaries. If you get them translated, you can't keep what they contain from Paul. He is your father, and you've never kept secrets from him. The other thing to remember is he was also Charlotte's husband. He has a right to know what they say." Hearing my aunt admit this is a huge relief, especially considering the gun problem.

"Nobody besides you and dad care that much about Charlotte's life, so there's no reason for him to ever talk about it with anyone but you." This point seems to momentarily calm my aunt, as she stares out into Mick's chaotic backyard. Then she says I obviously care about Charlotte's life too – otherwise I wouldn't be pursuing answers. I assure her I'm much more driven by curiosity than by any sense of emotional connection to my mother.

"I think Dad's more upset about all this than he's letting on, and you're the only one he can turn to. This isn't the time for the silent treatment," I admonish. My aunt continues staring out the window.

"I love you, Aunt Sally, and Dad loves you, too. We won't let this wreck anything, I promise."

"Dear, innocent Natalie – you have no idea what you're promising... no idea at all."

"You trust Dad, don't you?"

"Of course I do. Paul is the only man I've ever trusted."

"Then trust me, as his daughter, who, incidentally, you helped raise, to not do anything he wouldn't do... and trust him to help us figure this out."

"I don't really have a choice. But we need to end this conversation. I don't want to chance Mick coming home early and finding me in a state, then demanding an explanation."

"Do you know anything about a trust Charlotte set up in Switzerland? The lawyer mentioned it to me, and I don't think even Dad knows about that," I ask as an afterthought. My aunt first goes pale, then bright scarlet as she begins to tremble, saying nothing in response to my question.

"Seeing your reaction, it appears safe to assume you do know something about it," I finally say.

"Even from the grave, Charlotte has managed to once again crush the life out of me," my mother's older sister sighs, then carries the remaining cake into the kitchen to wrap up for me to take back to Santa Barbara.

"That's just not true, Aunt Sally. No matter what your sister tried to do, she didn't crush you. You're still here, and a lot of people love you very much, no matter what. Nothing Charlotte ever did can change that unless you let her – and since you're still alive and she's forever dead, there's really no point in giving her the upper hand," I stress, trying out a slight smile on my deeply distraught aunt.

"I can't deal with whatever this mystery is all on my own. I need to talk about it, and I don't see myself stopping the search for answers until I have some. That's just how I am, and you should know that, since you raised me. The problem is you have the answers, and you're not talking... and I don't know what to do with that. I don't even know how to think about it, Aunt Sally. You've never clammed up on me before – ever, and this is a really, really bad time to start."

For the first time since this saga began nearly four months ago, I find myself about to cry. My aunt pats my hand, says nothing more, gives me another tight hug, and then hands me the carefully wrapped, leftover cake.

"Emily needs to know about the blood clotting issue. It might be better coming from you, but I'll tell her..."

"I'll take care of telling her,"my aunt interrupts, obviously trying to take control the narrative around hers and her sister's lives.

Driving away a few minutes later, I can't help wondering whether she agreed to see me hoping to talk me out of looking into whatever my mother has left behind. But if that were the case, why didn't she offer to clear out Charlotte's things herself, throwing away what she didn't want to be found? On the other hand, she didn't know Charlotte had kept the letters and diaries and probably thought sorting through everything wasn't going to be a big deal. Either way, she's obviously very afraid of something. After an hour so deep in thought, I miss all three Santa Barbara exits off the freeway.

"How'd it go?" Emily asks when I finally arrive back to my mother's casita. Looking around, I see that except for the furniture, all the household items that are going to be donated have been placed in boxes, and things that are being thrown away are now in trash bags in the middle of the living room floor.

"I see what you mean about Aunt Sally not wanting to deal with what her sister left behind, and there's no point in pushing her. Also, I forgot to give her the jewelry. Could you take it and maybe give it to her later, when she's in a better frame of mind?"

"That might be sometime late in the next century, but sure, I'll put it someplace for safekeeping," my cousin says, taking the bracelet, ring, and two necklaces I thought my aunt might like to have – or not.

"I need to show you something," Emily says, walking over to a box sitting on the coffee table. She pulls out another pack of letters, carefully wrapped in tissue, separated from the others.

"These were under the menorah. Some of them look pretty old and must be important if Charlotte wrapped them separately."

"Hard to know," I say, putting them back into the box. Minutes later, I take the letters out again and carefully unwrap them to look at the postmarks. As far as I can tell, none were mailed after October, 1942 which, in the context of the letter I translated, sends a shock wave washing over me, nearly knocking me off my feet. Quickly sitting down on the couch, Emily stops what she is doing and sits down beside me.

"What's wrong? You look like you're going to pass out."

"Could you please get me a glass of water? I ask buying time to think about what to tell my cousin.

"You look like gin would be better – I'll see if I can find some."

"Water's fine, thanks." Fortunately, it takes Emily a minute to find a glass and take a handful of ice out of the freezer.

"Here you go. Now, tell me what this is about?"

"I'm not sure, Emily. There was another letter from a relative in Germany written in late 1942 that Dad found in the safety deposit box in San Francisco, and I was just wondering whether she sent any more. Based on these postmarks, it doesn't look like she did, which could mean she, and the people she wrote about, perished under Hitler."

"What did the other letter say?"

"Mostly about the war. It was a rough translation that might make better sense when we know what everything else says."

"About the other stuff… what was Charlotte doing with a menorah? And how would she know anybody likely to be in Hitler's cross-hairs?"

"I don't know, but hopefully I can find out." I'll take everything back to San Francisco with me and sort through it more carefully. I'm sure Dad can find someplace to store it all. He's sending his plane to pick me up tomorrow afternoon."

"I could find space for this stuff in our garage. You could store everything there until you decide what to do with it," Emily suggests. Normally, I would never try to finesse anything with Emily because, until now, hiding something from her never crossed my mind. It is becoming extremely difficult not to slip into deep anger with my mother for the problems she has created that are driving wedges into my most important relationships. I'm beginning to resent finding myself swimming in the heavy current of dark secrets floating around my family.

"It's no trouble to take them with me, and unless Aunt Sally asks you, it's probably best not to volunteer what we've found here."

"No worries, Natalie. I'm quite skilled at avoiding any topic that could possibly upset my mother. After a few minutes of companionable silence, my cousin points out that we need to start taping up the boxes I'm taking with me tomorrow, then suggests Chinese carryout for dinner.

"Sorry, I want Mexican," I answer.

"Are there no Mexican restaurants in Chicago?"

"I'm sure there are, but nothing like what I can get in California. It's not up for discussion, Emily. I really need frijoles and guac," I insist, not even trying to explain that I'm exhausted from trying to figure out a family that, a few short weeks ago, I thought I knew well and never wondered about. Now it seems we're a cesspool of swirling secrets threatening to suck us into darkness. Suddenly my life seems like a swamp filled with alligators which my aunt claims threaten to eat us all alive.

The charity shop truck arrives early the next morning to pick up the furniture and other household items, leaving only small details to attend to before Buster loads the boxes into our cars and Emily and I head to the airport, where, hopefully, Raynor is waiting.

Smiling his usual effortless smile, which I can never look away from, Raynor is standing outside the private plane terminal at Santa Barbara airport smoking a cigarette when we drive up. He borrows a dolly to unload both cars and put the boxes in the plane, then says he understands we have an errand to do before taking off. I nod, and, not wanting to explain anything to Emily, walk her to her car, profusely thanking her and promising to call her tomorrow. Then, with my handsome crush in the passenger seat, as I drive to the bank I ask him if my dad explained the situation.

"Not really. He said something about a gun you weren't sure was loaded and didn't want to touch. Hearing your name and the word gun in the same sentence was weird, but I didn't ask a lot of questions."

"Do you know a lot about guns?" I ask.

"Enough to know whether one's loaded or not. When I was flying combat missions in Korea, all of us pilots carried one, in case we got shot down, but I never did – get shot down, that is – so I didn't have much use for it. I turned it in after the war without ever firing it," he answers, looking out the window as I debate whether to confide more to him.

A few minutes later, we carry two empty boxes into the bank vault to empty out the safety deposit boxes. I leave the gun until last.

"Jesus Christ, Natalie – where the hell did this come from?" Raynor says when he sees the weapon.

"This is my mother's safety deposit box. Obviously, the gun belonged to her."

"You do know it's a German Luger and it's illegal to own one?"

"I don't know anything, Raynor." I say, suddenly near tears.

"German officers carried them in World War II. What the hell was your mother doing with one?"

"I have no idea, but if I did, I'd tell you, because right now there's nothing in the world I want more than for someone to help me understand this fucking mess," I say, clearing my throat before apologizing for my language.

Carefully picking the gun up, he examines it, declares it unloaded and safe to put in the box, which he does, burying it in the folds of the clothing.

"That's OK, Natalie. If I discovered my mother owned a German Luger, I'd swear too," he smiles. It takes great restraint not to kiss him.

Chapter Five
פרק חמש

San Francisco
Early Spring, 1971

Every journey, no matter where it leads, begins with a first step.

"I'll stack the boxes in the back bedroom closet," my father says as he unlocks the door to his penthouse at the top of the Fairmont Hotel, high on a hill overlooking downtown San Francisco. The thirty-nine-hundred-square-foot, four-and-a-half-bath space is much too large for one person but has a panoramic view of the Golden Gate Bridge across San Francisco Bay only a fool would voluntarily surrender. The largest bedroom is his; the second largest is still mine, even though I haven't lived here in more than ten years. The other two are spares.

"I'm going to change out of my suit before tackling the boxes, then we can raid the kitchen for something to eat while we talk," my dad says, explaining that he told his housekeeper not to leave dinner for us, since he wasn't sure when we'd be home.

An hour later, wearing a faded, San Francisco 49ers t-shirt and jeans with a hole in the back pocket, my dad rearranges the larger spare bedroom closet to accommodate the boxes. Back in the kitchen, we search the refrigerator for leftovers.

My dad settles on a roast beef and Swiss cheese sandwich smeared thick with mayonnaise. Having exchanged my Santa Barbara clothes for cutoffs and a ratty, gray UC Berkeley t-shirt, I open a can of tomato soup and prepare to grill a cheddar cheese sandwich, packed with avocado.

"I thought Herlinda threw that shirt out," my father remarks, referencing the only housekeeper he's ever had, who has been with him since the beginning of modern time. Herlinda, along with his equally devoted secretary, Mary, keeps him afloat day in and day out. He jokes that he has two wives – one at home and one at the office, so he never has to decide what to wear, when to eat, where he is supposed to go or how to get from one place to the next. Mary is so attentive that, if I didn't know better, I'd seriously doubt he's ever dialed a telephone. I am one hundred percent certain Herlinda has never allowed him to make his own bed, do his own laundry, cook himself a meal, or wash a dirty dish.

"She did throw it out, but fortunately I discovered it was missing and fished it out of the rag bag," I proudly explain.

"It's a t-shirt, Natalie, not an irreplaceable family heirloom. It's barely rag worthy," my dad opines, opening us each a beer. After making our sandwiches we sit down at the kitchen table next to a window overlooking California's most beautiful city as it lights up for the evening.

"OK – let's have it," he begins. Slurping my soup, I don't say anything.

"No rush – whenever you're ready," he adds, taking a bite of his sandwich.

"Since Charlotte had a very good job and you were paying nearly all of her living expenses, do you have any idea what she was doing with her money all those years?" I ask between bites of my own, deliciously gooey sandwich.

"I never asked her, and she never volunteered any information about her personal finances…"

"Didn't you wonder?"

"Not enough to make an issue of it. Why are you asking?" My father stops chewing and looks at me.

"She was funding a substantial foreign trust through the Bank of Geneva since about 1946 or 1947. I don't know exactly how much money is in it, but the lawyer indicated it would be well north of seven figures by the end of next week."

"How did you find this out?" my father asks. It might be my imagination, but I think he suddenly looks a little peaked.

"Her lawyer in Santa Barbara. He said it would be easier to break into Fort Knox than to find out the details, including the amount of money involved and how it is being distributed, which he assumes it is. He also said there was an American trustee appointed to oversee the trust in the event of Charlotte's death, but that person's identity is also confidential." My father's face is impossible to read as he twirls the neck of his beer bottle between his hands, neither looking at me nor saying anything. Minutes pass in silence.

"Did you mention this to Sally when you saw her?"

"I did, and I'm sure she knows something, but at this point, hell would freeze over before she'd reveal it." More silence follows.

"Sally called me last night," he says, returning to his half-eaten sandwich.

"It was late, but we still talked for more than an hour. She loves you so very much and would always want to talk with you about anything, but needs you to understand that, in this situation, she might not be able to do it, no matter how much she might want to. She's worried you'll think less of her if she refuses. It's obvious that whatever it is that's holding her back is very complicated, so don't push her. Give her time and then go slow... talk to me first."

"You and I both have a pretty good idea where this is leading, Dad... and I don't see what the problem is?"

"Until you told me about the gun, and now the trust, I would've agreed that whatever secrets Charlotte had weren't a big deal, but the existence of a seven-figure foreign bank trust changes the conversation rather dramatically. That and a German Luger move this entire scenario to a whole new level. I have no idea, in the name of all that's holy, what the hell your mother was doing with that gun, where she got it, and why she kept it. In my mind, that's as mysterious as the trust," my dad sighs, then inhales another deep breath before taking a long draw from his beer.

"Raynor mentioned that a lot of soldiers kept guns they'd confiscated from the enemy during the war. He also mentioned that owning a German Luger is illegal in this country."

"Soldiers sometimes tried to steal enemy weapons as souvenirs and sneak them back into the country after the war ended, but I can't imagine the nurses were armed, so how she came to have a gun, much less a German Luger, is a huge question. I assume you didn't mention that to Sally?" I shake my head no, then ask if he knows what she's hiding.

"Who? Charlotte or Sally?"

"Either one..."

"I'm beginning to develop some pretty good guesses."

"Care to share?"

"Not until I know more. What are your plans for the letters and diaries?" He asks, redirecting the conversation.

"Hopefully find someone to translate them. I'll start with the modern languages department at Berkeley. It's larger than the one at Northwestern, and a graduate student fluent in German might be willing to earn some extra money." My father continues working on his sandwich without responding.

"One question maybe you can answer... why was I baptized Catholic and Episcopalian?" I ask, keeping the conversation alive.

"I didn't know you were."

"I found two baptismal certificates. One was for Natalie Rebecca, registered in an Episcopal church, and the other one for Natalie Abigail, signed by a Catholic priest."

"Damn it! I had no idea Charlotte went ahead with that. But I suppose I'm not surprised."

"You're not? It certainly surprised me!"

"She didn't like having you baptized Catholic, which she knew I felt strongly about, even though I honor it about twice a year. Charlotte was very proud of her nurse's training, which she received from Catholic nuns, yet was insistently anti-Catholic, and the closer you got to being born, the more we argued about it. She agreed to a Catholic baptism, but she wasn't happy about it. Apparently, she decided having you baptized Episcopalian was the solution."

"The solution to what? If nobody knew about it, what difference did it make?"

"If I understood any of this, Natalie, I would tell you. Maybe she was just feeling rebellious... or maybe she thought Catholics were up to no good, which a lot of people would've agreed with. There were rumors that the Archbishop of Munich was turning a blind eye to the persecution of Jews and cooperating with Hitler. The Church ran a lot of care homes and many believed they were instrumental in carrying out Hitler's plan to euthanize the frail, lame, and mentally disabled. Being Episcopalian was white, Anglo-Saxon protestant America's answer to religion and very socially acceptable. Charlotte probably believed it was a safer choice at a time when anti-Catholic sentiment was pervasive."

"So, what am I – Catholic or Episcopalian?"

"Whichever you want to be..."

"Is my name Abigail or Rebecca, after some dead people in Elyria, Ohio, I've never heard of – one of whom spells her name Avigail and the other spells her name Rebekkah?"

"Again, you can choose. Personally, I prefer Avigail, because it means 'joy of the father', and you are certainly that. But it's your decision."

"Jesus, Dad – how am I supposed to decide these things?"

"It's only a name, Natalie. Think about it for a while, and if you want to change it, do it. It's a personal preference, not a national security crisis." Signaling his weariness with this conversation, my father stands up and begins clearing the table, motioning me to do the same. I put our dishes in the dishwasher, then follow him over to the corner windows in the living room. Side by side, we stare out at one of the most majestic cities in the world in one direction, and the magnificent Golden Gate Bridge, awash in light, in the other.

"Just so you know, Natalie – I'm never moving away from here. This view looks out over a landscape that has defined both our lives far more than you realize."

"I don't recall anybody suggesting you move, Dad. But I don't understand what you mean by a view defining our lives."

"The bridge – it's a reminder of how the war that changed everything about life as we knew it finally ended." I wait for him to continue.

"The headquarters of the eleventh naval district, which was home to the Pacific fleet that eventually defeated the Japanese, was in San Diego, but when the war was finally over Bull Halsey brought the victorious naval forces back through the port of San Francisco so his sailors first sight of home would be the Golden Gate bridge..." my dad reminisces, his voice growing husky.

"Bull Halsey?"

"Admiral of the Pacific fleet, along with Chester Nimitz... the two greatest naval minds in American history – at least in my opinion. Sally, Jane, and I took you, Emily, and Tommy out onto the bridge that day to watch the warships break across the horizon and sail under the bridge into port. It was a sight we knew we'd never forget, and you'd never remember, but I also knew that someday I'd want to be able to tell you that you were there. Halsey's flagship led a fleet of battleships, destroyers, and a couple of aircraft carriers toward the coast... returning victorious after defeating the greatest evil the world had ever seen. The Navy band was on the bridge, and as Halsey and Nimitz sailed into San Francisco Bay, we saw them both salute the flag hanging off the bridge as the band started playing the Navy Hymn in honor of the sailors who didn't return. The band members were crying so hard they kept missing notes and finally dropped their instruments and just started cheering. Sally, Jane, and I were bawling like babies. It was one of those moments that stay with you forever... and every damned time I look out this window at that magnificent bridge, I remember that day with a sense of pride I'd never felt before – or since."

"Where was my mother?"

"By the time Japan surrendered and the fleet returned, the war in Europe had been over for months, and Charlotte was still wherever she was. We figured we would've heard if she'd died, so assumed she was alive and wasn't coming back until she was good and ready, which we were beginning to think might be never." Recalling this, my dad gives me a quick hug and says it's been a long day, so he's going to bed.

I always sleep soundly back in the bedroom I grew up in, and by the time the sun wakes me up it's late morning. Herlinda, who, in addition to overseeing all aspects of my father's life and eagerly managing every detail of mine whenever I am in her reach, is in the sacred space she calls her kitchen cleaning the coffee pot. Within seconds of seeing me, she lets loose with a cheer, leaps at me with arms poised for a smothering hug, then asks about breakfast. I say I'll eat something later and not to bother.

"I live for you to bother me," Herlinda smiles, tucking a loose strand of hair behind her ear as she gets out the toaster. Wearing an apron I've never seen her without, she is a solidly built Hispanic bundle of unbreakable loyalty and eager-to-please energy a foot shorter than I am.

After drinking a cup of tea and enjoying three pieces of Herlinda's homemade orange marmalade-covered toast, I use the hall phone to place a call to the general switchboard at the University of California-Berkeley, hoping to get connected to the Department of Modern Languages. Eventually, the department secretary comes on the line. I briefly introduce myself and describe my need for a trustworthy German translator. She explains that the German section has a relatively small enrollment and a difficult curriculum, so off-hand, no one with the time to translate several diaries and letters comes to mind. She offers to pin a notice on the department bulletin board and suggests placing an ad in *The Berkeley Barb*, the university's infamous and widely-read student newspaper.

"There may be some native German speakers enrolled elsewhere in the university who would be willing to do it for the extra cash students always need," she points out. I stress that I prefer someone who takes the project as seriously as I do and am willing to reimburse them generously in exchange for that level of commitment.

"I'll pass your name and phone number on to the department head, Professor Jacques LaValle, and if he knows of anyone, he can be in touch, but I'm not hopeful," she tells me. I thank her and walk into the floor-to-ceiling windowed great room, wondering what to do with the rest of my day.

Normally, when I am in town, my Aunt Jane and I have a long lunch, but she and Charlie have recently moved to someplace outside Portland where Tommy recently opened a law practice, which I find very difficult to imagine because Tommy is dumb as a rock. The only way I can conceive of him ever receiving a law degree is from the back of a cereal box – a remark my father did not find amusing.

"We're a small family, Natalie – you need to keep your opinions about the relatives' intellectual capabilities to yourself, because we don't have that many of them," he admonished, suppressing a smile. Despite Tommy's questionable legal and other abilities, his mother and I have always gotten along and I wish we could see each other more often.

"The problem with returning to San Francisco is I no longer have any friends here. I suppose I could work on my book manuscript, which is still in my suitcase, but I'm not really in the mood to stress my brain," I mumble to the empty room.

Eventually, I take a shower, get dressed, and ride the trolley cars around town, which is my favorite activity when something is bothering me, or I'm bored and don't have anything else to do. I let Herlinda know my plans, including eating lunch on Fisherman's Wharf, and ask if she wants me to bring anything back. My polite offer results in a substantial grocery list and instructions to do the shopping last so the fish and vegetables are in the refrigerator as soon as possible. Promising to do as I am told, I'm out the door.

Arriving back just past four thirty, I unload the groceries while Herlinda digs into her apron pocket searching for a slip of paper.

"He say to call this number," she explains, handing me a crumpled wad of paper towel.

"Who?"

"Professor somebody. His English not so good. I only pick up because the phone keeps ringing and ringing. When I say hello, he just start talking – asks for you." Herlinda hates speaking English on the telephone and rarely answers it, so I'm somewhat surprised she took the message.

Despite being late in the day, I return the call and am pleasantly surprised when Professor LaValle himself answers the phone. After identifying myself, he asks for more information about my need for a translator, because he has an idea that might work. I describe the letters, notebooks, and diaries, explain how they came to be in my possession, stressing that my interest in knowing what they say is personal and has nothing to do with any scholarly effort.

"A few days ago, I met an interesting fellow here on sabbatical," Berkeley's Modern Languages Department chairman says, in charming, French-accented English. "He spent the last six years as the Vatican envoy to Germany and is writing a book on Pope Pius XII's relationship with Hitler and the murderous Third Reich. He's fluent in German and might be interested in doing some translating, especially documents from the era he's working on. If this sounds like a suitable possibility, I'll try to track him down and, with your permission, give him your phone number."

"This sounds perfect," I reply, smiling to myself.

"I don't recall his name and will have to make a couple of phone calls. It might take me a day or two," he says. I thank him and explain I'll be in town for another four days before returning to Chicago.

Less than five minutes later, my father telephones asking if I'm interested in dinner in Chinatown. I grab onto the idea and agree to meet him at Yees, our favorite place to gorge ourselves on authentic Chinese food, around seven.

"Phone calls this late are never good news," my dad grouses, unlocking the apartment door as the phone is ringing. After dinner, we spent some time wandering around Chinatown, then took the trolley home, and it's now after ten p.m. I offer to answer the phone, and he shakes his head.

"We've already had one person assume I'm dating a beautiful woman less than half my age – we don't need to fuel that rumor further," my father says, referring to a business colleague we met earlier in the evening. The portly older gentleman assumed Paul Barlow was having a clandestine affair with a much younger woman. Despite our family resemblance and the explanation that I was his daughter, my dad isn't convinced the man believed him. While I'm hanging my coat in the hall closet, my father calls out that the phone is for me.

"Someone named Adrian McCormick," he says, holding the receiver and questioning me with his eyes. When I pick up, a deep, melodious voice confirms that he is speaking with Natalie Barlow.

"I'm sorry for calling so late. Jacques LaValle from Modern Languages contacted me about your need for a someone to translate some German documents. He said that you were only in town for a few days, so I thought I shouldn't wait before trying to reach you," Adrian McCormick begins. I assure him the late hour is no problem, and briefly explain why I need a translator.

"I suggest we meet for coffee and allow me to have a look at one of the letters, or a diary. If it seems like something I am capable of doing, we can talk further. Are you by any chance available tomorrow afternoon?" he asks. I assure him I can be available any time tomorrow and volunteer to meet him wherever is convenient.

"Are you at all familiar with Berkeley?"

"It's the home of my misspent youth – at least that's how my father, who was paying the bills at the time, would describe it. Personally, I loved it and don't consider one minute of my time there to be misspent," I deadpan.

"I take that as a yes?" Adrian chuckles.

"I'm somewhat familiar with the area, although I'm sure things have changed since I left."

"There is a nice little bakery and coffee shop on Telegraph, next door to Moe's Bookstore – Ella's I think it's called. I can meet you there at three, if that's convenient. Whoever arrives first can grab a booth on the window side." I assure him I remember Ella's and the time will be fine, then thank him again for his interest.

"Looking forward to meeting you and hearing more," Adrian McCormick says, hanging up. Still holding the phone, I decide that if the man is anything like his voice sounds, I've just fallen in love. I walk into the kitchen, where my father is watching the end of a baseball game on Herlinda's portable television while waiting to find out who was on the phone. Briefly summarizing the call, I ask about borrowing his personal car tomorrow.

"My driver can take you over and bring you back," my dad answers.

"I'd rather drive myself. We might be a while."

"What about parking? Berkeley's mostly street parking, which there's not a lot of."

"Dad – I'm nearly thirty years old – I'll figure it out."

"Fine. Take the car, and call if you're going to be late. I'm too old to be worrying about where my daughter is." I start to protest, then decide it's pointless, so pat him on the cheek and kiss the top of his head goodnight.

The next afternoon my father's assessment of Berkeley's parking issues proves unfortunately correct. After a hunting expedition lasting far too long and irritating me to the point of screaming, the best I can do is a side street eight blocks from Ella's. I'm twenty minutes late, arriving frustrated and disheveled from a lengthy power walk better accomplished in shorts and running shoes, which was not my wardrobe choice for this meeting.

Both window booths are occupied – one by an older, balding man with thick glasses, wearing a plaid shirt missing several buttons and stroking a moustache covering the bottom half of his face as he reads a newspaper. Sitting in the other booth, partially obscured by a glass front refrigerator filled with cheese wheels, pre-packaged salami, a large jar of pickles, and an even larger crock of sauerkraut, is a remarkably handsome man wearing a black turtle-neck sweater. The sun shining through the window forms a halo around his tousled, dark hair slightly beginning to gray. One hand grips a coffee mug resting on a scarred wooden tabletop and the other holds a book commanding his full attention. While I'm standing in the doorway trying to decide which man is more likely Adrian McCormick, the man with the book looks up and smiles. To my great relief, the other man ignores me. *Maybe there really is a God after all*, I think, accepting the invitation to walk in the direction of the smile while extending my hand.

"I'm so sorry to be late, Mr. McCormick. Parking problems. I'm eight blocks away," I explain, tossing my head in hopes of rearranging my hair, which has come loose from the clip holding it at the base of my neck. *Thank God I didn't wear a sweater*, I exhale, suddenly feeling very warm.

"Please, call me Adrian… and I'm pleased to meet you. I was beginning to wonder whether you'd changed your mind," he says, standing up at the same time he gestures me to sit down.

"Before we get started, I suggest we order coffee and whatever mid-afternoon snack suits you. The granola chocolate chip cookies are addictive, and it smells like they've just pulled a fresh batch out of the oven. Alternatively, the cherry pie gives you a sugar high you'll be days coming off of."

"Coffee will be fine," I answer, while trying to pry my eyes off his chiseled, dark Irish face.

"Two coffees, and maybe split a cookie? You really should try one," he smiles, heading toward the counter along the far wall without waiting for my response, which affords me a desperately needed moment to compose myself. He returns to the table with two mugs of hot coffee and a gigantic cookie thicker than an ice cream bar and overflowing with chocolate chips. He hands me a mug before breaking the cookie in two and handing me the generous half, along with a napkin. Finally, he sits down.

"Do you prefer Doctor Barlow, Professor Barlow, or Mrs. Barlow?" he begins.

"In this situation, I prefer Natalie, and I'm not Mrs. Barlow."

"A man who said his name was Paul Barlow answered the phone, and I assumed…"

"Paul Barlow is my father. I'm staying with him while I'm home in California. How did you know I am a professor?"

"You must've mentioned it to Jacques, because he told me. And apologies for misunderstanding your situation."

"You're not the first person. Last night one of my dad's business associates came upon us eating dinner in Chinatown and assumed my father was clandestinely dating a much younger woman. I thought it was funny, but my dad wasn't amused," I smile.

"Lets begin with you telling me more about how you came upon these documents and what you know about them?" Adrian redirects.

I explain that my mother died in January, and I discovered them as I was sorting through her belongings. As an afterthought, I add that I also discovered several other things no one is sure what to make of, leaving out the part about the foreign trust and the gun.

"Like what?"

"A tapestry, a tattered yarmulke, a menorah, a letter that included a yellow cloth star, and more letters in a safety deposit box, just for starters. I assume these are family heirlooms, but I have no idea who they belonged to or what meaning they held for her. It turns out my dad didn't even know her real name, but that's a story for another time…"

"Your mother was Jewish?"

"Not that my father or I were aware of, but it now appears that she might've been. My father found a letter to her in a safety deposit box written in German and containing yellow cloth star."

"And these discoveries have created a family uproar?"

"That's one way of putting it. Other than curiosity, my dad and I don't really care what the implications are, but my mother's sister, who is also my dearly beloved aunt, is very upset. I have no idea why, and she's not talking. Right now, everything is mostly questions with no clear answers."

"Your aunt may have very good reasons for being upset. She and your mother may have had deep concerns about their Jewish heritage being discovered. Keeping their true identity a secret would have imposed a very heavy burden upon them both, but it also kept them safe during periods of very ugly antisemitism in this country. After so many years, your aunt probably believes it best not to risk the truth."

"I honestly don't understand what there is to be afraid of?"

"Being labeled a lifetime liar and being publicly identified with a culture, religion, heritage and ethnicity a lot of people hate are two possibilities that come immediately to mind."

"You sound very compassionate regarding this dilemma," I remark, looking into liquid brown eyes, emphasized by faint smile lines in each corner.

"To be perfectly frank, this dilemma as you call it, is framed by deep fear, ugly politics, profound distrust, evil men and the darkest side of human nature, even here in America. It's part of what I am exploring for the book I am working on, and is one of the reasons your project is so intriguing. These diaries and letters may contain insights into how Jews suffered during the reign of Pope Pius XII, formerly the Archbishop of Munich. The Pius XII era lasted for nineteen long years – from 1939 to 1958 – plenty of time to do a lot of harm. Not to sound too dramatic about it, but sometimes a gift just lands in your lap, and that was my reaction when Jacques mentioned your needing German diaries from that period translated."

"And the letters."

"All the better…"

"How did you make a possible Jewish connection just from the information I gave Professor LaValle?"

"Any German diaries written during this time period are likely to at least mention the rise of Nazis and the emergence of the Third Reich, thus are automatically interesting to me. At the very least, they provide rich background material, which is always valuable in historical research."

"I brought the earliest one I've found, so far. I've not unpacked everything yet," I explain, pushing the manila envelope I brought with me toward him. He very carefully removes the notebook, opens it, then asks how many I have.

"There are several. The later ones are partly in English and perhaps written by my mother. Many have a lot of blank pages and the only thing I can think of is someone wrote in them for a while, maybe during a period of acute personal angst, and when whatever was so upsetting finally passed, they stopped writing… until the next upset. They aren't all the same handwriting, so it might take some sleuthing to figure out who wrote what, but in any case, they aren't likely to be the thoughts of a dedicated journal writer. They're more likely a receptacle for intermittent frustrations, with nothing connecting one set of entries to the next."

Adrian reads through the first entry while I try not to stare at the gentle face sitting across from me. Eventually I distract myself by refilling our coffee mugs. After several silent minutes, he looks up.

"What was your grandmother's name?" he asks.

"According to a headstone in Elyria, Ohio, it was Nathalie Avigail Weiss Rosenblum."

"You knew her?" I shake my head.

"You were named for her?"

"Apparently, although even that isn't entirely clear. My name is spelled slightly differently and Avigail might actually be Rebekkah. It depends on which baptismal certificate you look at." I take a sip from the coffee mug.

"There's more than one?" he asks, raising his eyebrows slightly.

"Two – a couple weeks apart. One Catholic and one Episcopalian. My dad didn't know anything about the Episcopalian one."

"Which was first?"

"Catholic, why?"

"Someone, perhaps your mother, was very concerned about your being identified as Catholic which, at that time could be almost as risky as being identified as a Jew. Whoever arranged for two baptisms was trying to protect you."

"That was my dad's guess. My cousin thought concerns about becoming possessed by the devil might've been the motivation."

"Back then, some people thought Catholics were the devil, and many still do," Adrian smiles, then returns to the diary, which he studies for several minutes.

"It appears this was begun on the journey to America. It contains the Shema – the central prayer of Jewish faith, written in Hebrew and phonetic Hebrew, suggesting whoever wrote it, and my guess is it was your grandmother, was learned... had several years of formal education. Perhaps she feared forgetting the prayer, or perhaps just writing it down was comforting. Regardless, she knew it well, it was important to her, and she wrote in a clear, beautiful hand. In my opinion, this is a sacred document created by someone who left all that was familiar behind to travel, alone, to a strange country and face an unknowable future... the prayer probably consoled her." Adrian remarks, then graciously stays silent, allowing me a few moments to absorb what he has translated. Staring into my coffee, I blink back sudden tears, then say I vaguely remember someone, probably my Aunt Sally, mentioning that my grandmother had immigrated to America from Germany, so what he says makes sense.

"It was a casual remark a long time ago, and I don't recall any other details. I never thought about it again, until recently. I can't even begin to imagine doing what she did – leaving everyone she'd loved all her life, knowing she'll never see any of them again... going to a strange country alone. She must've been nearly paralyzed with fear and loneliness."

"It's pretty clear she was Jewish, Natalie. That might have something to do with why she left Germany."

"I don't know anything about her reasons, but the Jewish part doesn't surprise me." I exhale a breath I didn't realize I was holding.

"Just at first glance, it's also pretty clear she was strong, brave, smart, and remarkably articulate. She writes quite descriptively, at least in this part." When I don't respond, he asks what I know about the Jewish culture and religion.

"Basically, nothing. I was raised by a non-observant Catholic father and was never exposed to, nor particularly interested in anything else.

"Unless you are protestant, religious freedom in America is largely a myth. Early in the century prejudice against Catholics was pervasive in this country. Irish and Italian immigrants were both universally Catholic and the largest population groups entering the country, and the more of them there were, the greater the anti-Catholic sentiment. By the 1920's the Ku Klux Klan was well organized and, in addition to murdering Negroes, was focused on promoting the belief you couldn't be loyal to America and to the pope, so Catholic immigrants were viewed with suspicion and distrust, labeled papists, and on the receiving end of a lot of nasty rhetoric."

"What about the Jews?"

"In the beginning, there weren't enough to matter, to be perfectly honest. But as more came, most were very clannish – creating their own communities and tending to isolate themselves from wider society. Eventually, Catholics targeted them because they thought Jews threatened to overtake them as a religion. It was politically advantageous to Catholics, who were just as clannish, to stop the Jews before they became too powerful. Basically, it was religious gang warfare on a national scale led by a Detroit priest who appointed himself to lead the nationwide charge – and others followed. His radio program broadcast his vitriol to thousands across the country. It wasn't the Catholic Church's finest hour."

"Detroit isn't far from Cleveland. If my mother was growing up there, she probably heard of him."

"Starting in the early 1930's Father Charles Coughlin began spewing antisemitic rhetoric right out of Hitler's playbook. He blamed Jewish bankers for the 1929 stock market crash, which resulted in the worst economic depression in American history. Everybody was hurting, and wanted someone to blame, and Coughlin handed them the perfect scapegoat. It didn't matter that he was wrong – it worked."

"Which is nothing new. I'm not a historian but my impression is that, throughout history, whenever things go bad, blame always lands on the Jews. I suppose that's what happens when you're accused of killing Christ."

"There were a lot of outrageously false, antisemitic canards that, unfortunately, caught on. Coughlin supported many of Nazi Germany's policies, essentially creating a fascist agenda applicable to American culture. This firmly established Catholics as Jew haters, which ultimately put your mother in an untenable position. She would not have wanted her child to be in any way connected to a religion that hated Jews when her child was one, and if her husband, who was Catholic, discovered she was a Jew, she may have been terrified he would hate her."

"If that is how she felt, she didn't know my father at all. Like everybody, he has his flaws, but hating others isn't one of them. He loved my mother so much he never divorced her and continued to support her throughout her life, even though they only lived together for less than three of the more than thirty years they were married. He gives new meaning to the concept of lifetime commitment," I smile weakly, taking a drink of what is now lukewarm coffee.

"My dad loved my mother far above and way beyond most people's ability to love anyone, and he wouldn't have cared if she was Jewish, Mexican, East Indian, Chinese, Eskimo or tribal African. The tragedy is she didn't trust him enough to be honest with him about who, it now appears, she really was. My guess is this has hurt him deeply."

"With all the antisemitism swirling around her, most likely she was deeply afraid of the truth. She may have thought her being Jewish, if known, would endanger your father, and you... but this is all speculation. At this point, we have no way of knowing what was in her head. Maybe eventually the diaries and letters will help piece together some answers," Adrian counsels. I shrug, studying my coffee mug.

"What's important to keep in mind is that during those years, anyone in the wider society who wasn't white, Anglo-Saxon and protestant was vulnerable to hate, and to a significant degree, still is," he continues. "My Irish immigrant parents spoke about that a lot. There was plenty of prejudice to go around. It wasn't just toward the Jews, and it was all ugly. 'No Irish Need Apply' signs were as common in parts of the U.S. as Juden signs were in Nazi Germany."

"I guess I have a lot to learn..." I admit, sobered by the direction this conversation has taken.

"And even more to try to understand. The immigrant experience wasn't what it was cracked up to be. There is a quote scratched into the wall of one of the Ellis Island buildings – something to the effect that 'We were promised the streets were paved with gold, and when we got here, we found out the streets weren't paved, and we were expected to pave them'. I think it's credited to an Italian immigrant. The point is, many came here illiterate and full of hope, and ended up being exploited and no better off. In fact, they were worse off when you consider that they left their families and all that was familiar to them behind to chase a dream that never came true. Only the really lucky ones improved their lives enough to make all that they gave up worth it."

"You're saying what they got when they arrived was a lot of crushing disappointment, which isn't too surprising when the prevailing American value is free-enterprise, profit-motive capitalism. But that's a conversation for another time," I expound, frowning.

"Do you want to know what having a Jewish mother means, according to Jewish law?" Adrian asks, looking directly at me.

"I don't know. Do I?"

"I would, if I were you. I can tell you, but only if you promise that as you process all this, you won't do it alone, and will ask me, or someone, any questions that arise. It's not like you're discovering some distant relative rustled cattle for a living. This is much bigger than a merely interesting piece of family folklore… it's seriously life changing."

"I live in Chicago, Adrian… I don't get to California often, so your suggestion that I bring every question that arises or upsets me to you might be difficult."

"Last I knew, Chicago had telephones. My sisters and I call each other every so often with no problem," he points out.

"They live in Chicago?"

"In the general area. I was born and grew up there – just down the street from Wrigley Field. Many of the happiest days of my life have been spent watching the Cubs lose a baseball game."

"I like football myself, although watching baseball is a nice way to spend a summer afternoon," I remark, having no idea why I'm talking about sports at this moment, but very happy the conversation has moved toward something far less intense than my newly discovered Jewish heritage.

"Football is my second favorite. The Bears lose with the best of them and have a good time doing it, which is the upside to watching them play. Otherwise, their games are pure torture," Adrian chuckles.

"Now that we've established that there's a phone connection between Chicago and Berkeley and determined who likes which sports, go ahead with what you were going to tell me," I invite.

"By Jewish law, anyone born of a Jewish mother is a Jew…"

"Which makes me a Jew, even though my father is not Jewish?"

"That's right. This is one of the rare cases when paternity doesn't matter."

"No shit!" I exclaim, then quickly apologize for my choice of words.

"No shit that you're a Jew or no shit that paternity doesn't matter?" Adrian asks, with a slight grin.

"Both. It's not often that someone my age gets handed an identity crisis of this magnitude, and it's even more unusual to find out there's a situation where men don't have the last word. That part's really great, to tell you the truth," I smile enthusiastically.

"Just so I'm clear: I am in the presence of a lovely Jewish woman with a strong feminist streak who is facing an unexpected, sudden onset of a deeply personal identity crisis. Who knew this is how my day would turn out?" he shoots back, giving as good as he's getting.

"That's a fair assessment," I admit, smiling, then turning serious again.

"Honestly, learning about all this is a relief, and not that surprising. I've always felt there was something important about my heritage I wasn't aware of, and that feeling has intensified dramatically as all this has unfolded. Now I at least have a reason for why I've never felt like I fit into the Christian mold. Since my days in Catholic boarding school, it seemed like I was trying too hard to believe in something I should believe in... and couldn't. It was a classic case of trying to shove a square peg into a round hole – there was nothing I could do to make it fit. I believed in God, but not in Jesus as the son of God sent to save us from ourselves, which only makes sense as a fairy tale somebody thought up during an intense period of self-loathing involving strong, mind-altering substances. Same with the Holy Spirit – it's an interesting image, but otherwise useless. It's hard to explain. and I don't know why I'm confessing this to someone I met less than an hour ago. I apologize. I've embarrassed myself." *It must be his dark eyes... they're an open invitation to bare my soul,* I think, as Adrian and I look directly at each other.

"No apology necessary, and there's no need whatever to be embarrassed. You're embarking on an unanticipated emotional journey into a different life, and you need to travel that road with someone you feel comfortable with. If you decide you want me to do the translations, we'll be on this journey together, and I hope you will be comfortable with me as your traveling companion. As an added note – you'd make a great Jew. The one, and probably only, thing all Jews agree on is that there is one God and one God only."

"Truthfully, all this is a little frightening... but I'm in it now, and there's no going back. Would you like to see a copy of the letter with the yellow star? I bought a dictionary and made a stab at translating it myself. Frankly, it really tore me apart."

"If you're willing to share it, I'd love to have a look." He wipes his hands on a napkin as I take the copy out of the envelope and hand it to him. He picks it up, and I watch his lips move as he reads it. When he is finished, he puts it down and reaches for his coffee.

"It doesn't need much explanation, does it?" he says quietly. I shake my head.

"At some point the letters might contain enough information to at least try to find out what happened to the people she refers to..."

"How is that possible?"

"Between 1933 and 1945 Nazi Germany and its allies set up more than forty-four thousand labor camps, death camps, confinement ghettos and other incarceration facilities. After the war ended, various Jewish organizations began meticulously examining these records, as well as those the International Red Cross compiled as the camps were liberated. As you can imagine, ensuring that the name of every human being Hitler murdered is recorded is a massive labor of love and commitment that is taking a long time and is far from complete, but it might help you find out what happened to these people. If you decide you want to pursue it, I'll help you as much as I can."

"So, you're definitely interested in translating the diaries and letters?" I ask.

"Yes, but only with certain caveats we should discuss." I nod, encouraging him to continue.

"Translating between two languages is about word choices, and the results depend to a very large extent on the translator's vocabulary, among other things. I am a man translating diaries presumably written by a woman and no matter how accurate I try to be, I will use words that a woman translator might not choose. It's a matter of nuance, and nearly every language, including German, is more nuanced that English, so the translator makes judgment calls. Diaries written by a woman might be best translated by another woman. She would be better able to pick up on emotional undertones I might miss."

"Can you give me an example?"

"German has both familiar and formal forms for some words, including pronouns. English doesn't make that distinction, so in the phrase 'you are my friend' the form the word 'you' takes depends upon how well I know you: as a close, personal friend, as an acquaintance, or in the context of a more formal relationship."

"And you wouldn't pick up on that?"

"I might miss it occasionally. A good translation of the letters should reflect the nature of the relationship between writer and the recipient, and clarifying that sometimes means adding a word. If the form of the word 'you' implies a personal friendship, the translator would need to either footnote this or add the word 'personal' to bring forth the full meaning of the phrase, because otherwise, it would not be clear."

"I don't see how this is a problem, as long as you are aware of it."

"The problem is in the words I choose for clarification. I might say 'good friend' while a woman translator who intuitively understands female friendships would say 'intimate friend'. It's not a distinction without a difference."

"We're talking about private letters and diaries of a family member, not the secrets of the Third Reich's war machine. This is nothing more than satisfying my personal curiosity, and guaranteeing the level of accuracy you describe isn't that concerning to me."

"I just want to be clear on my limitations…"

"I appreciate that, but don't think the issue you raise is that important. If it makes you feel better, you could note places where you think there might be multiple or nuanced meanings, and if I have questions, we can talk about them."

"I'm happy to do that, if it satisfies you."

"I'm more than satisfied! I'm really happy you're willing to do this at all. We need to talk about how much to pay you."

"My preference is for you to give me permission to use the information gleaned from the letters and diaries as part of my own research for the book I'm working on… relevant quotes, for example."

"I hope you understand that I can't make that decision until I know what's in these diaries and letters."

"I don't expect you to decide anything right now. I see this as having access to a private collection of family documents possibly containing a wealth of useful background information. If they were stored in a museum somewhere or were part of a special collection in some library, I'd be translating them just for the information they contain. The museum or library might ask me for copies of my translations in return for allowing me access to the originals, but no money would change hands. I prefer we handle this the same way… as a quid-pro-quo arrangement that suits me and hopefully suits you as well. We can decide how far we want to take whatever is revealed later, but even if this ends up being nothing more than further informing how I think about my topic it will have been time well spent."

"This seems fair enough for right now. But we need to agree to discuss it again if something changes. I don't want to risk taking advantage of a good thing, and I am fully prepared to pay you," I add, unsure how comfortable I am with the arrangement.

"Since you're returning to Chicago in a few days, do you mind leaving this diary with me? I promise to be very, very careful with it."

"Not at all."

"How about the letters and other diaries?"

"Right now, everything's at my dad's. I can go through the rest of the boxes this evening and gather everything together. I'm sure my father won't mind arranging to get the others to you."

"Do you have time to meet again before you leave? I'd like to look at this more closely tonight to determine whether any specific questions come to mind. I can meet you in the city tomorrow afternoon, if that is enough time for you to go through the other boxes."

"Later tomorrow afternoon will be fine, as far as I know. If you'll give me your phone number, I'll call you if it isn't." Adrian takes a piece of paper from his shirt pocket and jots down a phone number in boldly confident handwriting.

"Unless I hear from you otherwise, I'll be on the bus from Berkeley that arrives at the Embarcadero at five. It's usually on time, so we can meet there, grab something to eat and talk about any details that still need ironing out."

"Thanks very much, Adrian. This really means a lot to me. I'd love to stay and chat a while longer, but I better get back to my car before it's towed. I'm parked in a two-hour zone, and we've been talking a lot longer than that," I say, reaching into my purse for money as I stand up. Adrian rises at the same time. Standing next to me, his shoulder is about four inches above my own, making him well over six feet tall.

"I run a tab," he says, handing the five-dollar bill I put on the table back to me.

"I don't believe you, but we can discuss it later," I chuckle. His hand lightly on my back, he guides me toward the door. Outside, he asks which way my car is parked, and I point to the left.

"That's basically the direction I'm going. If you don't mind, I'll walk with you, and if your car has been towed, I can help you find it. Unfortunately, I'm quite familiar with Berkeley's car towing protocol." *You have no idea how little I mind you walking with me*, I think, stifling what I know is a silly grin.

That evening, over a supper Herlinda prepared before she left for the day, I update my dad on what I've learned and the translation plan going forward, then ask how he feels about the Jewish connection?

"Although I can't say why, I'm not altogether surprised, and it certainly doesn't change anything. As long as you're not upset, I really don't care. You'll have to determine how it affects you, which will take time, and I have full confidence you'll figure it out," he smiles, then continues.

"Hopefully, you'll be pleased rather than upset. Despite their horrific persecution, across history the Jews have provided humankind with countless wonderful, valuable gifts and made many important contributions that immeasurably improved the human condition. Without them, we'd all be in a world of hurt. Being a Jew gives you a great deal to be proud of."

"What about Aunt Sally?"

"Sally already knows, Natalie – it's knowing you've discovered all this that's the problem for her, at least as far as I can tell. She needs to be able to control the information flow on her terms, so for the moment, this should remain between us... not forever, but for right now. In the meantime, just keep telling her how much you love her and how much she matters to you, and she'll be fine."

"I can't hold back for long. Emily and I talk a couple times a week, and she'll never forgive me for keeping a secret like this..."

"This isn't a telephone conversation, Natalie."

"It's not a felony conviction either, Dad. I think everybody's making too big a deal out of it."

"People feel how they feel and whether those feelings are justified isn't your call. You'll need to return to California sooner rather than later, and stay long enough for everyone to work through this together. Emily will certainly understand that when you explain it."

"The quarter ends with Memorial Day. I can come back after that and stay all summer. If Cal gives me use of the university library, and there's no reason they wouldn't, I can just as easily work on my book here in California as in Chicago. Logistically it might be complicated in terms of my data, but I'm sure I can figure something out."

"That might be a good idea... give everyone time to let all this sink in. You seem pretty impressed with your translator," my father says, shifting gears and looking straight at me.

"That's one way of putting it," I whisper, noisily stacking the dishes.

The following morning, opening the boxes Emily and I hadn't bothered with earlier, I discover more partially filled journals and packets of letters. I put everything in order as best I can, making it easy for my dad to pass them on as needed, then take a shower and start thinking about what to wear to meet Adrian. As I'm drying my hair, Herlinda knocks on the door and asks whether I want lunch?

"Thanks, but I'm probably having an early dinner someplace on Fisherman's Wharf," I answer. An hour later, Herlinda knocks again, then sticks her head in to find most of the contents of my closet emptied onto various surfaces in my room.

"Must be a very important dinner," she smiles, picking a shirt up off the floor.

"Tell me where you are going and who you are going with… I make suggestions," my self-appointed mother offers, moving a skirt to plant herself in the chair nearest the window.

"I'm meeting someone who has agreed to help me with a project."

"The person you drove over to Berkeley to meet?" she asks.

"That's the one."

"Is a man – yes?"

"Yes."

"And he's very handsome – yes?"

"Right again, Herlinda."

"And you know him how long? Maybe two hours?"

"Pretty close. And this matters how?"

"You tell me," she commands, then adds that I'm an idiot regarding men and good looks because I let them mess with my head. She isn't wrong.

"And your point is?" I push back.

"No point – just saying. When you marry that other guy, your Papa, he make grooves my waxed floors walking off worry. My hair get full of white too soon – very upsetting for me. We no want to go through that again. Muy hard on us both."

"It's an early dinner, Herlinda. He hasn't asked me to marry him, and your hair looks fine."

"If it's just early dinner, why are all your clothes all over the room?"

"I'm not sure. What do you think of this skirt with this shirt – or should I just wear slacks and a sweater?"

"Whatever you wear looks like a movie star – a paper bag is fine," Herlinda answers, standing up and shaking her head.

Eventually, having exhausted all options, I decide on a creamy white silk shirt, beige gaberdine culottes, flat shoes and a dark brown sweater. I put another diary and two packets of letters in my canvas messenger bag, write a note to my dad saying I should be home by ten, and wave to Herlinda as I walk out the door.

"Looking good!" she hollers.

The trolley ride across town takes forty-five minutes and I arrive at the Embarcadero just as the bus from Berkeley rolls to a stop. Adrian, wearing faded blue Levis, an open-collared, oxford shirt, brown tweed sport coat, and loafers with no socks, is the ninth person down the steps. Making eye contact, he offers me a smile that would melt glass.

"Hi Natalie," he says, gently touching my shoulder, causing an involuntary shiver that necessitates a deep breath to stop myself from dissolving into the sidewalk. *For god's sake, Natalie – you're not a teenager. Get a damned grip, I* reprimand myself.

"Shall we walk over toward the wharf?" Adrian invites. I nod in agreement, then don't move.

"I think it's this way," he says, gently taking my elbow and pointing me in the direction of the iconic San Francisco landmark I have been frequenting since I was old enough to walk. *Get a grip, Natalie.* I repeat, taking another deep breath.

"The bus ride okay?" I ask, unable to think of anything else to say.

"Fine. I come over here every so often just to wander the streets. I've been in most of the major cities in the world and, at least to me, San Francisco is the most beautiful. I can't put my finger on it, but there's something here that doesn't exist anywhere else."

"I was born and grew up here, so I guess I don't notice. No question it's very nice, but I never think about it," I stammer.

"I feel the same way about Chicago. I know the city is different from most, but I grew up there, so I don't see all the things that make it unique."

"Do you get back often?"

"It's definitely home, but I don't go back as often as my sisters and my aunt and uncle would like, especially while I was at the Vatican. Do you come to San Francisco often?"

"Three or four times a year." By now we are approaching the wharf, which is alive with the smell of fresh fish, screeching seagulls, and watchful pelicans.

"I hope this isn't too presumptuous, but since it's a Friday night, I went ahead and made dinner reservations at Alioto's for 6:30. If that doesn't work for you, just say so."

"That's fine. Gives us a little time to walk around."

"Did you sort through everything?" he asks.

"I did – and found more letters and diaries. I brought a couple with me.

I also discovered one I think is my mother's, which might not be as useful to you as the earlier ones. None of them seem complete. Mostly the entries are a few pages of what looks like random thoughts."

"Everything up to the end of Pius XII's reign is potentially useful. Obviously, the far-reaching effects of his influence didn't stop with his death, but at some point, I have to cut it off. Otherwise, I won't live long enough to finish the book."

"That's sort of how I'm beginning to feel about my mother's story. It will take a lifetime to peel away all the layers, and even then, I might not uncover the core truths."

"Want to turn down Pier 39 and visit the sea lions… see if we can figure out what they're discussing among themselves this evening?" Adrian asks, shifting the conversation and the direction we are walking.

"I heard they're going to open Alcatraz for public tours. You know anything about that?" Adrian asks, looking across the bay where the infamous federal prison sits on a rock, surrounded by strong currents and shark-infested water that made trying to escape a very bad idea.

"It has fascinating historic significance, but whether I agree with making a notorious federal prison into a national monument is another question."

"I take it you don't?"

"Off hand, I'd say no. I don't see how enshrining what has been generally considered the most inhumane prison in America serves any higher good, except as a capitalist, profit-motive-driven revenue source that feeds off the American fascination for violence and brutality. But until this minute, I haven't really thought about it."

"Did you know Al Capone was once a prisoner there?"

"I did not, but I don't know a lot about him, other than he made some unusual career choices."

"Living in Chicago, you really should read up on him. As mobsters go, he was one of the best and is a big part of Chicago's very colorful history." Hearing this, the sea lions start barking. For several minutes we stand next to each other in silence, listening to the playful creatures converse.

"Do you ever wonder what they're saying?" Adrian asks.

"Not really," I answer, fearing I'm starting to sound like the least interesting person the handsome, erudite man standing next to me has ever met.

"When I was little and came here with my dad, he said they talked about things like what they were going to eat for lunch and what they wanted for Christmas. I must've found it a satisfactory answer because I can't say I've thought about it since," I explain as Adrian chuckles.

"Do you ever think about all the ways there are to communicate? We humans are the only ones who use words, but words are only one way to convey meaning. There are millions of other ways for humans, other animals, and even plants, to exchange information," he continues, standing slightly closer to me than necessary. I don't move away.

A few minutes later, after giving up on trying to understand sea lion language, we continue toward the restaurant. The salty breeze off San Francisco Bay blowing on my face and through my hair is slightly intoxicating and I finally begin to relax into the experience of being a tourist in my own hometown.

"You are very lucky – a table next to the far window has just become available. You will be able to see the sunset," the maître' d smiles when we arrive at Alioto's. He leads us to a back corner table next to a window with a panoramic view of San Francisco Bay like no other.

"This is a stroke of good luck," Adrian smiles, sitting down and picking up the wine list, then asking whether I'd like to order something before dinner. I explain that I don't generally drink, and he suggests ordering a large glass of wine we can share while celebrating our chance encounter with the fantastic view.

It turns out splitting one glass of wine lasts a half hour, which is an opportunity for me to ask Adrian more about his book project and how he came to be writing it.

"You want the long or short answer?"

"Either one. I'm in no hurry."

"I majored in history at Loyola-Chicago, then went to the seminary, and eventually was ordained to the Catholic priesthood in Rome," he begins, looking straight at me, making it easier for him to gauge my reaction to what he is saying. It can't possibly escape his notice that my reflexive response to his first sentence, confessing that he is a Catholic priest committed to avoiding the temptations inherent in relationships with women, is to suck in my breath and exert a white-knuckled grip my wine glass.

"Let me finish, Natalie, please..." he implores. I release my wine glass and place my hands in my lap, preparing to listen very carefully while, at the same time, noticing that my stomach is suddenly clenching as if Adrian just confessed to being out on bail after having been accused of unspeakable crimes against humanity.

"After ordination, I was sent to law school at Georgetown then, immediately after finishing, was called back to Rome and assigned to the diplomatic corps. My first job was to apply what I knew about international monetary law to an assignment as one of several assistants to the Vatican Secretary of State, then as the executive secretary to the Vatican envoy to Germany. I spent six months incarcerated at the Vatican language institute learning German, then went to Munich."

"Sounds very interesting, actually," I acknowledge, trying my best to sound nonchalant when I feel like I've been duped, although I'm hard pressed to say why or by whom.

"It was fascinating, and as I explored the history of the German Catholic Church, I became fascinated with Pius XII, who, as Archbishop of Munich, I strongly suspected, and the Church vehemently denied, had trafficking with Hitler. I spent every spare minute in the libraries of whatever German city I was in, trying to figure out why the Church, as a moral arbiter of good versus evil had failed to take a stand against the greatest evil in modern human history. In the process, the horrifyingly ugly underbelly of the institution I had committed my life to serving was laid bare, planting the seeds of disillusionment." He stops to take a deep breath and another sip of his wine.

"I was propelled into a personal crisis on par with your discovering your Jewish bloodline. But unlike your situation, mine was not a positive discovery – it was like a black death. I struggled with it for a year, then my parents both died within weeks of each other. No longer having to answer to them, and having come into some money, I had choices I'd never had before. The first thing I did was apply for a leave of absence from the active priesthood. While the application was working its way through the bureaucracy, I decided to write a book about Pius, Hitler and the rise of antisemitism in America. I pulled together a proposal I titled *Hitler's Pope*, which a mainline publisher quickly accepted, offering a generous stipend to complete the book. I knew I had to leave Rome and reached out to a former seminary classmate who was teaching at Berkeley. He told me about a three-year fellowship in the history department. I applied and was accepted… and here I am. I do three guest lectures and two seminars on my topic per semester and spend the rest of the time researching and writing. It's a pretty good gig, to be perfectly honest."

"How much longer is the fellowship?"

"The first year ended December 30, so two years, less about four months. By then, I need to have a solid draft of the book in the publisher's hands."

"Do you think you'll make the deadline?"

"Right now, yes. I'm pretty much where I want to be. I'm expecting the letters and diaries will help flesh out a lot of background details."

"Then what?"

"I don't know, to be truthful. I was granted a five-year leave from the priesthood, so I have some time."

"What, exactly, is a leave from the priesthood?" I ask, taking shallow breaths and not moving from my original position directly in front of the handsomest man I've ever sat across the dinner table from. Out of the corner of my eye I see small white caps breaking on the silvery ocean surface as it flows through the bay, illuminated by the setting sun's translucent golden glow.

"Basically, it's unpaid leave. I can't administer sacraments or perform any other religious duties and am on my own financially. This is frequently the exit strategy for those intending to permanently leave the priesthood and want time to figure out a path forward before burning all their bridges. If they find options, they never return to the active priesthood. Some purists request an official dispensation from their vows, which takes a while to work its way through the tangled bureaucracy. Those who decide to remain in the priesthood apply for reinstatement to active ministry, and if they haven't been arrested for sodomy or fathered a child, reinstatement is generally automatic."

"Arrested for sodomy?"

"Half of the active priesthood is homosexual, Natalie. It's a good cover for that lifestyle, if one is discrete."

"I didn't know that," I admit.

"Most people don't. It's not something the Church is eager to advertise when it recruits for humble laborers in the vineyards of the Lord."

"No, I suppose not. How many priests who take a leave eventually return?" I ask, faking a casualness I don't feel, trying not to sound too interested in his answer.

"I don't know... some do, but my guess us most don't. It seems to me that the longer the leave, the harder it would be to return to active ministry, unless it's the only option. The priesthood isn't a particularly healthy lifestyle and very few are truly suited to it. A surprising number of priests decide religious life isn't for them and leave. Sadly, many who stay do so for the wrong reasons and often become alcoholics... or worse."

"At this point, I suppose you have no idea where you're at with it all," I venture, buying time to absorb my persistent visceral reaction to what I've just learned, which is that Adrian is married — just not to a human being. Admittedly, one would have to be both blind and extremely naïve to assume that someone as charming as he is, is not encumbered by other commitments of some sort, but my guess would've been they involved a woman, not a religious institution.

"If I can find permanent work that I'm qualified for and is truly meaningful to me, it's hard to imagine returning to the active priesthood. I can't see myself living with the corruption and politics undergirding the Church for the rest of my life. They're too pervasive, too embedded in the church's MO and too vital to its survival to change in any significant way, and I haven't been able to rationalize that enough to remain a part of it. Don't get me wrong – there are a great many things about the Church I deeply love, but the only reason I would go back is if I came to truly believe I could work from within to make the institutional Church better, and I just can't envision how that would be possible."

"A lot of people do that, though – try to change institutions they care about from within," I point out.

"That's true, but the other issue is that once the book is in print, I'll be labeled a pariah, so they won't want me back."

Adrian's voice reflects resignation, and his eyes reveal a melancholy I interpret as a plea for understanding. In addition to being a sucker where good looks are concerned, I have always been too willing to take on other people's problems, and I feel great compassion toward his dilemma.

"This must upset you," I reflect.

"Not as much as you might imagine. I've had plenty of time to think about it and I have options a lot of priests don't have, a big one being that supporting myself isn't a huge worry. Truthfully, the bigger issue for me is not wanting to spend the rest of my life alone and wondering whether any woman would have me," he answers. While I'm thinking about my next question, the waiter interrupts to ask if we are ready to order.

"What's good here?" Adrian asks.

"Everything," the waiter and I answer simultaneously.

"Then I'll have what she's having," my dinner companion says, nodding toward me while closing the menu. I order pasta with vegetables for two and grilled shrimp as a side for Adrian, then spend the rest of the dinner talking about the logistics for managing the translations after I return to Chicago. Occasionally, we stop talking to enjoy the glorious view surrounding us as the sun slowly drops behind the Golden Gate Bridge.

"This is why I think San Francisco is the most majestic city in the world," Adrian exclaims.

"My dad took me out onto the bridge to watch the Pacific fleet sail into the bay at the end of World War II. I don't remember it, but he chokes up every time he mentions it," I say.

RED ANEMONES

"I'd choke up too if I had witnessed that. It's not something you'd ever forget," Adrian remarks, taking a deep breath.

The rest of our meal is punctuated by less intense conversation, and when we are finally finished eating, Adrian suggests walking off our dinner by wandering over to Ghirardelli Square for an ice cream cone, insisting the mocha is like nothing I've ever tasted before. We both succumb to the temptation of gigantic, two-scoop cones. We continue walking and talking until he says he has a dental appointment early in the morning and needs to catch the 10:20 bus back to Berkeley, offering to leave me off at the nearest trolley stop.

"I'll walk back to the Embarcadero with you and catch the trolley there," I say, wanting to stretch out our time together as long as possible. Fully aware that becoming emotionally involved with an unavailable man is flirting with heartbreak, I still don't want to say good-bye to Adrian any sooner than necessary.

"You sure? I'd love it if you're willing to do that, but it's out of your way."

"I'm sure..." We walk along quietly, continuing to lick at the cold, rich ice cream. Occasionally, Adrian lightly touches my shoulder to point out something he finds interesting, and in response, I tilt my head closer to him.

My trolley arrives at the Embarcadero at about the same time we do, but it takes a few minutes to turn around before passengers board, so we sit down to continue working on our our ice cream cones while we wait.

"I've really enjoyed the evening," Adrian says.

"So have I," I admit.

"I guess one thing we have in common is we're both in the middle of a shifting identity crisis we hadn't planned on but found us anyway," the priest who isn't a priest smiles, looking at me.

"It appears that is definitely true, although mine is just beginning and yours is closer to the middle," I say, watching the turn style move the trolley around a circle to face forward in the direction it came from. As the bell clangs, Adrian stands up next to me.

"Mind if I hug you?" he asks. *I wouldn't mind if you kissed me*, I think, placing the arm that isn't holding what's left of my ice cream snugly around his back and planting my face firmly into his neck.

Chapter Six
פרק שש

New York City
Late fall, 1912

If things are not as you wish them to be, wish them to be as they are...

The journey from leaving my old life behind to beginning my new one was so many tortured days of never-ending seasickness I lost count. I arrive in America accepting that I have died and gone to hell, and am too weak to care. *This is what I deserve for leaving home when I should've listened to my heart and stayed,* I tell myself again and again.

Assuring me my feelings are not unusual among new arrivals having suffered a rough crossing, Malka agrees I'm too weak to travel on to Cleveland, which I am unable to even think about. Guiding me to a bench near the dock, wraps Maman's shawl around me, and begins searching for help. Surprisingly quickly, she finds a Jewish family living on Manhattan's lower east side willing to take me in until I recover my strength.

"You stay with us as long as you need to make yourself strong again. We help you become well and on your way to your new life," Guta Petrosky tells me in rapid fire Yiddish, with Malka as my interpreter. I am barely able to understand the open-hearted Polish woman as she pulls my emaciated body close into her more generous one. Seeing my puzzled look, she repeats her welcome a second time, much more slowly, accompanied by universally understood facial expressions and hand gestures designed to communicate when words fail.

"Try harder, Nathalie – you're lucky she's willing to take you in," Malka scolds my still blank face. The kindness radiating from the Polish woman's eyes soften her otherwise coarse features and her grandmotherly, take-charge manner, offers comfort. I nod as I slowly follow her across the street toward an outside wooden staircase up the side of a building.

Malka explains that upwards of one million Jews are crowded into less than one square mile enclosing the Petroski's noisy, chaotic neighborhood, landscaped with blowing trash and heaps of garbage only the rats appreciate. Despite their own hardships, many willingly take in newly arrived immigrants until they can settle themselves. While grateful for the solid ground beneath my feet, nothing I see reminds me of the refined German life I left behind. I am among strangers I have a fractured ability to communicate with yet, at this moment, am entirely dependent upon. The future is a deep black hole, and the past is quickly disappearing. Already, the memory of Maman's yeasty challah baking in the oven is growing dull in my brain.

"I will telegram Eitan that you have arrived and need to rest before continuing the trip, promising him you will be in touch soon. This is my address in Detroit. Write to me after you arrive in Cleveland," Malka instructs, handing over a piece of paper as she bids me goodbye at the bottom of the stairs. Offering only a weak smile, I tuck the paper among my travel documents and bid my only friend in America a sad good-bye, with no expectation of ever seeing her again.

The Petroski two-room apartment, up a long flight of stairs I am barely able to navigate, is one of many in a building that smells of raw sewage mixed with peculiar cooking odors I don't recognize. The combination further challenges my already queasy, untrustworthy stomach.

I can't get rest in this small space filled with fighting and yelling, I moan to myself a few minutes later as Mrs. Petroski, still chattering in Yiddish, motions three squirming children away from the bed she indicates will be mine, located in a room with four other beds covered in colorful handmade, well-worn quilts. Grateful that the floor isn't moving, I smile my thanks, then lay down facing the wall, squeezing my eyes shut, trying to hold back tears escaping my eyes, blurry with loneliness and grief. I can't stop wondering why I was so gullible I willingly believed life in America was worth leaving Germany. This is the last thought I have before awakening sometime later to see five children of various sizes, smelling of boiled cabbage, fried onions, and unwashed bodies staring at me, suppressing giggles.

"Come quick, Ma. Her eyes are open," the tallest of the five shouts in some combination of Yiddish and fractured German. Mrs. Petroski, a squirming baby on her hip, rushes into the room and, wiping her flour-covered hands on her apron, instructs her eldest daughter to show me the bathroom at the end of the outside hall. Reluctantly, I follow the smell to the putrid, public toilet at the end of the hallway.

"Fill the basin so she can wash up," Mrs. Petroski shouts in a shrill voice that would wake the dead. At least I think this is what she is saying. A few minutes later, I walk into the room that is not the bedroom just as Mrs. Petrosky is filling a large pot with various vegetables. Looking around, it is amazing she manages to cook anything in the small corner space containing only a single burner hot plate and a metal pan doubling as a sink. I don't see any evidence of running water.

"Shabbos begins in one hour. I make familiar foods for you so your stomach does not revolt against nourishment, if you eat slowly," she instructs, using the Yiddish term for Shabbat. She enhances her words with a unique sign language like nothing I have seen before but does help me to understand her. I want to ask how she knows when Shabbat begins when, from these tiny windows clouded with grime, it is barely possible to see the sky at all, much less find three stars signaling the beginning and end of Shabbat observance. But the anticipation of taking part in the familiar, universal ritual central to the Jewish family life brings a welcome comfort I don't want to disturb, so I stay silent.

Shabbat officially begins with a surprise when I discover thirteen people of various ages standing at the table. As best I can understand, they are all speaking Yiddish, with a little Polish or an occasional German word thrown in. My second surprise is discovering Mr. Petroski is Hasid, which means, among other things, that the family keeps kosher. Seeing the look on my face, Guta is quick to explain that Hasid in America isn't quite the same as in the old country.

"We adapt – a little," she whispers, guiding me toward the Shabbat table as she covers my head, then stands aside while, lighting the candles, I pray in Hebrew. *Barukh ata Adonai Eloheinu, Melekh ha'olam, asher kid'shanu b'mitzvotav v'tzivanu l'hadlik ner shel Shabbat.* "Blessed are You, Lord our G-d, King of the universe, who has sanctified us with His commandments and commanded us to light the Shabbat lamp."

"You can decide on shul in the morning," Lottie, the older Petroski daughter whose job it has been to shepherd me through the afternoon, whispers in barely passable German she claims she has learned from playmates scattered throughout the tenements, adding that she can read, write, and add numbers in German, sort of.

"Nobody to practice words with," she shrugs, waiting for her father's signal to begin eating.

"Thank you. I appreciate everything you are doing for me," I reply, patting her hand. I start to ask her about school when Mrs. Petroski interrupts me.

"Eat slowly... small bites," she cautions, passing me a plate with a minuscule helping of potato and the tenderest bits of brisket. My response to her kindness is to swallow hard, choking back the ocean of unwanted tears pressing behind my eyes, threatening to escape at any moment.

A few days later, after the midday meal, I retreat to the tiny, windowless room overcrowded with beds, intending to rest. The children are either napping or outside playing and I am hoping for the blessed relief of crying alone, because holding back tears most of the time I am awake quickly drains what little energy I have. Just as I am dozing off, Guta sits down on the bed. Struggling to speak some form of understandable German, she takes my hand and offers her conclusion that sadness is sucking the life from me, keeping me from growing stronger. I signal agreement, shrugging that I don't know what to do about it.

"You are sad for your home you left behind. It feels lost to you forever, with no hope of return," she sighs, placing her warm, greasy hand in my own, cold one.

"For us, escaping the Czar and his pogroms overflowing into Poland made us happy to come here, and many families come together... move home in Poland to home in America. We find other Jews and make a new life with them. It's working out. Some ways are better than before, some ways worse, but we adjust and focus on living. For you, was different. Life in Germany was happy, and you come to America alone. Even with a marriage waiting for you, you are still without family. You don't know what to expect, and you are afraid. With your hat on my head, I would be afraid too."

Staring at the wall, I realize this illiterate Polish immigrant woman knows exactly how I am feeling. Yet, instead of being grateful for her understanding, I am angry, because by giving voice to what I have been trying to hide from and am unable to face, she's just made everything worse.

"Perhaps you gave up too much and you should return... would not be a failure. You tried, and it didn't work out. You are not the first bride to change her mind at the last minute. I did it myself, twice, before finally marrying Igor, and look how that turned out... maybe better, maybe worse than with the others. Who knows?" Guta chuckles. The confession captures my attention, because she is putting what I can't stop thinking about since my first step into America into simple words that make sense. The only thing holding back a decision to return is the thought of another

Atlantic crossing, which I do not believe I could survive. Just considering the possibility makes me dizzy. I am trapped in a place I don't want to be, longing for the home I love and cannot return to.

"You must decide, Nathalie," Guta continues. "You cannot go forward dragging the sadness of wishing for something different with you. You do that and you go nowhere... might as well give up and die now." I can't argue with her conclusion, because it's one I've already arrived at.

"Accept your inheritance from the Jews before you. We are world experts on leaving our life behind and moving on to a new one. It is our destiny – your destiny. Start acting like the Jew you are and move forward into the unknown in joyful anticipation. It's not hard. Just do it. Sadness will follow you, but you must not allow it to make your decisions. You are stronger than that, especially if you stop wasting your energy feeling sorry for yourself." These last words jolt me. I cannot ever remember anyone – not Maman, Papa, or Levi – ever speaking to me as harshly or as directly as this humble, plainspoken woman.

"All I can do is try," I choke.

"Try is not good enough. If Jews only try, we still be slaves in Egypt. You either stop being sorry for yourself and make your mind determined move forward with marriage and life in America or return to Germany. These are your choices," Guta commands, standing up.

"We are Jews. Suffering is our destiny, but we find joy in life anyway... find reasons to celebrate anything...make life worth-while." Readjusting her head scarf and retying her apron, she indicates she has said what she has to say and has important things to do.

"You will always be sad about leaving Germany and your family, but you survived a long trip across a black ocean ready to swallow you up at any moment. You can survive not being in Germany," she declares, closing the bedroom door, hanging by one hinge. A moment later, she opens it.

"You rest enough now. Come to the kitchen and help with peeling potatoes and carrots. Many hungry faces here soon."

Facing the smudged wall next to the bed, my mind won't let me ignore what I have just heard. With all the uproar over Irina and the twins, Maman never spoke frankly to me about marriage – what it really means to be with a husband, or even how to be married day in and day out. What I know about marriage comes from watching her and Papa, who seem very happy with each other most of the time. But my father never asked my mother to leave her family, who she sees often, to be with him, so there was not a great deal of sacrifice involved in their marriage. Levi's marriage with Irina seems fine for him but not so for Irina, who is drowning in babies and, even with two mothers helping her, spends her days either hysterical or sleeping. Knowing I will never have even one mother helping me brings on another fit of sobbing and feeling even sorrier for myself, followed by angry frustration that I am not stronger. Mrs. Petrosky commands my name again, forcing me to give up my self-indulgent wallowing and drag my body out of bed into the kitchen.

Three weeks later, finally having gathered myself together during most of my waking hours, I am standing in the middle of a large, confusing building called Grand Central Station, bidding Guta Petroski a surprisingly tearful goodbye. Being jostled by people moving in many different directions unnerves me and hanging onto my suitcase while juggling the large basket of food she packed for the eleven-hour train trip to Cleveland is clumsy. Although living in the Petroski household was never-ending chaos, it comforted me, and I am sad to be leaving.

"Maybe the train breaks down and you'll be stuck somewhere for G-d knows how long. I know this happens, and if it does, you'll need to eat, so no argument," she instructs when I object to the food basket. Pointing out that it has taken nearly three weeks for my stomach to settle down after its tumultuous ocean voyage, Guta refuses to listen to any excuse for not traveling fortified with at least a week's worth of food. Although she can neither read nor write, she also insists I promise to send letters from Cleveland.

"Lottie can read to me what you say and write back what I say to you," she proclaims with no small amount of pride. I promise to keep in touch and mean it. Hugging the courageous woman who exchanged agrarian life in rural Poland for a dangerous, overcrowded New York City tenement jammed with people of all ages, languages, traditions, and cultures, I don't feel nearly as brave or as robust as she is... and I doubt I will ever overflow with the loving kindness, common sense and generosity that comes naturally to her. Taking a deep breath, I wave a last goodbye to the woman who saved me from my despairing self and board the Baltimore and Ohio Railroad's night train for Cleveland.

Pulling out of New York, my attempts to push down the uncertainty about what awaits me when Eitan and I see each other for the first time in nearly two years are only marginally successful. *Maybe after so long we won't know each other anymore. Worse, maybe we won't even like each other,* are among the heavy thoughts floating through my mind, in a steady rhythm that matches the motion-driven sound of metal wheels rolling rail cars along steel tracks, shaking the food basket filled with rye bread, ripe cheese and fragrant kielbasa. *Guta obviously cheats on keeping kosher,* I chuckle to myself.

Arriving in Cleveland the next day, after a trip that was supposed to take eleven hours took sixteen, I see Eitan standing on the station platform before he sees me. He looks the same, but I am sure I do not. Yet, when our eyes meet, we recognize each other at once, then move slowly closer. I am surprised to see tears in Eitan's eyes, and disappointed none flow from my own, which I hope my promised husband does not notice. After weeks of nothing but crying, I am just too exhausted to do it anymore, even for a happy reason.

"I thought this day might never come," Eitan tells me, picking up my suitcase. I smile and tell him I hope his job with the railroad includes improving efficiency because American trains certainly don't run with the German precision we are accustomed to.

"You made me very worried. Are you feeling well now?" Eitan asks, walking slowly.

"Much better, but not perfect yet... too easily tired. The train I managed, but the ship was a misery impossible to describe. I will die in America because I can never board another ship again. Just thinking about it turns my body inside out." This truth, which I have desperately wanted to deny, brings on the tears seeing Eitan did not.

"Don't say that, Nathalie. You won't die. We have too much to look forward to... somebody dying is not part of the plan," Eitan insists, opening the door to the car he proudly wrote about in the last letter I received before leaving Germany. He asks about the strong smell coming from the basket. When I explain it is part of Mrs. Petroski's traveling care package, he reminds me we are not peasants.

"I have a house in the town called Elyria I think you will like. Three sleeping rooms, a large kitchen, parlor and eating room – and indoor plumbing with running water and electricity! And a front porch to sit outside in the evenings. I can't wait to show you." I am too fascinated by the car he drives slowly along a street lined with houses spaced apart instead of connected together to pay attention to what he is saying. Coming from life in a city centre apartment, this arrangement is very strange, and I'm not sure what to think.

"I hope this house is in the city centre, because otherwise, I won't like it," I tell my soon-to-be husband as we pass house after house, with no shops anywhere nearby.

"It's different here, Nathalie. There is no city centre as we know it. Only poor people live in apartments above the shops, and we aren't poor.

Everyone who can lives in a house. You'll get used to it. And being with other Germans is better, I think, at least in the beginning, as you adjust. You won't feel so alone." What he says is true, and I take reassurance in knowing I will be among other German speakers, even if they aren't all Jews.

"But how do you shop when you are so far away from everything?" I fret.

"You take the trolley. Some women are even learning to drive an automobile. Maybe you will, too."

"I don't want to drive an automobile, Eitan. I want to walk to the butcher and the greengrocer… to the mercantile… get outside air every day… visit with neighbors also shopping."

"You will have a yard with grass… room for a garden. You can grow flowers or vegetables… almost like living in a park. You'll like it if you give it a chance. I promise." Looking around, I can't dispute that, compared to where I just spent the last three weeks, houses surrounded by trees and grass look very appealing. The bare branches of trees gone dormant for winter, reach out in a welcoming presence on the streets, offering the birds a place to land. But the idea of digging in the dirt and trying to grow anything is not even vaguely appealing.

"Hanukkah is coming soon, Eitan. Will we have someone to celebrate with?"

"I have arranged for you to stay with Mrs. Sophie Meier, our neighbor next door, until our marriage. She is a native German speaker and very nice. You will like her," he says, not answering my question.

"She is willing to have me until we are married?"

"I am already living in the house and thought you would not want to be there with me until our marriage, which can be very soon. All we need is a license from the local government office, then an official marries us as soon as we sign the paper and pay a small fee. It's not complicated. We can do it tomorrow or the next day."

"But a Jewish wedding is what I want, not some government official making a few words into a marriage five minutes after we sign a piece of paper. That is not a marriage, Eitan – it's a government procedure."

"I wait for you two years, Nathalie. How much more waiting do you expect from me?"

"I will go for the license and move into the house with you, but I will not be your wife until a rabbi says we are married, Eitan. Marriage is not a government form and a five-minute spoken agreement – it is a spiritual commitment, a religious tradition, a lifetime promise. It takes thought and planning, and celebrating with other Jews blessing us going into our new life together. Already I have given up a lot to be here with you; don't ask me to give up a proper religious marriage too."

"This is our house," Eitan says, ignoring my complaining as he slows the car in front of a two-story, four-square white clapboard house surrounded by dormant, brown grass, with a broad, welcoming front porch up several steps from the street. Eitan parks the car and, carrying my suitcase in one hand, guides me to the door with the other.

Inside is as he described, with minimal plain, functional furniture, blank walls, clear windows and a few faded, well-worn Persian carpets. Considering he has been living here alone, with no one looking after him, the interior is surprisingly bright and clean. Seeing the bouquet of flowers in a jar on a small table in the front hallway reminds me how hard he is trying to make me feel welcome in my new life and comforts my frightened heart.

"I have what we need to begin living here. The rest is up to you to make it into the home you want," Eitan explains, taking my hand and leading me into a small room just off the kitchen, where a sewing machine, affixed to a dark oak treadle table with four drawers for thread and scissors, is placed near the small window, catching the natural light.

"For you to make the curtains and anything else you want," he announces with obvious pride. His thoughtfulness brings forth my first spontaneous smile in more than a month, happily surprising me by the lack of effort it demanded.

"I really like it, Eitan," I exclaim, fingering the spool holder on the shiny, late-model Singer sewing machine. It will be much better than my old one. You are very kind to give it to me. Thank you," I say, reaching to him for the first time since he met me at the train and found me too shy to do anything other than walk up to him.

"I want you to be happy here, Nathalie. We have the promise of a good life together, but if you are not happy, we will both be miserable. I know following me to America was a very big sacrifice, but if you allow yourself, what you receive will be more than what you gave up."

"I want to be happy too, Eitan. Otherwise I would not have agreed to come to you. But I am not adventuresome like you. It will take me time to learn a new language and get used to different customs for living everyday life… and to be a wife."

"You will be a good wife," my promised husband assures me, gently taking my hand to show me the other rooms in the house. Moments later, as we are walking into the kitchen, the front door opens and a tall, slender woman with honey blond hair piled high on her head enters, hands outstretched.

"You are Eitan's beloved Nathalie! He has been beside himself awaiting you! I have never seen a man so excited as he has been," she says in rapid German.

"You must be Sophie. Eitan told me about you!" I exclaim. Hearing a familiar German dialect I easily understand, and from someone who could be my friend, pushes me to relax slightly.

"I am looking forward to having you with us until your marriage. My Miriam is grown up, with a family of her own far from here. I miss another woman in the house to talk to, and now I will have you!" Sophie chatters, her dark brown eyes wide with enthusiasm.

"Eitan tells me your journey has been very difficult, but it is over now. Come for tea and cake to refresh you," she insists, guiding me out the door, leaving Eitan standing alone in the parlor.

A few minutes later, sitting next to a sunny kitchen window, Sophie offers me a generous piece of warm apfelkuchen, smelling of cinnamon and nutmeg, and a cup of hot, strong coffee.

"This is wonderful," I say after the first bite.

"I will give you the recipe," Sophie smiles.

"I'm not much of a cook," I admit.

"It is simple; the first time we will make it together. After that, you can do it any time you wish, and use different fruits... peaches, plums, even berries."

"My Maman sent with me the recipe for her wonderful honey lemon cake, which requires fresh butter, new honey and juicy lemons. Perhaps you can help me make that?" I ask.

"Of course. I will enjoy trying a new recipe. Honey and lemon flavors are favorites of the Sephardic Jews. Your mutter, she is Sephardic?"

"No – Français-Deutsch, from Strasbourg. Who knows – perhaps there is Sephardic somewhere in her background, but no matter – the cake is delicious," I insist, feeling an all too familiar sadness descend over me as I reminisce.

"You should be excited about your new life, but your eyes betray you. Something is deeply bothering you," Sophie probes.

"I worry I will disappoint Eitan..."

"Disappoint him how, dear?"

"As a wife. I am not submissive. Deferring to the wishes of another is not natural for me. I came to America because Eitan wanted it, not because I did, and so far, it has been much more difficult than I expected. I have lingering doubts about whether I did the right thing leaving my family, perhaps forever."

"Eitan is a kind, gentle man, Nathalie. He will never ask more than you can give."

"That's not true. He asked me to come to America despite knowing how I felt about it," I frown.

"Marriage involves compromise – willingly doing things you might not want to do, but you do them anyway, because you love your husband and want him to be happy. Somehow, it all works out, most of the time."

"And the rest of the time?"

"The rest of the time, you accept that nothing is perfect and do your best to carry on."

"And the husband does the same for his wife – does things he doesn't want to do, but does them anyway, to make her happy?"

"Eitan has worked hard to welcome you here in ways he believes will please you. He was very excited about the sewing machine and even painted all the rooms in the house to make them bright and clean and ready for you to decorate however you wish. Every spare minute he was painting and cleaning. I'm sure there were many other things he would've rather been doing."

"The skills a wife needs: washing, ironing, cooking… they don't interest me. Please understand that I love Eitan very much but the possibility that marriage sentences me to a boring, uninteresting life frightens me."

"The routine tasks holding a home together are indeed boring, Nathalie, but soon enough you will have children and never be bored again, I promise you."

"I'm not sure I want children. Watching my sister-in-law, it's obvious that caring for children is hard work, and changes your life in ways you might not want it to change but have no choice, because the child, who is demanding and dependent, forces the change. My brother's wife, Irina, finds motherhood very difficult, with little pleasure involved, and I don't want a life like hers."

"Motherhood is very, very hard work, but also delightful and loving… not describable with words and possible to know only through experience. I'm sure your sister-in-law will discover this eventually," Sophie smiles knowingly, as she pours more coffee.

"I have many interests. I love to read, to sew and knit, and even to write bad poetry. These activities interest me much more than being a wife and mother. I am trapped between loving Eitan and being unwilling to accept what this love asks of me. I tried to explain this to Eitan, but he didn't listen… said my mind would soften as I grew more accustomed to thinking about our life together. The problem is my mind isn't softening, and I feel like a fraud who came here under false pretenses," I confess to a women I met only moments ago, making no effort to hide the tears streaming down my face.

"You are overtired. Too much change happening too fast, added onto suffering the nervousness every bride-to-be feels, has exhausted you. This upset will pass much more quickly if you don't give in to your doubts. Dry your eyes and we'll go upstairs to draw a hot bath. You'll feel much better after that, and there will still be time for a nap before Shabbat," Sophie smiles reassuringly, handing over a handkerchief and motioning me to follow her. Ascending the stairs, I offer to help prepare the Shabbat meal.

"We will have plenty of time together in the kitchen later. Right now, you need rest," my gracious hostess answers.

Our Shabbat celebration includes, in addition to Sophie, her neatly groomed, bespectacled physician husband, Dr. Heinrich Meier, Eitan and me. The Meier family came to America fifteen years ago from Dresden, bringing their six-year-old daughter and nine-year-old son with them, intending to stay only one year.

"I had a fellowship to study a new surgical technique with a physician in Cleveland, and one thing led to another. I had to make the difficult decision between returning to Germany, where I was needed, or remaining here, where I was also needed. Sophie wanted to return, and I wanted to stay."

"So of course you stayed, because it was what you wanted," I grumble under my breath in an attempt to conceal my irritation at his getting his way despite his wife's objections. If anyone notices, they ignore me.

"After making a trip back to Germany and discovering how much had changed in just one year, we decided to return. We moved to Elyria because there was no operating doctor for many miles. Sophie didn't disagree, but remained hesitant. Fifteen years later, she is content and has mostly adjusted to the peculiarities of this infant country," the doctor explains jovially, smiling at his wife. I ask for more about his views of American life, hoping they are more positive than Malka's.

"This is an immature country – barely able to stand on its own feet. It is still figuring itself out and is in no way ready to be part of the world. The government is like a laboratory experiment – trial and error to see what works and what doesn't. The wealthy and the leaders harbor some ridiculously mistaken notion that the nation has a divinely ordained destiny commissioned by G-d, which is an excuse for bad political decisions. Imagine the arrogance of believing the mind of G-d is knowable by mortal man!!" the learned doctor gestures, his voice rising as he reaches up to catch the yarmulke falling off his head.

"There is too much freedom without the maturity to accept such huge responsibility. Every individual is for himself only, and there are very big, very serious problems with that approach to life. Unfortunately, Americans haven't figured that out yet, and we all must suffer through her growing pains. For the lucky ones, there is much opportunity; for others, not so much. But Europe, where most people come here from, is growing more and more unstable, so returning is not an option either." Frowning, Eitan nods his agreement at this assessment, adding that he has concerns about the railroad's rapid expansion plans.

"We will be laying track across land people who have lived there hundreds of years consider sacred and depend upon to live. This isn't right, but if the people who were there first object, the United States Calvary overtakes them by force, then removes them to a different location. It's the American version of a pogrom."

"Despite what you promised, you are admitting America is no different from Europe, Eitan. Jews have always faced pogroms when a government decides it doesn't want them or wants something they have – like land. The government confiscates, forcing them to move on and punishing them if they resist. It frightens me to think America does the same thing." I admit.

"There are similarities, but Jews are not who America is forcing off their land, so we have nothing to worry about. And this is not a problem for us in the cities. Here, we are safe."

"I'm not sure about that, Eitan, but no need to worry your bride with things that might never happen," Dr. Meier cautions, offering a second helping of deliciously heavy, traditional almond honey cake to anyone who wants it. The remaining conversation is lively, but makes no reference to any connection with a local shul or Jewish community. Finally, I ask.

"There are several Jewish communities in Cleveland," Dr. Meier answers.

"Closest to us is Temple Banzai Abraham – a young Orthodox congregation. We are not such committed Jews… more like Shabbat every so often, with friends, Passover, and synagogue on the High Holy Days. To be perfectly honest, it is difficult enough being German, without adding Jewish onto the burden. Besides, Judaism is a collection of various practices one can engage in or not, so blending in or standing apart depends upon the choices we make," the kindly physician explains, obviously more comfortable with his relaxed approach to his Jewish identity than his wife, who is frowning.

"I grew up in a strict kosher home and prefer more observance," Sophie says.

"I bake a challah every week, and special foods for the holidays – Purim, Sukkot, Passover. I have made a few like-minded acquaintances and one or two good friends to share gossip and confidences. They are all nice people to know, to speak German with, celebrate Passover together. I appreciate them very much," she smiles, looking directly at her husband, whose scowl shows he does not entirely agree with his wife's social connections.

"I am away frequently, so if these people keep Sophie free from loneliness, then I cannot complain too loudly," Dr. Meier says, standing up to signal the meal is over, and inviting Eitan into another room to join him in a Jägermeister while his wife and I clear the table.

"I agree with Heinrich about blending in as much as we can, but I draw the line at celebrating Christmas," she tells me, adding that she doesn't mind the decorations and finds the music rather pleasant, but the holiday itself is meaningless and too materialistic. I don't disagree, adding that I was surprised Christmas decorations were everywhere, both in New York and upon arriving in Cleveland.

"It was hard for the children – surrounded by all the festivities and seeing their playmates receiving all kinds of presents from Father Christmas, who their friends referred to as Santa Claus. We became much more serious about Hanukkah to make up for it," she explains as I continue scraping and stacking plates.

"Leave the dishes in the sink, Nathalie. Sumi comes in the morning, and she will clean up," Sophie instructs, referring to her young Negro day maid. "Your day has been long. Let's go upstairs and prepare you for a restful sleep."

The quiet corner bedroom awaiting me, smelling of clean sheets and lavender soap beside a washbasin, convinces me I have now entered heaven. With freshly shampooed hair and refreshed after a long, soaking bath earlier in the afternoon, my eyelids are heavy as I eagerly anticipate falling into the most restful sleep I have had since leaving Hildesheim. Then, Sophie sits down in the chair near the corner window, signaling that sleep is not coming as soon as I hope.

"Eitan says you will be married in the city hall in a few days," Sophie begins. I nod, explaining that I agreed to go along with the civil ceremony but will not consider myself married until a rabbi performs a traditional marriage ceremony.

"I have no idea how to bring this about, but am not willing to forgo it," I say.

"Eitan must love you with the patience of Job to wait so long for you."

"He understands a Jewish wedding is important to me, but we have not discussed how to arrange one."

"No worries. I can organize a wedding very quickly," Sophie smiles, clapping her hands together.

"There is a traveling rabbi who will perform the ceremony… and you can use your sewing machine to make my wedding dress fit you."

"You brought your wedding dress from Germany?" I ask, astonished.

"No, but I sent for it for my Miriam, and then she didn't like it and wanted one of her own. It is a beautiful dress – fine silk and Belgian lace. Someone should wear it again, and we are nearly the same size – making it small enough to fit you should not be difficult. It will be perfect, and you will be beautiful wearing it," Sophie states with a conviction that does not invite further discussion.

"The rabbi comes tomorrow. We will meet with him and arrange for the wedding. It will be wonderful, Nathalie – I promise."

Sophie's wedding prediction comes true and, except for the absence of both our families, the day is perfect for both Eitan and me. The small Elyria Jewish community welcomes us warmly and joyously, happy for any opportunity to celebrate, especially a wedding, even if they don't know either the groom or the bride.

"It doesn't matter, liebling. Jews automatically know each other; nothing else is needed," the rabbi insisted when we met. It turned out he was saying the truth. Many of my fears take flight as the rabbi's prayer of gratitude at the end of the ceremony, under a chuppah the congregation made especially for us, wraps Eitan, me, and everyone present in love.

Baruch Atah Adonai Eloheinu Melech Haolam Shehehcheyahnu Vekiyimanu Vehegianu Lazman Hazeh, Amein: "Blessed are you, Lord our G-d, King of the universe, who has kept us alive, and sustained us, and enabled us to see this moment." Everyone repeats the Amein, first in Hebrew then in German.

Earlier, I decided not to tell Maman I made my head covering from the delicately crocheted table covering she gave me, intending that it grace the Shabbat table. When Sophie questioned this decision, I point out Maman would be embarrassed I made myself into a bride by wearing a tablecloth on my head.

"Perhaps, but she might also be very happy something she made you was with you on your wedding day, even if it wasn't the use she originally intended. You should not deny her the pleasure of knowing she was holding you close on this very important day in your life," Sophie replied, causing me to burst into tears.

"You must discipline yourself not to cry so much, dear. It gives the impression of weakness and those of us who have come here to make a life are not weaklings. Show the world the strong, brave woman you are, even when you don't feel that way," Sophie admonished, trying not to sound too impatient with what she apparently considers to be an excess of emotion always lurking just beneath the surface of my life, ready to erupt with volcanic energy any moment.

"Everything gets easier with practice," the older, very much wiser woman assured me.

Chapter Seven
פרק שבע

Chicago
Late Spring, 1971

In America, everyone is a lonely immigrant
searching for a place to fit in...

Arriving back in Chicago tired, thoroughly upended by Adrian McCormick's unsettling effect on me, and happy to be home in my own apartment, I make myself a cup of tea before sitting down on the couch to sort through the mail. A hand-addressed envelope from Dr. Cohen is among the tree-killing junk I throw into a pile on the floor. Inside is a hastily scribbled, barely legible note.

> *Natalie – Your test result came back positive, but not to worry, we'll deal with it. I have a plan. Stop by the office when you have time, and we'll discuss. Dr. C.*

Two days later, more anxious than I anticipated, I'm sitting in Dr. Cohen's cramped hospital office, watching him flip through a stack of files haphazardly scattered across his desk. My chair is the only uncluttered space in the room.

"Here we are – Natalie Barlow. Did you have a good trip home to San Francisco? Beautiful city... I'd go in a minute if I could afford to live there. But it's not an option with six kids to educate and a mother I'd have to physically pry out of Skokie – or send in the Russian army to forcibly remove, and even then she might not leave. A mind of her own, that one," the dry-witted doctor casually remarks, pushing his round, wire-rimmed glasses back up his nose as he reads through the first page of my medical file.

"San Francisco was fine, thanks; although informative might be a better word," I answer, returning to his original question, then suddenly feeling my face flush for no reason. To calm myself, I tuck a loose strand of hair behind my ear.

"As I mentioned, the test is positive for the clotting disorder we were checking for. Your clot time is slow, but I've seen worse," Doctor Cohen explains in a non-alarmist, matter-of-fact monotone I imagine him using when telling someone there is absolutely nothing wrong with them, or breaking the news of an incurable, fatal disease requiring them to get their affairs in order before sunset. It's reassuring to know that, apparently, not much rattles him.

"My mother, my aunt, my cousin, and now me, all seem to have this condition, so that's four for four," I point out, staring down at my hands resting in my lap while shredding a Kleenex.

"It behaves differently in different people; some are more acute bleeders than others. Generally speaking, the individual tendency doesn't vary much over a lifetime, but for some, it can get worse, as appears was the case with your mother. We don't know why that occurs, but it's not common. According to her surgeon, her blood spurted like water out of a fire hose, which neither of us believes was always true. At minimum, she would have had chronic, very heavy bruising, which would have been impossible to ignore." He stops speaking while he thumbs through more notes.

"Keeping everything in mind, here's my plan for you, and it's very simple," he says, looking at me in a grandfatherly way despite not being old enough to be one.

"We regularly check you for anemia, which I have already done, and you do not currently have, but could develop. It doesn't always happen, but it's not unheard of – and if it occurs, we fix it."

"How?"

"High doses of gigantic horse pills packed with concentrated iron and vitamin C. You won't like them, but trust me, the shots are worse. Transfusions are only necessary in the most severe cases, and because we are paying attention, yours would be unlikely to ever reach that level. Eat plenty of meat. It helps mitigate the potential for anemia considerably."

"I'm vegetarian," I interrupt.

"Of course you are! Why make this easy? Eat your spinach – three generous servings a day, like our old friend Popeye."

"I don't really like spinach," I interrupt.

"My cholesterol is higher than the Illinois tax deficit, I believe vegetables are poisonous and exercise is cruel and inhumane punishment, and I haven't had brisket on Shabbat since the Eisenhower administration. If I can deal with all that, you can eat the damned spinach," Doctor Cohen says, rolling his eyes as he's looking down at my chart, then up at me again.

"We would manage a pregnancy very carefully. There's a somewhat greater risk of miscarriage with this, and you'd automatically go on iron shots. Delivery would be by cesarean section because controlling postpartum bleeding is much more effective that way," he explains. I've always assumed I could have children if I wanted them, and hearing this assumption challenged is a jolt I hadn't seen coming.

"With cesareans we're able to surgically remove the placenta and be sure your uterus is completely cleared out." Dr. Cohen continues.

"Isn't that more dangerous?"

"Childbirth is inherently risky, and in situations where we can't predict how the pregnancy might affect the blood's ability to clot normally, cesareans are far less dangerous than unexpectedly gushing like Old Faithful during a normal delivery. As long as there are no surprises, and we'll do all we can to be sure there aren't, everything will be fine. Being well-prepared for complications automatically makes them less complicated. My colleague, Doctor Schwartz is a genius in the delivery room – delivered all my wife's babies pro-bono because he believes in doing his part to replace the Jews lost in the Holocaust. He has six kids of his own and convinced me to have six if he delivered them for free, then conveniently forgot to offer to pay for their college educations... but I digress. He's a fine doctor; you and baby will thrive." Hearing this, I am bereft of words.

"You look a little shell-shocked," my trusted physician tells me, after the silence between us grows too wide to ignore.

"Maybe a little. I'm not sure how I feel. Thankfully I'm no longer married nor interested in doing it again, so being pregnant and having children hasn't been a burning question in my life. But it also never occurred to me it could be a problem."

"You're not listening, Natalie. It's not a problem. It's a situation we manage before it becomes a problem, and that's what we're going to do. The goal is preserving your options. You might fall flat on your face in love with some man you can't live without and want to give him children. It's been known to happen."

"To other people, maybe. I really doubt that will happen to me."

"You have no way to know the future. My advice is to go ahead and live your life and don't worry about this. Your mother's death was a freak occurrence that was avoidable if she had mentioned the bleeding possibility to her surgeon ahead of time or, frankly, if he'd checked more thoroughly, which is generally routine before any procedure."

"She was a nurse, and a very smart woman. I'm sure she knew she was a bleeder, and consciously chose not to mention it," I say, giving voice to a suspicion that has been tickling the back of my mind since learning of my mother's sudden, unexpected death.

"Don't jump to upsetting conclusions, Natalie. You'd be surprised at the things people forget to tell their doctors: 'oops, I forgot to mention somebody punched out one of my kidneys a few years ago – I didn't know it was important. Yea, I had a couple heart attacks – maybe three, I'm not sure. I didn't think coughing up a little blood now and then was a big deal...' We don't like surprises, but patients think we're mind readers who can figure things out all on our own... frustrating as hell."

"Still, the more I think about it, the only thing that makes sense is that she knew about the bleeding issue and didn't say anything on purpose," I insist, then ask whether her surgeon explained why he was operating on her?

"She had a benign cyst on her gall bladder that was causing troublesome digestive issues. Under ordinary circumstances it's an easy, straightforward procedure to fix a common problem, and she would've been fine. She probably viewed it as the quick surgery it normally is and didn't give it anymore thought – and neither should you."

"Perhaps, but I'm not one hundred percent convinced."

"You're far more likely to be hit by a San Francisco trolley than to die from this. You're young, otherwise healthy, don't have any bad habits that I know about, and seem to take good care of yourself. You're doing fine. Just file this away for safe keeping and get on with your life."

"I think I remember my cousin Emily mentioning iron shots when she was pregnant... said something about a needle the size of a broom handle and being more constipated than John Dillinger."

"How could your cousin possibly know John Dillinger was constipated? That's not the sort of thing people talk about. My patients never admit it even when they're gassier than a Goodyear blimp and their stomachs are harder than a cement sidewalk," Doctor Cohen shares, looking up from his desk.

"Emily went on vacation in northern Wisconsin, where Dillinger hid out when he was on the run. Apparently, he had to make a quick escape and left behind a grocery bag full of Ex-Lax she discovered in the display cabinet in some lodge."

"I'll be damned. A constipated gangster on the run... Not too surprising, if you think about it. Life as an outlaw wanted dead or alive is very stressful and doesn't promote good eating habits or regularity which, medically speaking, leads to chronic irritability that tends to exacerbate any tendencies toward violence... explains a lot about Dillinger's career choice. Regardless, it's not a useful comparison to grab onto as you're thinking about your iron intake," Dr. Cohen cautions, half smiling.

"Do you have any questions about anything I've said?" he then asks, shifting the conversation back to the reason I'm sitting in his office.

"None at the moment," I answer, shaking my head.

"I don't want you worrying about this, Natalie. I told you my mother has the same problem, had several kids anyway and now she's pushed way past eighty – how far past depends on which day you ask her. She makes blintzes to die for and I can only dream about, and despite her last license application being denied because she flunked the test, is still driving, which I worry about a hell of a lot more than her blood clotting time," Doctor Cohen says, patting me on my shoulder as he guides me out the door.

Later that evening, I update my dad on the doctor's report and raise the possibility that my mother purposely hid her bleeding problem from her surgeon. The intensity of his reaction surprises me.

"Your mother was many things, Natalie, but self-destructive wasn't one of them. You've got plenty of things to figure out without adding this to the list You'll never know what was, or wasn't, going on in her head before she died, so do us both a favor and drop it," my father instructs, sounding surprisingly irritated at the direction our discussion has taken. I reluctantly agree, knowing I'll always wonder whether my mother passively committed suicide.

Since I've been back in Chicago, Emily calls more often than previously. She knows someone is translating the letters and diaries but hasn't asked a lot of questions. Mostly we talk about all the things in her life that keeps her perpetually irritated: her husband, her son's basketball coach, little Charlotte's ballet teacher, her mother-in-law's refusal to learn English, and my boring social life. Sometimes she goes off on Aunt Sally, which I feel is a little harsh, but I'm in no position to opine on mother-daughter relationships. So far, she's not said anything about the blood clotting issue, which I hope my aunt has explained to her, and I'm tempted to ask her about, but...

I generally call my aunt on Tuesday or Thursday afternoons, when Mick is at the union hall playing cards or shooting pool. Sally views the telephone as useful only in times of extreme duress and has never been one for long, stream of consciousness phone conversations about nothing important, so we don't talk long. The important thing is she knows I'm thinking about her. She writes often, sending samples of yarn she's knitting, a pattern I might like, or newspaper clippings she guesses might interest me. She never asks about the letters or the diaries, and I don't bring them up.

While I cherish the close connection with my family, the person I long to talk to the most hasn't been in touch since I returned to Chicago. Adrian McCormick is living rent-free in my head, and I can't seem to evict him. Sometimes I'm forced to walk a mile or two along the lake shore to keep from calling or writing to him, although I'm not sure how I'd do that since I don't recall him giving me his mailing address and I'm not sure what I did with his phone number. We didn't make specific plans for him to contact me after I returned to Chicago, and he did say he has other, ongoing obligations in addition tot he translations. Rationally, I know I shouldn't be upset that I haven't heard from him, but can't help wishing that, by now, I had.

On the other hand, despite his theoretical unavailability, as handsome and charming as Adrian is, it's hard to imagine he doesn't have a woman in his life who keeps him occupied. He might only have time to work on the translations when she's busy doing something else, which probably isn't very often. It's also possible he's more married to the Catholic Church than he lets on and doesn't want the complications of even a casual relationship with a woman. Maybe the diaries contain such vulgar information he doesn't want anything to do with someone with that kind of family background and has changed his mind about the whole project. In my worst moments, the possibility he got hit by a car, eloped with an irresistible girlfriend and is on an extended honeymoon in Tahiti, or was recently diagnosed with a fatal illness all occur to me. When my fantasies are finally exhausted, I feel like smacking myself in the head for being unable to stop thinking about someone I spent less than eight hours with over a month ago. *You're being ridiculous, Natalie – knock it off*, becomes my silent mantra every time Adrian enters my mind without an invitation, which is several times a day.

Attempting to distract myself, I've begun reading up on Judaism, and find it wonderfully interesting. One Friday evening I wrangle an invitation to the Hillel Jewish students' Shabbat celebration from one of my graduate students and enjoy myself very much. The meal is my first direct exposure to an important ritual that has spanned millennia of Jewish life, and taking part in a tradition that ancestors who, until a few weeks ago I never knew I had, also participated in, is deeply emotional for me. The connection between us feels fragile and weak, but slowly I am beginning to believe it is real.

I also ask to sit in on the Basics of Judaism class offered by a professor of world religions at the divinity school who is also a rabbi. He agrees to accommodate my request, with the understanding that I don't intrude on student discussion time by asking too many questions and don't turn in any papers he is expected to read.

I soon realize that cultivating my new identity more deeply also involves finding a rabbi who will take me as a conversion candidate, and the obvious choice is the professor. But when I approach him, he explains that since my mother was Jewish, I am already Jewish, and can't convert to something I already am. He adds that he would be happy to recommend a couple of books that will tell me everything I need to know. His casual approach to what I an experiencing as a profoundly life-changing discovery about myself is off-putting and, in my view, arrogant.

"Sorry, Rabbi, but just reading a few books isn't going to do it for me," I bristle, sitting in his book-jammed office, badly in need of a good airing out.

"Lesson number one, Dr. Barlow, is that rabbis speak with authority. Don't raise problems with a rabbi if you don't want to accept the rabbi's solutions. My solution to your request is to read the books I'm recommending. Judaism is a lived religion and culture celebrated through shared ritual in community with others and in the home. Chicago has many Jewish congregations to choose from. Find one you like and start taking part. Buy some nice dishes and learn how to keep kosher. Do these things, and pretty soon being Jewish sinks in," he instructs, smoothing his poorly groomed beard while pawing through a pile of papers strewn across his desk and avoiding further eye contact. Realizing this is as much as I'm going to get from him, I mentally add "find a synagogue I like" to the list of things I need to explore further and leave, angry at his dismissively patronizing tone.

A few days later, recounting this to Elena, I say Judaism sounds as bad as Catholicism in terms of being authoritarian and patriarchal.

"Not really. If you don't like one rabbi, just keep looking until you find one you do like. Rabbi shopping is no big deal – all Jews do it, and there are several kinds of Judaism to choose from. The other thing to know is Jews don't all agree on anything. It's our nature to question and argue. Two Jews have four opinions and as soon as somebody agrees with you, you're obligated to change your mind. It's what keeps us alive and once you get used to it, it's kind of fun. No Jew cares whether you agree with them… it's the argument that matters," she laughs.

"If you say so. I don't enjoy conflict that much," I admit, then ask about the possibility of joining in her family celebrations and maybe going to synagogue with her sometime.

"You're more than welcome to join us, Natalie," Elena smiles, sitting down next to me at the worktable beside the large window in my office, then biting into an apple before continuing.

"The thing is, Shabbat involves a lot of preparation, and I have a full-time job plus three boys with the combined energy of an Apollo rocket. Even if I wanted to, which I don't, I can't spend all day Friday chopping vegetables, baking bread, and marinating meat. Shabbat happens because David's mother, Adva, comes weekly and takes over the cooking, including baking challah, but she's complaining a lot and any day now she'll announce it's all too much for her and quit. Passover is a nightmare because the boys can't sit still long enough to get through the Seder, and they hate the food, which they sneak under the table to the dog. Last time, between the prayers over the egg and the matzoh we had an emergency trip to the vet to dislodge parsley from Pogo's esophagus, which cost $400 because it was an after-hours, life-or-death crisis. The dog damn near died, the kids were hysterical, and Adva wailed over and over that interrupting the meal to save a family pet insulted G-d, our ancestors, and Jews around the world, plus ruined her carefully prepared rack of lamb. She refused to acknowledge that the lamb and our ancestors were already dead, Jews world-wide were focused on their own Passover celebrations and didn't give a rip about ours, and the dog still had a chance if we acted quickly. We go to synagogue for High Holy Days, weddings, funerals, and bar mitzvahs, which our oldest has totally blown off because he thinks Hebrew school is intentional cruelty and a stupid waste of time better spent doing other things. Last week the rabbi caught him and two other boys shooting craps in the alley behind shul and suspended him. To get him reinstated, David promised he'd have a talk with him as soon as he gets around to it, which we all know will be never, and has my mother-in-law very upset because she might die before celebrating her oldest grandson's transition to

Jewish manhood... but I'm blathering. We'd love for you to join in any aspect of our Jewish life that interests you."

Barely able to hide my amusement, I assure my best friend it all sounds wonderful and I'm looking forward to it. I even offer to bring something, which Elena says would insult Adva directly into the grave, which wouldn't necessarily be a bad thing for someone her age.

Meanwhile, I'm not making much progress on the book summarizing my last five years of research on women, poverty, and public policy I'm supposed to be writing. I keep telling myself I'll have all summer to catch up and still meet the publisher's deadline. But I'm overwhelmed by all that has occurred in the last few months and I've lost interest, at least for the moment. This lapse is heavy on my mind on a Friday evening in early May when the phone rings at the same time the apartment lights flash in concert with a window-rattling clap of thunder. Fearful of talking on the phone during thunderstorms, I avoid answering it, but whoever is calling is persistent and the phone keeps ringing until I finally pick up.

"Natalie, this is Adrian McCormick – I guess I woke you up," a melodic baritone voice says.

"You didn't wake me up, but I hate talking on the phone during a thunderstorm. I'll call you back," I answer, hanging up before he has a chance to reply. Immediately, I remember I'm not sure I still have his phone number.

An hour later, after frantically rummaging through my purse and canvas messenger bag with a flashlight, I finally locate the scrap of paper with Adrian's phone number. By now, it's midnight Chicago time and there's still no electricity, but the post-storm darkness adds a touch of romance to the necessity of returning Adrian's call by candlelight. Clearing my throat and hoping my voice is the right mixture of happy to hear from him but not too excited that he's home on a Friday night, I dial the telephone.

"Sorry about that. I've never gotten used to Midwest thunderstorms. I keep imagining the lightening will leap through the telephone directly into my ear," I explain. Adrian's response is a hearty laugh that instantly doubles my heart rate.

"How have you been?" I continue, anxious to satisfy the deep craving to hear his voice that has plagued me for weeks, and relieved that he cannot see what I am sure is a ridiculous grin spreading across my face.

"Busier than I want to be, but fine otherwise. You?"

"Good. I'm exploring Judaism a little, and it feels like I'm finding a part of myself I always felt was missing yet never understood what, exactly, it was. I can't articulate this very well, but it's real, slightly overwhelming sometimes – and very present in my life. But this isn't why you called," I say, pushing the conversation away from myself before revealing something I'll later wish I hadn't. Adrian is dangerous this way. Something about him invites confessional, soul-baring conversations which I succumb to all too easily.

"One reason I called is to find out how you're doing with everything. I'm glad you're learning more about Judaism, and a little envious, to be perfectly honest."

"Really? Why would you be envious?"

"At its core, Catholicism is a political religion, while Judaism mostly separates itself from Zionism and the State of Israel and seeks to do God's work on earth, without getting too complicated about it. Jews celebrate life. The rabbis don't get involved in politics; instead, they live by the Torah, which they are constantly discussing and re-defining. Unlike us poor Catholics, they aren't required to spend a lifetime doing penance simply for being mortal human beings."

"I've thought of Catholicism as a lot of things, but never as a political initiative. Why do you say that?" I ask, keeping the conversation alive as the lights in my apartment flash on and off.

"Power. The Vatican is an independent nation state intent on maintaining its power on the world stage. Other countries send ambassadors to the Vatican, and the Church sends envoys – papal nuncios – to most countries, partly because the pope is the undisputed leader of nearly one billion Catholics worldwide. In terms of raw numbers, the Vatican holds sway over a population several times larger than most countries in the world and includes fully half of Christianity. Those numbers alone carry powerful political influence."

"That's a lot of people, Adrian. There has to be some management or governing structure."

"True, but the reality is no other religion functions as its own independent nation. The U.S. doesn't send an ambassador to the Lutherans or Methodists, for example, but it does send one to the Vatican. Religion is the Vatican's GNP – what they produce to justify their existence and maintain a revenue stream."

"Israel's a nation state," I remind Adrian, struggling to get my head around what he is saying.

"It's also the Jews' ancestral homeland where several million Jews have lived for thousands of years. The problem is the Palestinians also believe Israel is their homeland and want the Jews gone, which means Israel has to be political in order to survive, but it separates this from religious practices. Religion is not the economic engine driving the Israeli economy. Culturally, Israel as a nation embraces the traditions and practices of Jewish life and faith, but that's as far as it goes. It accommodates the wide variances in Judaism's religious perspectives and admits to being foremost a political entity. Israel can't help that its nickname is The Holy Land, whereas the Vatican puts itself forth as the headquarters of the One True Church with all the answers, which is damned arrogant, if you think about it."

"I honestly had no idea. I spent a lot of years in boarding school with the nuns, but they didn't talk politics."

"They wouldn't, and I'd be surprised if even the most devout realize how political the official Catholic Church is or view the pope as a political leader. I certainly didn't, until I went to Rome and saw it first-hand, then participated in it. But it's past midnight on your end, and this is a discussion to continue another time."

"That's OK – it's very interesting," I interrupt, not wanting the conversation to end.

"The other reason I called is I've been working on the translations and wanted to catch you up... and assure you they're a real treasure. You should start thinking about how to preserve them – donate them to a library or something. They're part of the Jewish-American story and of Jewish history, and are far too precious to sit in a closet."

"I haven't thought about what to do with them."

"We can talk more about it later, but it is something to start thinking about. I finished the first diary you gave me, which is mostly about leaving Germany and settling into America. Your grandmother has a very strong sense of herself, an independent streak that runs through much of what she writes. You come by this honestly."

"I'm not that independent."

"I disagree, but it's not an unattractive trait, so don't worry about it."

"I'm not worried about it; I just don't believe it."

"Glad to hear it isn't keeping you up nights," Adrian chuckles, then asks if I have a minute, because he wants to read a little of what he's translated and get my opinion on whether the translations should be literal, as written but perhaps more difficult to understand, or as grammatically correct as possible, which makes it an easier read.

"Personally, I favor the literal. It honors the writer by respecting what he, or she, in this case, has written and comes closest to what she was intending to say. Literal translations tend to subtly reveal more about the person but can sometimes be hard to follow." Adrian explains.

"I agree. Change as little as possible."

"Before deciding for sure, see what you think about this literal excerpt from your grandmother's journal:"

> *Sophie made us a nice wedding. She invited many people who were happy celebrating with us, but I was sad and missed my family… Eitan said he understood, and maybe so, because he did not insist I come to him that night, which was his right as my husband. After I wrote to Maman and Papa about the rabbi making a proper wedding, I finally felt married enough to go into Eitan's bed. He was gently glad to have me, but not too glad, and didn't insist on anything that made me uncomfortable. Sleeping with someone, rather than alone, as I have done all my life, is not as difficult as I imagined, and I am getting used to it. Sometimes Eitan snores, which is upsetting when it keeps me awake and I am irritable the next day. But he is gone parts of every week, so I still sleep alone some of the time.*
>
> *I am in America four months now, and every day I still wish for Germany. Eitan talks about having children making everything better, but I don't believe he has any idea what he's claiming. Every time I think about being a mother, recalling Irina and her screaming babies drives the thought away. How she complained!! She was so upset that being a mother turned into a milk cow, and comforting her was impossible, because she wasn't wrong. No matter how much Eitan wants children, it terrifies me, but letting fear control me now, when I've not let it control me before, is nonsense, so I'll probably try for children anyway… someday… maybe… if I can ever imagine life with children but without Maman to tell me how to be a mother, which is something I cannot do alone, because it is hard and I know nothing about it.*
>
> *Eitan is working on the garden he promised me, which I tell him is silly because I am not a farmer – all I know about growing things is watering the flowers Maman plants in the window boxes every spring. He says I will*

enjoy planting seeds and watching them grow, but what I think he means is growing plants will put me into the frame of mind to grow a baby. I don't say that remembering to water the dirt when the plants are thirsty is not the same as satisfying a baby when it is hungry. I decide to plant flowers, which will remind me of home and help me feel happier. Sophie says vegetables would be better, but they are a lot of responsibility... what I don't eat or give away I have to preserve, and I don't like cooking well enough to get involved in all that. She claims she's never heard of a Jewish woman who didn't love cooking for her family, so doesn't understand my insistence on being a committed Jew but unwilling to feed a crowd at a moment's notice. I don't understand either, but it's how I feel, so I can't pretend otherwise. Weather is warming and there is more sun so I will plant soon... maybe include one tomato plant, but that's all...

Listening to Adrian read from my grandmother's diary transforms her from an abstract concept into a once-living person, which is not the reaction I expected. I need to catch my breath before saying anything, then I start laughing. Adrian asks me what it is about what he has just read that is so funny

"Nothing really – it's just that I don't like cooking either. Maybe it's an inherited trait, or flaw, depending upon who you ask, that runs in the family. My aunt's not a great cook either."

"Claiming you can't do something you don't want to do is an inherited trait is a pretty weak avoidance tactic," he chuckles.

"Do you get the sense lot of what she writes is sad and lonely – and scared," I ask.

"Definitely. Imagine finding yourself in a strange country, unable to speak the language, doubting you'll ever see your family again, yet expected to be a proper wife and good mother. She must've been terrified, yet incredibly brave – and emotionally strong."

"I can't imagine it... just thinking about it makes me cry," I admit, searching for a Kleenex.

"She was a very courageous and determined young woman, Natalie. And from what I can determine so far, your grandfather was a good man. You come from remarkable people. You should be very proud."

"I wouldn't say proud so much as deeply grateful for the heritage. It feels like a gift I didn't know I've been waiting for all my life, which sounds a little dramatic, I suppose… but it's true."

"Christians call it being born again. Maybe not the best analogy, but the one that comes immediately to mind."

"I don't know about being born again. It's more like sudden turn in a direction I never anticipated going. But I haven't been at it long enough to describe it; maybe it will end up being born again – who knows? In the meantime, it's also a bomb waiting to go off in terms of my existing family relationships, at least concerning my aunt. I have no idea how this is going to play out with her and am not looking forward to finding out." Saying this, an involuntary frown overtakes the bright smile on my face.

"It might be a little like Mr. Toad's wild ride, with this one being through the family forest. It'll take a while to arrive at a clearing. In the meantime, try to understand how huge this is, especially for your aunt, who undoubtedly doesn't want her family secrets, whatever they are, revealed, nor does she want her identity challenged at this stage of her life. I hope you won't forget that we agreed you would reach out if you need to talk about it," Adrian gently reminds me.

"I won't forget."

"Promise?"

"I promise, Adrian. Honestly."

"Good. Now that that's settled, I can fill you in on the next entries. They're mostly about trying to have children, which apparently was difficult. It seems she had bleeding problems."

"Wow! She says that?"

"Basically. Why?"

"My mother died because of a bleeding disorder she apparently forgot to mention to her surgeon. My aunt, my cousin, and I all have it."

"Is it serious?"

"I'm told it's not serious as long as you know about it and take appropriate precautions; otherwise, obviously it could be. I've been told to live my life and not worry about it, but it is interesting that my grandmother had it too. My aunt thinks it's probably the reason we are a small family."

"So having children is a problem?"

"Not necessarily. Why?"

"Just wondering…" The lengthy silence that follows puzzles me.

"How do you want me to get these next sections to you? I can mail them or bring them when I come to Chicago," Adrian finally continues.

"You're coming to Chicago?" I exclaim, as my suddenly galloping heart begins pounding so hard I'm sure Adrian can hear it through the telephone as it sucks every cubic centimeter of air out of me.

"Next month. Any chance we can get together?" Adrian asks.

"I'm sure there is..." I respond breathless with an excitement I hope he doesn't pick up on.

"There are several things I need to do while I'm there. How about I call you again in a few days and we'll figure something out?"

"That would be nice... it'll be really good to see you," I reply, which isn't quite what I want to openly admit at this moment, but the words are out of my mouth before I can stop them.

"You've been on my mind a lot, Natalie... I've wanted to call you, but..."

"Call me any time, Adrian... really. I think about you, too, and..."

"Sleep well. We'll talk again soon." The phone clicks before I can say more. Hanging up, I realize the abrupt ending is probably for the best. Adrian disturbs me in ways I'm not sure I want to be disturbed and the more apparent this becomes, the more out-of-control I feel.

Although it's well past midnight, I'm now wide awake and spend the next several hours allowing my mind to wander aimlessly over the emerging landscape of my new life, trying out several scenarios that Adrian might possibly fit into. Dawn is just beginning to break over Lake Michigan when I finally stretch out on the couch and doze off.

A week after Adrian's phone call, I find a thick envelope containing several handwritten pages, held together with a paper clip and a folded note stuffed into my office mailbox. *I have to give Adrian my home address*, I remind myself while quickly glancing at the contents before putting everything into my canvas shoulder pouch to take home.

Later that evening, armed with a cup of tea, I sit down on my couch, tuck my stocking feet under my long skirt, and begin reading.

> *This is the last of the first diary. The entries aren't always dated, but they are in a sequence that makes sense. As you can see, they're mostly daily trivia written in loneliness, revealing mostly her state of mind and little else. The letters from this time are from your great-grandmother back in Germany and are mostly family news and neighborhood gossip. When she refers to Papa, I assume he was your great-grandfather. If he wasn't a rabbi, he was very involved in the Hildesheim Jewish*

community. I'm not finished yet, but enclosed is an example, written by your great-grandmother. I might get started on the second diary before coming to Chicago, but not sure. Hopefully see you soon – Adrian writes.

> *Beloved daughter – I write that the babies continue to grow and thrive and, at this moment, Irina is not expecting another one, which she is very happy about. This is because she is not living with her husband and instead is still living with us, which means there are little people walking and crawling everywhere. The noise is happy, but is also all the time. Papa is worried over the Kaiser building an army...says he will lead Germany to war, which will be a problem for everyone, especially the Jews. I say we have steady income, food on the table, a shul, and Levi has a job, a wife and children, so we are complete and don't worry about what might never happen. Papa says worrying is what keeps him alive, so now I am quiet and just let him fret. Only your voice he will listen to. He reads your letters over and over because you are strong enough to convince him to stop with his thinking bad things all the time. He is comforted that you are in America, so will survive whatever occurs here in Germany, and our family will continue... otherwise, it might not, and we will be extinct, he says. Such grim thoughts your Papa carries around with him, Nathalie... and it is worse because he is so much missing you. He even stopped playing his violin for a time. We are all of us missing you but comforted knowing you are finding yourself a happy life, even if it is hard and lonely and you don't fit in yet. Everything in life is hard and often lonely, and Jews never fit in, but we try to enjoy life anyway...*
>   *Long may we live to see each other again...*
>   *Your loving Maman.*

Finishing the translation, I return to Adrian's note, wondering about the "hopefully see you soon" sign-off. Frowning, I stress over what might prevent us from meeting when he is in Chicago for a full five minutes before telling myself to calm down and stop acting like a lovesick teenager. I read the translation again, this time more slowly, often staring out the window, thinking about the woman I am named for, until the telephone interrupts me.

"Natalie – it's Adrian."

"I just finished the letter you translated. It's wonderful, although that's probably not the right word. Maybe fascinating would be better... heartbreakingly fascinating," I say, realizing too late I should've brought forth a better beginning to the conversation.

"They were a family who loved each other very much. Not every family can make that claim. The downside, of course, is the pain that comes with being separated from people you love that much," Adrian offers.

"I have a hard time imagining how it would be possible to get past missing them enough to make a new life. The loss must permanently rearrange a person's psyche in ways they probably never fully recover from."

"I expect they carry the sadness with them always... just like the maudlin Irish poets claim."

"You're right. That kind of separation – knowing someone you love is out there, but you can't quite reach them really would be awful," I admit, suddenly caught in the thought that this could be exactly where Adrian lands in my life: as someone I profoundly love and can never reach. A deep breath I am sure Adrian hears, escapes me.

"I've looked at more letters, and the next diary. Most pertain to daily life up to 1914, when the war everyone feared erupts and things get ugly."

"You have more letters and another diary?"

"Your dad brought them over a few days ago." *Funny he didn't mention that,* I think, trying to remember the last time we spoke and whether he said anything about meeting Adrian, and I missed it.

"I can't promise I'll finish by the time I come next week, but I hope to."

"I thought you weren't coming for a month or so."

"Changed my mind after checking the Cubs schedule. I hope that's not a problem."

"No, of course not... I'm here until the end of the term."

"I'll be staying with my aunt and uncle who live across the street from my younger sister and a houseful of smelly teenagers. The upside is it's just a few blocks from Wrigley Field, which is very convenient for getting to ball games. My other sister lives west, about halfway to Rockford. She'll probably drive in, but if not, I'll go out there for a night with fewer kids but a loudmouth husband only tolerable in small doses. I also need to drive up to Lake Superior to check on a place I inherited a few years back... meet with the caretaker and check on the winter damage. That's a four-day road trip; otherwise, my only plans are a double header at Wrigley Field with some guys I grew up with, and whatever thoughts you have..."

"I certainly wouldn't mind a baseball game if the weather is nice."

"Seriously? I think I love you!" Adrian exclaims, sending an instant shiver through me, producing a weakness I hope I quickly recover from and don't reflexively respond with a similar remark, which would be highly inappropriate and nearly impossible to contain.

"I arrive next Thursday afternoon. Why don't we plan on dinner somewhere in Evanston Friday night? My plan is to go up to Lake Superior Saturday and come back Tuesday. The double header is Wednesday and, according to the schedule I carry in my wallet, which I'm currently looking at, there are also home games Thursday and Friday of that week. We could go either one of those days."

"What time is the game on Friday?"

"2:30."

"Let's plan on that."

"Fantastic! It gives me something special to look forward to," Adrian replies.

"Me too," I whisper, growing warm all over.

"Not that dinner won't be nice too," he quickly adds. "I'll call you Thursday night. In the meantime, decide where and what time. Anyplace that isn't Irish is fine. I'll take the EL to you, which is a straight shot north from my neighborhood and runs every 20 minutes or so. Should work perfectly. Talk soon."

He hangs up the phone before I can respond. *Apparently, he's pretty used to having the last word*, I conclude, still holding the telephone in my hand, wondering how, in a brief phone call, Adrian McCormick manages to thoroughly demolish my emotional equilibrium.

As the days wear on, the decisions about what to wear and where to have dinner take on an order of magnitude rivaling the launch of an intercontinental ballistic missile. What if the weather is bad? What if the restaurant is terrible? What if we really hit it off and our relationship soars? What if our relationship takes off then crashes? What if we don't have a relationship and I am imagining all this? What if I wear jeans and a black turtleneck and Adrian shows up in a suit and tie? What if I wear a dress and heels and Adrian chooses Levis and a sport coat? What if... what if... what if... and why do I care so much?

I propose these questions to Elena the next afternoon while we're in my office mindlessly sorting through data for future analysis. Her unhelpful response is that she thinks I'm losing my mind, which she finds deeply upsetting, because it used to function so well. It's a conclusion I can't readily disagree with since no man, including my former husband, has ever upset my life to the extent Adrian McCormick so effortlessly does – and I haven't a clue how he's managing to do it.

Thursday evening comes and goes without a phone call from Adrian, causing me to conclude either his plane crashed and has not yet been reported on the evening news, or he changed his mind about getting together. Disappointed and frustrated that I can't seem to stop myself from turning into a pitiful neurotic as concerns him, I go to bed early. Then, instead of sleeping I lay face up on my pillow, staring at the moonlit ceiling, feeling sorry for myself. When the phone rings I'm tempted not to answer, but then realize it's probably my dad, and he'll keep ringing until I pick up.

Without saying hello, Adrian begins by profusely apologizing for the late hour, explaining his plane was delayed, and he didn't want to wait until tomorrow to call, in case I'd decided he wasn't coming and made other plans. Instead of asking what kind of plans he thinks I'd be making in the middle of the night, I admit I'm very glad to hear from him, as I was a little worried. He asks about dinner tomorrow, which begins in less than five minutes.

"How about casual Italian?" I suggest having failed, after hours of stressing over the decision, to come up with a better option. He says that sounds fine, asks whether the six o'clock EL is still a good arrival time and requests directions to the restaurant. Drawing a sudden blank on how to direct him to Enzo's from the EL, I say I'll meet him at the station, then immediately regret it, fearing I sound too eager. He says he's looking forward to seeing me, then ends the call. *Maybe he just doesn't like talking on the telephone*, I think, once again listening to a buzz tone while holding the receiver in my hand.

The next morning, I call Enzo to request a six-thirty reservation for two at one of the booths near the window.

"Who died?" he barks when he picks up the phone on the third ring. I identify myself and quickly reassure him no one has died; I just want to make a dinner reservation. He points out that the restaurant isn't open because he is still in bed, sound asleep, then says that he always has room for me, and I don't need a reservation. I glance at the clock and see that it is barely five a.m. I apologize, thank him profusely, then hang up before he can ask who the person accompanying me will be and why this dinner is so important arranging it couldn't wait until the sun was up.

Adrian is the last person off the train, which is never late, but is late tonight. The endless minutes of waiting encourage my monkey mind to swing through various scenarios residing in the tangled jungle of my overactive imagination: a multi-car derailment with fatalities; a suicide on the tracks – although sometimes I think just riding the EL, which is less structurally sound than a condemned roller coaster, is flirting with suicide; a power failure electrocutes all the passengers; or a last minute Chicago rail workers strike. By the time I finally see him, my anxiety is so far off the charts it is nearly impossible to refrain from running up to him and collapsing into his arms as if he's just been released from the gulag after being shot down during a dangerous spy mission over Soviet Russia. Hugging me, I inhale the warm wool smell of his rich brown, crew neck sweater, which fits perfectly across his broad shoulders, nearly bringing on an old-fashioned swoon.

"Great to see you!" Adrian says, flashing his thousand-watt smile.

"You, too," I answer, not moving and hoping to continue breathing. The relief that my last-minute decision to wear Levis and a black cashmere turtleneck sweater and leave my hair hanging loose wasn't a mistake is palpable.

"Should we go to the restaurant?" he finally asks.

"We can walk there, if that's OK?" I respond. He takes my elbow as we continue down the platform stairs to the sidewalk.

"Lovely evening," I say, filling the empty air between us as we turn right toward the lake.

"Evanston's a nice town – great bookstores. I've always liked coming here," Adrian answers.

Fifteen minutes later, seeing us enter his restaurant Enzo gallops toward the waiting area, then stops, carefully eyeing Adrian.

"Natalie, I save a special booth for you and your guest… but first, introduce us to each other," he instructs, wiping his meaty fists on the apron tied around his generous waist.

"Adrian McCormick – Enzo Fanolli, owner of this extraordinary restaurant. Adrian is a friend from San Francisco who's helping me with a project," I explain. Enzo brings forth a meaty, vice-grip handshake that causes Adrian to wince slightly.

"I am Natalie's Chicago father. You treat her well or you deal with me. I have connections… they ruin your kneecaps," Enzo declares, continuing to pump Adrian's hand, not smiling.

"I have every intention of treating her well, Enzo, and I assure you I'm very fond of my kneecaps."

"Kneecaps no matter in the grave," Enzo responds, still not smiling. *Maybe we should've gone somewhere else,* I think, feeling a blush creep up my neck as Enzo firmly establishes his paternal claim on me, his status in Chicago's Italian community, and his mob connections. Finally, he remembers we are in his restaurant to eat and shows us to the last of the three booths along the window wall. A red checked tablecloth and a candle melted into a straw-bound wine bottle grace our table. Enzo lights the candle, which casts a pleasant glow across the space, then says he will bring wine, fresh bread, and olives, with antipasto coming later. I start to object, but he is already on his way back to the kitchen.

"He seems very protective of you," Adrian deadpans, not smiling.

"A couple times a week I stop in for carryout. It's a comfort food habit that breeds familiarity in a small neighborhood."

"Twice a week is a lot of spaghetti – you must be in serious need of comforting."

"Only since my identity began undergoing a major overhaul. Until recently, my emotional comfort level was in pretty good shape and once every week or ten days was plenty. Since coming more often, I've convinced him to give me half portions – otherwise I'd be forced to walk off a lot of pasta or suffer undesired consequences."

"I had that problem in Rome. The trattoria I frequented fed me like I was a war refugee. I couldn't resist the food and, as a result, I had to unload some weight when I got back to the U.S."

"Enzo and Marie never had children and somehow adopted me. Except for tonight, it's kind of cute. He's never reacted this way before, and it's a little embarrassing," I explain, picking at the candle wax on the bottle.

"Not embarrassing for me, but I have to ask, since you seem to engender great protectiveness in older men: If I do something your father doesn't like, is he apt to put out a contract on me?"

"He's not a violent man, so very doubtful. He generally trusts my good judgment and ability to take care of myself, although he slips into paternal, over-the-top protective mode occasionally, usually when I'm in his direct line of vision. It would drive me nuts if we lived closer and worries me a little if I decide to spend the summer back in California."

"You're thinking about spending the summer in California?"

"I don't think I have much choice. Discovering the diaries has created a lot of angst for my aunt and raised a lot of questions only she can answer, and these aren't phone conversations. If she's going to talk at all, which I'm not sure she will, it'll only happen when we're face to face. Upsetting her is the very last thing I want to do and I'm struggling with whether my desire to get to the truth is worth causing her as much grief as it seems to be doing, and how much right I have to do that?"

"Obviously that's a decision only you can make, Natalie…"

"The other issue is that living with my dad all summer would be difficult for us both. When I'm under his roof, he wants to know where I'm going and waits up until I get back. I don't like upsetting him, either, plus answering for my every move is a little irritating, but his house – his rules, so…"

"What is the alternative?"

"A summer sublet, if I can find one."

"If you're serious about this, and Berkeley would be an option, I might be able to help. Most of the history department empties out over the summer so faculty can pursue their research. Sublets are starting to show up on the faculty bulletin board. They go fast, so you should probably contact the department directly, if you're interested. I could also keep an eye out, if that would be helpful."

"Berkeley's definitely an option, so if you come across something, please let me know."

"Your dad won't be too upset?"

"I doubt it. He plays the 'I'm too old to lose sleep worrying about when you're coming home tonight' card too often not to be secretly relieved if I make some other living arrangement. He's protective, but not possessive – basically trusts me not to do something stupid, at least not without consulting him first. He'll be fine with the occasional phone call and dinner together every week or so."

"You sound sure about this summer."

"I guess I am," I smile, then ask about the translations.

"Frankly, I'm really enjoying them. Even the mundane parts reveal a lot about German life during the period of high migration to America. As I get further, I'm hoping to find out more about the antisemitism problem, which was probably significant much earlier than we generally believe.

Many claim it didn't really rear its ugly head in this country until around 1920, but prejudices like that don't just suddenly appear out of nowhere – they gain momentum over time. Your grandmother was pretty sharp, so I can't imagine she wasn't aware of whatever was happening, and probably makes reference to it somewhere."

While we ponder these details, Enzo returns with a bottle of Chianti, a plate of gigantic, beautiful green olives, and a loaf of warm bread. He knows I don't drink, and I object to an entire bottle of wine.

"You will be talking a long time – you'll drink it," he insists.

"Don't bother arguing with him," Adrian signals. I shrug as Enzo pours me a half glass, then pushes the bottle toward Adrian without filling his glass. If I didn't know better, I'd be tempted to think he is jealous of my dinner companion.

"On another subject, how is being back in Chicago?" I venture.

"It's always good seeing my family, in small doses. My sisters are consumed with wife, mother, and children responsibilities, so we don't have much in common. My aunt and uncle are loving, generous people who've lived across the street since before I was born, so we have history, which counts for a lot. But they never had children, and their world mostly revolves around neighborhood gossip, so it's hard to keep up much of a conversation. They are a big help to my younger sister, who is a single, working mother and living in our family home. I still have some friends from high school and a few seminary classmates I enjoy getting together with, so all in all, it's fine."

"If it isn't too personal, what do they think about you being on leave from the priesthood?"

"Who – my family or my friends?"

"Both."

"My friends, including those who are still active in the priesthood, don't care. My aunt and uncle love me no matter what and don't ask questions. My sisters are too busy with their own lives to pay much attention to mine, although my older sister, Bridget, who has been aware of my doubts from the beginning, said she was surprised I lasted as long as I did."

"You had doubts from the beginning?"

"Huge ones. I was never one hundred percent sure I wanted to be a priest, but as the first son of an Irish-Catholic mother, the collar was snapped around my neck out of the womb and from that moment forward, I never had a choice."

"That must've been difficult to live with."

"You have no idea. I had a high school girlfriend I cared for deeply. I was hoping she'd get pregnant so we'd have to get married, but Janie was so afraid of my mother's wrath she was extremely careful, so it never happened. We broke it off when I went to Rome the first time. I was crushed, but knew she deserved better, and I couldn't deny her that chance."

"Did you keep in touch?"

"Occasionally. She died in childbirth a few years later – left three or four kids motherless. I took it very hard but, for obvious reasons, could never talk about it. Grieving alone, in silence, is its own kind of hell." I have no idea how to respond to this.

"I've always been a restless priest, Natalie. I either overthink everything or don't think something through at all – and both tendencies have distinct disadvantages in terms of the priesthood."

I still don't know how to respond, especially since I'm finding what I'm hearing oddly comforting in the sense that Adrian might be more available than I think.

"We've never ordered our food," he suddenly remembers.

"Enzo takes care of that."

"Hopefully he won't poison me."

"Not as long as you don't give him a reason to. Besides, I think his citizenship application is still pending, and a murder charge would really screw it up," I chuckle. As if on cue, Enzo brings a large antipasto and two plates of spaghetti.

"I guess I'm a vegetarian tonight," Adrian remarks after we've divided up the food.

"I can get you some meatballs," I offer, rising out of the booth.

"Don't bother. It's Friday and I'm not supposed to eat meat anyway…"

"I thought that rule was relaxed."

"Not for priests."

"Enzo couldn't possibly know you're a priest."

"Don't kid yourself – when it comes to spotting priests, Italians have radar like air traffic controllers. I've never figured it out, but it's a natural instinct they're born with."

"Even when the priest is out with a woman?"

"They don't care about that. It happened all the time when I was in Rome."

It's nearly nine by the time we finish the meal, which includes Marie's freshly made cannoli and another warning from Enzo about treating me carefully before announcing the meal is on him.

"See what I mean? – Italians never charge a priest for a meal, either. They think free food builds good will in case they need a favor from the Church," Adrian chuckles as we're leaving.

We agree that we're both stuffed and need to walk off our food. Since it is a balmy evening with barely a breeze off the lake, we decide to walk toward campus. Slowly meandering along a tree-lined, lakeside street of old Victorian houses, Adrian asks where I live? I point to the well-kept house on the corner, explaining that the entire third floor is mine and I love every inch of it.

"The panoramic lake view promotes deep thinking and the fresh air off the water is perfect for sleeping… a little chilly in winter, but great otherwise," I say, inviting him up onto the wrap-around porch where we sit next to each other in the swing.

"Will this hold us both?" Adrian asks.

"I'm pretty sure it will, but it's not a long drop if it doesn't," I answer.

"Look at the moon… it's so bright you can read a book by it," he observes, pointing toward the giant ball of light made brighter by the reflection off the lake. Having seen the moon before, I really prefer looking at Adrian instead, which is a little too obvious as we sit, shoulders touching, slowly swinging back and forth.

"You don't have to answer this but are you… do you…" he stammers.

"If you're trying to ask whether there's someone in my life, the answer is no."

"Frankly, I'm surprised. I thought for sure your answer would be yes."

"It's my choice. I have serious reservations about marriage, which eventually becomes a problem in relationships, since most men want to be married. Basically, it's easier to just avoid the situation altogether."

"What's wrong with marriage?"

"Nothing, if that's what someone wants. I tried it once and I didn't like it."

"Was it the person or the actual relationship. Seems to me having someone to share your life with can be very fulfilling."

"It was definitely the person. But as an only child, I'm pretty good at entertaining myself and don't have a great need for companionship. The relationship aspect smothered me, and it was definitely a better deal for my husband, which offended my feminist sensibilities. I was twenty-two years old and the marriage lasted less than three months. We both went into it for the wrong reasons…"

"What reasons were those?"

"Sex was the main one."

"Sex?"

"We wholeheartedly bought into the Church's 'no sex before marriage' mandate, but wanted to have sex, so had to get married to do it. Twenty-four hours later, after what my cousin Emily referred to as the wedding of the century, I concluded sex wasn't what it was cracked up to be and I'd just made a mistake that cost my dad a staggering amount of money."

"Sex was the only reason you got married?"

"Basically. The marriage part wasn't a significant emotional investment for either of us. When all was said and done, the entire situation was harder on my dad and my aunt than on me... and I never admitted to either of them the real reason why I'd gotten married. It would be a little hard to explain to my father how losing my virginity had cost him more than Mayor Alioto's San Francisco re-election campaign."

"I can see how that would be difficult," Adrian chuckles, "but I've never thought of sex as the reason to get married." When I don't respond, he continues.

"I was twenty-four when Janie and I broke it off and I went to Rome, but we'd been together since high school, and known each other since second grade. Ending it was brutal – far worse than I expected, and I hated myself for not standing up to my mother and fighting for what I wanted. I loved the easy, natural intimacy of our relationship – and I don't just mean the sex, although that was nice, too. I liked that someone knew everything about me, forgave me my blunders, which were plenty, and loved me anyway. It touched something deep in me, and I still believe we could've been very happy together if I hadn't surrendered to the priesthood. It's my biggest regret in life, so far, and I am resolved to never again make the mistake of giving any institution that kind of power over my life."

"Loving you would hardly be difficult," I mumble, suppressing a smile.

"Sorry, I didn't hear you." Adrian remarks in such a way I'm not sure he's telling the truth. Ignoring him, I pick up the conversation where he left off.

"I quickly figured out the difference between sex and intimacy and realized intimacy was what really mattered, and that Liam and I didn't have any. When that realization sunk in, I didn't like him anymore, and any lingering interest in sex completely disappeared... vanished into thin air... gone with the wind, so to speak."

"What did you do?"

"Took a wad of cash to Tijuana and hired a Mexican lawyer."

"That was it?"

"To dot the i's and cross the t's, I also got an annulment. It turned out that was more difficult than the divorce because my dad had to cut a deal with the archbishop."

"What kind of deal?"

"Something about a new bell tower for the cathedral and paid-up dues at the country club…"

"That makes sense." Adrian chuckles, adding that it sounds like I had a huge wedding, so a lot to emotionally unpack.

"My dad claimed my wedding made future Queen Elizabeth's wedding to Prince Phillip look like a Saturday afternoon garden party in Alameda – but he tends to exaggerate to make a point. I personally found the whole thing boring and was very glad when it was over. Within a week after the divorce I had forgotten about the whole thing."

"How long ago was all this?"

"Seven years and counting…"

"And no one since?"

"Not really. I'm generally quite content with my life. No question it would be very nice to care deeply for someone, but I have never needed to be in a relationship to feel like I'm a whole person," I answer, choosing to ignore the unraveling effect Adrian is having on my well-ordered life.

"It's been nearly eighteen years since Janie and I parted ways, which seems like a lifetime. It's all a distant memory that's harder and harder to bring forth, which saddens me more than the outcome itself. It feels like an important part of myself I want to hold onto is slipping away, and there's nothing I can do about it."

"I guess, given your lifestyle, there's been no one else…" I probe.

"There was someone while I was in law school I could've cared for, but I was newly ordained and still focused in a future in the priesthood. To avoid the risk of eventual heartbreak, we agreed to put the brakes on before it went anywhere. Later, there was a woman in Germany. We were deeply fond of one another, but there was never any possibility of me remaining in Germany or of her ever leaving. From the outset, we both knew we were destined to go our separate ways at some point and never pretended otherwise, but under other circumstances, it probably could've been an enduring love. At least that's how I felt – I'm not as sure about her. I always sensed she was better at holding back than I was."

"All this happened after you were a priest?"

"The American church is the only one that even tries to present a façade of celibacy. It's different in Europe. Having a relationship with a woman isn't unusual or especially problematic if the priest is discrete, and most are."

"That seems pretty exploitative toward the woman involved."

"European women don't necessarily look at it that way. Anna certainly didn't. We both felt having someone in our lives who we were able to care deeply for was a rare privilege that doesn't come along often... a gift to be cherished for as long as it lasts. We enjoyed a loving relationship. It wasn't the transactional, quid-pro-quo, cost-benefit analysis business arrangement many American feminists seem to think male-female relationships are, which is very unfortunate, in my view. They miss out on a lot... including the sacredness of truly loving someone for no other reason than you just do."

"Are you still in touch with her?"

"I wrote to her from New York, telling her about the book. She sent a brief note back, wishing me well. That was more than a year ago." Without saying more, we sit in companionable silence, swinging slowly back and forth, watching the flashing lights from cargo ships move across the night horizon while digesting the confessions we've each offered the other.

"Do you think it's weird that a celibate priest has had more sexual experience than I have?" I ask.

"To be perfectly honest, I've never thought about whether Monsignor Adrian McCormick has had more sexual experience than Professor Natalie Barlow, so I can't answer that question. Is it important to you, for some reason?"

"No... just seems odd, that's all. You didn't tell me you were a monsignor."

"The title came with the job in Rome. I didn't earn it."

"What's the difference?"

"Not much. But getting back to the issue of priests and women..." Adrian says, obviously interested in pursuing the topic.

"It was an open secret that Pius XII had a woman in his life. Sister Pascalina. She met him when he was a young priest taking a rest cure someplace and remained with him until his death. She lived in the papal apartment and held his hand until his last breath. Around the Vatican she was known as La Popessa."

"What happened to her after he died?"

"She went back to her convent in Germany."

"Do you think it was a celibate situation?"

"He was Italian, and Italian men aren't known to eagerly embrace celibacy, so I doubt it."

"Really? A habit isn't the most attractive outfit a woman can wear…"

"It's the eyes that count, Natalie… they're windows into the soul. Nothing else matters as much to a man as knowing a woman truly sees him."

"That sounds pretty romantic, for a priest."

"I read a lot of poetry."

"You do?"

"Don't act so surprised. It's the burden of inherited Irish melancholy that suffers love and loss deeply. It doesn't have anything to do with being a priest."

"Was Anna a nun?"

"No. She was an interpreter – my interpreter. The circumstances required us to spend a lot of time together, which created a natural intimacy that took on a life of its own, even after I was proficient in German and didn't need her anymore." The similarity to our situation, with Adrian being the interpreter of my family history, doesn't escape me, although I keep this to myself.

"I should go soon. I have a long drive tomorrow and if I get moving, I can make 10:40 train back to the city," Adrian says, looking at his watch, then standing up and reaching for my hand.

"I hope you've enjoyed the evening as much as I have," he says, pulling me into a warm hug, holding tight as he kisses my forehead.

"I definitely enjoyed it," I tell his neck.

"I hope you don't mind that I pushed my trip back so I could see you sooner," he whispers. In response, I boldly kiss him on the lips.

"I'll take that as a no," he smiles, then kisses me again, causing a visceral meltdown that leaves me dizzy and desperate for air. Moving down the porch steps he says he'll call when he returns from Lake Superior.

In the meantime, I'll try coax my heart into beating normally again, I tell myself as I watch him walk toward the EL station. Fully aware I'm on a collision course with a free-floating chunk of emotional danger the size of the Polar Ice Cap, I'm not sure I can handle what is happening to me but also know I'm powerless to stop it. On the other hand, life continues to exist even in the most treacherous circumstances so there's at least some chance of surviving the emotional chaos overtaking me.

Chapter Eight
פרק שמונה

Elyria, Ohio
1913-1919

I will always be an immigrant. Nothing can ever change that.

Every day, in a thousand tiny ways, Sophie Meier encourages me to work harder at settling into life in America. She insists this does not require erasing Germany from my life, it only asks that I expand my loyalty to include both countries.

"No matter how long I live here, I will always be German first. I understand that missing Germany does not mean I can't learn to like America; it just means I won't ever be an American," I lament. Complimenting my ability to no longer cry so much, Sophie agrees this is a lot to sort through, but believes the adjustment is taking me longer than most people.

"Most people come to America to escape bad conditions. This was not true for me. I came to be a wife, because that was what was expected of me. Life in Germany was good. I wasn't running away from anything," I repeat yet again.

"Heinrich and I weren't running away from anything either. We decided to stay in America because there was a lack of physicians and Heinrich felt he could be of use. I would have preferred returning to Germany, but I was never unhappy about remaining here. We accepted our responsibility to do mitzvahs... good deeds that make the world better. You can do the same, if you put your mind to it," she scolds.

"You have such a lovely face, Nathalie, but your continual distress is making you old before your time," she admonishes as she stands up from the small table where we have been enjoying afternoon tea.

Sophie is very giving of her time, teaching me about American currency, where to shop, how to ride Cleveland's public transit system, and basic English. Each new step in independence brings me a little more happiness, and I am trying to be a quick learner.

"It's good you are catching on, dear. With Eitan being gone so much you need to be able to get along on your own," Sophie encourages.

I am using my new sewing machine to make curtains for every room in the house, and, by word of mouth, have begun doing mending and alterations for some of the women Sophie has introduced me to. Everyone is pleased with my work and pays generously. Because Eitan already earns a good living, I am saving my money, thinking perhaps I will open a dressmaking shop someday – a dream I brought with me from Germany and am not willing to give up.

On my own, I apply for a library card, then check out books to practice reading English, which is not terribly difficult. I recently discovered a monthly Jewish newspaper from Cleveland, published in German, Yiddish and English, that is very informative and I'm forcing myself to read it in English. Sophie promises that as soon as I feel comfortable, I am welcome in the book club she hosts each month. It is a challenge I eagerly accept and suggest joining now but, in the beginning, listening more than speaking. Smiling, she agrees this is a very good idea.

"We should speak English together so I can practice," I tell Eitan over dinner one evening during a week he is home rather than traveling somewhere.

"I speak English all day and look forward to relaxing into German at home," he answers, chewing on the tough piece of overcooked meat resulting from my failure to carefully follow the recipe in the cookbook Maman recently sent. Cooking bores me and I am easily distracted, which accounts for so few successes among the simple recipes.

"What works for you doesn't necessarily work for me, Eitan. You forget I don't get many practice opportunities," I respond angrily, pushing my portion of the meat aside. This leads to an argument that ends when I leave the table. A few minutes later, my husband apologizes, in English, making me smile. His even nature makes it very difficult to stay angry with him for long, and besides, the discussion has given me an idea.

A few weeks later, Sophie is sitting in my kitchen, enjoying a warm apfelkuchen, fresh from the oven.

"I'm not sure this will be good. Cooking still hasn't captured my attention, but Eitan likes to eat, so I am trying." I apologize, handing her a fork.

Sophie smiles, adding cream to her coffee. I think Americans are addicted to coffee, which explains why they drink so much of it. I've developed a taste for it myself, and believe this accounts for my recent miscarriage, although no one agrees with me.

"You're looking much better, Nathalie... almost healthy again. I hope you're still not sad about losing the baby. These things happen, and it doesn't mean there won't be a healthy baby the next time," Sophie assures me.

"Dr. Meier said I bleed too easily. But I am not sure about having babies anyway. I have no experience with them and no mother nearby to help me. And Eitan is gone so much – not that I expect him to provide the kind of help Maman could..." My voice trails off.

"I would help you with a baby, Nathalie. By now, you should know this," Sophie frowns, making no effort to hide her disappointment in my failure to fully acknowledge her many kindnesses. I apologize for not being more grateful, admitting that it is difficult for me to ask more of her when she is already so generous. After she compliments my apfelkuchen, I confess I've been thinking about something I want to do, making little effort to hide the excitement in my voice.

"Some of the ladies I mend for have asked me to make them dresses, which I have enjoyed very much. They pay me well and I have been saving the money. I think I could start my own sewing business." Smiling, Sophie acknowledges that a dressmaking business would be successful in Elyria, because there currently aren't any others.

"Normally, I don't think a married woman should do anything that interferes with making a home for her husband and children, but Eitan is rarely home, and you have no children – and you are very talented. It seems wrong to not encourage you. I know of a possibility for a little storefront shop, if you are interested," she says, adding that the location would be perfect. My face lights up in gratitude when she suggests the we walk five long blocks from our houses to a small building on Elyria's main street that might be suitable.

"Abe Rutkowski from shul owns the building and the only shoe repair business in Elyria. Maybe you remember him and Leah from your wedding. They were very enthusiastic to celebrate with you," Sophie says. I tell her there was so much happening I barely remember anything about the day.

"There is empty space in the back, with a side entrance that would be very private, which your customers would like. You could put a sign in the front under his," Sophie points out as we enter the disheveled shoe repair shop. Abe, hunched over a hand-turned sewing machine, is deep in concentration as he carefully stitches a piece of leather.

"Abe – this is my neighbor Nathalie. You celebrated her wedding," Sophie shouts over the rhythmic clicks of the sewing machine, hoping to get his attention. Abe keeps stitching. Sophie says he must've lost his hearing and repeats herself, adding that I would like to discuss renting the room at the back of the building. Suddenly Abe's hearing returns, and he looks up.

"You are the girl sewing for my wife?" he asks, looking at me. I nod.

"You are costing me a lot of money."

"She wants to set up a shop for sewing and I told her you have an empty room in the back that would be perfect – tall windows for natural light and a private entrance," Sophie explains to the grumpy shoemaker.

"Can we see it?" Sophie asks when Abe fails to respond.

"You can look, but I am too busy to be a landlord… otherwise, it would be rented," he says, motioning us to follow him through his shop and down a short hallway that opens into a clean, empty room large enough to accommodate a sewing machine, a cutting table, a platform, mirror, dressing screen, and several shelves for storage. Immediately, I know this will be perfect.

"How much do you want for rent?" I ask.

"I have no idea – how much you pay?" he answers.

"What is fair to you?"

"I think what is fair is that Nathalie will bring you more business, so she pays nothing," Sophie interjects. Abe looks first at her then at me.

"I don't need more business – already I have too much."

"Then get a helper and make a bigger business," Sophie pushes.

"I don't want a bigger business. I am happy with this one."

"Then you give her the space as a mitzvah for someone new to our small community."

"No, I want to pay something," I insist, impressed with Sophie's masterful negotiating.

"Pay me one dollar per month, and the room is yours… and maybe you bring me a cake once in a while to supplement," Abe finally agrees. Immediately, I make generous promises of cakes and other sweets I have no idea how to make.

"Danke, Mr. Rutkowski. This means very much to me," I smile. Abe answers in Yiddish, causing us both to laugh.

Within days, I begin occupying the new space. Sophie brings my sewing machine and supplies in the family automobile she recently learned to drive, and I bring a honey lemon cake, which is the one recipe I have successfully mastered. Abe surprises me with an old table suitable for cutting out patterns, and three sets of shelves, which he has affixed to the wall. I am so excited to be settling in that I forget Eitan who, after several days on the road inspecting new rail lines, is at home expecting supper. When I finally return, my husband's face is a mixture of worry laced with frustration that, after several long days away, he is greeted by an empty house – no wife and no food awaiting him.

"Where have you been, Nathalie? I was becoming frightened something happened to you," he says, with a mixture of relief and annoyance. Bubbling with excitement, I fill him in on my new business venture. Several minutes pass before I notice he isn't sharing my enthusiasm.

"Why didn't you discuss this with me?" my husband asks, struggling to hold back his anger.

"You weren't here to discuss it," I point out.

"You can't have decided to do this in the three days I've been gone. How long have you been thinking about it?"

"A while… but the opportunity to act only came on Monday."

"And you couldn't wait until I returned?"

"I didn't see any reason to. You already knew I was doing mending and alterations. This is merely the natural next step. I took you at your word that you want me to be happy, and this makes me very happy, Eitan. It can't be a surprise. We talked about it in Germany – you know it's something I've always wanted to do, and you can't expect me to spend all my time just waiting for you to come home."

"You make enough money to cover business expenses?"

"Of course," I say, not bothering to explain my token rent arrangement with Abe.

"What will you do when we have babies, Nathalie?"

"You're not home enough to make babies, Eitan – and they don't make themselves." I don't remind him that twice I expected a baby and twice the baby never arrived, but the look on his face says that he remembers, and he quickly apologizes.

"Doctor Meier says if G-d wants me to have a baby, I will have one, so in the meantime don't worry about it, and that's what I've decided to do," I tell my husband, without confessing my nagging doubts about motherhood and fears about winding up like Irina, who just had another baby. In Maman's last letter she wrote that the new one screams like all the others but at least this time it is only one, not two.

"I cannot imagine how many people are stuffed into our once comfortable, peaceful apartment... poor Papa is going crazy," I told Sophie after receiving Maman's letter with the news that I am, once again, an aunt.

"What does she say about political problems?" Sophie asked. I shrugged, then wondered aloud about the question. Sophie explained she has read in the Cleveland newspaper that the Kaiser is a bad leader and wants a war, which letters from her family confirm, making her very worried.

"Maman has written that things she doesn't understand too well are upsetting Papa, but day-by-day nothing changes, and life goes on as always. She tells him they are good Germans, loyal to the Vaterland, so there is nothing to worry about, but then complains he doesn't listen," I reported, adding that Maman didn't say more because she always tries to send only good news.

"Levi and Irina having another baby is, in her mind, good news. I'm not sure Irina would agree, but I will knit another blanket for the new one... or maybe a shawl for my sister-in-law. She probably has enough baby blankets by now."

Soon after settling into my new business, which now includes a selection of fabrics I ordered through a catalogue, I am battling heavy tiredness. With no appetite, my stomach revolts against even the smell of food. I know what this could mean but ignore the possibility. I have more work than I can manage efficiently and have put a sign in Abe's window asking for help. The next day, a thin, neatly dressed, dark-skinned youngster appears.

"My name is Tildie, and I wish to know about the work," she says, staring at the floor.

"How old are you?" I ask.

"Fourteen – almost fifteen."

"You don't look almost fifteen."

"Just little for my age is all... my mama says it can't be helped... you only grow as big as God wants you to grow – no more. I is always gonna be little and ain't nothin' can be done about it." Tildie answers, staring at the floor, nervously adjusting the little hat on her neatly plaited hair.

"I need someone to help me sew. Do you know how to sew?"

"Yes, 'um – I sew real good... real neat stitches – tiny and straight."

"I'd like you to show me," I smile, taken in by the earnest eagerness of a young girl barely out of childhood.

"I have a shirt that needs the collar turned and two buttons sewn on. I'd like you to do this. It will give me an idea of your abilities." Tildie walks over to the chair near the window.

"I'll work here, where the light is good," she says, gathering up the shirt and buttons.

"I'll leave it to you to select the scissors, matching thread and best needle size from the supplies on the far shelf," I say. Tildie spends several minutes carefully deciding which thread and needle she wants to work with, then begins repairing the shirt. Two hours later, she presents a shirt with a perfectly turned collar and three neatly sewed buttons. There are no stray threads.

"I sewed another button that was about to fall off, and fixed up one of the buttonholes coming undone. This shirt be frayed here and there, but got plenty life in it yet," she says, her eyes seeking my approval.

"This is beautiful work, Tilde, much better than I could do at your age. Where did you learn to sew this well?"

"My mama and grandma – they teach me. My grandma can sew up anything from my little brother's head to my big sister's weddin' dress. She make that real pretty. Everybody say so, and my sister – she a sight to behold wearin' it. She stitch up my dress I'm wearin' too, but I stitch the ribbon and buttons myself," she tells me, twirling around to show me a plain, neatly sewn, well-fitting dress.

"What about school? Won't that interfere with working for me?"

"I don't never go to school."

"Why not?"

"Ain't no school for my kind round here. All my learnin' come from church and home... and what I pick up on my own here and there."

"In that case, how soon can you start?"

"I start right now, if you want me. This ain't nothin' like what I expected – it a whole lot better. Sweepin' floors 'n' washin' windows is what coloreds mostly do. Just wait'll I tell my mama... she be so proud of me she bust a button herself," my new helper beams.

Over the next weeks, Tildie and I find our rhythm working together. Having basic reading ability and a grasp of some numbers help to make her a quick learner. As she becomes comfortable asking for help if she needs it, I give her more work. Soon she is doing all the mending, with many compliments and not a single customer complaint, freeing me to concentrate on custom-sewn dresses and shirts.

Late one afternoon, just as we are preparing to leave for the day, Abe comes into our room and announces that he is having the building wired for electricity so he can use a motorized machine to sew his leather. I mention that Singer has recently come out with an electric sewing machine and ask whether the wiring will reach to the back room.

"I don't know… might cost more." I offer to pay the extra if Tildie and I can have electricity, too, which would mean more lighting, allowing us to work longer days in winter. I could buy an electric sewing machine for myself and teach Tildie how to use my foot-pedal machine.

"We would be much more efficient… work faster and get more done," I tell Abe.

"Your husband's not going to like me arranging so his wife is gone even longer days than you are now," Abe frowns. I assure him this is unlikely. He shrugs something in Yiddish and says they are starting work on the building tomorrow, and it might be noisy.

The following week I buy an electric sewing machine on a payment plan, estimating that with the greater overall efficiency for both me and Tildie, I can pay it off in less than a year. Equally important, Tildie is beside herself over learning to use a sewing machine and takes to it immediately, accidentally pricking her finger only once.

"I sew faster than the wind, Miss Nathalie," she proudly exclaims, showing off an intricate mending job she just completed. There's no question she has natural talent. Often, if something needs patching, she selects fabric and a design that makes the garment look better than it did originally.

Despite how well things are going, I continue to lack energy and feel thick, dull and worn, like a faded old coat no one wants to wear anymore. It is impossible to continue ignoring my suspicion that something is wrong with me.

"You should have come to me sooner," Doctor Meier scolds when he confirms that I am nearly six months into what turns out to be another pregnancy.

"I've never been pregnant long enough to know what it feels like, so how could I be sure this was the problem?" I fire back, suddenly overwhelmed with mixed emotions flooding me like a summer thunderstorm. I am happy being a businesswoman, eager to please Eitan by giving him children, conflicted about motherhood, and consumed with fear of bleeding to death, all of which I reluctantly confess to the doctor.

"I can't solve all of these concerns, Nathalie, but I suspect that if you have come this far without developing a problem, this pregnancy will reach a successful conclusion," he reassures me.

"Why this one and not the others?"

"No one knows that answer, but perhaps this is a female, and the others were male. It is commonly believed that a male infant is weaker... far more likely than a female to succumb before birth or in the days immediately afterwards. We don't know why, but some speculate that because females bear children, they are naturally more robust than males. Or, it may be G-d's, or nature's, way of managing the population."

"I don't understand. Are you saying this baby could be weak?" I respond, panicking.

"That's not what I'm saying at all. Males don't need a lot of strength to create hundreds of babies, but women, though limited in how many babies they can produce, need to be physically stronger than men to do it. In other words, to guarantee the species continues, we don't need as many men as women, so nature fixes it that women are more likely to survive. But instead of fretting over what has been lost, accept my congratulations on what you can now look forward to, provided you follow my instructions very carefully."

"And what might those be?" I ask, alert to the impact this unexpected event could have on my flourishing dressmaking business.

"There are reasons pregnancies are referred to as confinements, my dear. In your case, you've failed to gain enough weight, which is a concern. We don't want to risk anything that will cause bleeding, so no marital relations, off your feet as much as possible, no heavy lifting, or strenuous activity, and eat more... quite a lot more. The baby takes everything from you, and if you don't add weight, you'll grow even thinner, allowing weakness to settle in." When I don't respond, Dr. Meier continues, instructing me to return in two weeks, again stressing his optimism that, with care, I will deliver a healthy baby without complications.

"I expected you to be more excited," he adds as I prepare to leave.

"I'm just surprised. I know Eitan will be excited enough for us both," I reply, putting on my coat.

"Remember what I've said about taking care of yourself, and returning in two weeks, weighing much more that you do now. I'll have Sophie make you some kugels rich with heavy cream and butter," Dr. Meier repeats, showing me to the door. Walking home, I ponder this news. I don't know how I feel about a baby, now that it appears likely one is actually coming. It seems like a good thing until I remember Irina – then it becomes something that threatens to suck the life out of me. As the days pass, I gradually accept that no matter what, I'm in it now. Haunted by all the suffering pregnancy and motherhood inflicted on my once-beautiful sister-in-law, I resolve not to let what happened to her happen to me, and push against any possibility of confinement or closing my thriving business.

On a particularly busy afternoon, a stately, well-dressed woman brings some mending to the shop and, seeing Tildie, announces she doesn't want the Negro girl working on her clothing. I start to say I'll do the work myself, then, noticing the struck look on Tildie's face, change my mind.

"Tildie sews as well as I do and we work together, sharing the work equally. If you don't want a Negro mending your clothes, you should go somewhere else, because I don't need your business," I tell her, opening the door to invite her out. Staring me down, she leaves.

"Negros been sewing and cooking for white folk since the beginnin' of time. They think the only reason we born is to do their bidding. Why she not want me doing what we always been doing for her kind since forever? I don't understand the problem," Tildie says, her voice shaking.

"I have no idea, Tildie. But we're partners, and if she doesn't like our arrangement, she can take her business somewhere else."

"Maybe that there is the problem, Miss Nathalie. She don't like we is partners… thinks I'm an uppity nigger don't know my place."

"Your place is beside me, Tildie. That's our arrangement and nothing is going to change it. I don't want you worrying about it."

A few days later, the woman returns, saying there isn't anywhere else to take her mending, and asking me to reconsider.

"I don't want to work on clothing worn by someone who doesn't know how to treat people with respect and am asking you to please leave my shop and not come back until you are ready to apologize to Tildie," I tell her.

"Nigger-loving Jew," the woman hisses, slamming the door. Overhearing the ruckus, Abe comes into the back room to ask what happened. After I briefly explain, and he cautions that I'm asking for trouble.

"I don't care, Abe. It's not right, acting like she did."

"Maybe not right, Nathalie, but it's not uncommon, and I don't want problems."

Over the next several weeks, a couple of other regular customers suddenly stop coming, but I am still making plenty of money and have more than enough work. Other than feeling bad for Tildie, I decide to write the incident off as typical American arrogance and stupidity I see happening around me more and more often. I am too busy preparing Tildie to take charge when the baby comes to spend time trying to figure it all out, but this latest incident causes me to worry over her.

"Don't worry 'bout me none, Miss Nathalie – people been bein' mean to me all my life for no good reason... I know'd it be their problem, not somethin' bad about me and real clear on how to take care of myself. Ain't nothin' lower than a nigger woman, and I don't like it, but don't let it hurt my feelings none, neither. Mama say Jesus God – he loves us all no matter what anybody thinks." Her confidence in what she believes shines through her words.

"You're very smart for being so young, Tildie. I'm proud of you... and envy your strength," I reassure her, reaching to squeeze her hand across our cutting table where we are laying out a pattern together.

"No need to go envying me. My mama say your people got your own problems to worry 'bout."

"I thought America was supposed to be safe for everyone," I muse as we continue measuring and cutting.

"Sorry to disappoint you, Miss Nathalie, but whoever say that was lyin'. Ain't nobody safe in America 'cept they be a Christian white man. Everybody else – they all on their own. My Uncle Raymond Lee say black folk's life in America ain't nothin' more than one long ride on a train goin' nowhere... whatever that mean." I tell Tildie I don't know what it means, either, but assure her we'll stick together, no matter what. She smiles her big, warm smile, again insisting she can take care of herself.

Meanwhile, Abe, alert for problems regarding Tildie, admits knowing that some white people want to hurt Negroes, and sometimes even hurt whites, especially Jews, who are friends with them.

"You're asking for trouble you don't need, Nathalie, but I'll do all I can to keep everything safe and calm," he tells me, taking a deep breath as he pushes his glasses from his forehead up into his hair which tends to explode on his head.

The next day I again reassure Tildie this sort of thing has been happening to Jews since the beginning of time, and still we survive, so she is not to worry. She listens, but because I'm white and she isn't, makes it clear she has a hard time believing me.

As the time for the baby's arrival approaches, Tildie suddenly grows more nervous about taking charge of the business.

"I'm thinkin' maybe I bring my mama to help me – she read and write some, and does money better than me," Tildie tells me one afternoon as we are tidying up. I assure her I am confident she can manage, but if having her mother come makes her more comfortable, I'm glad she has suggested it. Since Tildie will be earning more as the stand-in for me, I ask if paying her mother what I am currently paying her will suffice.

"Mama come for nothin' just to be helpin' me out. I don't think she like the idea of us working together and me bein' the boss of her," Tildie frowns. I tell her want to pay her mother anyway, and the two of them can figure out their working arrangements on their own.

Eitan is beside himself with excitement over a baby and accepts that, with each passing day, I feel more untouchable. He is very understanding, even offering to sleep in a different bed. He is much less accepting of my arrangement with Tildie and is insisting I close my business and stay home to care for his child.

"It's what mothers do, Nathalie," he repeats every time the subject come up, which is whenever he is home.

"Maybe so, but I gave up everything to come to America and be with you. It's not fair to ask me to give up something I love doing, and am very good at, to stay home and raise a child. I'm sure I can do both just fine."

"I want a wife who is perfectly happy at home caring for my child, not running a business," he counters.

"Then I guess you'll have to get another wife," I finally say, walking out of our parlor, slamming the door.

A few days later, our argument still unresolved, I give birth to a healthy baby girl I name Sarah Avigail. She arrives while Eitan is away identifying sites for new rail lines, and more than a week passes before he meets his daughter. When he finally arrives at home, I dare him to challenge my decision to name my daughter for living people instead of dead ones, as is the Jewish tradition. He says questioning his daughter's name never occurred to him.

The birth leaves me weak from blood loss but, as she promised, Sophie steps in as my substitute mother. Doctor Meier insists on two months convalescence to regain my strength. Haunted by my visions of Irina struggling with the twins, I take this news badly and am overcome with sadness, and confusion. Nothing in my experience of babies has encouraged me to consider the possibility of loving a baby as much as I have discovered I love Sarah, who does me the favor of crying very little. Yet I find motherhood boring and am eager to return to sewing sooner than my strength allows.

"The body, especially yours, Nathalie, needs rest while it adjusts to the demands of motherhood, your baby adjusts to the world, and the two of you adjust to each other. She will never need you more than she needs you now," Doctor Meier insists, leaving no room for further discussion.

The next day Tildie brings a soft woolen blanket she says her grandmother knit for the new baby. She is bubbling with reassurance that I have nothing to worry about as regards our sewing business.

"Between me and mama, we got everything under control. It all goin' real good... real smooth," she proudly proclaims.

"Bring me some mending, please, Tildie. I'm going crazy just lying here and I can do it while Sarah is sleeping."

"You sleep when the baby sleeps," Sophie interrupts, shaking her head to signal Tildie this is not a good idea. Realizing I'm never going to win this argument, I fall back onto the pillow, shutting my eyes, and everyone else, out.

Two days later, Tildie comes again. After reporting that things are going well, she hands me a letter informing me that Belgian lace is no longer available for export, and my order will not be filled. When I pass this news on to Tildie she frowns deeply, worrying that she has at least three pieces of work waiting for the lace.

"We'll have to make some ourselves," I tell her.

"I never done made lace in my life and ain't got no idea about how to do it," Tildie answers.

"Then I'll teach you," I say, frankly excited at having something to do besides care for my baby daughter, who is content with life and demands very little of me.

"You already know how to knit and crochet and make fine stitches – it won't be difficult to learn. We'll split the silk embroidery thread into finer strands and use our thinnest sewing needles to weave the lace into a pattern. Bring everything with you tomorrow, and I'll show you."

"If you say so, Miss Nathalie, but I ain't so sure this gonna work."

The next evening Tildie arrives near tears. She explains the lady wanting the lace collar for her dress says she doesn't want a nigger fixing up a substitute for the real thing, then grabs the dress away and leaves without paying for the work we've already done.

"It a perfectly nice dress the way it is, without the lace fancying it up. She shoulda paid us," Tildie frets.

"We only make things for women who appreciate what we do. If she changes her mind and comes back, tell her I said she needs to look for another dressmaker," I snap, unhappy to be facing this issue yet again.

Three days later, Tildie reports that the woman returned, and she told her what I said.

"She say there ain't no other dressmaker around for her to go to."

"Did she apologize?" I ask. Tildie shakes her head no.

"Then she's out of luck. Tell her we expect her to return the dress, and we're not interested in her business."

"You sure, Miss Nathalie – I don't wanna be no cause for trouble."

"I'm sure, Tildie."

"Well then, I be prayin' you ain't makin' no mistake…"

When Eitan hears about this incident, his response is to point out that being friendly with Negros is dangerous and he doesn't want me bringing unnecessary problems on myself. I just as firmly point out that unless he is willing to stay home and take care of Sarah while I sew, my business decisions are no concern of his. Unable to disagree, he claims he is worried for both Tildie and me.

"I can see why you're so fond of her, Nathalie, and I like her too, but there's bound to be bigger trouble sooner or later. Don't forget you're a Jew, and that's already against you," he insists. I can't help thinking how strange it is to be having this conversation with my husband who, when trying to convince me to follow him, had insisted being Jewish in America was not a problem. I can never remember anything this harsh being spoken between Maman and Papa. *Maybe this is what America has forced us to become*, I tell myself.

To my great relief, as the months pass Sarah never develops the habit of screaming constantly like Irina's babies did from the beginning. She sleeps soundly, is generally content and agreeable when awake, and I have not become the farm animal Irina claimed her body became the moment Levi made her pregnant. I bring Sarah to the shop with me and find it is not difficult for me to care for her and still sew.

"So far, motherhood isn't nearly as bad as I expected. If another baby happens, I won't be nearly so frightened," I admit to Sophie. What I don't tell her is that another ugly incident has occurred, this time involving a man who wanted me to make him some silk ties, a project especially well-suited to Tildie's fine stitching skills. As he was explaining what he wanted, I called Tildie over to listen. The man refused to speak with her, saying everybody knows Jews are better tailors than niggers. I told him if this is what he believes we aren't interested in his business.

"I heard you're a nigger-lover, but thought it was just a rumor. Obviously, I was mistaken," he says, slamming the door so hard Abe comes back to investigate. When I explain the incident, the old shoemaker, shaking his head and scowling, says he isn't surprised.

RED ANEMONES

"Some people don't need a reason to hate, they just enjoy doing it, and hating Negros is very popular in this country... no different than the Czar hating Jews. Nigger-lover is a label they can slap on us to make us less mainstream American and let them feel better about themselves." he mumbles, wiping at his eyes.

Having overheard all this, Tildie is uncharacteristically quiet for several days, until I finally ask her what's bothering her? She says she doesn't understand how hating someone makes anybody feel good about themselves and the trouble people hating her is causing me is making her very sad.

"I don't understand it either, Tildie – but Abe's right, it's the way the world works. People hate your kind, and they hate my kind. The only thing we can do about it is not become haters ourselves."

The incident is forgotten until, a few days later, a woman with kind eyes and a gentle smile comes in asking if I will make her wedding dress. When I explain I have never made a wedding dress, she claims she's heard that Tildie and I are the best seamstresses in the entire area, including Cleveland, and she will pay a lot of money for the dress if I am willing to make it. I explain that I can only agree to discuss it with Tildie, and to come back in a few days for my decision.

"I hope you'll do it," she smiles as she turns to leave.

Tildie expresses great excitement at the possibility of sewing a wedding dress and offers to bring her sister Jeenie to do the mending, so she will be free to help me.

"Most all of it ain't too complicated... nothin' Jeenie can't handle. This way, me and you can devote us selves to the wedding dress," she nearly begs me. After sleeping on it, I realize I'm too tempted to try something new, and too eager to work with the luxurious fabric a beautiful wedding dress demands, to turn the opportunity down. When the woman returns, I tell her Tildie and I have agreed to take on the project and work on it together. Expressing her pleasure at our decision, the woman introduces herself as Alice and says she'd like us to make six attendant dresses as well. When I hesitate, Tildie assures her we can manage this just fine, and pulls out our calendar to start setting up appointments. After the woman leaves, Tildie announces she'll bring her grandmother in to help, too.

"After she got them seein' glasses, she took to the lace making real fast. I only showed her once and she was off on it like a hound dog chasin' a rabbit. She'll help however we need her, Miss Nathalie. And if we need even more help, Mama'll come too."

"What about your mother's rheumatism, Tildie? I thought it was getting worse."

"It only worse when she don't wanna do somethin'. Ain't no way she passes up a chance to be here workin' with us on a wedding dress. A sudden miracle will be visited upon her, and we'll never hear nothin' more about any aches and pains." I couldn't help laughing at this accounting of Tildie's mother, whom I like very much and Tildie complains about constantly.

"It'll all be real good… real, real good. You just wait; we be famous!" Tildie exclaims, clapping her hands, then saying she's going to tell Abe, so he can prepare to make the wedding shoes.

The project takes many hours, but together Tildie and I, with help from Tildie's relatives, produce a white silk wedding dress so beautiful Alice and her mother both cry when they see it. We set up an assembly line for the bridesmaid's dresses, which is efficient, but requires a lot of notations to make sure we don't confuse the sleeve of one dress with the sleeve of a different one. Discussing this dilemma as we prepare to pin the patterns and cut the fabric, Tildie's grandmother comes up with the genius idea of using colored pins, giving each dress its own, unique pin color. Tildie sends her mother to purchase six different shades of nail lacquer, and we spend an entire afternoon painting dressmaking pins. The color coding works perfectly, and only once do we confuse two different reds, which is my mistake, no one else's.

At the last minute, we even manage to pull together something for the mother of the bride, who apologizes for not making the request sooner, but admits she wanted to see how everything else turned out first. Neither Tildie nor I are sure this is a compliment, until we are invited to the wedding and see all our hard work slowly walk up the aisle of St. Elizabeth Catholic Church with more grace than, in our wildest dreams, we could ever imagine.

Two weeks later, another woman comes in to request a wedding dress. Hearing this, Tildie beams, saying she loves working on beautiful dresses. I eagerly praise her enthusiasm because I have begun to suspect another baby is coming and will again need Tildie's entire family to show up and help keep things going.

Within days of confirming my pregnancy, Eitan comes home unexpectedly and announces that war has broken out in Europe.

"There's no way to know what this means, Nathalie. All we can do is carry forth and hope it ends quickly." We both know that by feigning ignorance he is kidding himself about what the war means. Jews across

Europe cannot possibly escape danger, but neither of us wants to admit this to ourselves or each other.

After years of frequent letters, suddenly months pass without any word from our families. When a letter finally arrives from Maman, it is the first news from Germany since the Austrian archduke was assassinated and troops mobilized. She says they are relatively safe at the moment but fearful and unsure about what will happen next.

Except for the blessed relief Tildie's chattering family brings, everyone around me speaks of nothing but war, propelling me into a new orbit of distress over being separated from my beloved family at a time of great peril. I have been sending money back to Germany for more than a year, as it became more and more obvious trouble was coming and Jews would not escape unscathed. Maman's next letter confirms my worst fears.

> *My dearest daughter,*
> *I am sorry to write the sad news that Irina's youngest brother Isaac, only months past his bar mitzvah, died in a battle he ran away to fight when he was too young to know what he was doing. We sat Shiva but Irina is not consoled and Levi is to angry to speak about it...says if the wars goes on long enough, it will claim his sons, too. Papa says to me that killing will continue until America enters the war and he doesn't understand why America isn't making all this stop. We do not know what will be left after the war ends but fear it will be nothing, and the Jews will be faulted.*
>
> *Eitan's brother, Moishe, came back one day unmarked by bullets but he is not right anymore. Papa thinks he deserted the army and would be shot if anyone finds him. Moishe refused to sing Kol Nidre at High Holy Days, and Papa is no cantor, so it was difficult for everyone. Months later, Moishe still refuses to speak words. Naomi and Sh'mul don't know what to do with their beloved son who sits all day staring at the wall to be fed with a spoon like a baby. Eitan must write his brother a letter and you must ask your president to make this war end. There is no one left to fight it, and no Germany left to fight for.*
>
> *The money you send is the only thing that, in our desperation, makes Papa smile. That and stories of little Sarah, who we ache to see for ourselves. Your letters keep us alive to read again and again while we miss you all*

day, every day. Long may we live to see each other one more time...
   Your loving Maman.

    While earlier letters from both my and Eitan's parents had been filled with family news and little concern for the future, after reading this one, I ache with fear, unable to escape feeling the same desperation and sadness I hear beating in my mother's heart and am helpless to do anything about. Being pregnant does nothing to soothe these feelings in me; instead it only makes everything worse, especially since the letter I wrote Maman, hoping to cheer her with news of a new baby coming, must've been lost, or stolen for the money it contained. Otherwise, she would've said something about another grandchild on its way to her. *How many other letters never got to them*? I wonder.

    All of this causes me to spend many hours thinking about whether bringing another child, especially a Jewish one, into this hostile, angry world is a good idea. Most of the time, I think it is not, but pregnancy has a life of its own and proceeds anyway.

    Sooner than anyone anticipated, Rachael Rebekkah arrives, kicking and screaming. She is healthy, but my blood loss is nearly fatal.

    "There can't be any more babies. Be grateful for the ones you have and do not spend time wanting more," Doctor Meier tells Eitan and me. I more easily accept this news that Eitan who, faced with no possibility of ever having a son, falls into great sadness. He loves his daughters, understands the risk of another pregnancy, and is unwilling to imperil me in any way, but still suffers with loss. My head, already overpopulated with thoughts of the war, has little patience with him.

    Tildie's mother comes every day to help with the children, allowing me to return to work sooner that I dared hope. Eitan, already upset, accuses me of running away from reality and I don't disagree. He doesn't understand that if I give the thoughts in my head too much space to expand, the blue-black darkness lurking there, always threatening to overtake me, will grow so strong I will be unable to push against it.

    Eitan complains that I should not speak German with Sarah who, once she begins school, will be expected to speak English, which she barely knows. I understand the importance of English, but it does not come naturally to her and as long as Eitan and I continuing speaking only German to each other, she will do the same.

    "I don't want to forget who I am and where I come from, and I want Sarah to realize who her grandparents are. Besides, our friends at shul are mostly German, although some speak Yiddish. Sarah will pick up English quickly when she is in school," I insist. Eitan counters that since war broke out in Europe, Germans are America's enemy, and this threatens to become a problem for us.

"No one will blame us here in America for what the Kaiser does in Europe," I claim.

"You are naïve, Nathalie. We are welcome here as long as there is no trouble, but if trouble comes, it's Jews and immigrants who pay."

Soon after this conversation, I receive another letter from Maman. This one says Levi has gone to fight, and the older boys are gone from school to earn money running messages for the German army, making my anxiety even worse. All I can think to do is send even more money which, since I earn it myself, I see no need to discuss with my husband. Later that evening, when telling Eitan about the letter, he says that while America has not yet joined in the war, he believes it is unavoidable, and will happen soon.

"What will it mean for us that America is in a fight against Germany?" I ask, frowning deeply. I don't admit I am less concerned for him, as a naturalized citizen, than I am for myself, who is not. I have no interest in renouncing my German citizenship in favor of pledging allegiance to a country that believes only whites and Christians are worthy people.

"I don't know, Nathalie. But I can't imagine it will be good," he responds.

Meanwhile, Sophie has organized the women at shul to make bandages, and I offer my left-over material scraps for padding. Every night Tildie, her mother, grandmother, sister, and I sit together to cut and fold scraps of material into squares. *Maybe we are saving a life, but it won't be a German life*, I think, haunted by visions of my brother, fighting for Germany, being attacked, maybe killed, by American soldiers serving the country where I now live.

Weeks later, Eitan forcefully insists we must stop speaking German outside the house. I explain this is impossible because Sarah speaks only German with us, no matter where we are, but he again insists Sarah either starts speaking English or stay home.

"Neither of us speaks the English of a native speaker, so what does it matter?" I ask, surprised at my husband's uncharacteristically angry outburst.

"We must show how hard we try to be good Americans. In Germany we knew what to expect. Here, we don't know anything." he answers, walking away from me, which is his preferred way of ending any discussion he doesn't want to continue. For the first time since the threat of war became real to us, I realize he is much more frightened than he is letting on. I decide ignoring him is the best strategy and set about teaching Sarah the Shema – in German and Hebrew. Eitan strongly objects.

"She is a Jew, Eitan, and needs to know how to pray the prayers her ancestors prayed. It will comfort her when trouble comes, and from what you say, it is coming soon," I counter, with as much fortitude as I can find in my tired heart. In the next breath I tell him I want us to go to Passover Seder at shul. He reminds me that he doesn't celebrate Shabbat, so why should he celebrate Passover? I accuse him of trying to erase being Jewish from his life, which I believe is something only a fool would try. For days we argue about how to be German, Jewish, and American all at the same time. Eitan claims that to be safe we must be American first. I admit he is right, but I am proudly German and Jewish and don't want to be American first, or much at all, for that matter.

"I have done my best to adjust, but Americans are self-centered, entitled, white-skinned protestants who believe they are better than everyone else, and I don't like how they treat people who are different. Money is what matters most and there is no desire to honor the common good... no moral core... nothing like Tikkun Olam to fix the brokenness surrounding us. I've met no one in America who is interested in using their life to make the world better. Here everyone is for themselves only, which turns people against each other."

"Tikkun Olam doesn't exist because there aren't enough Jews in America to promote it, Nathalie. Surely you realize that. If there were more of us, we might be able to make it be important, but right now Americans aren't interested in a common good, they're interested in opportunities for themselves, and you can't deny there are many opportunities here," Eitan insists, obviously growing very impatient with a conversation we constantly repeat.

"We should return to Germany, Eitan, while we still can. It might be a harder life than we have here, but only in some ways. Germany is our home... where our family is, where our children can grow up surrounded by that love. None of these things are true in America. If their grandparents walked into our house this minute, the children would not know who they are. This is a tragedy for everyone."

"You are romanticizing our old life, Nathalie. Germany is sure to lose the war and fault the Jews. Things will get very bad when that happens. We are better off staying here and downplaying our German, and Jewish origins. Telling the children about their grandparents will have to be enough."

"America already hates the Germans for causing a war, and this spills over onto all Germans, not just the Jewish ones. No matter where we are, somebody hates us, but in Germany we wouldn't be facing the hatred all alone; we would be surrounded with family who love us," I sob, releasing the buildup of frustration and homesickness that has again overtaken me. Frustrated, yet trying to comfort me, Eitan doesn't disagree that we are facing a "no good answers" situation but still insists pretending we are loyal Americans is the best solution.

"I can't do that, Eitan. I can't pretend I'm not German and not a Jew. And no matter what you claim, I don't think you can, either."

Weeks later, Eitan comes home excited to say America has entered the war, which guarantees it will end soon. The last letter we received from our families was months ago, and since then I have continued to imagine the worst. I hear what Eitan is saying as good news and accept that this means he will be fully absorbed with keeping the railroads running to support the war effort and be home even less than he is now. Without him or my family nearby, I am raising our two daughters alone, which both angers and saddens me. Sophie does her best to cheer me, but worry over rumors about a sickness that is spreading rapidly weighs heavily on her. They call it the Spanish Flu, but Sophie says this isn't because only Spanish people get it. Many are falling ill and dying.

Meanwhile, another letter arrives from Germany, addressed only to Eitan. Nearly three weeks pass until he come homes from a rail inspection trip to open it. As I am waiting for him, I am becoming more and more consumed with worries about what is happening to my family in Germany and about the spreading sickness, which is proving deadly to many. When I give Eitan the letter, he goes into another room to read it.

> *Eitan, dear husband to my beloved daughter,*
> *I write with great concern and fear since learning that 24,000 German Jews who immigrated to America were turned away – forced to return to Germany. I do not know what this means, but worry that your life in America is becoming difficult. If that is true, my Nathalie will want to return to Germany. I write to insist you remain in America, because no matter what is happening, it is better and safer there. Please take no consideration of your dear*

wife's pleas about returning to Germany because Germany is not strong enough to survive this war, and already the Jews are being faulted for the failures. The workers' leaders have been barred from the Reichstag, which has led to worker strikes and worse economic problems. The seeds for moral upheaval and dangerously bad politics that have been planted are flourishing.

I have reluctantly joined the Centralverein Deutcher Staatsbürger Jüdischen Glaubens because it offers protection for Jews and might keep us safer, but I have doubts. I do not like political involvement, but there is no choice. Your vater also has joined, worried for the same reasons. He says workers need the protections that are going away, which is making workers revolt. Who can blame them? But it causes problems.

I say none of this to my Sarah and please do not worry my Nathalie with any of what I write. Just know of these troubles, made worse by terrible flooding taking people's homes away from them and there is a sickness so many are dying from. Germany faces complete devastation. Please look for possibilities for us to come to America. To be admitted we need sponsors, and you are our only hope.

Long may you live, Eitan.

Mikael, loving father of your beloved wife.

"It was written several months ago – it's nothing important," Eitan answers when I ask about the letter. His eyes say he is not being truthful with me, and he offers no explanation for why the letter was only for him and not both of us. He folds it into small squares and places it in the inside pocket of his suit coat, then says he is hungry and would like something to eat. After supper he announces, without explanation, that he is going out for a while and might be late returning. This is not normal behavior for him; when he is home with us in the evening, he always stays home. I read for a little while after the children are settled for the night, then fall asleep before Eitan returns.

In the early hours of the next morning, while Eitan is still snoring deeply, I do something I have never done, and read the letter he tried to hide, addressed only to him. It causes me to cry, but I cannot share this fearful sadness with my husband without explaining what I have done. Days later, I ask about the letter again. Eitan again assures me it was nothing important, then forbids me to mention it again. I tell him I don't believe it was not important, but don't have the energy to argue with him.

Many months pass before another letter arrives from Germany; this time it is addressed to me.

> *Dear Nathalie –*
> *I write with the good news of the war ending. It is great relief that the fighting has stopped, and we don't hear guns shooting all day and night, but we are left in ruins with nothing of the future but slim hope. Since the Kaiser abdicated, we don't know how or where we will be led now, which Levi says is a big worry. I also send very sad news. Your Maman, Sarah, took very sick and died of a very bad sickness sweeping across Europe.*
> *Naomi, Sh'mul and Moishe are also gone. Levi and I recovered, but your Papa lingers without strength because his deep sadness has drained away his will to get well again. His violin gathers dust, and he cannot be persuaded to play it for us. We were all too sick to sit Shiva for Sarah, but every day your Papa says Mourner's Kaddish. I bring him to us to live, which he resisted but right now he is too weak to complain. Some say this Spanish sickness is killing more people than the war.*
> *Please write to us and to Papa. He misses you so much he cries. I am too busy to cry but cannot remember even a little of what happy feels like. The money you send is all we have to survive, and even that is complicated. Long may you live and please remain well. I heard the sickness is everywhere in the world now, even in your America.*
> *Your ever devoted, loving sister-in-law, Irina.*

After reading Irina's letter, I go directly to Sophie, who looks more tired than I have ever seen her.

"Today came a letter from Irina with so much sadness. If a war wasn't bad enough, now everyone is getting sick and dying. I can't imagine never seeing Maman again, yet know I will not," I wail, collapsing in a chair.

"The Spanish sickness is growing worse everywhere, Nathalie. I heard the rabbi has it, and Abe. The school has closed and Heinrich says we must stay inside, away from others. You must close your shop," Sophie instructs. I disagree, but don't want to argue with her.

Within weeks, Sophie, Doctor Meier, Abe and Tildie all catch the mysterious sickness and die. One day they were well, the next day they were sick, and one or two days after that, they were dead. Somehow, the virulent, highly contagious sickness did not overtake Eitan, even after caring for me when I became so ill I didn't care whether I died and almost wished I would.

As I grow slowly stronger all I think about is returning to Germany. Eitan claims there is no Germany to return to, but I don't care. Even the thought of crossing the ocean again is not enough to dilute my desire to return home, and home is in Germany.

"Maybe it won't be the old life, but we will be together with our families and people we love, who love us, Eitan. Here, we are alone. Our friends are dead, and my sewing business is gone. There is no meaning in our lives… nothing here for us anymore," I plead. Eitan acknowledges my hopelessness, but reminds me that many in our families have died so even if returning to Germany were possible, we would find it changed into something very different from what we remember. To calm me, he promises that when the sickness passes away, we will talk about moving to somewhere else still in America, but away from Ohio.

"The railroad is expanding further west. There will be new opportunities… a chance to start over."

"I don't have it in me to start over in America, Eitan. I don't think I can do it."

"Remember you are a Jew, Nathalie. Jews are always starting over. It is our destiny to always be moving somewhere," my husband reminds me. But with sickness everywhere there are no services at shul and this year, no Passover celebration. With no Jewish community around us any longer sometimes I almost forget I am a Jew, and think that my life has simply disappeared. Again and again, I wonder what, in this country, we have to live for?

"We have each other and our children, Nathalie. We are our own family, with enough money to live comfortably. G-d spared us from death the sickness brought to so many. We have so much to be grateful for that I don't understand how you can even ask that question?" Eitan repeats each time I voice my upset.

In a moment of clear honesty, I admit that I don't know if all we have is enough to fill the gaping hole in my soul. I feel trapped and alone in a country that so easily hates others, and I feel certain will eventually hate us, too… and there is nothing I can do about it. Eitan's face goes blank when he hears me say these things. He enjoys being a highly successful civil engineer with one of America's largest railroads and firmly believes life here is the best possible life, especially now that Germany is in ruin after losing the war. He is unable, despite his best efforts, to understand my despair. This I can understand, because much of the time I can't grasp it myself.

Chapter Nine
פרק תשע

San Francisco
May 1971

In the midst of chaos, unexpected gifts often appear…

"Your translator, Adrian McCormick, seems like a nice fellow," my dad remarks, handing me a Dos Equis beer while pushing the platter of Herlinda's spectacular guacamole and homemade tortilla chips across the kitchen table. Although the San Francisco Giants baseball game on the counter top television set is muted, he sneaks a look every minute or two. Waiting on my delayed flight from Chicago, followed by an additional ninety minutes pacing around the baggage claim until all three of my suitcases finally appeared caused him to miss the first three innings of the game.

"I didn't know you've met him," I respond, pretending I'm not aware that he went to Berkeley to personally deliver more diaries and letters to Adrian.

"Met who?" my dad responds, glued to the television set.

"Adrian – my translator. You said he seems nice, which suggests you've met him."

"Right… Instead of sending the things you wanted him to have over to Berkeley by courier, I took them myself. We met at the Rathskeller on Telegraph, had a beer, and watched a couple innings of a Giants game. He didn't mention it to you?"

"I haven't spoken with him in several days."

"But you speak to him regularly?"

"What's going on here, Dad?" I ask, hoping my face isn't broadcasting the memory of Adrian's lingering front porch kiss. Just thinking about it is experiencing it all over again. Unfortunately, my dad reads me like a cheap comic book, making it nearly impossible to hide anything from him.

"Nothing's going on – just making conversation..." he answers between base hits, looking at the television screen instead of at me, then changing the subject by asking how the translations are going.

"Pretty well, so far. They're mostly about settling into life in America, the run-up to World War I, the Spanish Flu epidemic, and finally, the end of the war. Adrian said there's no question it all took a severe toll on my grandmother, plus she doesn't paint a particularly rosy picture of life in America. My impression, so far, is she never really adjusted to being here."

"Sally called the other night asking where you were at with everything. I promised her you would be in touch when you got home."

"I talk to her fairly often. I wonder why she hasn't asked me?"

"Hard to tell, but she's definitely thinking about it. When do you think you'll know more? I can give her a heads up on your progress and see how she reacts."

"I would love to talk with her any time she's willing, so maybe start easing her into the possibility of a conversation fairly soon," I say, clearing the dishes from the table and excusing myself to unpack.

"I had a desk put in the back bedroom for you," my father calls after me as I walk down the hall itching to telephone Adrian but not wanting to explain it to my dad. Then I remind myself I'm a fully functioning adult and don't need my father's permission to make a phone call and begin dialing. There is no answer.

The hall telephone wakes me the next morning, but Herlinda gets to it first. A moment later she's knocking on my door asking if I'm awake? Hoping it's Adrian, I leap out of bed, nearly knocking her down as I rush toward the phone.

"How many people live with you?" Adrian asks when I pick up. Before answering him, I wait to hear a click signaling Herlinda has hung up the kitchen phone. My surrogate mother out-waits me.

"That was my dad's housekeeper, since before I can remember. She comes every morning but doesn't live here."

"I wanted to check that you arrived okay and let you know I finished up the next diary. A lot of mundane stuff, but some passages are interesting. When do you want to get together?" he asks.

"Is this afternoon too soon?"

"Tomorrow would be better," Adrian responds. Hearing this, I frown, disappointed that he obviously isn't as eager to see me as I am to see him.

"When and where?"

"Ella's – around one, after the lunch crowd?"

"That sounds fine. It'll be good to see you…"

"You, too, Natalie. See you tomorrow." He hangs up without saying more. I spend the next several minutes listening to the dial tone, puzzling over the abrupt conversation and wondering what changed during the three weeks since we last saw each other? Eventually, Herlinda interrupts me.

"Take a shower and I make you huevos rancheros. There's also some tres leche cake left over from yesterday, plus fresh juice. You feel better after that," she tells me.

"I feel fine now, thanks."

"You don't look fine," Herlinda snaps.

Breakfast takes on the intensity of the Spanish Inquisition as Herlinda uses all means possible to learn more about Adrian without asking outright. At loose ends, I finish unpacking, then waste most of the day aimlessly riding the trolleys around San Francisco. At least the sun is shining, which isn't always true in a city chronically plagued by fog. That evening, I ask my dad about borrowing the car to go to Berkeley tomorrow. He says Herlinda mentioned something about that and hands me the keys without further comment.

When I walk into Ella's, Adrian is sitting in the same booth we sat in previously. Seeing me, his face lights up, but not nearly as much as I was anticipating before our cryptic phone conversation poured ice water on my hopes for a romantic reunion. He stands up and draws me into a brief hug but doesn't kiss me. Quickly, we sit down across from each other.

"Adrian…" I begin.

"I don't see how this summer is going to work in terms of our seeing each other," he blurts out. I ask him to be more specific, then, before he has a chance to answer, excuse myself, saying I forgot to plug my parking meter. This isn't true, but I need to do something quick, before the panic overtaking me spirals out of control.

"You were saying…" I continue a few minutes later, taking several deep breaths.

"You're living with your dad who, despite your claims to the contrary, is obviously very protective. You won't be free to come and go as you wish and certainly won't be able to stay overnight here, or…" This is the first he's mentioned the overnight possibility, and he can't possibly miss the surprise exploding across my face.

"If you want to, that is… I don't mean to rush anything," he adds, reaching for my hand, then pulling back.

"I take this is about the sublet?"

"You didn't mention it again, so I figured you'd changed your mind."

"I didn't change my mind, but you didn't mention finding anything, and I assumed you'd had second thoughts about me coming over here."

"And you weren't going to bring it up?"

"You didn't bring it up, either."

"I don't know how we're going to have a relationship if we can't be clear with each other, Natalie. You could've asked me."

"You also could've asked me, Adrian. Instead, you just decided to be disappointed."

"I am very disappointed. I was looking forward to having you nearby… being able to see each other often… maybe every day, and let things happen, or not happen, naturally. But maybe it was all just wishful thinking. Maybe this is just a quid-pro-quo relationship and our kiss didn't mean anything."

"As long as we're occupying space in this deli, don't you think we should buy something? I'll get us a couple cokes," I say, standing up, trying to buy time to consider where this conversation is going. Minutes later, after putting two cokes and a large cookie on the table, I sit back down and look at Adrian.

"I take it you haven't found any sublets?" I ask, avoiding the relationship question for the moment.

"I told you – I was waiting for you to bring it up again, so haven't looked too hard. I do know of one possibility. It's a large studio two blocks from my place belonging to an adjunct professor in the history department who's going home to Boston for the summer. A while back, I did mention to her that I might know someone who would be interested. She said she was hiking the rent up to keep it out of the reach of students."

"Do you have the phone number?"

"Back at my apartment."

"Then before I leave, I'll call her. If it's still available, maybe I can see it today."

"You're serious?" Adrian asks, eyes wide and riveted on mine.

"Very serious," I answer, swallowing hard.

"You're sure?"

"Yes, Adrian, I'm sure. Why don't you believe me?"

"Because I assumed your dad was expecting you to stay with him all summer."

"I got here less than forty-eight hours ago. He and I haven't discussed the rest of the summer yet. I already told you I don't expect him to balk at the sublet idea. He knows it would be my decision and I don't need his permission, and he isn't expecting me to ask for it." I stop to take a breath and wait for Adrian to say something. When he doesn't, I continue.

"I know I mentioned the sublet when you were in Chicago, but I didn't think our relationship hinged on where I ended up living this summer."

"What do you think this is between us, Natalie? It's certainly not nothing... at least not to me."

"It's not nothing to me, either... and to be perfectly honest, I'm finding that a problem."

"Why?"

"You upset my equilibrium, and it scares me – a lot. On top of that, my reality is shifting, and I feel like I'm standing on beach sand while waves crash at my feet, knocking me off balance. I'm barely staying upright as I try to figure out who I am now, in the context of what I've learned in the last months. I like you a lot – maybe too much, but I'm not sure this is a good time for me to get involved with someone. I don't know myself as a Jew or how that new identity will play out in my life, and you don't know whether you're in or out of the priesthood. I don't want either of us getting hurt."

"I'm no good at just playing around, Natalie. I wouldn't be interested in pursuing this further if I thought there was a chance of either of us getting hurt. I really care about you and believe you care for me... and I very much want to see where that takes us. The Jewish part matters not at all to me. I thought I'd made that clear already," Adrian smiles.

"You're also a priest. That sort of limits your – our – options."

"I'm not an active priest, and I've got plenty of options, including never communicating with Rome again."

"What about the priest forever according to the order of Melchizedek, permanent mark on your soul, God's chosen, and so on? You can't just erase all that, and I certainly don't want to be the reason you decide to try. I'd feel too responsible for your decision, and the risk of eventually disappointing you is too great."

"My soul belongs to me, not to the Church; I decide what marks it. I wouldn't leave the priesthood permanently because you wanted me to, but I would leave it because I wanted to. Being with you would be an added bonus that hopefully works out."

"You're splitting hairs..."

"No, I'm not. I'd be leaving because I don't want to be a priest anymore and want to be something else instead... a husband, a father, an historian... something that isn't a priest. Right now, I'm leaning heavily toward ordinary human being, with all its ups and downs. Plain, ordinary Adrian McCormick is a very attractive option; priest on a pedestal is not."

"You'd forego all the power that comes with being a priest?"

"Being viewed as an elevated being with a direct line to God and the moral authority to proclaim the last word on the dilemma of the day is a burden I never wanted and was very happy to unload when I went inactive. Hearing confessions, passing judgment in the name of God on what was mostly ordinary human behavior, then handing out punishments to good people for being normal human beings was pure torture. And, you're forgetting that when we met, I was ninety percent out of the priesthood already, and you weren't any part of the decision that took me that far. At most, you've upped the percentage a point or two, which should make you feel better about any responsibility you bear for my life, which is basically none."

"Actually, it does make me feel better," I smile, sipping on my coke and breaking off a piece of cookie, then handing it to the extraordinarily handsome man I am longing to kiss as he sits across from me.

"So, what exactly does ninety percent out of the priesthood mean?" I ask a moment later.

"At this point, it's closer to ninety-five percent, but I didn't want to scare you," he smiles.

"It means I've not entered a church or had any communication with either Rome or my home diocese, which is Chicago, for nearly two years. I've separated myself from all that to feel my way through a decision about my future… figure out what I truly believe inside myself and not just accept what I was indoctrinated to believe. If I'm willing to take a chance on you and your identity crisis, which is in its early stages, can't you take a chance on me and mine? I'm much further along than you are and am pretty well equipped to deal with the ups and downs that come with deep personal transformation. I honestly do understand what you're going through and am able to give you the space you need to figure it all out. Think of it as the two of us as pilgrim companions on a journey toward an unknown destination." Instead of answering, I take another bite of cookie.

"Besides – you kissed me first, which suggests you're in better emotional shape than you think you are," Adrian teases. Feeling my face grow warm, I don't respond. "On a more serious note: Your dad's a great guy, but there's no bullshitting him. I'm sure he senses something between us and came over here to check me out."

"You're probably right. When I told him I wanted to get the next diary to you I thought he'd send it by courier. It never occurred to me he'd come himself."

"As I see it, our options are to tell him we're seeing each other or sneak around, and I definitely don't favor that…"

"Neither do I, but telling him about us could be a little dicey…"

"Why?"

"He's not neutral where Irish Catholics are concerned. My former husband was one, and my dad was opposed to it from the beginning."

"Because he was Irish Catholic, or were there other reasons?"

"He never really said – just implied there were cultural issues I would find difficult. My Aunt Sally was worse – hysterical is probably the best description. Her husband is Irish, and she could've done a whole lot better. Regardless, my dad understands I'm an adult and have the right to my own friends and my own mistakes. He's entitled to share his opinion on all of those things but doesn't get a vote. All this said, he did find the marriage-divorce fiasco pretty upsetting."

"Even if he wasn't your father, I'd like him and want to shoot straight with him."

"I think taking a summer sublet over here is shooting straight enough for now. If he wants to know more, he'll ask, and I'll answer honestly."

"The Giants are playing a double header against the Cubs in Candlestick Park tomorrow afternoon. Want to go?" Adrian smiles.

"Sure…"

"Want to invite your dad?"

"No."

"Maybe if he gets to know me better, he'll be more relaxed about us seeing each other. A baseball game is a perfect way to do that."

"I'll mention it to him," I concede as Adrian hands me another set of translations.

"These are the ones I mentioned earlier. Despite being an immigrant, your grandmother was a strong-willed, independent woman with a mind of her own. You're a lot like her," Adrian smiles.

"Is that a compliment or merely an observation?"

"Definitely a compliment…why?"

"Just wondering… I've been accused of that before, and the consequences weren't what I expected."

"If you're asking whether I can handle a strong-minded woman, the answer is yes. I've dealt with nuns, and while they seem weak and submissive, nothing could be further from the truth. Without even trying, they can back anybody into a corner and scare the crap out of them to get what they want."

"Good to know," I laugh.

"These entries indicate your grandmother suffered divided loyalties in three directions, and that can't have been easy."

"Three directions?"

"German, Jewish, and American. Your grandmother's loyalties were to being Jewish and German first. Being an American was a distant third, and that never changed. She was a deeply honest woman. That made everything about the life she was trying to live much more difficult."

"I'm not sure I understand what you're saying."

"She would have found not being forthright about exactly who she was and what she believed extremely difficult... more difficult than most people. She wasn't good at pretending to be someone she knew she wasn't and didn't want to bring up her daughters that way. It was a moral issue for her... went right to the heart of what she believed about living a righteous life."

"My brain's fried right now. I'll read these and think about all that later. I'd like to call about the sublet and see if it's still available," I say, folding the translations into my book bag. Walking out of the café, Adrian places his arm lightly around my shoulder and points me in the direction of his apartment. Relief washes over me as he notes that we have just survived our first major upset.

"I thought was just a minor misunderstanding," I tease, loathe to admit how crushingly unsettled I was when I thought we were over before we ever really began.

The sublet is a large, sunny, attic in a mission-style, former sorority house on the edge of campus. Eclectically tasteful, the room has dormer windows on four sides, a sleeping alcove, a tiny kitchen opening onto a fire escape large enough for two chairs, and a skylight in the antique bathroom. It will become available in five days, until the weekend after Labor Day.

"It's very pleasant here – quiet, and the others here keep to themselves," Professor Angela Milburn explains.

"I am aware the rent borders on exorbitant, but if you're interested, we can negotiate," she continues, giving me the first indication that she might consider renting to me. After some back and forth, the professor and I agree on twelve percent over the monthly rent she is currently paying, plus utilities and phone, with a one-month damage deposit in advance. I write her a check, and, in return, she hands me a set of keys and says she'll leave her contact information under the telephone. Showing me to the door, she adds that she hopes I have a good summer. The entire transaction takes less than an hour.

To celebrate my new address, Adrian suggests we eat supper in an Armenian restaurant a block from his apartment in the opposite direction. I don't get back to San Francisco until nearly midnight and find my father waiting up for me."

"You could've called... I was getting worried," he says.

"If something happened the police would let you know, Dad. Otherwise, it's safe to assume I'm fine... and a sensible, capable adult."

"A father always views his daughter as his little girl, and it's his job to worry about her, no matter how old, capable, or sensible she is. Otherwise, he thinks he's failing as a parent."

"Adrian and I are going to the double header at Candlestick Park tomorrow afternoon. Want to come?" I ask, cutting off the 'I'm the protective father – you're my little girl' conversation.

"Sure, if I'm caught up on my sleep," my dad answers, cracking a slight smile as he walks down the hall toward his bedroom.

A few minutes later I climb into bed, but am unable to relax into sleep. My mind swings from random thought to random thought like a great ape propelling itself from tree to tree, looking for a comfortable place to land. I can't decide what to think about... the sublet, my shifting relationship with Adrian, or the translations and what they're telling me about who I am and how this could change me. I wonder about how much of myself am I losing as the life I have been very happily living transforms into a vast, unfamiliar space I never expected to inhabit and know so little about. The landscape of my life is being bulldozed over and replanted, and I have no idea what the result will look like. Giving up on sleep, I get out of bed, wrap myself in my old bathrobe, sit down in the chair nearest my bedroom window and unfold the latest translations. Adrian's note explains that he found the enclosed newspaper articles about Negro lynchings and the Ku Klux Klan tucked among the diary pages as he worked. There are other articles about the war in Europe, mostly describing Germany's downfall. I carefully unfold the fragile, yellowed newspaper clippings and begin reading.

Well, this explains a lot, I sigh two hours later, carefully putting everything back in the envelope. The little I can recall of this historical era is that Germany did lose the first world war and even though Jews fought alongside German soldiers, they were blamed for the defeat. This set into motion a series of events that ultimately resulted in Hitler's rise to power, the establishment of the Third Reich, and eventually, to the Holocaust.

"I really have to find out more about all this. If Aunt Sally stays silent, maybe historical records will give me some clues," I mutter, setting the envelope aside, turning off the table lamp and climbing back into bed.

I oversleep, and the next morning find a note taped to my bedroom door.

> *The game starts at three. Tell Adrian we'll meet him at Candlestick's main gate half hour before. Whoever gets there first buys the tickets and we'll settle up later.*

"I guess that's a yes on the game," I mumble, dialing Adrian's telephone number. He answers on the second ring.

"The game's a go. We'll meet you at the entrance and first one to arrive is supposed to buy the tickets," I tell him.

"That's great. Should be a fun afternoon. Was your dad pleased to be invited?"

"Hard to say – he went to bed right after I asked him. There was a note on my door this morning saying he wanted to go."

"What did he say about the sublet?"

"I haven't had a chance to tell him yet, but he'll probably be happy. He was a little put out about how late I got home last night."

"He was waiting up for you?"

"Couldn't help himself, apparently."

"I can understand that. See you in a few hours," Adrian says, hanging up. I call him right back.

"I wasn't finished…"

"What else?"

"I couldn't sleep last night, so read through the news clippings. Do you know why the US started turning Jews back sometime before WWI?"

"It was probably an immigration quota problem, but I'll have to check further."

"These articles are sort of a tease. Obviously, my grandmother saved them because they were important to her, but they raise more questions. I need to fill in the context…"

"We can talk more about it later. I'll see you this afternoon." Adrian hangs up again before I've finished what I have to say, which I'm learning not to take personally.

My dad and I arrive at Candlestick Park, the San Francisco Giant's home field, thirty-five minutes before the first pitch and find Adrian waiting.

"Good to see you, Adrian, and thanks for the invite," my dad says, walking toward him, hand outstretched. Adrian returns the handshake and says he has three tickets along the first base line, thirty-six rows up.

"Candlestick's not the Wrigley Field of the west, but I think these are pretty good seats," he says.

"Perfect," my father grins, handing him several twenty-dollar bills, which Adrian refuses.

"Then the next game's on me," my dad responds, pocketing the money. Adrian nods and we begin winding our way up to our seats in the modern stadium lacking even a trace of the homegrown culture that defines the iconic Wrigley Field, one of America's last traditional, old-fashioned ballparks. I'm sitting between my father, who is wearing a faded blue SF Giants t-shirt and Adrian, wearing an even more faded red Chicago Cubs t-shirt. In a feeble attempt at neutrality, I'm wearing a Cal-Berkeley t-shirt with a large image of the infamous mascot, a sturdy, golden grizzly bear, firmly affixed to my unimpressive chest.

"Who are you rooting for – the home team you grew up with or the home team where you live now?" my father asks.

"Whoever scores," I answer as it dawns on me that this afternoon is about baseball. It won't be the same experience I had with Adrian when we sat in Wrigley Field enjoying each other at least as much or, in my case, more than the game.

"I must've missed something. When, exactly, did I pay for you to go to diplomacy school?" my father shoots back, then announces he's going for beer and hot dogs for anyone who wants them.

"A Bud and Chicago-style dog for me," Adrian replies without looking up from his intense study of the program, which includes the Cubs' starting lineup.

"Oscar Mayer with mustard or ketchup is the best we can do."

"I'll suffer through... Looks like Fergie Jenkins is the Cubs' starting pitcher," Adrian answers.

"We can handle him – no problem," my dad assures, taking the stadium steps two at a time.

The afternoon is an endless series of moans, groans, cheers, and jeers. One crack of a bat has my father on his feet cheering while Adrian lets loose with several expletives under his breath. A few minutes later, another crack of a bat has the opposite effect – Adrian is clapping loudly and my father has his head in his hands. Both offer running opinions on the home plate umpire's skills, regardless of which team is up. I am the only one within hearing distance who is surprised by the words coming out of my father's mouth when the Giants strike out with three men on base which would've put them two runs ahead and instead leaves them one run behind.

"You'll never make the midnight bus, and the next one isn't for a couple more hours. You're welcome to stay in the city with us," my dad tells Adrian as we are leaving the stadium after both games of the double header went extra innings. Hearing this, my jaw drops. The "getting to know each other better" opportunity Adrian referred to earlier has apparently worked quite well.

"We have extra bedrooms, and you can leave first thing in the morning if you're in a hurry to get back to Berkeley," my father offers. By now we are standing at Candlestick's main entrance and Adrian has to make a decision. He can come home with us or look for a cab to the Embarcadero, then wait two hours for the next bus to Berkeley.

"If it isn't too much trouble, I appreciate the offer to stay over," Adrian finally says, not looking at me. In response, my father whistles for a taxi and we all get into the back seat.

"This is cozy," I mumble, squeezed between the two most important men in my life.

The next morning Herlinda shakes me out of a sound sleep.

"Wake up. There's a man in my kitchen drinking coffee," she explodes, wiping her hands on her apron.

"Maybe it's a plumber," I suggest.

"He too good looking for a plumber and I no call one anyway," she insists.

"It's just a friend of mine – it's all right."

"Who you kidding? Nobody looks like him is just a friend." Herlinda sputters, pacing back and forth beside the bed.

"Señor Paul know about him here?"

"He invited him. The baseball game went extra innings, so he offered to have him stay here instead of going back to Berkeley on the late bus."

"So, this the Berkeley man? No wonder you can't decide what to wear. His looks – they dangerous, Natalie. I warning you right now."

"He's not dangerous, Herlinda. I'll get up and introduce you. Just give me a minute."

RED ANEMONES

"He too good looking – I no trust him, she declares, sitting down on the bed. I pull on the flannel bathrobe I have worn since high school and we walk into the kitchen. Seeing all four feet ten inches of Herlinda, with her hands on her hips, and me, a foot taller, and with my hair hanging in my face, Adrian laughs out loud.

"Good morning. You're a vision to behold early in the morning," he teases, grinning.

"If I wanted your opinion, I'd ask for it," I snap, instantly embarrassed that I'd failed to comb my hair, wash the sleep off my face, or put on something more presentable than my favorite threadbare leisurewear before entering the kitchen. This is not how I planned for him to see what I look like first thing in the morning.

"This is Herlinda – I forgot to leave her a note that you were here, and it startled her," I explain, clearing my throat. Adrian smiles and offers Herlinda his hand.

"Hello, Herlinda – I'm Adrian McCormick. I'm pleased to meet you and apologize for frightening you. Please – sit down for a moment and have a cup of coffee with me before I leave," he invites.

"I no drink coffee with strangers." Herlinda huffs.

"You sure? You make wonderful coffee."

"Where you find this guy anyway?" Herlinda frowns, acting as if I've just brought home a stray dog, which she might be more inclined to accept. Acutely self-conscious about how unattractive I must look standing barefoot in the kitchen, wearing a robe older than dirt covering a pair of gray gym shorts and a purple Northwestern Wildcats tank top, I don't answer. Herlinda pulls a stool from under the island and hikes herself up, never taking her eyes off Adrian.

"Would you like cream and sugar, or just black?" Adrian continues. *No wonder he was a career Vatican diplomat – he could charm the fangs off a venomous snake,* I think. Herlinda says a little sugar would be nice.

"How about you, Natalie – black or cream and sugar?"

"A little cream, thanks." He hands us both mugs of aromatic, steaming coffee.

"Tell me about yourself, Herlinda?" Adrian asks.

"I been totally in charge running this household since Natalie was in diapers," my motherly overseer declares, clearly unapologetic about the image she has brought forth. I continue studying my coffee while they make small talk.

"I hate to cut this short, but I would like to make the nine o'clock bus, so best get moving," Adrian says moments later, rinsing out his mug and placing it in the dishwasher. He assures Herlinda it has been a pleasure meeting her, then asks to speak to me. I follow him toward the hallway knowing he thinks we're out of Herlinda's earshot, which is a mistaken assumption.

"Now that you know what I look like in the morning, if you want to end things, I won't blame you," I say, not smiling.

"You're adorable in the morning, and obviously low maintenance," he chuckles.

"Did you sleep well," I ask, not really caring what the answer is.

"Are you kidding? Our first night together was twenty feet from each other and under your father's roof. I stared at the ceiling all night," Adrian responds without expression.

"Sorry to hear that… I slept just fine."

"What are your plans for the next couple days?"

"I was going to shop for my sublet, but it might be easier to do that in Berkeley, maybe on Saturday, if you don't mind me leaving a few things at your place for a day or so. I'll tell my dad about it tonight and probably move in on Monday."

"What about Herlinda? I don't see her thinking your moving to Berkeley is a good idea."

"I think you won her over with the sugar in her coffee. She usually drinks it black."

"I hope you're right; otherwise, she'd be a formidable opponent. Do you want me to take another diary or some letters back with me?"

"I'll bring them Saturday."

"Let me know what time to expect you," Adrian says, then asks whether kissing me goodbye is a problem.

"If you're asking whether Herlinda has eyes in the back of her head, the answer is yes. She also has an emotional radar detection system rivaling the North American Air Defense Command. She really ought to be working for the CIA instead of keeping house for my father."

"In that case – I had a great time yesterday and look forward to seeing you Saturday," he says, shaking my hand and opening the door. I wave slightly as he walks toward the elevator.

"Holy Mother of God – you no marry that man, you should be committed to happy academy," Herlinda pronounces, referring to the California State Mental Hospital.

"I'm not marrying anybody – remember? Besides, half an hour ago, he was the most dangerous man on the west coast. What changed?"

"He so polite... compliment my coffee... means he is a good man... not like the other guy... what was his name?"

"I can't remember," I smile.

That evening over the supper Herlinda prepared before she left for the day, I fill my dad in on my sublet.

"It makes sense, Natalie. Although I hate to admit it, I'm too old to be waiting up nights until you get home. And just so you know, I like Adrian. He's an honest, decent man. My sense is he's good for you..."

"And just so you know, Dad – staying in Berkeley isn't just about Adrian. I have other reasons to be there."

"If you say so, but you'll have to convince Herlinda of that. You'll need to break your plans to her gently – reassure her you know what you're doing and not making a mistake. She won't believe you, but you still need to say it."

"You might be wrong on that. She seemed to like Adrian."

"That's the problem, Natalie. She likes him a lot, and it alarms her."

"How do you know that?"

"She called me at the office this morning to report on meeting him."

"Seriously? Is there anything she doesn't report to you?"

"Generally speaking, she doesn't say much about what you eat for lunch. Before getting resentful, you need to understand that she's helped raise you since..."

"I know – since I was in diapers, which she informed Adrian of this morning."

"It's only natural she worries about you. Your divorce was very traumatic for her – she doesn't want a repeat."

"It seems my divorce was very traumatic for everybody but me, and I'm getting a little tired of being reminded of it. I was just glad to unload the guy and sorry it cost you half the California state budget to get it straightened out."

"It didn't cost quite that much, unless you include the wedding. Be patient with Herlinda; otherwise, you'll worry her into an early grave, which would be a tragedy not just for her..." my father admonishes, making me wonder whether he's projecting his own anxiety onto his beloved housekeeper. Unlike him, Herlinda's never had a problem expressing her feelings and there's never any question about what she's thinking. My father is harder to read.

"Let's plan on dinner every Wednesday. You can stay overnight and update Herlinda on your life in the morning, before going back to

Berkeley. That saves me from Herlinda's version of a congressional inquiry every week," my dad suggests, only half joking. I happily agree that's a good idea.

"Being devoutly Catholic, do you think she'll have a problem with the Jewish thing?" I ask, shifting the conversation to a not necessarily safer topic.

"I don't think she cares if you're Hari Krishna, as long as your chanting doesn't drown out her afternoon soap opera and you keep her informed about your life, so she feels like she has input. The more you talk to her, the less she grills me, and the happier we both are."

"I think I'm going to like it here," I tell Adrian the following Monday as I survey my sublet after bringing the last box up the stairs.

"Let's sit on the fire escape and catch our breath. We can watch the sun set while guzzling a beer."

"Good idea, but I don't have any beer."

"I did a little grocery shopping on my way over. Think of it as a housewarming present," he says, reaching into a paper bag and retrieving two frosty, long neck bottles."

"No opener, and I doubt this kitchen has one," I frown. In response, Adrian produces a Swiss Army knife from his pocket, snaps off the bottle tops, pulls out a bag of pretzels, and opens the door onto the fire escape. We sit quietly, elbows touching, as the sun drops in the western sky.

"I don't know about you, but this is a little like what I imagine heaven to be..." he smiles, tilting his bottle toward me.

Chapter Ten
פרק עשר

Berkeley, California
Summer, 1971

Sometimes there are no good answers...

"These move in a darker direction," Adrian warns, handing over a manila envelope with his latest translations. We're sitting on a wooden bench across from the campanile in Berkeley's central campus, licking drips off mocha ice cream cones while enjoying the warmth of the late afternoon summer sun. A few days ago, he warned me that my grandmother was experiencing an ugly side of the American promise, and suggested I do some background reading to help me better understand what she was feeling as she wrote about it. Taking this advice, I've just spent several hours in the university library squinting over microfilmed newspaper articles from World War I and the Spanish Flu epidemic before finally taking a break to enjoy what's left of a warm summer day.

"Did you learn a lot?" Adrian asks.

"More than I expected to, and much of it is information I wish I didn't know. After sitting in the Doe Library dungeon, shivering in controlled temperature archives with my face glued to a microfilm reader until my eyeballs no longer focused, I am really glad you showed up and suggested a break," I answer, patting his hand. A few licks later, I admit not being an historian is a significant disadvantage in this situation and ask what he knows about the era surrounding World War I.

"Not as much as I would like. There was a lengthy military buildup before Germany declared war on Russia in 1914. It seems the Kaiser and the Czar were in bed together until all of a sudden, they weren't," he remarks, catching the drips from his ice cream before continuing.

"The Kaiser was power hungry and filled with blind ambition; ultimately the Czar became an impediment to him. The other problem was the German economy was tanking at the same time the population was increasing and a half million Germans, which was a quarter of the available labor force, were unemployed – a problem that was rapidly growing. One sure way to rescue a failing economy is to start a war, and the Kaiser may have believed that was his only choice. He knew building a war machine was the quickest path to economic recovery and I doubt he worried that it would explode to involve the rest of the world or considered the possibility that Germany would lose. By the time it was over, ten million were dead including six million civilian casualties, the German economy was in shreds, and the Kaiser was forced to abdicate. The country was extremely unstable and despite most Jews being well assimilated into German life and culture, they were the scapegoats."

"That part doesn't make any sense to me," I admit.

"It doesn't make any sense, period, but Germans are proud people. They had to blame their massive failure on somebody, and the Jews were a convenient target. It wasn't the first time."

"I suppose it didn't help that the entire world was already angry with Germany."

"Particularly in this country. A lot of Americans deeply resented the pressure to get involved in the war, and by the time we finally did, Germans were being arrested for no reason other than being German. Catholic-instigated Anti-German, anti-Jewish organizations were springing up everywhere."

"Why were Catholics doing this?"

"I really wish I could answer that question. The political Church may have seen it as an opportunity to mitigate widespread anti-Catholic sentiment, thus increasing its own chances for greater social acceptance. The Church had to hit below the belt to generate significant antisemitism, because a great many German Jews who emigrated were secular and had no plans to cultivate their Jewish lifestyle. They came well-educated, culturally enlightened and fully prepared to assimilate into American society, which is exactly what your grandfather's plan was. Your grandmother felt differently, and very much wanted to keep her Jewish identity."

"I can hardly bear to think about how awful that situation must've been. If she and my grandfather disagreed on maintaining a traditional Jewish identity, it must've been a very lonely marriage for her," I say, just as the campanile strikes four o'clock.

"You'll get a pretty good idea from the next translations. Come over around six and you can read while I cook some spaghetti, then we can talk about them," Adrian suggests. I nod, thank him, and say that after sitting all day I need a long walk first. He gives me a quick kiss, then stands up and turns in the direction of his apartment, saying he'll see me soon. After sitting for a few minutes with my face to the afternoon sun, I open the envelope. The top page is a letter, dated January 10, 1919.

> *My dearest Nathalie,*
> *I write with sad news. Your nephew, Asher, Levi and Irina's son, has died from lingering wounds he suffered when he was delivering messages during the war. Despite his parent's objections, he ran away to the war before celebrating his bar mitzvah. We sat Shiva but Irina is not consoled, Levi is too angry to be comforted, and those who come to be with us are the same ones we sat Shiva with a week or a month ago. All of this after the sickness claimed so many lives is too much to bear.*
>
> *Your Papa has never recovered from losing your mother and says he is too weak to be any sadder than he already is and still continue breathing. Then I notice he added Asher's name to the list of the dead he says Mourner's Kaddish for every day.*
>
> *Many who came back from the war are not right anymore, including my son, Irina's brother. We think he deserted the army and would be shot if anyone discovered him, but he tells us nothing. He hides whenever we hear voices or footsteps, but otherwise stares at a wall, silent and eating almost nothing. Old Germany no longer exists and some days it is very difficult to carry forward, but as Jews, we always find a reason, no matter how bad things are.*
>
> *I am sorry this is such a sad letter but felt you should know what has happened to your brother's family and there is no one else with enough strength left to tell you.*
>
> *Long may we live to see each other again...*
> *Rute Bachmann, loving mother to Irina.*

This is the first letter not from an immediate family member, and reveals a heart filled with fear, desperation and sadness, but not hopelessness, which is what I would've been feeling if I found myself in the situation she describes. My grandmother, receiving this letter from her sister-in-law's mother, who she might not have known very well, must've felt helpless, lonely, and frightened. The guilt she must've carried because her beloved family was in such dire straits and out of her reach must have been overwhelming. I can easily imagine how desperate she was to return to her family – to comfort them and to die with them, if that was their fate. She seemed to believe that remaining in America and surviving into a future without them was worse than death itself. *In her shoes, I'd definitely return to my family, but that's easy to say when I've never faced the decision or the circumstances confronting her,* I tell myself. Mulling this over, I wander aimlessly around the campus for more than an hour, arriving at Adrian's just after six.

"You read the letter," he says, as soon as he sees my face. I nod as he pulls me into a hug, then walks me to his couch, where we both sit down.

"Maybe we put off reading any more tonight," he suggests.

"I'd rather do it when you're nearby to catch me if I dissolve," I say.

"In that case, sit here. I'll be in the kitchen if you need me."

"Adrian – if people you dearly loved were in danger, wouldn't you want to be with them and do what you could to save them?" He stops walking and turns toward me.

"Of course I would. But sometimes more can be done some other way. Your grandmother was sending money, and that was helping a lot, perhaps more than if she were with them and facing the same dangers without the money she provided, which offered some level of protection for them," he says, standing in the kitchen doorway.

"But if the people you love die and you don't, what do you do with the guilt, and the loneliness?" I ask.

"Find a way to live with it. Configure your own life in some way that makes meaning out of theirs – and plan on never being truly carefree and happy again," he answers.

"In other words, either way is a death sentence," I say, my eyes filling.

"In many respects. But much of life is learning to live with loss. Some losses are just much harder to deal with than others, and only the strongest survive them."

"And some are so devastating they are impossible to survive, no matter how strong someone is…"

"I wouldn't underestimate the abilities of the human heart, Natalie. And I certainly wouldn't underestimate your grandmother." When I don't respond, Adrian walks over to the couch and sits down.

"You're not going to feel like a big dinner. I'll save the spaghetti for later. How about I go down to the corner store and bring back some ice cream? I make a mean chocolate milkshake specifically designed for troubled times," he says, squeezing my hand. Although I've had enough ice cream for one day, I don't have the will power to refuse chocolate, and offer a weak smile in response.

A few minutes later, the door onto the back stairway closes. Aware that I'm alone in the apartment, I take out the next sheets of paper and begin reading.

Chapter Eleven
פרק אחד עשר

Elyria, Ohio
1920

Given all the hatred surrounding Jews, it is a miracle we survive…

With both the war and the Spanish Flu epidemic finally over, leaving behind deep loss and terrible sadness, it is hard for me to return Sarah and Rachael to school, even though that is where they belong. In the past two years the demands of caring for them and providing for their learning have gotten me through the day, and I am reluctant to give up the comfort this has brought me. But they want to be back in school, and that is not an opportunity I can deny them. Eitan is away most of the time, Sophie and Tildie are now buried, and my sewing business is gone. I have no one to talk with except my children. Neither is interested in what I have to say unless it directly involves them, but they still offer me an opportunity to be with someone other than myself.

Sarah is a bright, fast learner, and surpassed her grade level while at home. Upon returning to school, she is placed one year ahead. A happy little girl, she makes friends easily and enjoys learning new things. Rachael is different. She finds school boring and is a discipline problem.

"Your daughter quickly completes her grade-level work, and without anything to occupy her, spends her time disrupting the others," Miss Collins, Rachael's teacher, tells me just after the American Thanksgiving holiday. Primly dressed, although the garment fits poorly and the color is not well-suited to her pale complexion, she is a tall, sober young woman new to the school and nervous in her first teaching position. But her eyes are kind, and her seriousness reveals her commitment to her pupils, who span several grades.

"Although Rachael will be the youngest in the group, I recommend that after Christmas vacation she advance to the next level. With more difficult challenges, she is less likely to misbehave and we both will be much happier," the earnest young teacher says, looking directly at me, hoping for agreement. I nod an understanding of her concern, then ask about Rachael's ability in English.

"Both your daughters are quite proficient in English. Why do you ask?"

"I just want to be sure," I quickly answer, suddenly aware Miss Collins does not know English is not Rachael and Sarah's first language, but after meeting me will quickly figure it out. Realizing my innocent question could bring harm to my children causes my heart to beat so rapidly it begins sucking the air from my chest. Forcing back tears, I smile, firmly shake the hand of my daughters' teacher, thank her, and leave without saying more. That evening I caution Rachael about her classroom behavior, insisting she be more like her older, more compliant sister. She gives no sign she listens to me.

On the first warm day of spring, Sarah and Rachael arrive home from school crying. The ribbon is gone from Sarah's normally carefully combed hair and her favorite, light blue dress is smudged with dirt. The yellow gingham dress I made Rachael a few months earlier for her first school day is torn from her shoulder and the sash at her waist is ripped away. I tell them I don't want to hear what happened because I already know.

"They called us names... heiney and kraut and kike... and pulled my hair. They threw dirt and spit at us..." Sarah sobs, ignoring my request not to describe the incident.

"They ripped my dress, and I hit them back hard... shoved one boy's face into the ground," Rachael reports proudly, wiping tears from her dirt-streaked cheeks. *With her dark curls and blue eyes, she is so much my Maman's child*, I think, looking at her defiant face.

"A boy sang a song 'Sarah red head wets the bed' so I threw a brick at him – almost got him!" she adds, swinging her arm in a circle.

"Violetta says she can't be my friend anymore, because her mother says if she likes me, other girls won't like her," Sarah continues, sniffling. Sarah and Violetta have been friends since they played together in the park when both were just learning to walk. Over the years I have sewn many elegant dresses for Violetta and her mother and several shirts and ties for her father, always at lower cost, because I believed they were loyal friends. Now I see I was mistaken, and a rock-hard sadness takes hold of my heart.

As soon as I can breathe quietly again, I dry my daughters' tears, give them each a cookie and milk, then explain I am going to the school to talk to Miss Collins. I instruct them to stay inside the house until I return.

"If anyone comes to the door, don't answer," I say in a firm voice unfamiliar to my children.

Less than one hour later, hearing my knock on her classroom door, Miss Collins, sitting at her desk, looks up.

"What are you doing here, Mrs. Rosenblum?" she asks, making no effort to hide her annoyance. Frowning slightly, her mouth set in a firm line, she suggests that I am interrupting her and does not welcome me as warmly as the first time we met. I describe the incident involving Sarah and Rachael as carefully as I can and seek assurances that it won't happen again.

"Am I correct that you are Jewish as well as German?" Miss Collins asks. I nod, looking directly into her eyes.

"Let's face it, Mrs. Rosenblum, German Jews aren't very popular right now. Unfortunately, I can't promise that something like what happened to your daughters this afternoon won't be repeated. I insist the children are polite and kind to one another while they are here, but I'm sure you understand I have no control over what happens once they leave the school yard," she explains. The young teacher expresses no concern for how the experience affected Sarah and Rachael, or me, as a loving mother determined to protect her daughters.

"We are good people. We work hard for America, do our part for others and cause no trouble to anyone," I insist, looking directly at the young teacher's face.

"The Jews in Germany brought on a war America had to fight. American men, including the man I was betrothed to, died as a result of something that was not America's fault, but America had to fix. It cost my brother both his legs, and he wishes he were dead, which is the same as being dead."

"Please forgive me for disagreeing, Miss Collins, but you are mistaken. German Jews did not bring on the war. Germany was one of the central European powers and was forced into the war after Austria-Hungary declared war on Serbia. I am very sorry for what happened to your beloved and to your brother, but the Jews did nothing that caused any of this," I point out, straightening my back.

"Truthfully, I think it best if Sarah and Rachael don't come back to school here," my daughters' teacher finally says, staring down at her desk. I repeat that blame for the war rests squarely with conspiring events involving the Kaiser, not the Jews, but Miss Collins is having none of it.

Like everyone else, she wants to blame somebody for the war and the Jews are a convenient target.

Rather than argue, I leave without saying goodbye. Then, two days later, after Eitan returns home from an extended trip, I explain why our children are no longer attending school.

"America is a free country; our children are entitled to an education," he barks, pacing the floor.

"Entitled or not, I won't allow Sarah and Rachael to be among people who hate them. I have made up my mind we will find some other way for an education and don't wish to discuss it further," I say, in an unusual show of will against my beloved husband. Tears in my eyes, I add that this has happened to other Jewish families and there is a rumor our shul is going to open its own school as soon as a teacher is found.

"This is a good solution. Sarah and Rachael won't be afraid anymore and can be themselves… be good Jews and speak German when they want to. It will be safe for them."

"This is a solution for now, my wife, but eventually our daughters will have to learn how to live as Americans," their father insists.

A few months later, with Sarah and Rachael safe and thriving in the school run by shul, Eitan announces he has an opportunity to go to work for another railroad.

"The Union Pacific Railroad is expanding throughout the west, Nathalie. It offers new challenges, new opportunities, and more money. It will be a fresh start in a new place. No one will know we are Germans or Jews. As long as the work gets done, they won't care who we are."

"We are Germans, and we are Jews, Eitan. No matter how much you want to pretend otherwise, we can't change that, and the minute we open our mouths it is obvious we are not native speakers. Denial won't make any of these realities disappear. You are an intelligent man. I don't understand why you believe pretending to be what we are not makes it so." He doesn't answer.

Sooner than I expect, and without discussing it further, we are packing up our lives and moving west, to Bakersfield, California. I don't want to go but have no energy left in me to push against my husband's will. Soon after, we find ourselves living in a nice house in an ugly town.

I write to Irina more often now, not wanting to reveal my sadness because I hope my letter offers her a brief respite from the grief she suffers daily. Soon after arriving in Bakersfield, I describe our new home.

Elyria had flowers, shade trees, changing seasons, and an inland lake nearly as big as an ocean. Bakersfield is hot, dry, dusty, flat, battered by constantly blowing wind, with no water, not even a river or a stream, anywhere nearby. Everyone is busy all the time, so I suppose no one notices there's nothing nice to look at when you sit on your front porch in the evening. Eitan says this is a hub – a meeting place for many trains who bring what grows in a long valley between two sets of mountains to market and carry things back and forth between one side of America and the other, which keeps Eitan very busy. He encourages me to open another dressmaking business, but I reject the idea because the town is too small and too poor – mostly people coming here from somewhere else, looking for work because of bad conditions on the other side of the mountains. I see no one wearing well-made dresses and suppose most women do their own mending and sewing. I cannot imagine they are interested in hiring someone to do it for them and might not do not have money to pay for it even if they did want it.

One evening, while Eitan and I sit on our wide front porch drinking lemonade and fanning ourselves, he asks how I fill my time now that both Sarah and Rachael are back in school and someone comes daily to help care for the house.

"I am knitting baby blankets and caps to send back to Germany. Irina says things are bad – no jobs and people are hungry but still having babies. She knows people who need what I knit. We could also send money, Eitan. We have more than we need." He doesn't disagree but offers no assurances he will follow up. A few minutes later, he asks where I find yarn to knit?"

"I am spinning my own yarn from wool roving a sheep rancher's wife sells to me. She showed me how to card the wool and spin it into threads."

"So that is the big wheel you have in the parlor?" he asks. I nod, smiling as I point out I have been spinning yarn for months and he is just now noticing it.

"The wool is rough. I soak it a long time in vinegar water to make it softer. It is not ideal for a baby, but it is warm, and Germany is cold in winter, especially now, with everything is in ruins."

"This vinegar treatment is why the house smells like pickles! All this time I was hoping you were making fat German dills," Eitan remarks, laughing. It is a sound I have not heard in months. I tell him I'm sorry to disappoint him but have never pickled anything in my life and have no idea how to do it.

"Fortunately, I did not marry you because I expected you could cook," my husband teases.

As far as I can quietly determine, we are the only Jews in Bakersfield, which means there is no one to share Shabbat, Passover, Hanukkah and other celebrations, and no rabbi for the High Holy Days. Not preparing for these occasions creates a vacancy that affects me more deeply than the celebrations themselves fill me spiritually. Sarah and Rachael are growing up not knowing their G-d, Torah or their spiritual heritage, I lament, feeling that I am failing as their mother. A dense, heavy grief unlike anything I've ever felt settles over me, pushing me into a perpetual darkness I have no strength to resist. *Torah and Talmud have answers to this pain I feel, but it has been so long since I've been to shul I have no memories of hearing these comforting words*, I wail only to myself.

In the year I have been here I have made only one friend, Maya Stein, who is also German, and lives in the next block. I long to ask whether she is also Jewish but fear the question will end our new and fragile friendship. Maya's husband, Herman, also works for the railroad, and they move around a lot, going wherever he is needed.

"Most people in Bakersfield come from somewhere else and don't stay here long," she explains, offering me orange cake made from the fruit on the one tree in her yard, and iced tea. I have never gotten used to cold tea, but understand why, living in this dusty, parching heat, everyone drinks it.

"I don't blame anyone for leaving here if they can – this is not a pleasant place to live," I offer as we sit on her wide veranda which, other than the lonely orange tree beside her house, is the only shade she enjoys.

Maya's daughter, Alena, is between Sarah's and Rachael's ages and a sweet girl with good manners. Like my daughters, she is not supposed to speak German outside her family, but sometimes, when the girls are playing together, they forget themselves and slip into their mother language. All three children's English is good enough that no one mentions an accent or teases them, and they are making good marks in school. Overall, although I hate Bakersfield, which is mostly a barren desert with tall, strange-looking trees offering no protection from the hot sun, and could not be less like Germany, I cannot deny that both Sarah and Rachael seem happier here than in Elyria.

During the oppressive heat of our first summer, when no one wants to be outside in the sun, I teach all three girls how to knit. Sarah and Alena take to it right away, but Rachael isn't interested and prefers books. I try embroidery and then crocheting with her, but she doesn't like those either. She passes many hours on our porch reading and writing in a notebook she keeps under her mattress.

"She is of her own mind, and smarter than is good for her. Her teacher wants to skip her forward, which has already occurred once. I agreed, because she was bored and making trouble, but this move ahead makes her much younger than her classmates, and risks creating another kind of problem," I complain to Maya one afternoon as we sit on my small side porch away from the sun fanning ourselves.

At the end of an oppressively hot, dry and dusty summer unlike any I have ever experienced before, Maya announces her family is leaving Bakersfield.

"We are going to Los Angeles. It is much bigger than anywhere else we have lived, and I don't know what to expect," she admits. This news hits all of us hard, but me more than either Sarah or Rachael. Losing my only friend with no sure opportunity to make another one darkens my mood even more. Eitan, who has colleagues to talk with, doesn't understand the problem, until I explain that everyone goes to a Catholic or a protestant church, which is their way to have friends, but impossible for us.

"In Elyria people sometimes weren't nice to us, but we had friends at shul, so it didn't matter. Here we have no connections," I tell my husband, whose solution is to pretend to be Catholic, and go to that church, because Catholics also pray in a language that is not English.

"Catholics aren't much more popular than Jews, Eitan. But it doesn't matter, because I can't pretend to be someone I am not, so I am not going," I answer, firm that my mind cannot be changed. He finally tells me he is all out of ideas for helping me make friends or be happy but hopes eventually I figure these things out. What I cannot say, because he is tired of hearing it, is how much I still struggle with the question of whether the benefits of coming to America outweigh the losses I have suffered by leaving my home country and beloved family. Even after so many years, most days, my answer is "no". Despite the hardships Germany faces, I would rather be there, suffering together with my family than here in America, where I am outwardly comfortable, but inwardly miserable, consumed by guilt for having abandoned the people I love so dearly to a struggle they did not bring upon themselves, yet must deal with. *If I return to Germany, I am abandoning my daughters and husband to life without me... and I cannot live with that either,* I tell myself, wondering endlessly why the decision to come to America nearly twenty years ago continually thrusts me into an entrapped emotional darkness it is becoming harder and harder to push back from.

"I've been accepted at the normal school," Sarah calls out one late spring afternoon, as she enters our house, waving a letter.

"This means I can be a teacher!" she cheers, clapping her hands and smiling a happier smile than I have ever seen on her face. Achieving further education is very difficult for Jews and nearly impossible for women, and I cannot recall Sarah ever mentioning she had such a dream, much less intended to act on it. I always assumed she would remain living with us until she married and the news that she will be pursuing another goal to become a teacher, shocks me. It's not that I don't want her to follow her dreams, because I do want that for her. I just don't want her to make the same mistake I did and travel far away from her home and family to do it.

"How did you manage to do this?" I ask my elated eldest daughter, now planning to leave home at a mere sixteen years of age. If I had not allowed her, like her sister, to skip grades, I would have her for one more year at least. But they are both smart girls, and I didn't know what else to do.

"I lied – about my age, my name and my religion. I changed my name from Sarah Rosenblum to Sally Rose and checked protestant when the application asked about my religious preference," Sarah answers, revealing no shame at this successful deception. Horrified, I quickly realize that with Eitan's dark red hair, light brown eyes, and a name that isn't obviously German or Jewish, Sarah might be lucky enough that no one will question her background.

"That you deny who you are breaks my heart, Sarah..."

"I'm sorry, Mama, but if I admitted I was a German Jew I would not be able to do this. Suspicion of Germans and hatred of Jews is more widespread than ever, and it might never get better. It's just easier this way."

I cannot argue with my daughter's reasoning, and am happy she shows such self-confidence, but I don't have to like what she plans to do, or be proud of her for having the courage to lie in order to do it. I fear for her being out in the world, away from Eitan and me, and eventually cannot stop myself from saying all this. Her face shows her hurt.

"I wish you could just be proud and happy for me, Mama, and let everything else go," she begs.

Sarah's successful deception doesn't escape Rachael's notice, and I overhear many conversations about this passing between them. Among other things, Rachael is very upset about being left behind with "our sad and withdrawn mother" which is how she describes me. My endless lament that allowing Sarah to go away is inviting trouble wears on everyone, but I cannot help my worry. Eventually, Eitan reminds me that Sarah will be going whether we like it or not, even if we forbid it, and my constant fretting is only making it less likely she will ever want to return.

"Your sister is my only friend now that Maya is gone. We knit together and I tell her about my life in Germany. Remembering makes me happy, and there is no one else who likes hearing my stories," I tell Rachael one afternoon a few days before Sarah is leaving. Rachael appears to be listening but stays silent. Later, I hear her recounting this to her older sister, asking how to respond to my musings.

"Just listen, Rach. She doesn't expect a response," I overhear my older daughter advising my younger one.

"I won't be that far away. I'll try to get back as often as possible," Sarah promises on the morning she leaves for normal school in a town two hundred and fifty miles away, with the strange name "San Jose" which, like much of California, is another language instead of familiar English. Both Rachael and I know this is an empty assurance and Sarah will quickly become caught up in the new life awaiting her, rarely looking back.

My sister-in-law, Irina, now writes only once or twice a year. I fear the threads holding me together with my German family are so thin and fragile they could easily break and if that happens, I will break apart with them. Taking her sister's advice, Rachael doesn't respond to these laments, but I sense she is quickly tiring of my increasing emotional neediness and is beginning to pull away.

"I don't want you doing things for me I can do for myself. This will give you more time to do what you want to do – what makes you happy, Mama... please think about that, not about me," Rachael insists. But with her father gone many days at once and Sarah's letters exuding joy over her new life, instead of finding pleasure in more time for myself, life becomes less and less interesting.

Trying to cheer me during one of his rare evenings at home, Eitan casually mentions how lucky we are to be in a place where no one knows us as Jews or Germans because across America both are becoming even more unpopular.

"There are so few Jews no one notices, or if they do, they don't care. Ask any Chinese, Italian or Irish person and they'll tell you the real problem is no one likes immigrants, even when they are needed to do important jobs," Eitan says, adding that as long as his trains keep going where they are supposed to go, he is safe.

Rachael, whose English is only distinguishable from a native speaker if one listens very closely, asks her father whether being Jewish is as big a problem in Bakersfield as I claim. He admits that he isn't sure what locals think about Jews and has no interest in finding out. I point out that ignoring a possible problem doesn't make it go away and is also dangerous.

"There's no point in thinking about this, Nathalie. We can't move somewhere else right now… maybe later, but not now," he says, trying to appease both my ongoing sorrow and his overconfident daughter's curiosity.

"The only place for us in America is the place we make for ourselves and that is very hard when we live in the middle of nowhere with nothing but dust, wind and constant heat. If you die, there would be no minion to say Mourner's Kaddish for you, and no one to sit Shiva with me. I would be alone with my grief. Without Shabbat, every day is the same. Nothing matters anymore. I will never be at home in my life again, and when I think of this, which is always, I cry until I ache. There is no place for me here, Eitan. I am sorry – I have tried as much as I can." After exhausting myself into frustrated tears, I go to the bedroom, leaving my husband and our younger daughter staring at each other.

More and more, Eitan loses patience with my spells of bleak hopelessness. Although he has tried, his efforts to provide relief for my deep sadness and chronic upset are futile. He tells me my mind is wrapped like coiled wire on a spool, going around and around, repeating the same thoughts over and over again, growing tighter and tighter each time. He says he knows he has failed me but has tried his best and doesn't know what else he can do. His admission adds guilt onto my ever-present sadness, and for his sake, I know I must find a way to hide my all-enveloping darkness. Slowly, I become clever at making him think I am happy even when I am not. I do not know how long I can keep pretending this, but I convince myself that, for right now, I'm trying as hard as I can, and this is enough.

"If I go to Germany, America will refuse to let me back. I think that might not be so bad, but Irina says there is no Germany anymore to return to… that I would not know it as home because that home no longer exists," I tell Eitan during one of the increasingly rare times he asks me what I am thinking, and I answer him honestly.

"You romanticize Germany, Nathalie, remembering it as it was when you left, and that is what you want to go back to. The war ruined everything and that Germany is gone; it only exists in your memory, and you cause yourself great distress wishing otherwise. Listen to Irina… she says the truth, my husband insists." I shrug, not confiding the truth that with Rachael nearly grown, Sarah happily successful pursuing her dreams and my husband able to get along on his own, I feel more and more useless and less able to find meaning in a life where no one needs me.

Chapter Twelve
פרק שתים עשרה

San Francisco
Summer, 1971

*No family is perfect, but family is family,
and the ties that bind don't break.*

"Have you spoken to Sally lately," my dad inquires as he is attacking Herlinda's fabulous guacamole and homemade tortilla chips while we wait for the rest of our meal to reheat.

"Not for several days. Why?" I answer, munching on a chip.

"She called last night, wondering whether you are still working on the diaries," he says, handing me a glass filled with my half of the beer we agreed to split.

"They're coming along, getting more and more sad. World War I and the Spanish flu epidemic took their toll, antisemitism was on the rise, and Germans clearly weren't popular in this country. My grandmother's world wasn't a happy, hopeful one. They moved from Ohio to Bakersfield, which is a pit of dirt and dust now and was probably worse then. It can't have been an improvement over Elyria, but there's much more to go through before I'll have a full picture."

"That might be a way to approach Sally. Instead of asking her about what the diaries contain, ask her what she remembers about a particular time, like moving from Elyria to Bakersfield. That had to be a culture shock, and would be a great way to open the conversation."

"I can't imagine anyone living in Bakersfield voluntarily, I add."

"My guess is moving there had something to do with the area becoming a railroad hub for agriculture in the Central Valley, which would've been an advancement opportunity for your grandfather. After the first world war, the railroads reverted to private ownership and quickly expanded in search of greater profits," my dad casually explains, moving chopped up lettuce, tomatoes, and shredded cheese from the refrigerator to the table, then handing me hot pads to take a bubbling casserole out of the oven.

"I'll call her tonight. Maybe I can go down this weekend," I say, filling a taco shell.

"Let me know what you decide. If the schedule works, maybe Adrian would be interested in taking in a ball game while you're gone." Hearing this, I stop eating and stare at my father, starting to comment, then change my mind. We finish the meal talking about who's going to challenge Joe Alioto in San Francisco's upcoming mayor's race, the FDR biography my dad just finished reading, and questioning whether, had he lived, Roosevelt would've dropped the bomb in Hiroshima to end the war in the Pacific. My father has his doubts.

"Why would he order it developed, if he wasn't going to use it?" I ask.

"We were fighting a global war on two fronts, against vicious enemies, one of which was an imminent threat to the continental United States. It would have been a severe dereliction of duty for our president to not develop the best weapons arsenal possible. Roosevelt was sworn to protect this country, and that included supporting an arms buildup, but that doesn't mean he would've used every weapon at his disposal."

While my father clears the table, I call my aunt and ask whether it is convenient for me to visit over the coming weekend.

"Of course you can, sweetheart. I'm always thrilled to see you. Mick will love showing off his new chicken coop. Our house needs a lot of work, but that coop's fancier than a Beverly Hills pool house," Aunt Sally chuckles.

"Mick won't mind?"

"He spends most of his time in his recliner watching television through his eyelids. The biggest inconvenience for him will be remembering to close the bathroom door; otherwise, he'll barely notice you're here."

"It's a six-hour drive, so I won't get there until Saturday afternoon, if that's OK."

"Come Friday. There's an estate auction I've been looking forward to on Saturday morning. We can go together, but need to get there early in case there's something worth bidding on. Afterwards, we'll eat lunch somewhere."

For as long as I can remember, my aunt's favorite pastime has been going to estate auctions, amassing an incoherent collection of things she doesn't need just because she thinks they're a good deal. Not wanting Mick to know the extent of her addiction, she pays out a fair amount of cash in monthly rent on storage lockers scattered throughout the greater Los Angeles area. She has a network of friends on call to help with her haul, if need-be. I've been with her when we've gone directly from an auction to renting yet another storage facility to accommodate her latest good deal.

"Somebody can sort it all out after I die," she laughs whenever I ask about her eventual plans for this accumulation of what looks to me like junk rather than anything of actual value.

"I can do Friday, but it'll be weekend traffic. It might be close to dinner by the time I get there."

"That's fine – we'll wait. Mick can make a tuna casserole. That always keeps," my aunt who hates to cook promises.

"I might get a late start; it'll be easier if I stop on the way," I quickly respond, wiggling my way out of one of Mick's infamous casseroles, which are generally unfit for human consumption. The tuna concoction is especially bad. My guess is he gets a deal on the fish because it was hanging on the dock a little too long.

"Don't forget to bring your knitting," Sally reminds me.

"Never go anywhere without it. The pattern I showed you isn't turning out exactly as I expected, but it looks nice, especially the color. You can tell me what you think," I answer.

"Drive carefully, sweetheart… can't wait to see you. And love to Paul," she says, hanging up.

"She sends her love, and doesn't sound particularly anxious about me coming," I tell my dad.

"I've reminded her several times that she doesn't have to answer any questions she doesn't want to answer and can always talk to me about whatever you uncover. Once that finally sunk in, she seemed to relax. But she loves you too much not to be excited to see you, no matter what," my father declares, starting the dishwasher, then walking into the sitting room. I can't help asking when he started cleaning up the kitchen, and he claims Herlinda finally put her foot down and showed him how to run the dishwasher so she isn't greeted by a sink full of dirty dishes every morning and can spend her time on more important things, like ironing his bed sheets.

"I'm going to read for a while. You're welcome to watch television in my den if you want to," he offers. Sitting in his favorite chair beside the window, he glances up to see the city's night lights just beginning to flicker in the distance.

"I think I'll knit – maybe go to bed early since I'm going to drive to

Los Angeles on Friday," I answer, sitting down on the sofa and reaching for the raffia knitting bag my aunt crafted for me when I was ten years old.

"Pretty color," my dad remarks as I take out the periwinkle blue and white wool shawl I've been working on.

"It's for Aunt Sally – something I decided to do on the fly when I was in Santa Barbara. The yarn is spun from wool and silk… really smooth to work with, but the pattern's a little tricky. I probably should've used a smaller needle. But why your sudden interest in a knitting project?" When my dad doesn't respond, I look up and see him engrossed in his book, not listening to anything I've said.

As my needles weave the yarn back and forth through the loops, I sink into the deeply meditative state the repetitive practice brings, which never fails to clear my mind of whatever junk it sometimes insists on holding onto. My thoughts light on my left-handed aunt's patience as she taught me how to knit – a skill Emily was never interested in mastering. It took several tries before my aunt realized teaching me how to knit left-handed would be easier than battling my right-handedness, and it was, until I was ten or eleven years old and wanted to learn how to read patterns, which are written for right-handed knitters.

"The pattern is a guide we follow, but we never really know how it will come out, and it won't necessarily be the way you expect. Just keep knitting and don't worry about it. If it doesn't work, unravel it and start over. You'll figure it out eventually," she smiled as she walked me through the frustration of transposing patterns.

"Knitting is an act of love… a deeply personal revelation about yourself, so it's important to use natural fibers you can trust to be themselves, not synthetic ones that might look nice but aren't real. The yarn must be real and true to convey a message of love that is real and true," she instructed. To my ten-year-old ears, this advice sounded like she was telling herself a nonsense story I pretended to understand but had no idea what she was talking about.

"Choose your colors very carefully because the colors are a statement. Choose colors that speak clearly and be sure they say what you want them to say. Never bother knitting something intended to be an ordinary statement," she advised.

Several knitting years passed before any of this made sense to me, but when it finally did, I realized she was imparting wisdom that a mother normally would impart to her daughter, because that was the bond holding us together. Now we are facing something bigger than either of us can fully grasp, and neither of us knows where it will lead. For this reason alone, she deserves to be wrapped in the love I knit into this shawl, stitch by stitch, the way she taught me, as a little girl, to put yarn over needle, making a loop and pulling the strand through again and again. An unexpected tear falls down my cheek.

Kissing me good-bye shortly after lunch on Friday, Adrian says he plans on having the next translation finished by the time I return Monday, unless he and my dad decide to go to the third game in the three-game series between the Giants and the Cincinnati Reds.

"Fat chance that won't happen," I smile.

With Berkeley in my rear-view mirror, I begin wondering what, if anything, my dad has told my aunt about Adrian? *I guess I'll find out soon enough,* I think, hoping it hasn't come up. On the other hand, over the years, my dad has relied too heavily upon his sister-in-law to allow any secrets between them, especially as concerns what's going on in my life, so she probably knows about Adrian and is waiting for me to say something.

A few hours later, with the television blasting and Mick snoring in his recliner in the other room, my aunt and I are sitting in the kitchen eating honey lemon cake.

"The TV is really loud. Is Mick getting hard of hearing?" I ask.

"Only when he wants to be. He says he needs the television loud enough to hear it when he's sleeping, and that's not an argument I'm ever going to win," she chuckles. Then, turning serious, she asks why I'm living in Berkeley instead of San Francisco with my dad.

"It's easier on us both. He doesn't have to worry about my coming and going and I don't have to worry that he's worried," I answer through a mouthful of my favorite cake. She takes her time responding.

"Paul mentioned something about you spending a lot of time with the translator," she says, looking straight at me. *Here it comes,* I grimace.

"He's a nice guy and he's being very helpful."

"Paul seems to like him…"

"They enjoy going to baseball games…"

"You don't have to tell me anything you're not ready to tell me, Natalie, but for god's sake, don't get into another mess like the last time. That damned near killed me. I was years getting over it."

"You and a lot of other people… and in the last month every one of them has reminded me of this."

"We all want you to settle down with someone, sweetie – it just has to be the right someone, that's all," Sally smiles, patting my hand.

"As far as you and dad are concerned, I'm not sure that someone exists," I mumble, finishing the large helping of cake.

"Let me show you my knitting," I say a few moments later, changing the subject as I reach for my yarn bag. Aunt Sally looks at the shawl, feels the stitch tension and checks the pattern before commenting.

"You're doing a nice job on this. Maybe the needle should've been a little smaller, but this works. Do you know what you're going to do with it?"

"Give it to you," I smile. My aunt bursts into tears.

"You taught me to knit twenty-five years ago. I thought it was about time I made you something besides potholders," I explain as my aunt blows her nose following a reaction I never expected.

"I love those potholders, Natalie. I still have every one of them."

"And I still have every sweater, hat, scarf and pair of leg warmers you ever knit me. I'm saving them for my own little girl someday."

"Meanwhile, my little girl is growing up..."

"That kind of happened a long time ago, Aunt Sally." Then I say something I never expected to come out of my mouth.

"If I ever get married again, will you crochet me a wedding dress?"

"I tried crocheting one the last time and you know how that turned out... both the dress and the marriage were a failure."

"Point taken. If I. Magnin's hadn't been willing to sell us that floor sample at the last minute which, luckily, fit me, I would've walked down the aisle wrapped in a bolt of tulle and a bed sheet."

"I never understood why you weren't more upset about it being two weeks before the wedding and no wedding dress. I was practically hysterical, Herlinda was on her way to a nervous breakdown, and you didn't seem to care. I'd followed the crochet pattern more carefully than devout Christians follow the Bible and it still didn't come out like it was supposed to. That's when I knew the marriage wouldn't last," my aunt reflects.

"Well, if I ever do it again, I can assure you it'll last."

"You look like you'll do it again."

"How can you possibly know that?"

"It's obvious you're falling in love, Natalie. Any fool can see that, and I'm no fool," my aunt declares.

"How, exactly, does falling in love look, Aunt Sally?" I challenge, not sure I want to know how something so personal can be so obvious that others easily pick up on it.

"It's impossible to describe. It's something that's either there or it isn't, and Herlinda and I both agreed it wasn't there when you were preparing to marry what's his name. You just didn't have the look of love and were acting like your wedding was nothing more than a very expensive prom date." My response is silence, accompanied by an intense stare.

"I've obviously missed something. When was it you became a mind reader?" I eventually respond.

"When Emily was born, obviously," my aunt answers, with a devilish grin. I continue staring at her.

"You've had a long drive, and we have a big day tomorrow – it's bedtime," she finally says, standing up to clear the table, then hugging me tight before reminding me the bedroom that has always been mine is waiting for me.

"I unraveled the entire wedding dress and remade it into the cover on your bed. It came out beautifully. I've been thinking about giving it to you," she says as we walk down the hall.

The estate auction is in Pasadena, a little more than an hour away. I offer to drive and my aunt, the undisputed queen of fender benders, thankfully agrees.

"I have a friend who'll come back with a van if I get something we can't fit in the car," she says confidently, adding that mostly she's interested in the antique china-head doll collection that's included in the first auction.

"We're going to more than one?"

"Maybe – depends on how the first one goes," my aunt winks.

"I still have the doll you fixed up for me when I was little. It's on my dresser in my bedroom at home."

"If these are in anywhere near decent shape, I could fix up one for little Charlotte… or donate some to a charity auction… or save them for when you have a daughter. Doll clothes are a fun way to use up scraps of leftover fabric and swatches of lace," Sally explains.

It turns out she falls in love with the dolls and successfully bids on all ten of them, dropping over a thousand dollars. I ask her whether they're really worth that much.

"To me, they are," she smiles as we very carefully place the fragile purchase into the car.

"There's a new Mexican restaurant with a lovely outdoor patio a couple miles down Pasadena Boulevard that would be perfect for lunch," she suggests, knowing I live for authentic Mexican food.

A half-hour later, after we're seated under a large red umbrella near the outdoor fountain, my aunt shocks me by ordering a margarita.

"I didn't know you drank margaritas," I remark, surprised, because I've never known her to drink at all.

"This is a special occasion, and I'm not driving," she smiles. After my iced tea and her cocktail arrive, she takes off her sunglasses, then inhales a deep breath.

"I know you have questions, Natalie…"

"I have a lot of questions, which may, or may not, be answered when the translations are finished. Mostly, I'd like to better understand my mother, because right now, I don't have the slightest clue about who she was and why she did some of the things she did."

"If I understood Charlotte, I'd have been awarded a Nobel Prize for psychological insights."

"I don't think they award a Nobel for that," I remind her.

"Regardless, I'd win some kind of award. The truth is, I don't think anybody understood her. She was masterful at keeping everyone off balance and on guard… I seriously doubt she understood herself," my mother's older sister answers, watching herself draw circles on the tablecloth with her finger.

"Dad explained how she left me with you and signed on as a Red Cross nurse. But you already had Emily and a job. Weren't you angry about that?"

"Furious, but not about taking care of you, which was the good part. Jane offered to help, and Paul hired Herlinda, who was a heaven-sent angel willing to do anything that needed doing. The house was big enough that we weren't overcrowded, and we knew we could make it work. But there was no question in anybody's mind that when the war finally ended and Charlotte returned there was going to be hell to pay. I thought about it all the time… how would she explain herself to her husband and a daughter who had no idea who she was? And how in the hell was I supposed to suddenly give up being your mother? You weren't somebody's pet gerbil I was looking after until its owner returned – you were the baby I held in my arms moments after you were born and felt an instant attachment to. You'd grown into a very happy little girl, and Charlotte had no right to disrupt that, but I had no way to stop her. I lost a lot of sleep worrying about it."

"What did dad say?"

"Not a lot. He figured Charlotte would come back eventually but didn't have any more idea about what would happen than I did. You were attached to both Jane and me, but more to me. I was the only mother you knew; we were a tight bond, and you and Emily were inseparable. She couldn't just suddenly stop being your big sister. and I couldn't just take Emily and walk away from you, shredding the only life you knew. Paul and Jane both understood this and worried about it as much as I did. We had a problem none of us could figure out how to solve."

"You must've been terrified..."

"Terrified and mad as a hornet. Charlotte couldn't just walk right back into our lives – mine, Emily's, Paul's, Jane's – and yours too, and claim you, expecting everything to be fine and life to carry on as before. But knowing her, I felt sure that was exactly what she was going to do, and when she found out everything had changed while she was gone, then what? Neither Paul nor I was sure what Charlotte might do, but agreed we had to protect you. And I was very sure that I would never give you up to a stranger, which is who Charlotte had become – to all of us. Making everything worse, if possible, was that, at one time, Charlotte and I were very close, and I missed my sister." My aunt's eyes fill with tears.

"Dad's been vague on the details. What happened when Charlotte finally returned?" My aunt takes a large gulp of her margarita, allowing a bright pink alcohol flush to light up her face as small beads of perspiration erupt along her hairline. I've never seen my aunt this nervous.

"You know, even after all these years, it's hard to talk about..." she begins. I reach for her hand, gripping it tightly.

"When the war in Europe ended, things changed quickly. Paul had been remodeling the Fairmont Hotel in the city and in partial payment they offered him the penthouse apartment, with a roof garden and those wonderful views. The only hold-up was waiting for the war in the Pacific to end. Nobody thought Japan would surrender, but three months later, it finally did. No longer having to worry that we might get bombed into extinction at any moment was a huge relief, and we began believing in a future. Paul had a job waiting for Charlie when the war ended and sold the house we were all living in to he and Jane." I nod, sipping my tea.

"Mick stayed in the Army to help liberate the German concentration camps, so didn't come back for several months, and when he did, he was in pretty bad shape. The army sent him to a treatment center at Fort Sam Houston. It took nearly a year to get his head straightened out – to the extent Mick's head has ever been straight, which is debatable," she says, in a rare admission of her difficulties with her husband.

"Paul and I both wanted as little disruption as possible, and since Mick wasn't coming back right away Emily and I, along with Herlinda, went ahead moved into the city with him. I enrolled Emily in Regina Coeli

Academy, where you would be going the following year, and we waited."

"No one heard from my mother?"

"After nearly a year with no word Paul contacted the International Red Cross and was told she had only worked with them for a few months. They suggested that, if she was still alive, she could be helping treat concentration camp survivors, or working for another relief organization somewhere in Europe. Otherwise, they offered no concrete leads to her whereabouts. We both believed she was still alive and would show up eventually, which was like waiting for the other shoe to drop. I knew I was going to have to deal with Mick's return at some point, and expected that would be difficult. Most days I tried not to think about Charlotte at all."

"The entire situation must've been really hard…" I comment. My aunt nods her agreement, murmuring something to the effect that there are no words for how hard it was.

"One afternoon, a few months after the letter from the Red Cross, Charlotte called Paul's office. She was in San Francisco and asked him to pick her up someplace – I can't remember where. He settled her into a hotel, explained that a lot had changed, and she couldn't expect things to be like they were before she left… said the best thing would be for him to rent her an apartment for a while everything got sorted out. She became very upset and days later, on a Saturday afternoon when we were at Jane and Charlie's trying to figure out what to do next, Charlotte rang the doorbell…"

"Huge shock…" I interject.

"Yes and no. Jane said she'd been expecting Charlotte to show up at the house sooner rather than later. Emily, who was old enough to understand what was happening had been insisting that she'd kidnap you and run away forever if Charlotte tried to take you away. Everyone was already upset, and the shock of seeing Charlotte wasn't as much as you might think. She was bone weary and far too thin, yet exotically beautiful….like there was an electric aura surrounding her. She was alive in a way I'd never seen before and I just stood there staring at her, unable to say anything. You hid behind me holding Emily's hand, and Tommy hid behind Jane. Charlotte asked to come in, and then called to you, saying she was your mother. You started screaming and ran up the stairs. Emily and I followed you while Paul, Jane, and Charlie showed Charlotte into the living room. She became very agitated, and I could hear her raising her voice, lashing out at Paul and Jane. Eventually, Paul asked Jane to go into the kitchen to make some coffee. Charlie followed, carrying Tommy, and told Jane to go upstairs and send me down to try to calm Charlotte, then take Tommy, you, and Emily down the back stairs and go in the car for ice cream. Jane reminded him that she didn't know how to drive a car, and he barked at her to figure it out. You have no memory of this?" My aunt asks me.

"None whatever... honestly."

"Well, thank God for that. You needed an axe to cut through the tension, especially after I went back downstairs to try reasoning with Charlotte."

"Where was Charlie?"

"He stayed by the kitchen telephone..."

"She was that bad?"

"Worse every minute. She was paranoid, screaming obscenities at Paul, accusing me of stealing her daughter and her husband – totally out of control. When she started throwing things, Charlie called the police. It was awful, and I was terrified, but Jane, ever calm, just kept circling the block, waiting for Charlie to give an all-clear signal. The real miracle is they figured all this out on the fly and Jane didn't wreck the car, or worse."

"So, Charlotte went to jail?"

"Paul prevailed on the police to take her to the hospital instead. She was admitted to the psych ward, which solved the immediate problem, but left us all wrung out, with no idea what to do next. The answer came a week or so later when her doctor suggested she be placed in an in-patient facility to receive intensive psychotherapy for her war-trauma depression. Paul arranged for her to go to an upscale rest and recuperate, talk therapy facility in Santa Rosa, but she didn't respond to this treatment plan and eventually shock treatments were recommended. Paul and I resisted this option, until we had no other choice."

"She had electro-shock treatments?"

"A lot of them. Paul had her transferred to a place in San Leandro that specialized in cutting-edge mental health treatments, and once she was there, they recommended waiting six months before visiting her, to see how she responded. What amazed me was that during all this time you never asked about who Charlotte was or why she showed up claiming to be your mother, and amazingly, Emily didn't ask a lot of questions either. You both seemed to write the whole thing off as a bad Saturday afternoon, and forgot about it. We tried to live every day as normally as possible, and Paul bought you and Emily a puppy as a distraction."

"I remember getting the puppy, which was pretty exciting. But everything else is a blank."

"Do you remember going to visit Charlotte?"

"Not really… maybe vaguely if I try hard enough, but certainly no details."

"When things seemed settled down, the doctors suggested Paul and I bring you to visit Charlotte. Neither of us thought it was a good idea, but the doctor convinced us to try. We told you we were visiting someone who knew you as a baby and wanted to see you again, banking on your not remembering what Charlotte looked like when you saw her a few months earlier. It was a warm day and while we were waiting in the garden you picked her a little bouquet of flowers. The attendant brought her out and sat her next to the bench where we were sitting. Paul asked how she was feeling, and she didn't answer. We weren't sure whether she hadn't heard him or was just fixated on you, which made me very uneasy, to be perfectly honest. I didn't know what she might do. You walked over and handed her the flowers. She took them, looked at them, then threw them on the ground and signaled the attendant to return her to her room. Seeing you stand there looking at the flowers on the ground was the saddest thing I've ever seen, Natalie. Paul reached out for you, and you climbed onto his lap. 'I don't think that lady likes me' you said. Paul told you she was sick and couldn't help it. You turned to me and said you didn't want to come to visit that lady again and I promised you didn't have to. Paul said we'd go for ice cream and if we hurried, we'd get back to the city in time for one trolley ride before bedtime. You were happy with that plan, and we left."

"I guess that explains my therapeutic relationship with the San Francisco trolley system. But I honestly don't remember any of this."

"Thank God you don't. I wish I didn't," my aunt says, using her napkin to catch a tear rolling down her face. That's when I notice that sometime during this conversation a second margarita has appeared in front of her, and that we haven't touched the gorgeous guacamole we ordered, which has been sitting so long it's turning slightly brown.

"I hope you understand this is a two-margarita conversation," she half smiles, taking a big gulp before continuing.

"The doctors recommended against visiting again for at least a month, but Paul and I agreed that taking you for another visit at any time was a very bad idea. I tried visiting her a couple of times and it always ended badly. She accused me of stealing her daughter, turning her daughter against her, and so on. It was more than I could take, so I stopped going. Mick was due to be released from his treatment and wanted to go back to Los Angeles. I said I couldn't leave you and he finally agreed to work in Oakland for the time being. We found a place across the bay and little by little, I began going back and forth. Sometimes I stayed in the city, sometimes Jane came for a day or two, and sometimes you and Emily came over to Oakland. Herlinda was the steady hand through all this – even agreeing to the puppy, which really was asking a lot. When you began school and were thriving, I began thinking about going back to teaching."

"How long was Charlotte in the hospital?"

"I can't remember, but three or four years at least."

"Seriously? What did they do to her all that time?"

"I don't really know. Shock treatments, medication trials, psychotherapy are three things Paul mentioned. Mick said that's what they did at the place where he was and kept insisting that Charlotte could snap out of it if she wanted to, but obviously, she didn't. He wouldn't cut her any slack, and I didn't know whether to believe him or not. Paul and I both felt you should not see her again until you were old enough to better understand the situation. We figured you had to know your family was different from your friends' families, but you never asked any questions, so we had no idea what you thought, or how you felt about any of it."

"I don't remember ever wondering about anything pertaining to the family. If I did, it didn't matter much, because I was happy."

"Paul was firm that Charlotte could not return to a family situation, because he didn't trust she would remain mentally stable. His thinking was in terms of what to do with her when she was well enough to leave the hospital."

"What did happen?"

"She was eventually released and decided to get a graduate nursing degree at San Francisco General, then moved to Santa Barbara and got a job. She did well with her studies and managed fine on her own, as long as no one tried to get close to her in any kind of emotional sense. It was all over between us in terms of any kind of a sister relationship, so I kept my distance."

"So, she eventually got well."

"I wouldn't say well so much as she became functional – more or less. Don't you remember anything at all about this time either?"

"Not really. Dad and I talked about it occasionally over the years. I saw her a few times, but only briefly – for a treat someplace, maybe lunch once or twice. He encouraged me to try to get to know her, but never forced the issue, and I had no real interest. I had you, Jane, dad, Emily, Herlinda, Dominic, my cocker spaniel, and even Tommy, although I didn't much like him. It wasn't like I was lacking emotional warmth or love. I didn't need another mother when I already had three perfectly good ones plus a loving father, faithful dog, older sister and even a pain-in-the ass brother, sort of. If you think about it, that's more than most kids have."

"I still worry that Charlotte abandoning you left a lasting wound. We all hoped that wouldn't happen but sometimes I don't see how it could not have impacted your life, and not in a good way – even if you aren't aware of it."

"If it did, it can't be too bad. I'm doing fine."

"You don't think marrying Liam had anything to do with trying to get someone who was totally incapable of loving anyone to love you? It would be finishing the script Charlotte began writing for your life when she left you."

"I married Liam because I wanted to have sex. That had nothing to do with my mother or trying to get someone to love me." The wide-eyed look on my aunt's face when I say this says I've fired off a good one.

"I had the stupid idea that I had to be married before having sex. If I hadn't been such a tight-ass, Liam and I could've gotten it out of our systems and then gone our separate ways. My strongest memory of my wedding night is sitting in the bathtub thinking my father had just paid out many thousands of dollars for me to have an experience that lasted about fifteen minutes and wasn't nearly as great as I thought it would be."

"I really wish you would've discussed it with me, Natalie. I might've been able to help you make a different decision, my aunt says, trying to suppress a smile.

"I thought about coming to you, but I didn't know how to start the conversation. Emily said you weren't great on 'the talk' and yelled a lot."

"Emily was pregnant, unmarried and hadn't finished college. Of course I yelled a lot. I was upset."

By now our food has been in front of us for ten minutes, untouched. Since the greatest of all sins is letting good Mexican food go to waste, I ask for another iced tea, and we both start eating.

"I hope I answered some of your questions," my aunt says, chewing on a beef burrito.

"And I hope talking about these things hasn't upset you too much," I answer.

"Mostly, I feel unburdened. Paul helped me understand that there was a lot we never talked through, for various reasons… being overwhelmed with everything or because we were afraid of upsetting Charlotte, and there is no earthly reason to allow her to hold us hostage any longer. After thinking about it, I decided he's right," my aunt says, flashing a two-margarita smile, then turning serious again.

"Exactly where are you with the translations?" she asks.

"Adrian's working on one written after the family arrived in Bakersfield. After that, there seems to be a several year gap, and the next ones are probably written by my mother."

"Bakersfield was very difficult."

"How?"

"I finished high school and went on to college. Charlotte, understandably, resented being left behind to deal with our increasingly depressed mother. I didn't blame her for being upset with me, but I wasn't going to give up my dream of being a teacher, either. But this is a conversation for another time. Right now, we need to get going. Emily's bringing little Charlotte tomorrow. I want to show her the dolls – let her pick out her favorite for me to start working on. She's not as interested in knitting as you were at her age, but she likes embroidery, which you never did. Mick's grilling his special T-bone steaks and foil-wrapped baked potatoes, and I'll do another lemon cake."

"I haven't seen little Charlotte in two, maybe three years. She probably doesn't remember me."

"She remembers you, because Emily talks about Aunt Natalie all the time."

"Sounds wonderful – all of it," I smile, truly meaning it, especially the part about Mick's Sunday meal choice not being tuna casserole.

"I need to stop at the greengrocer and pick up something for you. Maybe a couple artichokes or an eggplant sound good?"

"Either one, or both, sound fine," I answer, picking up the check. After leaving a generous tip and throwing a handful of coins in the courtyard fountain, making secret wishes, we walk out of the restaurant and down Pasadena Boulevard arm in arm.

Chapter Thirteen
פרק שלושה עשר

Los Angeles
Mid-summer, 1971

Truth is like the sun – you can hide from it,
but it always breaks through eventually…

"I'm going to need some time before I can talk about the Bakersfield years," my aunt says. We are sitting in her recently repainted kitchen eating breakfast before I return to San Francisco after a wonderful visit. The sun is shining directly onto my corn flakes swimming in milk, and we're both feeling a little sad about saying good-bye.

"There's no hurry – take all the time you need," I assure her.

"I kept a diary of my own back then. It's the only thing from that time I saved, and I'd forgotten about it until you started talking about finding diaries. I took mine out of the box on the top shelf of my closet, not even sure whether I wanted to open it. The binding is coming loose, the pages stick together, the ink is faded, and it smells old, just like me…"

"You're not old, Aunt Sally."

"When my diary is so obviously old, it's pretty hard to believe I'm not old, too," she smiles.

"That little notebook holds the stories of my past… the details of my life I want to forget, to pretend never existed, but at the time believed were important and worth remembering. The pages have all of that… what was real and what I only pretended was real… still pretend is real, even though I know most of it is not. But it doesn't matter. The illusions hold me together, and I can't let them go…"

"You're making it sound like your life has been stolen from you…"

"It feels that way, Natalie. I have been forced into deciding how much I want to remember, and wondering whether questions with no answers, except the ones I make up in my own head, are worth asking. I'm just not sure I can go there. Burying it all is so much easier... so much safer." I sense my aunt doesn't expect a response and I don't offer one.

"The thing is, sweetheart, sometimes the truth extracts a huge price. I have to figure out whether I can afford to pay it. I know you deserve explanations, but they won't come cheap – they'll cost you something, too – and there are no refunds, because once you know something, you can't unknow it. I'm not sure how to prepare you for all this..."

"Keep this in perspective, Aunt Sally. We're only talking about a little family history. We're not a family of mobsters whose pictures are plastered on post office walls, or cold war spies the FBI is hunting down because somebody sold nuclear secrets to the Russians... at least I don't think that's what we're dealing with."

"Sometimes it feels that way, Natalie. I'm so afraid you're going to be hurt by all this, and there won't be anything I can do to stop it..."

"This isn't making any sense to me. How, exactly, am I going to be hurt?"

"You're going to find out things about your heritage..."

"For example?"

"Your grandmother was a deeply conflicted, tortured woman, not a loving mother who baked cookies and read bedtime stories. She and our father disagreed about life in America. He felt we should blend in, and she wanted us to be proud Germans, yet believed being German in America was dangerous... that if people knew who we were... knew everything about us, they would hate us. She passed this fear on to Charlotte and me. Obviously, I can't speak for my sister, but I do know it's taken me years of concerted effort to put all that behind me... to the extent I've been able to do it at all. Even after all this time, some days are still better than others. There's no question this affected Charlotte deeply also. To blend in, we both were forced to deny our heritage and live as who we weren't instead of who we were. You have no idea how difficult living a life of lies is... constantly hiding from yourself, wondering when you will be found out and what the consequences will be when it finally happens. I learned to live with it, but Charlotte was more deeply affected. She struggled in ways I didn't understand. I wasn't too surprised she eventually developed lifetime mental problems." As she is speaking my aunt's breath grows shallow and her forehead begins to glisten.

"I really, truly hate how much this is upsetting you, Aunt Sally, but I still don't see how any of it can hurt me, or you. What you're talking about is ancient history... nobody cares about Germans, Italians, Irish, or anybody else enough to target them."

"You'll just have to trust me when I tell you there is much more to this story, and unearthing it is taking a huge risk. Your life could be upended in ways you never saw coming… never even thought possible. Once that happens, there won't be any way to right the family ship again,"

"I'm in it now, Aunt Sally, and we'll just have to deal with it. And just so you know, I'm not worried about the family ship being in danger of sinking. You and I both know Dad would never let that happen," I smile, gathering up my breakfast dishes.

"Let me know you're back home safely," my aunt reminds me, gripping me in a hug so tight I can't breathe.

"Anything that hurts you, hurts me worse, Natalie. It reflects my failure to protect you."

"You can't protect me from life, Aunt Sally. I'm all grown up now and you've prepared me for adulthood just fine. I can cope, so be happy about that, and let me deal with the rest." With that proclamation, I kiss her goodbye and walk to the car. Pulling out of the driveway, I decide to return to San Francisco along the narrow, coast highway. It's a longer, more congested route, but the rhythmic ocean landscape, the smell of salty sea air and glimpses of bulging swells exploding into majestic whitecaps, make up for the inconvenience.

Besides, I want to spend time wallowing in the joy of the weekend, which was a trip back to the days when everyone was easy with each other. Whatever cares we had weren't important enough to fracture our happy moments together, laughing, complaining, and generally sharing the minutia of our ordinary, uninteresting lives. For the most part, Mick managed to be his less obnoxious self when he was awake, which wasn't very often.

"He's wearing out," Sally admitted when we returned late Saturday afternoon and found him snoring in his recliner, with his mouth half open and the television blasting. He didn't wake up when we shut the television off, and it's pretty obvious he doesn't have the energy to go on a rant over anything.

The only person missing from the visit with my beloved aunt and cousin was my dad who, when we called to invite him, begged off for business reasons that most likely involved golf clubs. He knows Sally can talk to him any time she wants to, and he probably felt she and I needed this time with just the two of us. He wasn't wrong.

Thinking more about my conversation with my aunt while I'm stuck in the perpetually congested Pacific Coast Highway 101 traffic, I begin wondering how much further I should crack open the Pandora's box I've discovered. I'd be doing it out of curiosity, not necessity, so what right do I have, really, to upend the lives of people I love dearly just to satisfy my own inquisitiveness? Is the knowledge I might gain worth the risk of hurting others? Pondering these questions, I nearly miss the Lompoc exit that leads to the fish shack where I always stop to gorge myself on conch fritters.

"How was your weekend," my dad asks, walking into the hallway just as I open the door.

"It was really nice… a lot like the old days. Mick still cooks food only his animals love and Aunt Sally's still filling storage lockers with auction treasures she pays too much for and are valuable only to her," I answer, smiling as I hand him the car keys.

"That's been going on for years. She must have what – twenty or more lockers by now?"

"I doubt she knows, but my impression is quite a few, scattered throughout Los Angeles County."

"I just hung up with Sally – she called to see if you were back yet."

"I'm surprised to find you here at four in the afternoon…"

"I brought some work home. I wanted to be here when you got back, in case things didn't go as you planned, and you needed to talk about it."

"Not much to report. Mick's fading – he doesn't have the ability to raise a ruckus about anything. The auction queen and I went to Pasadena Saturday – she spent over a thousand dollars outbidding somebody for ten china-head dolls in various states of disrepair. After that, we went to Abuela's Authentic Mexican Cuisine for lunch and the rest of the time just hung out with each other. Emily seemed a little distracted. She didn't ask any questions about the diaries, which surprised me, but on the other hand, she has never seemed that interested. Little Charlotte isn't so little anymore. She turns thirteen in a month, and is very pretty."

"That's a headache I'm familiar with," my father remarks, adding that Emily has her hands full with Joey finishing high school just as Charlotte is about to start because, for parents, eight years of high school is about seven and a half years too many.

"Did you and Sally have a chance to talk?" he asks.

"Didn't she tell you?"

"Not really – just said it was a nice visit and to let her know you got home OK."

"We talked some."

"And?"

"The thought of me digging around in the family secrets still distresses her – a lot. I don't quite know what to do about the battle raging between my personal curiosity, my desire to understand my mother, my ever-stronger commitment to living an authentic life, and my love for my aunt," I sigh.

"Did you and Adrian see a game?" I ask a few seconds later, changing the subject to something less upsetting.

"Saturday afternoon. Great game and went to Guido's for pizza afterwards. He's very interesting to talk to… a walking encyclopedia of baseball statistics. He ought to go on some TV quiz show – he'd win a lot of money."

"I need to get moving if I'm going to catch the 6:20 back to Berkeley. Do you mind calling Aunt Sally and reassuring her I've arrived safely?" My dad nods.

Back in my apartment, I open my windows, unpack, and then call Adrian.

"Relieved to hear from you. I was getting a little worried," he says before I identify myself. I have no idea how he knew it was me on the telephone but with my aunt and Herlinda having the same ability, I'm becoming aware that there is a limit on how many ESP experts I can tolerate in my life.

"I'm fine. It was a great trip, but I'm glad to be back. Dad said you saw a good game Saturday afternoon."

"We did. He really knows the game. My guess is we both harbor secret wishes to be professional baseball players… hit a four-run homer out of the park… pitch a no-hitter… win a World Series… do something meaningful with our lives…"

"He implied the same about you."

"Coming from your father, that's a high compliment! On another topic, I finished the Bakersfield diary. It's the last one for your grandmother and isn't an easy read. She experienced those years as very unhappy ones… feeling increasingly isolated and unable to find her footing in the community. Overall, there's no evidence she was ever happy in America… at least nothing I've read so far indicates she was. She always felt like a stranger in a strange land – homeless, yet with a roof over her head. She missed the family she left behind and seemed unable to bond with the family she had in America in the deeply connected ways that make life feel safe, and worthwhile. Making friends was difficult and she didn't feel like she fit in anywhere," Adrian summarizes.

"Loneliness like that wears away at the fiber of the soul... it becomes harder and harder to find reasons to keep going. I've seen it in my research: poor women with no resources and no connections actually prefer living in homeless shelters, which can be pretty bad places, over their own apartments, because at least the shelter has staff who care about them and people like themselves to connect with and talk to. It's weird, but not unusual. The thought of my own grandmother suffering such alienation and emptiness makes me very sad."

"She certainly shines a different light on the immigrant experience from the one we've been encouraged to believe, and is definitely not the image America likes to perpetuate."

"You mean the myth that claims America is the promised land and savior for the poor, tired, oppressed and downtrodden? Maybe for some it was, but from what I've read so far, my grandmother was none of those. She voluntarily left a comfortable, satisfying life in Germany for love and traditional expectations. She followed an ambitious man, then quickly figured out that was not good a reason to abandon a life she loved. She was caught in a battle between traditional social, cultural, and religious expectations and her own dreams, then ended up the victim of a pervasive anti-German, anti-Jewish sentiment gaining a foothold in rapidly expanding America, where she came hoping to make a life with someone she loved. According to my aunt, her mother lived in chronic fear of being found out as German – a trait she passed on to her daughters. Setting aside the complication of also being Jewish, her disappointment with her life must've been overwhelming, and the feminist in me really rankles at this, Adrian. She gave up everything to wrap her life around a man's dreams and ended up with none of her own."

"Try to remember that her decisions reflected the times she lived in. Inserting your 1970's feminist mentality into an early 20th century experience risks drawing conclusions that might not be entirely correct," he cautions. When I don't respond, he continues.

"If you'd rather be alone while you think about all this, I'll postpone bringing the translations over until you're ready to deal with the next part of the story."

"I had this great idea to bring you some conch fritters, but they didn't travel well and are a little soggy, so I'm pretty thin on food around here. But I'm never too tired or upset to see you – surely you know that."

"I'll get a couple sandwiches at the deli and be over in an hour or so."

"Thanks. I'll be really glad to see you," I say into the dead telephone.

A few weeks ago, we had discussed the idea of moving in together, after having fallen into the habit of spending most nights either at my apartment or Adrian's. Since each of us had already left toothbrushes and a few other things at the other apartment, officially living together made sense. But after a lengthy analysis of the pros and cons, we agreed that I need space and freedom as I work through this transformation in my life, and adding anything else would be too much right now. Adrian glossed over the fact that he's not one hundred percent free to adopt the living together relationship lifestyle either. Nevertheless, I got the sense he was a little disappointed. Since then, except for my weekly Wednesday nights in the city and last weekend's trip down the coast, we have yet to spend a night apart and obviously are kidding ourselves about living together.

An hour later, over sandwiches and beer, I report on the weekend, including Aunt Sally's parting remarks.

"She's got a point, Natalie. New truths replacing old ones we've believed in and have found out are not now, and perhaps never were true, takes a lot out of someone. Making room for a new reality involves giving up the old one and the loss triggers a grieving process. That's the cost she was probably referring to, and you pay it in emotional currency."

"Maybe, but I think it's more than that. She asked for time before talking about the Bakersfield years."

"After you read the translation, you'll have a good idea why. They were tough years, and I get the impression your grandmother died unexpectedly, raising still more questions."

"I wish I knew her. Occasionally, I do feel like something's missing in my life because I didn't have grandparents." Adrian's response is that he's felt this too, having met his grandparents only once, when he stopped in Ireland on one of his trips to Rome.

"If it's any comfort, it wasn't the emotionally intense experience you'd expect. I was just passing through, so no one was invested in trying to build a relationship. I enjoyed meeting them, and I think they felt the same way, but they'd never been part of my life, and we all knew one brief encounter wasn't going to change that." What he is saying makes sense but is still sad.

"The last diary, which is more like a notebook, is your mother's, which she writes partly in English and partly in German. I've not figured out why one over the other."

"It probably depended on what she was saying, and how it might affect whoever read it."

"Or maybe she was just practicing her bilingual language skills. Do you want to read any of this tonight?" he asks, handing over several pieces of paper held together with a paper clip.

"I've had enough for now. I'd rather just sit here and watch an old movie on TV. See what you can find," I suggest, handing over the TV guide. Adrian discovers *Casablanca*, one of my all-time favorites, begins in an hour. Finishing our sandwiches, then cleaning up the kitchen, we curl up together on the couch and flip on the television to suffer through Humphrey Bogart's and Ingrid Bergman's star-crossed, wartime love affair.

Adrian returns to his apartment just after nine the following morning, leaving me to settle into a sunny window with the translations. I turn to my mother's diary entries first.

> *We came here to Bakersfield in California more than two years ago, and it has not been a happy place. Our Papa promised it was a good move for us... he will make more money, and we can leave Elyria behind and start again... not be Germans or Jews, just be Americans. He seems to think even though we are Germans and Jews, which we can't change even if we wanted to, we can just ignore that fact and enjoy life. Mama tells him pretending we are someone we are not doesn't make it so and gets very upset with him when he talks this way... says he is stealing her life from her, and taking the life of his daughters away from them... that running away from problems is impossible, and we might as well have stayed in Elyria where we know people and people know us for who we are, and don't care that we are German Jews.*
>
> *Papa disagreed and never asked Sarah or me if we wanted to move away, which we didn't. He just said we had to go where he was sent to keep the trains running, and Bakersfield was important because trains passing through here carry food grown nearby to market and carry things back and forth between one side of America and the other.*
>
> *Most people just come here to do business, but don't stay. Mama says the local people are too poor to afford a dressmaker, and there is only so much knitting a person can do in a day, so she is bored. I know how she feels,*

because school is boring me every day. My teacher wants to skip me forward, but Mama says that's already happened once and doing it again makes me two years younger than my classmates, and she thinks that is not a good idea. There are no Jews that I know of here... no one for Shabbat or Passover, or Hanukkah celebrations that are so important to Mama. She doesn't talk about this much, but she told me that when she was born her Papa and Mama promised her life to G-d, because that is the best life... and honoring Jewish rituals and traditions are part of keeping that promise. She feels like she's breaking the lifetime promise her parents made for her. No wonder she is sad – promises are important to keep, and I would be very sad if I broke any. I heard her complaining again to Papa about Sarah and me growing up not knowing how to be Jewish and claimed she is failing as our mother, then started crying. German and Jewish are all she ever talks about, and it always makes her sad. I'm tired of hearing it.

I have a new friend, Norma Salgado, who is Mexican, and lives on the other side of town. I told her I am Jewish and German, and she asked what that meant? After I explained, she said "so what?" and told me her mother says people hate Mexicans, but not to let it bother her, because the problem is with the hater, not the person being hated. I wish Norma's mother could teach Mama to believe this.

Norma doesn't know how long her family will be here. I told her I don't blame her family for not staying any longer than they have to, because there are a lot of nicer places, like Elyria, Ohio, which I liked much better than here. She says Bakersfield is nicer than Sonora in Mexico, where they came from. Sometimes we do homework together and on Sundays she goes to sit in a church in the town center that speaks Latin. She doesn't understand it but likes being there anyway. I start to tell her about Hebrew being the language of our religion, then change my mind.

In a few weeks Sarah is going away to study to be a teacher. I am upset she is leaving and making me responsible for Mama, who is changing into someone who never smiles or even talks much. I wonder if I know her anymore... or if she has any idea who I am. Sarah says she understands me being angry with her and is sorry to abandon me to Mama and her constant bad mood but wants to live her own life.

I don't need Mama or Sarah to do things I can do for myself... but if Mama doesn't do these things, she won't have anything to do at all. She knows this and has started being even more upset. Sometimes she yells at me for nothing, breaks dishes, cries loudly and then stays in bed for days. Other times, she talks about returning to Germany... says Papa doesn't need her and I can take care of myself, so I don't need her either... when no one needs her, she doesn't have any life... and because her family in Germany needs her, that is where her life belongs now. Papa gives up and says he doesn't want her to go but he can't stop her. He's away most of the time and doesn't understand about her dark moods and fits of anger that scare me. I tried telling him and he said don't worry about it – she would never hurt me. I explained that's not what I'm worried about... that I want Mama to go to Germany if that will make her happy. With her gone, life would be much calmer, and I wouldn't have to wonder about her next time to start screaming or throwing things. I can't invite Norma over in case Mama is in one of her moods. Sometimes I worry she might try to hurt herself.

Mrs. Salgado always has cookies for us after school. She smiles and talks to us while we eat as many as we want.

After finishing this section of my mother's diary, I pause to reflect on what her childhood was like and how different it was from my own. She lived with an angry, fearful mother, and had worries no child should have to contend with, while I had a devoted, loving father, was surrounded by people who cared for me, was secure in who I was and had no fear of anything. Our early lives could not have been more different, which is, perhaps, one reason we were never able to feel anything toward one another. It wasn't something either of us had any control over – it just was. On the other hand, her sister experienced the same upbringing, and she and I are woven together tighter than a tapestry, so my reasoning, while slightly comforting, is flawed.

I'm not sure how long I stare out the window, watching sparrows fly back and forth among the branches in the tall eucalyptus tree nearby. The sun shines on the sidewalk across the street where flowers bloom in the front window boxes of the little neighborhood café whose outdoor tables surround a lush, low-hanging pepper tree. Eventually, I take a walk, ending up, not too surprisingly, at Adrian's front door. He opens on the first knock.

"You read it?" he asks, looking at me.

"How did you guess?"

"Your eyes," he answers, guiding me toward the kitchen table, where I sit down while he pours two mugs of coffee, then reaches into the refrigerator for fresh cream.

"What emptiness my grandmother must've felt, Adrian… staring down a dark, bottomless well of loneliness nothing and no one could pull her out of. For her, coming to America was committing suicide without knowing it. She went on a journey she thought was bringing her to a new life and instead led her into a dark abyss that became its own death. I don't think I've ever read anything so sad. The burden of being forced to carry her mother's pain was so unfair to my mother and my aunt as young girls."

"I had a hard time with it, too. I wanted to hug them all."

"What do you think ultimately happened to my grandmother?"

"It's hard to say. I doubt she returned to Germany and then came back to America, but whether she stayed, went, or returned, the outcome was probably the same. Leaving Germany again easily could've been too much for her. My guess, based upon what your mother writes, is that, either directly or indirectly, your grandmother took her own life."

"I'm not sure what you mean by directly or indirectly taking her own life, but if you mean she died of a broken heart, then I agree with you," I say, slowly stirring the cream into the mug of dark, rich coffee.

"Her heart definitely broke, either by her own hand or by life handing her more than she could manage any longer. How it happened doesn't really matter… the result was the same. She lost any desire to live." As Adrian is speaking, he offers me a segment of the orange he is peeling.

"What do Jews believe about an afterlife?" I inquire.

"It depends on who you ask. The answers vary from 'this is it and there's nothing more – the ashes to ashes, dust to dust perspective' to some version of 'there isn't any afterlife because life never ends', implying that death is the means for life energy to evolve into a higher state as the soul is liberated from the body to return to its original source and eventually reappear in some other form, which is the perspective I personally find most appealing."

"So, she could have felt that she wasn't ending her life so much as freeing her soul to be what it was supposed to be – go where it was supposed to go?"

"She could have believed that – or felt it without being able to articulate it. I expect most people who take their own lives do so hoping to move on to something better."

"Or just want to end the pain of this life. I guess we'll never know. The problem for me is that I don't know how to think about this, Adrian. I just don't."

"Try to understand it from her perspective, Natalie. The evidence suggests she felt she was living in a world she perceived as ugly and meaningless, and felt helpless to do anything about it. There are limits on how long any human being, no matter how emotionally strong, can tolerate a life without meaning, and she couldn't seem to find that lifeline. She could've easily started wondering which was better – being dead in this world or taking a chance on life in the next? But this is all speculation."

"I want to believe she was driven by the desire for a better life than the one she had and did what she needed to do to find it. But that perspective requires a gigantic leap of faith, and faith is merely the triumph of imagination over observable reality. She was obviously intelligent, but other than repeatedly expressing a desire to live a faithful Jewish life, she doesn't reveal many details about her spiritual beliefs," I reflect.

"You're a very sharp social scientist – you know that not everything is objectively measurable. This doesn't mean something doesn't exist, it just means it's not scientifically provable – yet. Just because the needed measuring tools don't currently exist doesn't mean they won't exist at some point in the future. It's possible faith really is factual reality, and we just don't know it, yet choose to believe anyway. Perhaps that's how your grandmother thought of it."

"That's a good point… a very good point, actually. It would've been wonderful to talk with her about it."

"My suggestion is that you sit with this for a while… find out all you can about the era, and think about the social and personal realities your grandmother had to deal with. You may not find many answers, but you will achieve greater understandings." When I don't respond, Adrian offers another idea.

"I know a rabbi at the divinity school who might be willing to talk with you about some of this. He's a wonderful man. I'm sure you'd like him."

"How do you know him?"

"I took his seminar on Jewish scripture and spiritual beliefs and we struck up a friendship when he discovered I was a renegade priest. He's been helping me with my book – reading drafts, suggesting resources, and telling stories. He's a deeply spiritual man with gifted insights."

"You sound like you know him well."

"I've been honored, and it really has been an honor, to share a few Shabbat dinners with he and his wife, and he's spent several hours discussing my manuscript with me as it progresses. He's been extremely generous with his time because he believes in the book and strongly supports my effort to shed a brighter light on the realities surrounding Pius XII and Nazi Germany. I've mentioned that I'm translating some original German diaries and letters from around the same era for a friend of mine and I imagine he would love to talk with you."

"Seriously? That would be wonderful." I smile.

"He has an interesting background. He came to the U.S. from Poland as a youngster and the family settled in New York City, among other Polish Jews. He grew up speaking Yiddish and eventually was accepted into rabbinical school at Hebrew Union. When Hitler began invading eastern Europe, the letters from family back home became fewer and fewer and then stopped entirely. In the meantime, it was becoming more obvious that life for American Jews was increasingly difficult, and he began helping in any way he could, including traveling to places where there was no local rabbi. Fast forward to the end of World War II, and he and his only brother went to Poland in search of extended family, then stayed to help as the camps were liberated. It was at a rehabilitation spa for survivors that he met his wife, Rivka, a lovely young woman who had managed to survive Auschwitz. They fell in love, married, and then remained in Germany five years hoping for news of their families. They learned Rivka's mother survived Buchenwald but died of typhus a month after the liberation. The rest of her family, as near as they were able to verify, perished. Same for Saul – the extended families of both his mother and father, including grandparents he could remember knowing, either turned up on extermination lists or were untraceable. With no evidence of family left, his parents became despondent and ultimately both took their lives, together, about a year after Saul returned."

"Together?" I interrupt.

"They shut their apartment windows, put their heads in the oven and turned on the gas. Saul believes their survivor's guilt led them to decide it would be an honor to die in the same way family members died, and saw what they did as an act of love." Hearing this, I shake my head, closing my eyes in a feeble acknowledgment of the deep pain this story reveals.

"An added sorrow was that, because of the medical experiments Nazis performed on Jewish women in the camps, Rivka was unable to have children, ending her family line. Saul told me that the moment they learned there was no hope for children, they had a decision to make – to live the best life they could anyway, or to let the Nazi's claim two more Jews, and after all that had happened, what was a couple more Jews anyway? He entered a very dark period in which he admits he drank too much and acknowledges that any other wife would've left him. Eventually, he sobered up and decided to dedicate his survival to ensuring the Jewish story is not forgotten, and he's done that – as a teacher and as a writer."

"How did all this affect Rivka?"

"She was more accepting of her fate... believed she was spared for a reason and began caring for the camp orphans while she waited for Saul to gather himself together. When he finally stopped drinking, they decided to return to America and she became a social worker for Jewish Social Services... something to do with adoptions."

"They never adopted children themselves?"

"One – an infant whose mother died within days of the liberation. They had him for nearly five years, until family found him. An aunt wanted to raise the boy, which they knew was the right thing for him, but giving him up was extremely painful, and they decided not to adopt again."

"They both sound very remarkable."

"More than remarkable. Once meeting them, you immediately realize you're in the presence of greatness – spiritually, intellectually, and as human beings. The time we've spent together will remain with me for the rest of my life. I hope you'll get in touch with him, because you'll both benefit. Just don't be put off by his health situation."

"What do you mean?"

"Although he stopped drinking years ago, he continued smoking like a thousand-acre forest fire and has severe breathing problems. But he's careful about shutting off his oxygen before lighting his pipe, so an explosion isn't likely," Adrian smiles reassuringly.

Chapter Fourteen
פרק ארבעה עשר

Berkeley
Mid-summer, 1971

America the beautiful isn't so beautiful after all.

Depending upon one's viewpoint, Rabbi Saul Werner's crowded office is a hoarder's paradise, a fire trap, or the physical manifestation of a chronically thirsty mind. Crowded with floor to ceiling bookcases on three walls and, except for a large window, most of the fourth, the two tables in front of the bookcases are stacked with more books and loose papers. The man sitting behind the desk, surrounded by a thick veil of pipe smoke swirling around an oxygen canister, is barely visible over his typewriter.

It would take several lifetimes to accumulate this many books, I think, standing in the doorway wondering whether a great rabbinical scholar died, and the learned rabbi inherited his entire library.

"Come in, Natalie," a raspy voice invites as the rabbi stands up, snuffing out his pipe and fumbling for his oxygen cannula, which he loops around his ears and pushes in the general direction of his nose. I look around for an empty space to place the large vase of yellow and white daisies I brought with me as a gesture of gratitude for his time. *Hopefully, he isn't allergic to flowers and his color improves when he begins breathing better air,* I think, alarmed at his dusky, blue-gray complexion.

"Please, find a chair and sit down, and forgive the snake around my head... the result of a youthful sense of invincibility, a bad habit, and a government who refuses to regulate the tobacco industry, which flourishes in this free-enterprise, profit motive economic system gone awry. But you did not come to listen to an old man complain about a world gone to hell," he smiles, struggling for a few deep inhales of life-giving oxygen.

"Where would you like me to put these?" I ask, gesturing toward the flowers.

"Maybe here, by the telephone," he answers, sweeping a pile of papers aside onto the floor. Setting the vase down, I look around for an empty chair and, seeing none, offer to bring one from the hallway.

"Perhaps the best solution. There is one in here, but where exactly is not obvious," the rabbi says, adjusting his yarmulke, which is perched on a head of thick, gray hair giving the impression his finger is stuck in a light plug. Thick, wire-rimmed glasses compete with his oxygen tube for space on his nose. The intensity in his eyes as he looks at me is a little disconcerting.

"Thank you for seeing me, Rabbi Werner. I am very grateful."

"How could I refuse such a compelling story… and a chance to welcome you to the tribe," he smiles.

"The tribe?"

"An inside joke. Every Jew belongs to one of the twelve tribes of Israel. Which one is impossible to know but be assured you belong to one of them… we all do."

"I did not know that. There is much about being Jewish I don't know, as I mentioned when we spoke on the phone."

"No Jew knows everything about being Jewish. How can one person know five thousand years of history in one lifetime? It's too much information, so we learn what we can and don't worry about the rest. If it is important, it will be revealed. If we need to know something, it will find us whether we seek it or not. Adrian – such a beautiful man he is – tells me something you did not seek, has found you," this obviously holy man smiles gently, before a deep, raspy coughing spell overtakes him.

"Thank you. That's a nice perspective on everything that's happening to me."

"And now you want me to help you to understand it."

"I would like that very much, but Adrian speaks so highly of you I wanted to meet you regardless." Not acknowledging the compliment, the rabbi peppers me with questions about my background and current life. After half an hour I gently remind him of the reason I am here and suggest we begin with a summary of what Adrian has already told him.

"All I know is he is translating dairies and letters found after your mother's recent death – may her memory be for a blessing – and that they describe a family history you know nothing about but has revealed you to be the Jew you didn't know you were. Mazel Tov!" *So far, not much of my mother's memory is any kind of blessing*, I think, resisting the urge to say this out loud.

"The diaries are mostly from my grandmother who immigrated from

Germany as a young woman; the letters are from the family she left behind. There are some notebooks belonging to my mother, both in German and in English, but I don't know a lot about those yet. The diaries strongly suggest my grandmother was very unhappy for most of the years she lived in America. I don't know what happened to her – whether she returned to Germany and died there or remained in America and died here. I don't know how she died – illness, accident, intentionally, or she simply gave up on life and died heartbroken. The truth is, rabbi, I know almost nothing. I've never even seen a picture of her." I pause, choking down sudden, unexpected tears.

"And you say Mourner's Kaddish for her?"

"I don't know the Mourner's Kaddish..."

"It is the most vital of all Jewish prayers because it honors our ancestors... keeps us connected to them. What could be more important? I will be sure you have knowledge of it before you leave today, but first, tell me what is distressing you right now."

"After immigrating to America, it appears my grandmother was compelled to deny being German and being Jewish, and passed this fear to her two daughters, one of whom was my mother. My aunt, her sister, is having a very difficult time with the contents of the letters and diaries being revealed and has been very reluctant to discuss any of it. She believes the risks are too great and a lot of people will be hurt. Honestly, I don't understand any of this, and Adrian believes you can help me."

"First, understand that America's founders only intended for this to be a great country for white, Anglo-Saxon, protestant men and no one else... not for women, the dark-skinned, the circumcised, not even for the native people who were already living here for centuries. The colonists were so arrogant they believed they were entitled to have what they wanted and getting it was all they cared about. Now we are left with the inevitable mess this misguided attitude has created. Such a travesty!" In a sudden burst of energy, the rabbi completes his sentence by sweeping his right hand through the air, attempting to move this despicable history out of his direct line of vision. I can't help smiling at this brief, remarkably accurate interpretation of American history.

"By the time your grandmother arrived, there was much for Germans and Jews in America to fear, beginning before World War I, when immigration generally was becoming increasingly unpopular, and remained that way up until the end of World War II. Your grandmother was not wrong in her assessment of her surroundings, and she may have been very wise to do what she needed to do to protect herself and her children.

Hitler was not the only person in the world who actively persecuted the Jews; across human history there has been no shortage of political leaders eager and willing to kill us. But more important for you right now is to think about this: if a German Jew is forced to deny being German and deny being Jewish, what identity is left to them? How do they answer the simple 'who are you?' and 'where do you come from?' questions?" Looking me straight in the eye, he waits for my answer.

"It would seem there is no identity left, and it would be impossible to answer those questions," I finally admit, looking into the space above the rabbi's head, hoping another episode of tears I feel forming don't start dripping down my face.

"Precisely! There is no identity... nothing to hold onto that validates someone as a living, breathing human being. Think of it as being adrift, alone in the treacherous ocean they crossed to come here. They aren't fish, they are air-breathing, land-loving humans facing deep panic at not knowing where they belong or how to survive in all that water. Nothingness surrounds them, and living beings cannot survive for long in a state of nothingness."

"She had a husband and two daughters to hold onto. They must've occupied huge space in her life," I posit.

"Yes and no. They gave her purpose for getting out of bed in the morning, but they could not give her an identity," Rabbi Werner huffs through his oxygen apparatus, fixated on the identity issue.

"They gave her an identity as a mother and a wife."

"No, they gave her roles to play; performing a role is different from having an identity. She had responsibilities to fulfill, but wife and mother do not define a person as a human being in the same way ethnicity, culture, heritage, and beliefs define them."

"Or being a woman..." I interject, beginning to follow his parsed reasoning, which is a little like going deaf from the sound of splitting hairs.

"Before she was anything else in life, she was first a human being, then a German Jewish woman. Then she became an actress playing roles in the various stage plays of life... as a wife, as a mother. Eventually the play ends, and the role ends with it. If there is not something else – a core identity – to carry the person forward onto the next stage where the next play, with different roles, will be performed, the person is left empty. If I understand correctly, you know nothing of your grandmother's life beyond the point where her role as a mother is nearly over."

"Her diaries end at about the time my mother – her youngest child – is around fourteen or fifteen years old and her older daughter is already away at school. My grandfather apparently traveled for his work with the railroad, so most of the time my grandmother was home either alone or with only my mother for company. She makes no reference to longtime friends, but does remark about the loss of connection to a Jewish community when she came to California."

"Judaism is a communal religion celebrated together, and Jews are clannish, which is what happens after five thousand years of depending upon each other for survival. We butter each other's bread, mind each other's business, and stick together no matter what, because our lives depend upon it. No one can exist isolated and alone, and Jews know this better than anyone... it's in our blood to know it. Your grandmother faced too much loss... identity and sense of belonging. There was nothing left for her to attach herself to. Humans, by nature, need attachments – things to cling onto – no matter the circumstances. Even Jews in the death camps made attachments and clung to each other. So what that Jews get carried away with this? It's not something we can help," Rabbi Werner says, exhibiting a proud smile, until he is interrupted by a fit of deep, tortured coughing that turns his face dark blue and red, causing me to rise out of my chair.

"Not to worry, liebling. Today is not the day I will die," he assures me. Looking at him, I have no idea how he can be so sure of this, but take his word for it as I sit back down.

"Your grandmother's decision to deny being Jewish and avoid being identified as German was not unusual.

"I'm not sure she decided... it's more that denial was forced on her as part of assimilating to life in America," I interrupt.

"Many Jews of her era and beyond chose denial, either directly or indirectly, and passed this choice on to their children. But many others chose not to go on. We must look upon both mercifully, because denial is also death. Forgoing who you really are in favor of trying to be someone else is living as an impostor... always with the threat that someone finds out, and not knowing what will happen then? A job is lost, a friendship ends, your business is vandalized, your house is burned, you are tortured... the possibilities are endless. This fear is a crushing burden to carry for a lifetime, Natalie. It is not difficult to believe physical death is so much easier."

"You're making it sound like she took her own life."

"Took it or just gave up on it. Either way is the same and a possibility we cannot ignore in this quest to understand her. I'm sorry, liebling, but that is the reality."

"What, exactly, was she afraid of? I know there were bad feelings toward Germans after the first world war, and that the Jews somehow were blamed, but I don't see how that reached all the way into her life directly."

"She could not have avoided it. Remember, America is, at its core, a white nationalist, Christian nation that harbors a belief in a doctrine the founders created, then labeled Manifest Destiny – a G-d-given right to conquer anyone who stood in the way of what they believed was their entitlement. Of course, there is no theological or other evidence to support the notion that G-d has ever given anybody a right to do anything. The whole idea was something they dreamed up to justify taking whatever they wanted, even though it wasn't rightfully theirs. This is not a suitable moral foundation upon which to build a nation, but it is how American expansionism justified its treatment of the native people, and this is what it has continued to do to anyone who isn't white and Christian, just in more subtle ways that no longer involve soldiers riding horseback and shooting rifles." The rabbi again stops to cough. I remain silent while he takes a few moments to catch his breath.

"It's terrible – then and now. Foreign-born immigrant labor was welcomed to advance the national agenda, but there was never any intention that immigrants be recognized as social equals. Africans weren't the only people Protestant white America enslaved. There was no hesitation about mistreating anybody who was in any way different. In many respects, the Germans, being industrious and better educated than many others, and Jews, being disciplined and clannish, fared better than average – certainly better than the Irish and Italians. But this success also set Jews up for jealousy to arise against them. People began fearing their ability to succeed."

"I'm embarrassed to admit that while I've heard of the doctrine of Manifest Destiny, I've never given it serious thought. Hearing you explain it, I feel as though I should be apologizing to someone," I frown.

"Come – let me show you something," Rabbi Werner says, rising slowly from his desk. I am surprised that, although stooped, he is nearly as tall as I am. Wheezing slightly, he walks toward the bookcase nearest the window.

"If you can be so kind, please hand me that box," he asks, pointing to a brown cardboard container above my head. After some juggling and shuffling around, I finally hand over the box.

"I have some things you need to see," he says setting the box on the nearest table and opening the dusty cardboard flaps, bringing on yet another consumptive coughing fit.

"These are posters from the era just before and then after the first world war. In addition to being nailed on lampposts and telephone poles, they also appeared as advertisements in newspapers, and as signs carried in parades. All were sponsored by various white nationalist groups," he explains, unrolling yellowed tubes of paper.

"This one depicts Germans as villains and questions their American loyalty. It was a dramatic reversal of fortune for Germans who, despite the unfounded prejudices against them, were industrious and for the most part, educated, and had generally managed life in America more successfully than other immigrant groups. Suddenly ten million Germans were no longer welcome, and most did not understand this sudden shift; it made no sense to them," he explains, holding up a poster with four corner holes, indicating it had been publicly visible somewhere. Handing it to me, he begins thumbing through several scraps of paper and news clippings, until he finds a photo of what appears to be a memorial.

"This was a terrible event. Robert Prager, a German immigrant was lynched after being accused, with no proof to back it up, of spying for Imperialist Germany, which he denied, all the while professing his love for America. They stripped him naked, marched him in the streets, forcing him to sing patriotic songs and walk over broken beer bottles, then took him to a tree and shook him by the neck. Eleven men were tried for this unspeakably heinous act, and none were convicted of murdering an innocent man. This is how the local newspaper reported about the verdict." He hands me a yellowed newspaper clipping from Collinsville, Illinois.

"The community is well convinced he was disloyal," the newspaper article reads. *"The city does not miss him. The lesson of his death has had a wholesome effect on the Germanists of Collinsville and the rest of the nation..."*

"This is horrible," I say, knowing how hollow my words sound against such ugly brutality in my own country.

"It was a widely reported incident, and news travels faster than the speed of light among Jews. Your grandmother may easily have learned about it, including all the details. But this was not the only occurrence; other bad things happened," Rabbi Werner continues, sitting down on the chair I had been standing on. I lean against the table and continue listening.

"The concert master for the Cincinnati Symphony – a great musician, was incarcerated. German as a language was suddenly verboten in the schools; the German-American press was heavily censored; libraries had to pull German books off the shelves; German-American organizations were targeted, because non-Germans believed that knowing a German meant you were sympathetic to the Hun – a negative term for being German – similar to using 'nigger' to refer to Negroes. Being friendly with a German was no different from being a nigger-lover, and few things invited more trouble than showing deference to Negroes." I admit I'm having a very hard time grasping all this.

"It gets worse, Natalie. If you spoke German, it was assumed you thought like Germans, who were perceived as vicious, heartless people lacking a soul. Defiant Germans dug in to become even more German but many others, as a matter of survival, shed their German identity as quickly as possible, at great personal cost. But it backfired, setting the stage for terrible times to come. Most people believed that the only reason to deny being German was having something to hide, automatically creating suspicion without reason. It was a lose-lose situation. There were no good answers."

"And being Jewish only made everything worse," I acknowledge, taking a deep breath at the same time.

"Worse than you can imagine," Rabbi Werner emphasizes, now coughing frequently, which I take as signal he is growing tired and needs to stop speaking. I thank him profusely for his time and promise to return soon to continue our wonderful conversation. Another coughing fit causes him to wave me off without saying good-bye.

Walking the two miles back to my apartment, I don't stop for an ice cream cone from the vendor claiming the corner across from the entrance to campus. In light of what I have just learned, anything pleasurable seems sacrilegious.

By the time I unlock my apartment door, I have decided to call my department head at Northwestern and request a leave for the fall semester so I can remain in Berkeley and take Rabbi Werner's seminar that Adrian mentioned earlier. I realize this is an impulsive decision, but it's not often anyone has a chance to be in the presence of a truly great mind, which the dear rabbi clearly has, and I'm not going to pass up this opportunity. The phone rings a long time before the department secretary finally answers. She doesn't think Martin Clark, my overly dramatic sociology department chairman given to fits of pique that can last for months, has already left for the day and will try to locate him. A few minutes later, he comes on the phone.

"Professor Barlow! Fortuitous you should call! I've been meaning to get in touch with you about your fall schedule. Connie Delavan has resigned – health problems. I need someone to teach her advanced women's studies class. The content's a little too specialized for a graduate assistant, so I immediately thought of you."

"Next fall is the reason I'm calling, Marty. I need to take the semester off. I know this is late notice, but I'm hoping a sabbatical can be arranged."

"No chance of that, my dear. Next year's sabbaticals have already been budgeted."

"Then I'll do it without pay," I impulsively respond. Since I'm making what we both know is an unreasonable request, I bite my tongue to avoid to reminding my department chair that calling a colleague "my dear" is demeaning, disrespectful, and intolerably irritating.

"I hope you realize this would require some significant juggling around on my end. Mind explaining why this suddenly urgent request?" he asks, a little louder than necessary for me to hear him.

I am at a loss to make the request sound anything like urgent, so I play the tenured professor card and stress an unexpected opportunity to advance my overall knowledge. I go back and forth with my department head for a half hour before he finally agrees to allowing me to take personal leave for all of fall term, with the condition that I continue to oversee my well-funded research program, am available by phone to my graduate students, and am willing to travel to Chicago if something comes up with the research protocol that can't be handled long distance – all for one-third salary. This is a better deal than I dared hope for, and I end the conversation quite satisfied with myself.

My next task will be finding somewhere to live, since the lease on my sublet expires Labor Day, and most fall rentals were already spoken for by the end of last spring term. Putting this problem off for the moment, I begin sorting through several days' mail I've thrown across my desk unopened and find a letter with Professor Helen Milburn's return address. She writes that the university has extended her leave, so she won't be returning for fall term as planned and would appreciate it if I would post a notice on her department bulletin board for another renter for fall term. *Looks like my fall housing problem just got solved*, I smile. A few minutes later, the telephone rings.

"This is Adrian McCormick calling. I've been instructed to invite Dr. Natalie Barlow to accompany me to Rabbi Saul Werner's home this Friday for Shabbat, if she is available and willing to allow me to escort her," the deadpan voice says.

Chapter Fifteen
פרק חמש עשרה

Berkeley
Late summer, 1971

*Life is acted out on an emotional stage where the
best performers are true to themselves.*

"Rivka cornered me in the kitchen to tell me we are a good match. She said I shouldn't wait too long to make my intentions clear because someone else will claim you," Adrian proclaims, squeezing my hand as we walk home after the wonderful Shabbat supper with Rabbi Werner and his lovely wife, who made no effort to hide her enthusiasm for playing matchmaker.

"I'd have to agree to be claimed," I point out, smiling at the absurdity of any man trying to pull something like that with me.

"My favorite part of the evening was Rivka showing me how to light Shabbat candles and inviting me to say the prayers with her. She even wrote them in phonetic Hebrew for me! This connected me with my grandmother in a way I've not felt before – almost like she was smiling down on me. And I also felt like I was being welcomed into a family."

"You probably were, although it's probably more accurate to refer to it as being welcomed into the tribe."

"Either way – it felt wonderful!" I exclaim. In response, Adrian settles his arm around my shoulder, staying silent as we walk through shadows cast by old-fashioned, pole-mounted street-lights.

"I've finished more entries in your mother's diary," he says a few minutes later.

"And..."

"She held her emotions close and doesn't reveal a lot about how she felt about things, but it's obvious she was a very complicated person – exceptionally intelligent, and her own mind was the only one that really mattered to her. After reading this, I imagine you're going to want another conversation with your aunt, and it might be a difficult one."

"Let's enjoy the afterglow of this lovely evening and leave any heavy discussions for later," I say. We walk the rest of the way in companionable silence, guided by the faint light of summer's last full moon.

It's not until after breakfast the following Tuesday morning that Adrian hands me the translations, suggesting I sit on the fire escape, warmed by the morning sun while I read them.

"I'll be at my desk working through a manuscript glitch. Let me know if you need anything," he says, walking into the other room. Then he stops and turns around.

"Could I request a favor?" he asks. I nod.

"I'm having a devil of a time with this current chapter. I've been working on it for nearly three weeks and getting nowhere. When you have a chance, would you read it and see what you think?"

"I'd love to read it. I've been a little disappointed you haven't asked."

"Believe me – I've wanted to. Your opinion would mean a lot, but I figured you had enough on your mind."

"It's an honor, and a welcome diversion." I smile, carrying my coffee onto the fire escape, then kicking my chair close enough to put my feet up on the rail and begin reading the translations.

> *Sarah has come home from her school and is promising to stay for three months, until things are settled into a routine without Mama. She doesn't say she wants to do this, but I am glad she is here. Papa doesn't say much at all. Sarah insists one thing we must do is go through Mama's things – decide what to keep and what to give away. She is right, but it's not something I want to do. A few days later, while Sarah was at the market, I looked in one of the boxes in Mama's closet and found letters from Germany. I read several and set one aside to show to my sister.*
>
> > *My dearest Nathalie –*
> > *As always, we are grateful for the money you send. Without it we would starve as the Reichsmark is worthless – four trillion marks to the U.S. dollar is a number much larger than I am able to*

understand. Where would enough paper to print that much money come from? But it doesn't matter – it buys us nothing. Without what you send, we would be living on state welfare, which is empty promises everyone knows the government can't keep. The newspapers write of a worldwide depression, and the struggle to hang on has brought a rise in German nationalism that is not good for Jews, especially because of persistent rumors we are trying to take over the world – as if that were possible!

We talk among ourselves that we would leave if there was somewhere safer, but we know of no such place. Your Papa, of course, would refuse to move on, and Levi would never leave him behind, so we aren't going anywhere even if we could. Every day Papa goes to your Maman's grave to say Mourner's Kaddish. It is no life, but he says doing this every day is the only reason for him to stay alive. On warm days he takes his violin and plays for your Maman, but he refuses to play for anyone else.

We hope you are well, and Sarah and Rachael are happy... Long may we all live to be together again someday...

Lovingly, Irina.

Sarah and I discuss the letter and decide we should write to Irina about our mother. I want to send money and know where Mama kept some. We find more than ten dollars, so we go to the bank to get paper money to enclose with the letter. We do not know what to say about the sad news that Mama has died, so decide to just say it, and promise to keep sending money, which we will explain to Papa when he returns. I can save from the allowance he gives me, and Sarah says she will do what she can but doesn't know how much help ten American dollars is, but at least we are trying, which is better than not trying.

I stop reading and stare into the distance, sipping lukewarm coffee and frowning. This is the first direct reference to my grandmother having died, and I'm not sure what to think about how my mother has reacted. Adrian breaks my spell by walking out onto the fire escape and asking whether I want to talk about what I've just read?

"I still can't tell whether my grandmother died in Bakersfield or somewhere else. Maybe she isn't buried in Elyria and they just put a headstone for her there when they buried my grandfather."

"Cemeteries keep records. They usually know who is buried there. If it's important to you, try calling them," Adrian suggests.

"I don't know how important it is, but I'm curious."

Two days later, over breakfast, Adrian asks whether I've been in touch with the cemetery in Elyria.

"The man I spoke with said their records were in the county courthouse, which burned to the ground twelve years ago. He had no idea whether Nathalie Rosenblum's grave holds an actual body, or if Eitan's does, either. He told me that often, particularly among Jewish immigrant families, they placed a memorial headstone next to an actual grave of a family member. If she died in Germany, he thought it very unlikely her body was shipped back to America for burial because people didn't do things like that back then – or now, for that matter. He said Jews want quick burials, preferably before sundown on the day of death, if possible. This all made sense, especially the part about a quick burial, which was my mother's wish also."

"Basically, you didn't learn anything."

"That's not quite true. He said I could go to Ohio and search death records, or to Sacramento and search California death records, but cautioned that the records offices are not well organized and don't necessarily include the names of people who weren't citizens, and I don't think my grandmother was. The records offices aren't very helpful unless there's a compelling reason to search, and satisfying personal curiosity isn't one of them."

"And so far, we've not found any clue about where your grandmother is buried – or how she died."

"Based upon her strong desire to return to Germany, my guess is if she died there, that's where she's buried. I can't imagine her wanting to return to America just to be buried here. But this is all conjecture, unless my aunt is willing to talk about it, and so far, that doesn't sound promising."

"She might not know for sure herself," Adrian correctly points out.

"That's true, and there are other things that are much more important to me to know about, so I'll probably not ask her outright. If it comes out somehow, great, but otherwise, I'll just leave the question alone."

"Wise decision, Natalie."

"I hope so. Meanwhile, I want to continue reading what my mother wrote, but not until after I get back from San Francisco. Tomorrow's my standing dinner date with my dad, and the next morning is my command appearance in Herlinda's kitchen. I'll be back mid-afternoon. Give me your chapter to take with me, and we can talk about it when I get back."

"I'm having dinner with the chairs of the history and language departments tomorrow and won't be home until later in the evening myself," Adrian says.

"Are they preparing to offer you a faculty appointment?"

"Not a permanent one. They're thinking about cross listing some classes in German history and language and want to thrash out some ideas for how to configure it."

"And what you might be willing to teach?"

"That, too."

Back in Berkeley by midday Thursday, I stop off to tell Adrian how wonderful his chapter is, offering only a few, minor suggestions, along with a request to read the entire manuscript. He's a talented, insightful historian and I imagine myself learning a great deal from his book. Shortly before supper, I return to my apartment and my mother's diary.

> *Today my teacher tells me she wants me to move ahead of my class. This means I will graduate two years sooner than is normal for my age. Papa seems happy about this... says I must begin thinking about what I want to do next.*
>
> *Sarah is keeping company with a man, Edwin Hall, who came home with her on one of her visits so he could meet us. He's very handsome and seems nice, but Papa doesn't like him because he doesn't have a job, and he thinks a man without a job has no business courting a woman. Sarah told Papa to be more understanding since there aren't any jobs, except for the railroad, and Edwin isn't mechanical, so the railroad wouldn't be interested in hiring him. Papa didn't directly ask Edwin where he gets his money, but I could tell he wanted to. I like Edwin, but it is strange hearing him call Sarah 'Sally' and even stranger hearing my sister giggle and watching her smile*

all the time. She never did any of these things before.

I told Sarah I've decided I want to go to nursing school. She says being accepted will be difficult and made me promise not to fill out applications without her help.

I received a letter from Sarah today. She said not to tell Papa that she and Edwin are married and told me if I want to get into nursing school, I have to figure out another name. She said Charlotte Rose sounds better than Rachael Rosenblum, which is very Jewish, and to ask school to change the name on my records, which is what she did to apply to normal school, and they didn't refuse.

A letter also came to Papa from Mama's father. Papa let me read it along with him. My opa says violence is growing and the safest thing is to denounce Jews and deny being Jewish, but he cannot do this, although he encourages Levi's family to do it, which caused a big argument because some agreed with him, and others didn't. He says Jews are in great peril but does not believe the rest of the world realizes this, so will not help them, and they are on their own. His letter is very sad. He sent tattered news clippings about the bad conditions in Germany and growing political problems. After reading all this Papa spent the rest of the evening in his private room with the door closed.

"You're right that I need to visit with Aunt Sally again. I'm going down to LA tomorrow," I tell Adrian later that evening.

"If she'll talk to you, it ought to be an interesting conversation," he confirms.

"I knew we'd be having this conversation eventually," Aunt Sally tells me the next afternoon as she holds the side door open so I can walk into the house through the kitchen. I've brought dinner with me, using the excuse that the visit is on short notice, and I don't want to be a bother. I'm sure my aunt knows the real reason for my generosity is avoiding the risk of one of Mick's infamously creative wartime army one-dish meals containing mysterious, life-threatening ingredients.

"I'm not sure if he makes these because he honestly thinks they're good or just wants to be sure nobody ever comes to our house for a meal again," my aunt remarked several years ago, after a particularly awful concoction Mick served that she was convinced contained duck eggs and raccoon meat. Not even the dog would eat it.

"I didn't expect to see you tonight," Mick burps after finishing our deli soup and sandwich dinner.

"It's a quick trip. I need to talk with Aunt Sally… some stuff about my mother," I explain as vaguely as possible.

"Bet she left a mess. Making things easier for other people never much interested Charlotte," Mick mumbles, walking into the living room, where he retires to his recliner and flips on the television so loud it would cause a normal person's eardrums to explode. My aunt signals me into the kitchen as she prepares to cut into yet another honey lemon cake, made from fresh lemons growing on the lovingly tended tree in their backyard. It's the house's finest feature. Closing the kitchen door to shut out the television, then sitting down to pick at her cake, she asks where I'm at with the diaries.

"The entries I've just finished reading are from when my grandmother apparently died, or disappeared somewhere, until Charlotte is preparing to apply to nursing school. What do you remember about that time?" I ask, watching my aunt pour herself a generous glass of sherry. Until our margarita-soaked lunch a few weeks ago, I've never known my aunt to drink at all, but apparently her sister's death has created so much stress she feels the need to fortify herself before she can talk about it.

"Mama's death was a surprise…" she begins. "We didn't know what happened. Charlotte said she'd been gone for a while but was expected to come back. The next thing either of us knew, she had died. Papa never said much about it."

"Where did she go?"

"That was never clear, and there are several possibilities…"

"Like what?" I ask, suddenly sitting up straighter.

"In the year before I left for normal school Mama changed dramatically. She was never what anyone would describe as ebullient, but for the most part she was pleasant enough to be around, until she wasn't. Her dark moods got darker and more frequent; she didn't leave her room, or sometimes even her bed, for days. Then, suddenly, she'd snap out of it and was perfectly reasonable, acting as if everything was fine and she hadn't disappeared into her bedroom for days, or weeks. Other times, she was in a blind fury that came out of nowhere, and she took it out on Charlotte and me… yelling, hitting us, throwing things, and so on. When we returned from school, we never knew which mother would be waiting for us: the reasonable one, the angry one, the sad one sobbing in her bedroom, or the one who went to bed several days ago and was yet to get up."

"Obviously, she was suffering from kind of mental issue," I remark."

"Undoubtedly, but Charlotte and I were both too young to understand that. We suddenly found ourselves scared of our mother and unable to grasp what was happening. All we knew was that we didn't like her anymore and didn't want to have anything to do with her, in case we accidentally set her off. I was on my way to teacher's college, so I didn't care that much, but Charlotte didn't have any way to escape and with Papa working so much, she was left to face this alone. More than once, Charlotte told our Mama to go back to Germany if that was what she wanted to do, insisting she could get along fine without her. But instead of comforting Mama, it had the opposite effect and made everything worse."

"Did she go back to Germany?"

"I seriously doubt it, but I don't think she returned to Elyria, either."

"Then what happened?"

"My best guess is Papa had her committed to a mental hospital. Looking back, it's clear she was a victim of moods she couldn't control, and he may not have had any choice. It's not something he would ever tell us."

"Do you think she died in a mental hospital someplace?"

"The only possibilities are Germany, Elyria, Bakersfield, or a hospital, and the hospital is most likely."

"This is a hard question to ask, but do you think maybe she committed suicide?"

"I don't want to think that, but I can't deny the possibility," my aunt admits, her bottom lip quivering.

"As an adult looking back on this, I understand that she suffered some kind of mental illness, probably depression. She gave up everything to come to America, and if I recall correctly, several family members died in the first world war and then in the Spanish flu epidemic right afterwards, so she'd suffered tremendous personal losses that would be extremely difficult for anyone to recover from, and perhaps impossible for someone who already felt alone in a strange country thousands of miles away."

"Maybe it wasn't mental illness so much as being consumed by overwhelming grief and not knowing how to cope with some pretty powerful emotions, particularly without friends to lean on," I offer.

"That's as good an explanation as any, but families didn't understand things like that back then. They swept any unpleasantness under the nearest rug and moved on with their lives. When Mama died, Papa insisted we continue as if nothing had happened. He may have even been relieved... I kind of was. Charlotte admitted she had often wished Mama was dead or would just go away someplace. After Mama died, Charlotte never tried to hide how glad she was to not be dealing with the problem anymore and focused even more on herself... not that she didn't always do that." It's impossible to miss the sarcasm dripping from my aunt's voice.

"Charlotte was at an age when she still needed a mother, whether she admitted it or not, so I stayed home with her for a while. I felt bad about going back to college when I did, but she didn't seem to care. Of the two of us, I felt much worse about Mama than Charlotte did... at least that's how it seemed to me. Charlotte wasn't one to let anyone get close enough to know what she was thinking or how she felt about anything. We were sisters and all we really had was each other, yet we lived a life of mostly peaceful co-existence without a lot of emotional connection. I always suspected I felt this more than Charlotte. There were brief periods when when we were close, but that abruptly ended when she left for the war, and we never recovered any kind of relationship." As I'm listening to my aunt, it doesn't escape notice that she never refers to her sister as Rachael, her given name.

"Is that why you got married soon after your mother died... you didn't feel connected to anybody?" I continue.

"It's hard to say. I'd finished teachers' college and didn't want to return to Bakersfield but had been unable to get a steady teaching job. It seemed like getting married was a good solution, which was wishful thinking with no basis in reality. I loved the feeling of being loved, and Edwin was very loving. He made marriage seem like a very appealing idea at the time."

"Charlotte apparently liked him."

"Nearly everybody did. Edwin was handsome, charming, and very easy to like. The problem was he didn't care much about holding onto a steady job and relied on gambling to support us, which was a dangerous lifestyle, not to mention a very unstable income source. He got in deep with loan sharks and suddenly took off... never saw him again. Eventually I got a divorce on grounds of desertion. Fortunately, there were no children, and soon after I was offered a permanent teaching position. But the marriage wasn't a total mistake."

"What do you mean?"

"I learned a valuable lesson about never being dependent upon a man again," my aunt proudly tells me, almost smiling.

"Edwin was a thirty-second degree Mason, which was helpful because, as his wife, I was able to join the women's auxiliary organization. That connection opened doors for me. I'm still active, and these women are my closest friends. Emily joined the daughter's group when she was old enough and enjoyed it all through high school, then moved up to the adult organization when she turned twenty-one. It's been a very important part of both our lives… still is. We both attend the monthly meeting."

"The Masons are a Christian organization that doesn't admit Catholics and certainly not Jews, which is why you had to keep being Jewish a secret," I acknowledge.

"By then I'd totally shed any remnants of a German accent and virtually everything about being Jewish, so I no longer thought of myself as a German or a Jew. I was liked, accepted, and never viewed with suspicion or distrust. Months would go by and being Jewish never crossed my mind. Occasionally, if I thought about it, I would panic at the possibility of someone finding out, but those times never lasted long and there were never any close calls. Eventually, I met Mick, got married again, had Emily, and never looked back, because there was no reason to… except one."

"What was that?"

"I worried that I was going to be like Mama, subject to uncontrolled fits of anger and deep sadness. I saw these tendencies in myself, and they scared me."

"You've always seemed the epitome of steady to me, Aunt Sally. I don't think you have anything to worry about."

"You haven't seen the times when I've taken out after Emily, and gone off on Mick like a trapped bear. It's not pretty."

"It can't have upset Emily too much; she's never said anything."

"That's because she has the same tendency. She really blows her stack at the kids sometimes – all out of proportion to the situation. I grimace every time I see it."

"You've never been that way toward me."

"I know, and I'm not sure why. The only reason I can think of is that, looking back, the happiest days of my life were during the war when I was living with Paul and taking care of you. Despite everything going on around us, Paul, Jane and I, together with Herlinda, you, Emily and Tommy, we were a well-functioning, happy family. It wasn't until later that I began feeling darker impulses."

"Do you think it's something that's inherited?"

"It's crossed my mind, especially when I saw how Charlotte was after she returned. She was prone to terrible outbursts and there was no way in hell Paul could allow her to come back home and live with you because if you did something she didn't like, she couldn't be trusted not to hurt you."

"Is that what he said?"

"He didn't have to. He knew I supported whatever he needed to do to keep you safe. She was my sister, and I loved her, but she had an ugly, angry streak she was unable to control. There was no question she was mentally unstable, and thankfully, Paul quickly recognized this. But if he hadn't, I'd have pointed it out. Whether it was genetic inheritance, or the result of whatever happened to her when she was off doing whatever it was she did during the war, is unknowable."

"Mick has to be aware of all this... what does he think?"

"He's always thought my outbursts were female trouble, which saved me from having to come up with an explanation. As far as everything else goes, he doesn't know much, and I want to keep it that way. The fewer questions he asks, the better. We just deal with the moment in front of us and don't dwell on either the past or the future."

"Isn't that lonely?"

"It's safe, and that's what matters most to me."

"What role do you think chronic denial played in the family mood swings, for lack of a better way to describe what you, my mother, my grandmother, and Emily have all suffered to varying degrees?"

"I have no idea, Natalie. I've never thought about it except to be grateful you've never shown the same tendencies. Thankfully, you inherited Paul's even temperament and none of Charlotte's, or my, volatility."

"Dad and I have never lived lives of denial and fear, Aunt Sally, and it seems to me that denying who you are and living in fear that you'll be found out would take a terrible toll... that not living a truly authentic life would be exhausting, and very depressing. My grandmother appears to have felt this deeply and perhaps, ultimately, my mother did, too."

"Perhaps. But I can honestly say it wasn't that difficult for me, and I doubt it was for Charlotte, either. We both knew the alternative would've been much worse. And denial gets easier with time. You absorb it into yourself and think about it less and less."

"Maybe, but I can't imagine it disappears entirely. A part of you realizes you're being dishonest with yourself, and others, and that has to wear on you, even if you get used to it," I point out.

"I never saw it as dishonest. I was just doing what I had to do to protect myself and survive. Imagine what would happen if Mick found out I am Jewish and have been pretending I wasn't all these years?" my aunt asks, looking straight at me, both hands in her lap, as if defying me to reveal her lifetime secret.

"I doubt much would happen, Aunt Sally. Mick couldn't raise a serious fuss about anything anymore."

"I wouldn't bet on that. And what would my friends think of me if they found out I was living a lie… had been lying to them about who I really am? I could never explain this dishonestly to my sisterhood. It's a Christian organization and none of the members would knowingly befriend a Jew. They would be horrified and never believe anything I said ever again, not that it would matter, because I'd be expelled." Saying this, my aunt puts her head in her hands and sobs.

"Then I guess we don't tell them," I say, patting her arm.

"Just how is that going to work, Natalie? You, my niece, are suddenly Jewish by birth, but I'm not? Jewish identity passes through the mother, and since your mother is my sister – we're either both Jewish or neither of us is Jewish. There's no half-in-half-out. If you embrace your Jewish heritage, it casts a wide net that includes me and Emily and both Emily's children."

"It might not be as bad as you think," I quietly suggest.

"That's true. It might be a lot worse than either you or I can imagine."

"Emily knows about the diaries and hasn't asked a single question about what they contain. She can't be that curious," I reassure my aunt.

"She's smart enough to have figured out she doesn't want anything to do with any of this. Joe's a Muslim and while he doesn't especially like that Emily is a Christian, she's not religious, so he can live with it. If he finds out his wife is a Jew, all hell will break loose. He'll nullify the marriage, claim the children under Muslim law, then take off for the Middle East. She'd never get them back – probably never see them again."

"Jesus…" I whisper.

"If Jesus could fix this, I guarantee you we wouldn't be having this conversation," Sally grimaces, rolling her eyes. "I'm not saying any of this will happen, but you need to understand that it could and understand precisely how great the risks involved in this possible scenario are. The stakes are higher than you can possibly imagine," my aunt cautions me, looking hard into my eyes.

"Emily must've said something to you?" I ask.

"She mentioned finding Charlotte's diaries and casually wondered what might be in them. I told her to ask you. If she hasn't done that, then she doesn't want to know."

"But denying our Jewish heritage is failing to honor our ancestors,

RED ANEMONES

most of who were probably exterminated in German death camps. Don't you feel any responsibility to honor their legacy, especially since we might be their only bloodline survivors?"

"I try very hard not think about that."

"You're comfortable ignoring our family history entirely?"

"I didn't say that, Natalie. There's a difference between ignoring something and broadcasting it."

"But what you're claiming is that if I continue the pattern of denial and bury all this, everything stays the same and everyone goes on living a false life as someone other than who they really are. If I decide to live my life authentically, as the Jew I was born to be, and am, the ripple effect could be devastating. Is that what you're really saying?" I ask, my voice quavering as the enormous cost of claiming a life that increasingly means so much to me begins enveloping me like a thick, heavy fog.

"Unfortunately, that's exactly what I'm saying, sweetheart. A lot of people could be badly – irreparably – hurt. Lives would be ruined forever, with no chance of repair."

"Then I guess I have a decision to make," I say, standing up.

"You don't have to make it tonight," my aunt responds, rising from her chair to pull me into one of the tightest hugs she's ever given me. It feels like she's hanging on for dear life.

"No, but I can't stop thinking about it either, so I'm heading back to San Francisco."

"Not now. It's nearly midnight. You'll be driving all night, and Paul would never forgive me for letting you do that. Stay here and when you wake up in the morning, if you still feel you must go, leave then."

"I can't, Aunt Sally. I'm sorry, but I just can't. I have to deal with a problem I didn't create, isn't my fault, and profoundly affects me. You're asking me to reject our common Jewish heritage just like you and my mother did. You want me to live an artificial life others created for me that denies who I am just to support the status quo and not upset a lot of people. Surely you know that's asking more from me than any person should ever be asked to give up."

"No, Natalie, I don't know that. There was a day not so long ago when women didn't tear families apart. They worked hard to hold them together. That was all that mattered, and I honestly don't understand any of what's going on with you," my aunt sighs, holding her head with both hands.

"Those days are over, Aunt Sally. Women have found their voices and are claiming the right to live their own lives. It's not meant to hurt anybody else; it's just to stop others from continually hurting us." My aunt looks at me like I've just confessed to planning the overthrow of the federal government.

"Maybe it was Berkeley. I told Paul that university was full of wacko ideas and sending you there would come to no good. He said he wasn't worried, but hearing you talk like this, I imagine he's plenty worried now."

"I don't think so. He believes we all love each other too much to let anything come between us, and in the larger context of what's important in life, that's the only thing that really matters. Everything else is just noise. He trusts everyone else feels the same way and no one has any intention of proving him wrong."

"You do realize that your mother and I faced the same dilemma – to risk being who we were and face the consequences or to deny our heritage and be assured of a safer life... a better life, with more opportunities. We both chose denial, and it worked out."

"Until it didn't, Aunt Sally. Can't you see that? I'm sure part of what drew Charlotte into the war in Europe was a desire to reclaim herself. She might not have been able to say that, but I can't imagine it wasn't part of whatever it was that compelled her to go."

"And look what it cost her, Natalie. She paid an exorbitant price for what was essentially a very selfish decision. Choosing to be a Jew is taking a huge risk. You might be giving up much more than you realize and creating a lot more problems for yourself, and the rest of us, than you can possibly imagine, while gaining very little, if anything, in return."

"I don't know what to say, Aunt Sally. I honestly don't see it that way," I admit, swallowing hard.

"Believe me when I say I'm not enjoying this any more than you are, and another conversation very definitely needs to happen."

"I know, but I'm angry right now, and I really don't want to say something I'll regret. I don't think it's fair to ask me to continue this charade and pretend to be who I'm not just because that's better for everyone else. Except maybe it's not better. This isn't like being told not to bring my favorite chocolate cake to a family potluck because Mick prefers apple pie. We're talking about accepting or continuing to reject our core identity as human beings. You can deny that identity until the second coming of Christ, but it isn't going to change one damned thing. We are Jews, whether you like it or not. And whether you want it to be true or not true, it is true. And now that I know this, I can't just unknow it. I love you like life itself, Aunt Sally, but this is my truth, and I want to own it."

Finished with what I have to say, I walk out of the kitchen toward the hallway leading to the bedroom where I left my suitcase. It feels as though

RED ANEMONES

I'm setting out on the Bataan death march, fully aware it may be a very long time, if ever, before I walk down this hallway again.

"I really wish you'd wait until morning, sweetheart. You'll be driving through some dangerous neighborhoods to get to the freeway. They're no place for a woman alone at midnight," my aunt begs.

"I'll take my chances. And maybe that's what everyone else in this family who is afraid of the truth should do… stop letting fear control them and start being themselves," I suggest, letting the outside kitchen door slam as I walk to my car wondering whether I'll ever pass through that portal again. Reflexively, I stop and turn around to wave goodbye. My aunt is standing in the yellow glow of the back porch bug light, her face a study in agony. With tears running down her face, arms tight around herself, she's barely holding herself together.

"I'm glad you're finally home. Sally called at midnight hysterical," my father says, apparently having heard me unlock the door just before seven a.m. He is standing in the foyer in his ratty brown bathrobe and duct-taped slippers that he retrieves from the trash every time Herlinda throws them away. Looking at the dark shadows under his eyes, it's obvious that after my aunt's phone call he was awake the rest of the night.

"I'm not real calm myself," I say, tossing his car keys onto the table.

"She filled me in. We can talk about it now or after you've had a good night's sleep."

"I don't even know how to talk about it, Dad. How the fuck do you respond to someone you love very much and who has always loved you for exactly who you are and now is suddenly asking you to be someone you're not?" I scowl, taking a deep breath after using language I never use around my father.

"You're my daughter, Natalie. I have every confidence you'll figure it out," my eternally loving father smiles, turning around and walking toward the kitchen.

"There's fresh coffee. I'll make cinnamon toast if you want some, but first I have to let Sally know you're back," he calls out.

After a couple pieces of gooey cinnamon toast dripping butter and sugar, washed down with black coffee rich with fresh cream, I explain that I need some time alone and after a shower, am going back to Berkeley.

"You realize the reason this is so difficult is because there's so much love involved?" my dad asks. "If you and Emily and Sally didn't love each other so much this wouldn't be such a big deal. But you love each other a gigantic amount, so this entire scenario is emotionally off the Richter

Earthquake Scale. Be sure to remember that as you think this through and try to understand that Sally is scared she might be losing you."

"For god's sake, Dad. It's not like I'm going to the convent, or disappearing into some ashram deep in the interior of India, never to be seen again," I grouse.

"It feels that way to her."

"It's not like she and Emily can't come with me on this journey. There are no words for how much I'd love it if we were doing this together."

"Why don't you spend the morning riding the trolleys around the city – it might help clear your head. We can meet on the wharf for a late lunch, and you can catch the 4:30 bus to Berkeley," my father suggests. He knows that, over the years, grinding up and down San Francisco's steep hills in an antique wooden trolley that could break loose at any moment, crash into a million pieces, and yet people love riding anyway, is a very helpful distraction when I'm struggling to put any number of life's problems in perspective… and this is definitely the biggest life problem I've faced.

"Thanks for the suggestion. I'll see you at DiMaggio's around three," I tell my dad, kissing the top of his head and hoping to get a shower and leave before Herlinda shows up and goes all motherly on me.

"I take it the visit didn't go well," Adrian says, opening his apartment door to find me standing there.

"Is it that obvious?"

"To me, it is. I've already eaten but I can reheat something for you," he offers, pulling me into a hug. I shake my head to say I'm not hungry.

"Then it's two beers on the fire escape," he says, walking into his kitchen. A few minutes later we are sitting side by side, feet on the railing, each holding a bottle of cold, soothing beer. Adrian waits for me to speak, and when I don't, finally asks if I'd rather not talk about it." In response, I sum up the conversation with my aunt, explaining that my reaction was to leave.

"Maybe I should've stayed – tried to talk it through," I say.

"From what you've described, emotions were running too high for that. You were probably right to leave before either or both of you said things you couldn't take back," Adrian replies, patting my arm.

"I'm pretty irritated that all this emotional crap is being dumped on me… that what I do will, according to my aunt, 'rip the family apart' which everybody expects me to understand, without making any effort to see any part of this from my perspective. Never mind that the route they chose, and my aunt prefers, caused everybody a boatload of mental problems that drove them to the brink – and maybe beyond," I whine, taking a long swig of beer.

"As much as you'd like for all these revelations to not change things, it's pretty naïve to think they won't, Natalie. This is way too big for that."

"That's what my dad said this morning, and again at lunch. Somehow, try though I might, I just don't see it as being as monumental as my aunt thinks it is. To me this is not a lot different from deciding to change my hair color, or political affiliation, or career choice – it's a personal issue and not something everybody else is entitled to a vote on."

"Speaking personally, I like your hair color and hope you don't change it. Changing your political affiliation is an entirely different matter, and I have to warn you ahead of time that I don't see myself spending the rest of my life eating breakfast with a republican," Adrian teases. At least I think he's teasing, but I get his point: what seems relatively minor to one person, another person might view as catastrophic, which is precisely the situation I find myself in.

"The question is how things will change, and there's no way to know that ahead of time. It's a process you have to ride out. You're in it now, and there's no turning back," he continues.

"That's not quite true. If I stop this search to know my mother, pretend I'm not a Jew and get on with my life as before, knowing I'm denying who I am and living the family lie, nothing changes. It's pretty simple, actually."

"That's one option, but frankly, it won't work, because things have already changed. Pandora's box has been opened, and the contents have escaped. Besides, how will you ever understand your mother, or know who you really are, if you stop now?"

"I won't. I very much want to understand Charlotte, and I resent my aunt for not respecting that and instead, pressuring me to just drop this whole thing, especially since she knows I'll never do it."

"Your aunt understands that you have every right to know your mother, Natalie – she's just scared, and she has every right to be. There's plenty to be afraid of in a scenario like this."

"Obviously. It occurred to me yesterday that maybe my aunt fears knowing my mother more will make me love her less, which is ridiculous. My aunt is my mother. Charlotte was the incubator that enabled me to grow big enough to enter the world, but no way in hell was she ever a mother to me."

"Your mother was a truly unusual, very remarkable woman. It would be a real tragedy for you not to know her and treasure that knowledge for the gift that it is."

"She was definitely remarkable in that she has a hell of a lot of power over the people in her life – even from the grave. But I don't agree that there's any gift involved in this situation. I want to live an authentic life and for me, that is embracing the Jewish heritage she denied, yet bestowed upon me. The downside is that going down that road is going to cost me dearly."

"Maybe not…"

"I don't see how you can say that, Adrian. This journey into a new life is going to be very expensive in terms of relationships that matter to me as much as life itself. There's no way to avoid it. At some point, even Herlinda's going to get upset about it, and god knows that won't be pretty."

"So far, the consequences everyone is talking about are merely speculation, flowing from fear of the unknown. Often the things we fear the most never materialize," he reminds me.

"That's easy for you to say since you're not in the middle of all this," I snap, a little irritated at his Pollyanna-ish, everything will work out fine, attempt to minimize what feels like life in an emotional volcano about to erupt at any moment.

"It seems to me the best choice is for you to let this work itself out in its own time. You don't need to do anything other than what you're already doing. Don't force anything. Give the situation as much time and space as it needs to resolve itself and, one way or another, it will."

"If what you suggest is true and time is what's needed, then maybe it's a good thing I'm not returning to Chicago in three weeks."

"You're not?"

"I decided to stay here for fall term and finagled a leave. As it turns out, my sublet is available and given what's just occurred, it appears the impulsive decision to remain here is a good one in terms of the unresolved chaos in my life, even if I didn't think it through in those terms ahead of time."

"Why didn't you say anything?"

"I just decided a few days ago and then went down to Los Angeles. This is the first chance I've had to tell you. If you don't think having me around all fall is a good idea, just say so."

"Why would I think that, Natalie? I love having you around and wasn't looking forward to summer ending and your return to Chicago. I was not looking forward to traveling back and forth to Chicago every chance I got. On the upside, I would've experienced ice, snow, and the brutal winter wind off Lake Michigan again, and who doesn't enjoy that?" Adrian says, trying to lighten the conversation.

"I didn't make the decision based upon any assumptions regarding us, at least not consciously. But I probably should've discussed it with you anyway. It happened fast, and if it makes you feel any better, I haven't said anything to my dad yet, either."

"What made you decide to stay?"

"Wanting to take Rabbi Werner's seminar on Jewish spirituality you talked about is a big reason, among others."

"Seriously? I'm repeating it. There was too much to absorb the first time. I presented this dilemma to Saul, and he said he learns something new every time he teaches it and encouraged me to repeat it as often as I want to."

"Maybe we can be study partners," I smile. Adrian draws me into a one-armed hug and kisses the side of my head.

"That's a lot of brain power concentrated in one place," he teases.

"Yea – and doesn't even approach what the wise and learned rabbi brings to the table." We sit in amicable silence, until I ask the 'elephant in the room' question.

"Are you sure you don't mind me hanging around all fall? You might be looking forward to being on your own again and not want to say it."

"I might be looking forward to getting a root canal without Novocain, too, but it's highly unlikely. I hate flying, but for you, I was willing to do it as often as necessary," Adrian chuckles. "I mind you being around here all fall about as much as I mind sitting in Wrigley Field watching the Cubs. In other words, I can't think of anything I mind less. I'm really glad you're staying. I wasn't happy about what I knew was coming, which was going to be painfully missing you every hour of every day."

"That's a much more romantic answer than I was expecting," I smile, reaching for a kiss.

"Has it ever occurred to you that your mother saved the diaries, and all the things she had stuffed into them, because she wanted you to know everything?" Adrian asks a few minutes later.

"Not really. I've thought more along the lines of her forcing a choice between my living the life I'm entitled to, which her family turned their backs on, or living the life they decided to live, and denying my own identity. I've also considered the possibility she hadn't given any thought at all to the letters, diaries, or other stuff, which seems to me to be the most likely scenario."

"Maybe. But she could've destroyed all the evidence, and she didn't, so she must've been saving everything for a reason. Perhaps she struggled over the entire situation, and hoped you'd find these writings and shine a light on all that deceit and denial, bringing it to an end and giving you the life she always wanted and was never able to have herself."

"There's no way to know. She died suddenly, so maybe she intended to destroy everything and just never got around to it."

"That's one possibility. Eventually, you might get a pretty good feel for her intentions, which are hard to parse right now, when everything is in chaos. When emotions quiet down, a lot of times things become much clearer."

"You're sounding a little like a therapist. Maybe I should lay down on the couch, stare at the ceiling, and call you Dr. McCormick."

"I had a two-credit pastoral counseling class in seminary I really grooved on, which automatically makes me an expert on other people's lives. I discovered I really enjoy crazy people. They're much more interesting than predictably normal people."

"Good to know, Adrian... and I hope you're right about all this, because to be perfectly honest, right now I feel a little crazy."

"I think I'm beginning to understand why your mother wrote in German," he says, getting back to the diaries.

"Why?"

"It probably was to ensure that if anyone found the notebook, they couldn't read it. Evenutally, she was basically practicing medicine without a license and among other things, helping women resolve problem pregnancies."

"So, in addition to everything else, my mother was an abortionist?" I interrupt, astonished.

"It's possible, based upon what she writes. But she also provided other kinds of care, so it's hard to be one hundred percent sure."

"Jesus. I hardly know what to say. This just gets better and better..."

"You don't have to say anything. You weren't the one breaking the law."

"But it adds one more complication to the 'who should I tell what?' question. Should I tell my dad his wife was an abortionist – tell my aunt her sister was a criminal?"

"If your dad asks about what was in her diary, then be honest with him... same with your aunt. Otherwise, it's up to you what you want to volunteer."

"If it was up to me, I'd have chosen a different mother."

"My impression is a lot of people feel that way. It certainly crossed my mind from time to time," Adrian mumbles. We sit in silence, nursing our beers in the gloaming as the sun drops behind the neighborhood trees.

"She was an incredible woman, Natalie. Flawed like everyone else, yet so much more remarkable than most women of that era, and so far ahead of her time. Knowing more about the circumstances that shaped and defined her will make you feel better about everything."

"I don't see that happening. I don't even understand why having her as a mother is, as you suggest, a gift."

"Most people have ordinary mothers who do ordinary mother things… cook, keep house and care for the children… scold them, when necessary, pat them on the back when they get one hundred percent on their weekly spelling test, dry their tears and bandage their skinned knees. Those are all worthy and important tasks, but performing them results in a limited, clearly defined life without much wiggle room. Your mother wanted more."

"Obviously, since she did none of those things and instead did a lot of other things nobody thought were a good idea."

"True, but I'm getting the sense those were big, important, heroic, brave, and remarkable things most women never do, even in their wildest dreams. She left you a legacy few daughters receive. Someday you might decide that legacy is worth the cost to you, and to everyone else who knew and loved her."

"Maybe, but I definitely don't see it that way now."

"Try to trust me that eventually you will. You might not ever love her, but I'm sure you'll come to admire and respect her. Time and distance are great healers, Natalie, if you allow them to be."

Chapter Sixteen
פרק שש עשרה

Los Angeles
Fall, 1933

I vow to do no harm...

Today is my first day of nursing school. Having lied about my name, my age, and my religion to be here, I expected to be nervous, but I'm not. Instead, I feel proud to find myself, at seven o'clock on this Monday morning, sitting in the deep, circular amphitheater of Divine Providence Hospital, operated by the Catholic Church, and staffed by the Nursing Sisters of Divine Mercy. Divine Providence is Los Angeles' largest public hospital. When my sister, who is teaching in the south Los Angeles barrios heard this is where I would be coming, she said it was a great place to learn how to be a nurse because every imaginable illness, injury, and human tragedy eventually passes through its doors.

The large, haphazardly remodeled four-story, red brick building takes up an entire city block. Wide steps lead up to a cavernous, institutional entrance echoing with an emptiness that does not inspire comfort and healing. A gigantic cross jutting upward from the center of the roof assists ambulances unfamiliar with south Los Angeles to identify the hospital's exact location. I've never seen such a large building and my first glimpse yesterday afternoon extended to several minutes standing across the street, facing into the sun and staring at it. I would have stood there longer, but my nursing school acceptance letter included a general information sheet cautioning that the hospital neighborhood is not safe for young women alone.

I am disappointed to discover the run-down hospital and the surrounding neighborhood are worse than Bakersfield – if that is possible. The city is bigger, and noisier, and has more automobiles, streetcars, people, and buildings. The trees, with tall, skinny trunks and long, spiked leaves, look like like long handled floor mops sticking straight up out of the ground.

To qualify myself for acceptance into what is widely considered the best nursing school in California, I falsified my application. I was admitted as Charlotte Rose, Catholic, age eighteen years and three months. No one knows I am Rachael Rosenblum, Jewish, and one month shy of my seventeenth birthday.

A few weeks ago, I learned my father is keeping company with a young widow who introduced herself as Mrs. Edna Winfield. I harbor no feelings about Mrs. Winfield one way or the other but did not appreciate her view that nursing is not a suitable profession for a young woman of my privileged background. I told her she was entitled to her opinion but it might change if she ever got sick and needed more care than home remedies and untrained female relatives know to provide. She said caring for a husband and children is a more suitable life's work for a woman and I should set my sights on finding a man and having his babies. I pointed out everyone is entitled to their own choices, and my choice was to leave dusty, grimy Bakersfield for better opportunities.

"Girls are supposed to get married and raise a family, and that's what you'll eventually do. Expecting your father to send you to nurses' school is a waste of his money," she admonished. I smiled sweetly and walked away.

"Since Papa hardly notices I'm here, he probably won't notice I'm gone," I told Sarah as I was getting ready to leave home. She said he's sure to marry Edna Winfield, a young, childless widow, before too much longer, because men don't like being alone and want a woman to cook and do other things for them. She did not elaborate on what the other things were, or how she knew this. Mrs. Winfield is younger than Papa and I hope the other things don't include babies, because I don't see her as an endlessly devoted mother, and the possibility of a baby sister or brother obligating me to return to Bakersfield and help raise it clenches my stomach.

Orientation begins precisely on time, when everyone stands up from their seats as a tall, squarely built nun enters the amphitheater. With a voice like a foghorn, she identifies herself as Sister Immaculata, the Sister-in-Charge of Divine Providence School of Nursing, then proceeds down the stairs deftly managing not to trip on her long, heavy white dress which seems to me to be an impractical wardrobe choice for a nurse. I hope we will not be expected to wear something similar, because it would be very awkward to put that many clothes on each morning and then drag them around all day.

Everyone's eyes follow Sister Immaculata as she paces in a circle around the table in the center of the amphitheater, her arms crossed, hiding her hands somewhere in the deep sleeves of a flowing costume designed to totally obscure her identity. The sound of her shoes clicking across the tile floor combine with the wooden beads affixed to her leather belt crashing together to create the only noise in the room. The strong smell of formaldehyde lingering after a human anatomy class recently dissected a corpse is making me a little dizzy. To avoid passing out, I focus on the light through a small stained-glass window near the ceiling, depicting an image of someone looking remarkably like Sister Immaculata. The reflection casts an eerie, green glow over the nun's starched white clothing hiding all but her stern face. *She probably hasn't smiled in at least fifty years, but it's impossible to guess how old she is, and even if she wanted to smile, that stiff, tight cap wrapped around her head can't possibly allow her face to move that much*, I tell myself.

After clearing her throat, and making some sort of sign on herself, from her forehead downward, then across both shoulders, Sister begins with a several minute lecture emphasizing how seriously she takes her responsibility as a nursing instructor. She views being a nurse as a divine calling equal to the call to religious life and expects each of us to think of nursing in exactly the same way – as a vocation we are being divinely called to fulfill. Every person in the room is riveted on Sister Immaculata's inhale and exhale, unconsciously matching our own breathing to hers as she speaks. I've never been as afraid of anyone as I am of this nun.

"This hospital's sacred mission is to fulfill the Holy Gospel's mandate to care for and to heal others," she continues. "Our commitment to loving all of God's children because we love the God who created them defines our compassionate response to victims of crime, accidents, explosions, and other life-threatening situations that continuously arise in a city of just over one million people of various races, creeds, emotional conditions, financial circumstances, life-experiences and cultural backgrounds. We welcome the needy, indigent, diseased, and those suffering afflictions this city's other hospitals refuse, for various reasons, to treat. We are the hospital of last resort for those no one else wants. With the nation suffering a deep economic depression, millions are homeless, hungry, and wandering the streets, and Divine Providence willingly opens its doors, and its loving arms, to all of them. As a result, we are overrun with desperately ill and injured people having nowhere else to turn. Each of these individuals, no matter their physical or mental condition, is a living, breathing human being God created in His image, and is deserving of the best care we can possibly provide... and when we cannot save them, we bear witness to their death with deep compassion, empathy, and respect for the life they lived while they were on earth among us. No one, and I mean no one, in this hospital ever dies alone, unattended," Sister emphasizes, raising her voice several octaves at the same time she lands her fist on the dissecting table.

She goes on to explain that Divine Providence Hospital School of Nursing is the larger of only two accredited nursing schools in California and, due to the overwhelming demand for acute care, is currently staffed jointly by the Sisters of Charity of St. Catherine and the Sisters of Divine Mercy, the religious order to which she is solemnly vowed. The sacred, holy responsibility to which God has called her is to train eager, carefully chosen young women in the best practices involved in caring for the sick and dying, and those of us fortunate enough to be among the applicants she has meticulously selected for admission are expected to become exceptionally skilled in the art and science of professional nursing. Pausing for a moment, she then acknowledges that the rumor she turns away eight of every ten applicants is true.

"Despite being among the carefully chosen few, not all of you will succeed. Some of you will, for various reasons, leave before this first week is over; others will be dismissed for failing to pass your first or second exams, or doing poorly on subsequent ones; others vomit too easily or faint at the sight of blood – a sure sign you don't have a vocation to care for the sick and injured. Some will marry before completing the training program, which is automatic expulsion, or be asked to leave because of discipline problems or rule infractions. Those of you who survive our rigorous training program all the way to graduation will be damned fine nurses who will uphold the honor of the profession with grace and dignity, and will leave this hospital destined for greatness in the broad field of medicine," she barks, projecting deep conviction.

Sitting next to me, my nursing dorm mate, Callie, whispers that she thinks she just heard a nun swear – or maybe it was her imagination.

"I definitely heard it, but why is it a big deal?" I ask. Sister Immaculata, who can apparently hear just fine despite all the material covering her ears, immediately singles me out.

"So you have something to add to my remarks?" she challenges. I am too frightened to respond.

"Speak up, young lady. I didn't hear your answer," the nun commands.

"No, Sister. I have nothing to add. You've been very clear," I choke out.

"Then keep your mouth shut, your attention on me, and your random comments to yourself." I feel my face growing bright red and hot. Ignoring my embarrassment, Sister goes on to explain that our first week will be orientation to the massive hospital which she points out is both Los Angeles County and Southern California's largest charity hospital.

"This means, in addition to responding to accidents, fires, earthquakes and other public catastrophes, we treat the patients no one else wants... the alcoholics, the homeless, the prostitutes, gunshot victims, wives of heavy-handed husbands too fond of the drink, the destitute and indigent, the lame, the insane and the slow of mind, body or spirit other hospitals refuse. Every one of these individuals is, before anything else, a human being created by a God who loves them," she reminds us again.

"As nurses caring for these poor souls, we must never forget that treating their physical afflictions includes loving them as persons worthy of love. Each person we meet, no matter their condition or circumstances, deserves the same dignity and respect we automatically offer to the wealthy and fully competent. We treat a vicious murderer with exactly the same care and concern we extend to our own brother, sister, or parent. If any of you feel unable to offer the less fortunate the same respect and loving tenderness you offer your own loved ones, please leave now, so I can assign your place to one of the more than one hundred qualified young women on our waiting list. I hope I have made myself clear," Sister Immaculata forcefully emphasizes, then stops speaking to allow anyone who wishes to leave to do so. Everyone remains stone-still in their seats.

"You are expected to pass all of your examinations with at least a ninety-three percent score, meaning you must answer nine out of every ten questions correctly and answer at least three exceptionally well. If you score between eighty-five and ninety-three percent, you will be allowed to retake a different form of the same exam once. If you fail the second time, you will be dismissed from the program. This may seem harsh, and it is. You are dealing with human lives, and mistakes are matters of life and death. The margin of error is extremely narrow," the nun scowls. *So far, our orientation is mostly a test of who is brave enough to risk the wrath of a humorless, extremely determined nun,* I conclude after listening to her rant.

"Upon successful completion of your course work, clinical assignments, and examinations, you will be well-prepared to take the national licensing exam. Only after you have passed this exam will you be capped, receive the pin signifying completion of this hospital's nursing program, and be entitled to be called 'Nurse Jones' or whatever your surname is. Prior to that time, you are Miss whatever your surname is."

Our studies include anatomy, physiology, chemistry, biology, Pharmacology, and basic physical and mental health. We are also expected learn, through clinical experience, the skills associated with nursing care, including medication management, infection control, surgical assistance, and patient comfort. We are offered electives in community-based midwifery and pediatrics, public health nursing, emergency response and crisis care, surgical nursing, and sub-specialty care of choice. I already know I want to care for distressed women, because they often need female-specific care and are unlikely to receive it. With this in mind, I am looking forward to as many of the relevant learning experiences as possible. Nevertheless, Sister Immaculata strikes fear of failure in my heart, and I realize nothing in my life at this time is more important than giving my full attention to learning how to become a nurse. There is no question in my mind this goal is within my reach – as long as no one discovers I'm Jewish and too young to be here.

Each hospital ward is headed by a nun and staffed by a combination of nursing sisters, regular nurses, medical and nursing students, doctors completing their training and staff physicians. Because the wards are always overflowing and perpetually understaffed, Sister Immaculata stresses that students are badly needed extra pairs of hands and are often plunged into situations for which we have little to no formal training, sometimes forcing us into quick, life-or-death decisions we are unprepared to make, with only our common sense to guide us. Without explaining how, she says we should emotionally prepare ourselves for these eventualities. Hearing this, I send Callie a questioning look. She responds by folding her hands in prayer, something I know absolutely nothing about.

"Every possible disease and injury you can imagine, and many you can't even begin to imagine, pass through our doors seeking our help. You will be expected to fully participate in caring for these suffering human beings and ask as many questions as you need to ask while you're doing it. Each encounter is a learning opportunity as well as a challenge to refine your intuitive sense... and you must never, ever underestimate the importance of intuition and simple common sense in caring for the sick and injured, because you will never become a good nurse without those attributes," Sister Immaculata proclaims so forcefully her voice bounces off the back wall. Watching her pace back and forth across the amphitheater, *She sounds more like a drill sergeant in General John "Black Jack" Pershing's infamous Allied Expeditionary Force than a healer of the sick,* I think, recalling that lesson in history class last year.

"Nursing is the noblest all professions. For as long as you live, you must always remember that it is a profound privilege to be called to minister to God's suffering people, and you will meet this challenge with humility, dignity, devotion, and unwavering determination to heal the sick, attend the dying and relieve pain in mind and body wherever you find it – and whenever it finds you. Most importantly, when all else fails, you must intuitively know when to back off and let God take over." She repeats the last sentence several times, then falls silent for what seems like hours as she looks at each of us directly. Finally, she asks for questions. When no one is brave enough to raise her hand, we are dismissed with instructions to move to a table where another nun, dressed identically to Sister Immaculata, is issuing the student nurse uniforms we will wear for the next thirty-six months. She doesn't smile, either.

"Did you notice all the patron saints of nursing?" Callie asks, referring to the larger-than-life windows depicting St. Agnes of Sicily, St. Elizabeth of Hungary and St. Camillus of Lellis in stained glass. An even larger window image of St. Catherine of Siena adorns the hallway leading to the auditorium where we just spent the last ninety minutes. I nod, wondering what, exactly, a patron saint is? Walking down the hall, Callie asks me whether, after what we've just heard, I think we'll survive the program all the way to graduation.

"Of course I do – don't you?"

"I guess so, but that nun scares me, and I'm pretty used to irritable nuns. She's a lot worse than most. If they're all like her, I'm not sure I'll stick it out."

"Sister Immaculata scared me, too, but I won't let her foul disposition stop me," I declare.

"I heard the nun in charge of the emergency department carries a gun," Callie says, wide-eyed, as we approach the table where Sister Immaculata stands at attention, supervising the distribution of our uniforms.

"Do something with your hair, Miss Rose. Either cut it off or braid it and pin it tightly to your head. Cutting is preferable," a stern-faced nun, with no visible hair of her own, directs me after I sign for two light blue dresses with red belts and dark blue cape. I am very relieved to discover we will not be required to wear yards and yards of heavy white material fashioned in the medieval costume apparently reserved just for the nuns.

"Cut your fingernails, Miss Moynihan. Long fingernails breed germs,

germs spread infections, and infections kill people," she instructs Callie, handing her a pair of manicure scissors and pointing toward a waste basket. The next person in line is told to wash the makeup off her face and the person after that is scolded for wearing too much perfume, which, among other things, invites unwanted responses from male patients and other hospital personnel. The harsh rebuke causes the nicely smelling student to burst into tears.

"If you can't take criticism you won't last until the end of the week," Sister Immaculata grumbles, handing the girl a Kleenex and stepping forward to clap her hands for our attention. She reminds us that cleanliness is next to godliness, and this is achieved with soap and water, not makeup and perfume, neither of which have any place in a hospital setting. A few of my classmates groan in response. *They won't last long either,* I think.

"From the sounds of it, I guess we better develop a personal relationship with those saints, because we're going to need all the help we can get," Callie sighs, referring to the larger than life images we passed earlier. We receive textbooks, notebooks, and satchels at the next table, then are told to return to the dorm, change into our uniforms and report to the nurses' dining room by noon for lunch, and reconvene in the amphitheater at one o'clock.

"How do I look?" Callie asks, her Irish blue eyes dancing as she adjusts her belt." "Like a student nurse," I respond, hassling with my thick hair.

"I've wanted to be a nurse since I was five years old, but never believed my mother would agree to me leaving Riverside to come all the way to Los Angeles for nursing school… and now, here I am," Callie reflects, sounding as if she might cry.

"What made her change her mind?"

"She didn't. She died and my dad said if I got into nursing school it was fine with him, as long as he didn't have to pay for it. He viewed me leaving as one less kid to worry about, although he wasn't happy about it because he depended on me to watch the little kids and take care of the house, which is my little sister's responsibility now. How about you? How'd you end up here?"

"Similar story. My mother died, my older sister was already in college, my father works for the railroad and isn't home much… and is probably going to remarry soon. He didn't object to my coming and never made an issue about the cost. If your dad's not paying, how are you affording this?" I ask.

"Our parish priest agreed to front the money, with the understanding than when I'm finished, I return to Riverside and work in the local hospital, which happens to also be run by this order. Seemed fair, so I agreed. Where are you from originally? Rose isn't a common name around here," Callie asks, continuing our casual, get-acquainted conversation from the previous evening. Having answered this question in my admission interview, I repeat that I was born in Ohio and ended up in Bakersfield when my father accepted an opportunity to work for the expanding Union Pacific Railroad.

"But what kind of name is Rose?"

"Danish."

"You don't look Danish," Callie challenges.

"Not all Danes are blue-eyed blonds... those from further south frequently have darker hair and eyes," I say, hoping European geography wasn't one of Callie's stronger subjects in high school. By now I have finished securing my hair to my head and buttoned the top button of my uniform.

"I'm ready if you are," I say, hoping to change the subject.

"We have a few minutes. Let's unpack the rest of our stuff," Callie answers, pulling her suitcase from under her bed. All we were required to bring with us were stockings, ugly, low-heeled oxford shoes, underwear, nightwear, and basic toiletries and it takes less than ten minutes to put these away in drawers.

"What's that?" Callie asks, nodding toward a leather-bound book I'm holding.

"My sister gave me a dairy as a birthday present, and at the last minute I decided to bring it with me. I've never kept one for very long, but after listening to Sister Immaculata, I'm pretty sure I'll appreciate doing it now," I answer evenly, carefully placing the small book in the bottom drawer of my chest for the moment. Now that it has been discovered, I'll either have to hide it or fill it with meaningless nonsense I don't care if anyone else reads, which defeats the purpose of keeping a diary. If I want to be honest about what I write, it is best kept under my mattress and written in German, which is a way to keep one connection with my real self, but is risky. *If someone finds it, they won't be able to read it, but I might also get accused of spying,* I caution myself.

Leaving our room a few minutes later, I see a gigantic cross with a dead man hanging on it affixed to the wall at the end of the hallway. Somehow, I had failed to notice this gory, oversize depiction of human suffering earlier.

"What the hell is that?" I gasp, having now uttered more swear words in the last two hours than in the nearly seventeen previous years of my life.

"It's the crucified Christ – obviously. How did you not know that?" Callie frowns. I start to explain that I've never seen anything like it before, then remember I'm supposedly Catholic and should know what a crucifixion looks like.

"I'm just surprised I hadn't noticed it before now," I stammer.

"He's hanging everywhere, so get used to it," Callie winks, adding that obviously I don't take being Catholic very seriously – an accusation I decide it's better not to deny.

"My mother put a crucifix on the wall beside my crib. It was the first thing I saw when my baby eyes began to focus," Callie continues.

"Didn't it scare you?" I ask, finding it hard to imagine sleeping with such a thing hanging above my bed, staring down at me.

"Not really. I was five or six before I understood what it was, and began to understand Catholic guilt, which is, as you are no doubt aware, never-ending. Truthfully, I still have a hard time believing we are born sinful and Christ died to redeem us from this unfortunate condition over which we had no control and automatically blighted our soul, obligating us to spend the rest of our lives apologizing. Seeing him hanging on the cross is a constant reminder of what we drove the poor guy to and keeps you from feeling too good about yourself, which hardly seems fair. How did you manage to grow up not knowing this?"

"My family wasn't very Catholic," I stammer. Anxious to end this conversation, I duck into the lavatory, claiming my hair is coming loose and I need to re-fasten it in front of a mirror.

"It'll be a lot easier if you just cut it all off," Callie calls after me, tossing her own head of short red curls in a circle. She's probably right, but entering to nursing school has already forced me to give up too much of myself in order to become someone others will find acceptable, because who I really am is somehow unacceptable. *The Jewish version of Catholic guilt,* I muse, taking slight comfort in the realization that I'm not the only one struggling with chronic unworthiness. Feeling suddenly rebellious, I resolve to never cut my dark auburn hair.

Six students disappear during our first two weeks – proof that Sister Immaculata's claim that several of us will leave immediately was not exaggerated. The struggle to keep up with studies and become oriented to the hospital routines evolves into an endurance contest that, so far, I'm managing only because I've never needed much sleep.

Mornings begin on the wards at six, when doctors make their rounds, checking on their patients; afternoons are dedicated to lectures and labs, learning biology, chemistry, and human anatomy. Evenings are spent studying, except for twice-weekly night duty, one of which is always spent in the emergency department. Sister Agnes, head of emergency nursing, explains she has never understood why most medical crises occur between nine o'clock at night and five o'clock in the morning, but they do.

"Those eight hours of darkness are when people are most likely to shoot each other, stab each other, beat each other up, set themselves or someone else on fire, get hit by cars, kicked by horses, break various bones or suddenly become sicker than they were during the daylight hours. It's also when the drunks show up looking for a warm place to sleep it off. I promise you will never be bored here, nor will you ever shut your eyes or catch your breath," she tells us, cleaning a spot of what appears to be blood off one of the generous, sleeves she's somehow managed to wrap tightly around her arm.

My first night rotation on emergency services involves the crib death of an undernourished infant the mother registered as Misty Sullivan. The circumstances arouse Sister Agnes' suspicions and she instructs me to report the incident to child welfare because there are several other children in the home and "there's something off about the mother" who refused to give us her name or an address. Saying I'm a little reluctant to report someone to a government agency based upon nothing more than a hunch, I press for more information. All she will say is that she doesn't like the mother's response to her baby's death and suspects it wasn't accidental, which makes it likely the mother is abusing her other children, and she wants their situation investigated. Sensing my reticence, she launches into a fifteen-minute lecture on the art of saving lives which frequently involves deferring to well-developed intuition.

"A nurse is only as good as her intuitive knowledge, Miss Rose, and if you aspire to be a good nurse, work on your observation skills and pay attention to your own internal reaction to what you see," she instructs.

"If, for whatever reason, something doesn't seem right, it probably isn't." My impression is that the nun is a little too willing to dismiss the lack of hard evidence in favor of first impressions and gut feelings, but I am in no position to challenge her and do as I am told.

Later that night an unidentified man, labeled a John Doe, dies from bullet wounds to his stomach. I sit with him through his final moments because, as Sister Immaculata hammered home to us, no one in her hospital dies alone, and everyone else is too busy trying to save lives to prioritize a dying man's final moments. It is my first direct experience with death, and I find it deeply calming and much less frightening than I imagined.

"I think he knew I was there… he might have squeezed my hand," I tell Sister Agnes, as the nun pronounces the man dead.

"I'm sure he did, dear. But hurry on to cubicle seven. The nurse there needs help with a stabbing victim," she replies.

The stabbing victim, a young man smelling of life on the streets, is sent to surgery. While I'm cleaning the cubicle in preparation for the next patient a woman identifying herself as Molly Leary staggers through the door claiming her husband beat her up. Regardless of whether this accusation is true, her nose is broken, a cut over her right eye is bleeding profusely, her other eye is swollen completely shut and her jaw is misaligned. I ask Sister Agnes about reporting the assault to the police.

"Why do you think the police care about a husband beating his wife? It happens all the time, especially among the Irish, who are always getting in their cups and insisting the world done them wrong. He'll claim she deserved it, and they'll believe him. There's no point in reporting it," the nun growls. Knowing from my own family experience that not all husbands beat their wives, I start to argue with this assumption.

"The only way a woman can avoid this kind of thing is to not get married in the first place," the nun frowns knowingly, allowing a trace of an Irish brogue to leak into her words. *You're wrong*, I think to myself, but decide against expressing myself out loud.

Among the other badly hurt women needing emergency care on my first night are two more wives, two runaways, and three prostitutes. Sister explains that the prostitutes are managed by men she calls Johns, who often beat them when they don't earn enough money, which makes no sense, because a beat-up prostitute earns even less.

"I'm not an expert on prostitution, but it doesn't take a mental giant to figure that out," she says, shaking her head as she cleans up the cubicle after stitching up the young woman's face in three places, then sending her to the hospital's overnight observation ward.

Eventually, a child welfare worker shows up to interview the still nameless mother of the crib death infant. She agrees with Sister Agnes that the mother's explanation doesn't add up and that, for their own safety, the other children must be placed in orphan care until she can investigate further. When I ask how she can do this when the mother refuses to reveal her name or provide an address, I'm told they "have their ways." This hasty decision, based on impression over verified facts, bothers me greatly. A mother who just lost one child to death is now losing her others to the welfare system, and since she is obviously impoverished, uneducated, and without a husband or apparent means of supporting herself or her children, having them ever returned to her is unlikely. When I raise this with Sister Agnes, she points out that the children's safety and overall welfare comes first and assures me the mother has an income, just not a legitimate one.

"Don't be surprised if she shows up here some night in as bad, or worse, shape as the woman we sent upstairs a few hours ago," the nun cautions.

By the end of the shift, I am in tears, both from exhaustion and my first glimpse into the ugly underbelly of human existence. Sister Agnes' response to this display of deeply felt emotion is a lecture on toughening up; otherwise, I will be a useless failure as a nurse and am wasting my time, her time, and everyone else's time. *I had no idea life could be this horrible,* I think, reflecting on the brutality I've seen in just one night and wondering, for the first time, whether I have the emotional stamina to deal with it.

The other night duty assignment students routinely receive is in maternity because babies are born when they want to be born and nights are just as busy as days. The first birth I witness is twins, and one is dead because the cord is knotted around his neck. Sister Hildegard, the maternity floor night supervisor, seeing that the baby has never drawn a breath, says there is no need to baptize it, whatever that means, and instructs me to take it away at once. Even though the baby's mother is begging to hold her child who, until a few moments ago, was alive inside her, the nun insists it is in her best interests not to see or hold her dead infant. I delay until after sister and the doctor leave the room, then take the lifeless infant to his small, rail-thin mother, who is barely old enough to bear a child. When the nun unexpectedly returns and discovers what I've done, she lets loose with a loud scolding. Through her tears, the mother comes to my defense, pointing out it is her fault… she wanted to hold her baby and I only did what she begged me to do. The outburst ends with Sister Hildegard demanding I apologize for my insubordination and vowing to obey orders in the future. I follow the request for an apology but not before mentally hollowing it out by reminding myself that I'm not sorry for breaching hospital policy and allowing a grieving mother a moment with her firstborn, who never took a breath of life-giving air or saw the light of day.

"I did the right thing," I insist, recounting the experience to Callie, who listens without comment.

My second birth experience occurs six nights later, in the hospital elevator, on my way back to maternity after taking a break in the all-night cafeteria. According to the mother, who says her name is Consuelo, her seventh child is coming much faster than the others. She is correct about the fast part because near the third floor, a baby appears. The elevator operator, first complaining about the mess in his elevator, then announcing he is going to faint, stops between floors so he can sit with his head between his legs. The warm smell of blood, fluid and tissue filling the cramped, airless space is making me feel faint too, but the baby, with the placenta still attached, is bringing forth lusty cries that demand my attention. I yell at the operator to get a grip and do his job so we can get this mother and baby up to the fifth floor where they belong. Afterwards, I report to Sister Hildegard that I managed everything very well considering how scared I was, then confess that the part about birth being a miracle completely escaped me.

"From what I have observed so far, having a baby is a very painful, extremely messy and exhausting experience," I say, between deep breaths. Sister Hildegard shrugs, walking away.

"All's well that ends well," she grumbles over her shoulder, fingering her beads.

The following day, I barely stay awake through my first two written exams. A few days later, prepared for the worst, I am shocked to learn I scored second highest in my class on one and third highest on the other. I am very proud of myself, until Sister Immaculata points out the first exams are purposely less difficult to acclimate students to the rigid testing standards required of aspiring nurses.

Despite this accommodation, five students fail badly and are told to leave. Two others decide to leave voluntarily, and twelve will be retaking one or both of the exams in two days. Breathing a sigh of relief, I return to my dorm room to lay down for a half hour before the three to eleven emergency room shift. The next thing I know, Callie is shaking me awake, yelling that Sister Agnes is on a rant looking for me. Yawning, with my hair falling down and wearing a uniform I've slept in, I arrive in the emergency room in less than fifteen minutes, greeted by an angry nun insisting that there is no place in the nursing profession for anyone who prefers napping over hard work.

Having survived the first six months of my three-year training period, I request an extended clinical rotation in the new midwife program the hospital is launching. Its purpose is to train nurses to provide care to expectant mothers who, for various reasons including a fear of hospitals, distrust of male doctors, an inability to pay, or all three, refuse to seek prenatal care, choosing instead to have their babies at home, attended by a female neighbor or relative. These women know that if complications arise they, and their babies, will most likely die, yet prefer that risk over a safer, medically supervised pregnancy and birth.

The program will serve the heart of the south Los Angeles barrios, personally visiting pregnant women living in squalid conditions throughout the area, many of whom are here illegally and neither speak nor understand English. Frequently, their babies, who are often low birth weight due to maternal poverty and lack of prenatal care, do not survive. The same is true for the mothers. Sadly, the outcomes for both would have most likely been different in the hospital.

Sister Michael Joan, the formidable midwife program supervisor with little patience for anyone except the mothers-to-be she cares for, is determined to improve the survival odds for home births. Her approach to preparing us to meet this goal is similar to Sister Immaculata's and involves a complete lack of patience and a lot of frustrated yelling at everyone but the patients she is caring for. For someone who has never had a baby herself, the nun exhibits amazing compassion and love for the women, whether it's their firstborn or their tenth.

"When all else fails, we pray, but only after we have done everything we possibly can for the mothers and babies, and we can do plenty. Don't get in the habit of giving up too soon, thinking prayer is the answer, because it's not. We nurses are the answer," she stresses again and again, beginning with our very first moments shadowing her.

"She's two people – a loving, compassionate one and an enraged one. I've never seen anyone as tough as she is. She takes on anybody and doesn't back down until she gets what she wants," I tell Callie after the first time I follow Sister Michael Joan on her rounds.

"Most of the time the women are grateful for our help, but the men in their lives are often angry and drunk. Sister tells them to get lost and not come back until they're sober and ready to act like responsible husbands and fathers; otherwise, they'll have her to answer to. My guess is most of them, not wanting to risk another encounter with a nun who hates men and would happily castrate them all, are never seen again. Honestly, it's probably good riddance."

"Does she carry a gun too?" Callie asks, wide-eyed.

"I haven't seen one, but it wouldn't surprise me," I answer.

Functioning as visiting nurses as well as midwives, we treat the common diseases of poverty we encounter every day – malnutrition, scabies, ulcerated leg sores, lice, and chronic respiratory problems – in addition to emaciated mothers who can't make enough milk, causing their babies to be labeled "failure to thrive". These infants often manage to hold onto life, but their grip is weak. Sister Michael Joan always baptizes the babies, even those who die, which comforts their mothers, who claim theirs is no life to bring another human being into anyway. In their minds, dying isn't as bad as a lifetime living in squalor with no hope of ever escaping. Even though I have rarely pondered the existence of an afterlife, and carry no personal beliefs about the possibility, I can't disagree about death being the better option when life is as horrible as what some of these women endure, with no chance of ever getting even slightly better.

Not infrequently, nurse midwives encounter women pleading for help to stop a pregnancy from advancing. They threaten that, if Sister or one of her nurses don't do something, they'll take care of it themselves which means they'll very likely either bleed to death or die from infection, leaving their already existing children motherless. When the over-distraught mother is reminded about the risks of a self-induced abortion and her responsibilities to the children she already has, the common response is that her life is barely survivable as it is and another baby will kill her, so she is dead either way.

Sister Michael Joan rarely turns her back on these women. After observing her efficiently perform what she calls a "corrective procedure for a complicated pregnancy", it isn't difficult to figure out what she is doing, which is against the law and the rules of the Catholic Church. After thinking about it and becoming concerned about the illegalities involved, I approach the no-nonsense nun. Before my first sentence is out of my mouth, she silences me, then proclaims some things are worth going to jail for, and she'll worry about going to hell later. She forcefully commands that I do as I am told and keep my mouth shut, then informs me that we will never speak of this again.

The conversation occurs while we are taking a short break, sitting on the wooden steps leading up to the dark, third floor of a warehouse storing equipment for the Long Beach oil rigs. An enterprising landlord divided the area into several windowless two-room apartments sharing a single kitchen and bathroom, then making them available to oil workers' families cheap, as part of a "compensation package" that includes housing. What the arrangement really means is the rent is deducted from the workers' paychecks, and if they lose their jobs, their families lose the roof over their heads – if the tin sheet covering the top of the building can even be called a roof.

"This place ain't fit living for stray dogs," Sister Michael Joan groans, hefting her bulk onto her feet and trying not to take a deep inhale of the surrounding air contaminated by the strong odor of urine mixed with crude oil, stale food, overflowing toilets, and rotting fish. She motions me to follow her.

While I am deeply immersed in learning midwifery, I receive a letter from my father announcing he is marrying Edna Winfield and asking me to come to Bakersfield to attend the ceremony and a small reception afterwards. I'm not interested in either witnessing or celebrating his marriage and use the demands of my nursing program as an excuse for being unable to attend. A few days later, I receive a letter from Sally saying she isn't going to attend our father and Edna's marriage either, and that she and Edwin are divorcing.

Edwin wanted me to stop teaching and start having babies, and I refused. He always claimed otherwise, but never had a job for more than a couple weeks, and it didn't make sense for me to quit working or start having babies when I'm the only one earning a regular paycheck. I love teaching in the barrios, where no one else will go, which is how I kept my job after marrying Edwin. It would've been impossible to hire someone to take my place if I was made to leave because I was married, so they let me stay. I use my own money to buy extra food and clothes for the children because if they are warm and fed, they stand a greater chance of maybe learning something, my sister writes. I never envisioned her having any kind of commitment to the poor, but based upon what I am exposed to every day, I find it deeply gratifying that she does.

As my first year of nursing school ends, I am very proud of myself. I rank second in some classes, third in others, and first in clinicals. Both Sisters Agnes and Hildegard give me good reviews, and, to my great surprise, Sister Michael Joan sings my praises loudest of all. I report all this to my father, assuring him the money he is spending on my nursing school education isn't wasted. Normally I wouldn't bother, but I harbor a nagging suspicion of Edna and her motives for marrying a much older man, and it wouldn't surprise me if she objected to my father spending their money on my tuition. I don't think he would agree with her, but I don't want to give her any reason to open the conversation, either.

Year two begins one week after first-year final exams are over and includes more advanced classes as well as extended clinical time. Second-year students spend longer shifts on the wards, taking care of the same patients for several hours. We also rotate through the pharmacy, learning how to compound medications, which is a lot like chemistry lab, or cooking from a recipe, provided we can read the doctors' handwriting on the prescriptions. I far prefer treating patients over mixing medicines, and find the pharmacy boring but Sister Helena, the chief pharmacist, continually stresses that safe medication management is vital to patient care.

"If pharmacists make a mistake, they can just as easily end a life as save one, so get over being bored and pay careful attention," she scolds when I complain. Callie insists the pharmacy exam is the hardest one, which I believe because, although I studied much harder for it than usual, I only scored ninety-three – barely passing. Over half the class including Callie, had to retake it.

"I'd rather be taking care of people instead of mashing X and Y together and then mixing it with lubricants, alcohol, saline, distilled water, or something I don't even want to think about," I complain to my sister on one of her infrequent visits a few days later. Her response is to explain that she has shown up unexpectedly to tell me she is getting married again and wants me to be with her at city hall for the brief ceremony. She doesn't say much about her soon-to-be second husband but describes him as very different from Edwin in every possible way, including natural charm and good looks.

"He isn't Edwin, but he holds down a job, knows how to fix things, and shows up when he says he will. I can't ask for more than that," she insists, with a surprising lack of enthusiasm about this change in her life. As much as I want to be with her, I explain the best I can do is try, but I can't promise.

Two weeks later, wearing my cape over my uniform because I didn't have time to change my clothes, I rush downtown, arriving just as my sister is reciting marriage vows for the second time. As soon as the ceremony concludes Sally runs into the bathroom. I follow and find her throwing up. Sobbing uncontrollably, she announces she is pregnant and terrified. I don't know what to do other than try to comfort her and promise to keep in closer touch.

Less than an hour later, riding the streetcar back to the hospital, I wonder whether, considering how upset she is, I should have asked her whether she wants a baby. I raise the question a few nights later, when I call to check on her. She admits she's not sure she wants to be a mother yet, but her husband has already guessed about the pregnancy so it's too late to do anything about it now.

My new brother-in-law, who goes by Mick, is squarely built, already balding, and considerably shorter than my tall, slender sister. He seems nice enough, although a little rough around the edges and not nearly as charming as Edwin who, despite his basic character flaws and tendency toward laziness, I was fond of. Mick works in the oil fields near Long Beach, not far from where Sally spends her days teaching the oil rig workers' children how to read, write, and add simple numbers. She and Mick are an odd match, and I can't help wondering what my sister sees in him.

The following month I begin a rotation in community nursing, the umbrella under which the midwife program functions. The nurse midwives do pre- and post-natal maternal care, deliver babies, and follow their development for a year, if they can keep track of a mother for that long. The community nurses take care of everything else, treating a wide variety of diseases and patients, wherever we find them, including local jails, flop houses, slum apartments, tents, city parks, aimlessly wandering the streets, panhandling, or sleeping in doorways. Both programs dispense birth control, even though the nurses work for a Catholic hospital and the Catholic Church forbids the practice. Since the patients are transients who never stay in one play for long, there is almost no chance either the hospital or the Church will find out what we are doing.

Sister Nora runs the community health program with such enforced determination, discipline and precision I often wonder whether she was a military officer in a previous life. She freely dispenses condoms, and after watching her do this for a few weeks, I can't resist asking where, as a Catholic nun, she gets them and how she justifies the practice.

"The answer to both questions, Miss Rose, is between me and my God. I strongly recommend never raising this issue again – ever," she commands. I can't help marveling at the amazing amount of self-confidence she holds regarding her decision to go against both her hospital's policy and her church's directives. If caught, she faces dire consequences, including expulsion from her religious community and excommunication from the Catholic Church. The certainty and courage with which she forthrightly carries out the courage of her convictions is admirable.

For reasons I don't understand, it appears the hard-working, no-nonsense nun is slowly beginning to trust me. Occasionally she specifically requests my help in treating several "mothers in distress," as she calls them. After several months of providing this kind of care to profoundly desperate women, I determine that Sister Nora is exactly the kind of nurse I want to be and eagerly help her however I can, wherever she sends me. Soon I am setting simple fractures, stitching up wounds, treating bedsores, infected insect and rat bites, and supplying whiskey to dying patients, along with whiffs of chloroform and whatever else I can concoct to relieve their suffering… and I am performing abortions.

One evening, after a particularly difficult delivery, Sister Nora tells me I "have what it takes" to be a truly good nurse. She suggests choosing electives that offer additional time in maternity and in the emergency department, which is the best preparation for community nursing.

"Learn as much as you can in those rotations, and I'll teach you everything else you need to know," she smiles – a rare gesture among the nuns I've met so far. I soon learn the value of a procedure called a dilation and curettage, performed to clean out a uterus that won't stop bleeding. It is a useful procedure for performing abortions as well as treating post-partum hemorrhaging which, if not brought under control quickly, is fatal to the mother. I learn how to cut and then repair an episiotomy needed to widen the birth canal and to use forceps when a baby is stuck and needs help coming into the world. A forceps delivery brutal for the mother, but sometimes necessary to extract a particularly large or poorly positioned infant. Whenever possible, I offer the mother a generous amount of whiskey to help her endure this barbarian, yet life-saving procedure.

"In a hospital doctors perform these procedures, but out in the community there are no doctors and we're on our own," Sister Nora explains as we assist Sister Michael Joan with a particularly gruesome delivery that nearly tears the mother apart but ultimately results in a robust, wailing eleven-pound baby.

"By the way, a baby that big means the mother probably has sugar diabetes. You'll need to check her for that and if she does, get her some insulin and teach her how to inject it," the exhausted nun adds as our late-night streetcar bumps along toward the hospital. A moment later, her head is bouncing off my shoulder.

I soon realize that many of our maternity patients are women who have been raped, beaten, suffer from venereal diseases and pregnancies they don't want, and are attached to bad men. Despite the harm these men inflict, the women somehow convince themselves they love them and believe everything will be fine when he gets a job, quits drinking, stops gambling, or gets out of jail, because she is sure he learned his lesson this time. When none of these hopes materialize, she blames herself for not being a better wife or girlfriend.

"The biggest problem these women have is no way to safely escape their abuser. They know not to expect the police to protect them, but there's nowhere else to turn," Sister Nora explodes following a repeat visit to a frightened young mother of six whose husband has rearranged what was probably a once beautiful face so many times her own mother would no longer recognize her.

Late one night, six months after Sally's marriage, I receive a panicky call from Mick saying Sally is in labor at Long Beach Community Hospital.

"Something ain't right, Charlotte – you gotta come," he pleads. Despite desperately needing sleep, I leave the dorm, arriving at Long Beach Community just as the doctor is telling Mick the baby has died and Sally, very weak from blood loss, is barely hanging on.

"We don't have any blood on hand but have put out a request to nearby hospitals. I hope to have some within the hour – two at most. Hopefully this will be soon enough," the doctor says. I interrupt to explain I'm Sally's sister, and if our blood types are compatible, he could do a direct transfusion. Half an hour later I'm stretched on a portable gurney next to my sister's bed with a tube running between us. Sally moans, then screams. I can't tell whether she's in physical or emotional pain – or both. When the screaming continues, I ask the nurse to give her something to calm her down.

"We don't usually give mothers anything at this stage. We don't want to affect the baby," the nurse answers dismissively.

"Her baby's dead – it doesn't matter. Give her some goddamned morphine," I shout with a vengeance that rivals Sister Michael Joan's, and I didn't know I possessed. My tortured outburst momentarily silences my sister.

A doctor finally appears, quickly examines Sally, and says to prep her for a deep episiotomy and high forceps delivery so he can extract the dead fetus, whose head is lodged high in the birth canal. The nurse clamps off the tube joining me to my sister and removes it, while another nurse hangs a bag of fresh blood on a pole near Sally's head. No one directs me to leave, so I stay in the room, still holding my sister's hand. A few minutes later, the doctor forcibly extracts a floppy, dark blue baby girl from my sister's body. He cuts the cord and hands the lifeless infant to the nurse.

Sally is wailing again and this time it's clearly from both pain and sorrow. She squeezes my hand and through her sobs whispers that she was going to name the baby Rachael if it was a girl, but since she is dead, she doesn't need a name, then lets out an exhausted sigh and goes quiet.

Moments later, with my sister in a state of twilight sleep, I go into the hall looking for the baby. The first nurse won't tell me where she is, and the second one says Sally isn't her patient and she doesn't know what happened to her baby. As I am clearly informing these nurses of my very poor opinion of their patient care skills, a young woman walking in the hallway overhears me and pulls on my sleeve. When I turn around, she jerks her head toward the opposite hallway, saying I should follow her toward what appears to be a closet.

"They put my baby in there. He was too little to survive," the young woman tearfully explains. Thanking her, I open the door and find a still newborn wrapped in a blanket laying in what appears to be a cardboard shoe box. My sister's name is written on a piece of paper under the baby's head. I pick up my namesake and hold her for a while. "No matter what anybody says, you'll always be Rachael to me, little one," I whisper.

Because of bleeding problems that require several transfusions, Sally remains in the hospital twenty days and is remains weak when she is finally discharged home. My request for compassionate leave from school to care for her is granted, and one evening after supper, while Sally is resting, I ask her husband to sit outside on the cement stoop with me.

"Sally shouldn't have any more babies, Mick. You should see to it that she doesn't get pregnant again," I tell my brother-in-law, who hears this as meddling in his marriage and explodes.

"Ain't none of your goddamned business whether Sally gets pregnant again," he blasts at me loud enough for the neighbors to hear.

"There are things you can do to insure she doesn't," I press, resolved to not allow his tantrum to stop me from saying what I need to say.

"Like what? A man has urges. You can't expect me to ignore them, for Christ's sake," he shouts, stomping his feet on the front sidewalk as if he's killing snakes. *Maybe I should've waited to bring this up when he hadn't had so many beers – although I have no idea when that might be*, I think, then decide to continue the conversation anyway, because I might not get another chance.

"You can use condoms. I can get you as many as you want." I say evenly.

"Hell no, I ain't using no rubbers… them's like putting a raincoat on my dick. It ain't natural." For emphasis, he stomps the concrete again.

Hearing the commotion, Sally leaves her bedroom, where she has been staring at the wall for nearly three weeks, and follows our voices outside.

"We didn't mean to wake you," I apologize.

"I want you to get rid of the crib and take the baby clothes away – now," Sally instructs, hanging onto the porch railing to steady herself. Mick and I look at each other, shrug and move toward the house. We spend the next couple of hours silently doing as my sister asked. I seal the baby clothes in a box and put them under the bed in the spare bedroom I am currently occupying. Mick takes the crib out to the garage, covers it with a sheet and places it against the back wall, then claims it is an accident when he rams into it driving the car back in.

A week later Sally announces she is returning to teaching, and the following Monday, pale and weak, she walks into her poor excuse for a classroom, in a building that should have been condemned years ago, to face the thirty-eight unruly urchins eagerly waiting for her. That same day, I return to the hospital.

Meanwhile, the massive economic depression gripping the country continues, with no end in sight. Sister Immaculata calls the students together and tells us to prepare for a tsunami of life and death medical problems because people don't have enough food or clothing, are living on the streets, depending on soup kitchens, becoming alcoholics, and suffering diseases arising from unclean living conditions and constant violence that no one should be expected to endure, yet has plagued them for too long – and in spite of all this, are continuing to have babies. Shaking her head in resignation, she scowls at this last pronouncement.

"The despair men in particular are feeling is driving them to suicide, leaving women without husbands and forced to raise children without a father or an income. Most patients are unable to pay, so wait until it is nearly too late before seeking medical attention. As a result, we are facing the inescapable reality that too often there is very little we can do for them, and many who could have been saved will die. Only by the grace of Almighty God, working through us, do any survive. Always remember that we can't accomplish anything without Divine assistance and never forget that we will continue to fulfill the gospel mandate to relieve suffering where we find it, despite our resources being stretched so far past our limits we've no hope of ever catching up." Pushing her foghorn voice to full capacity, the head of the nurses' training program speaks with such force I'm convinced what she is saying will be a question on our next test.

"These times are no different than wartime, except right now the war is here at home, and the enemies are poverty, despair and hopelessness surrounding us. Nurses are desperately needed, and if you fail the licensing exam, you will not be a nurse; instead you will have wasted your time and ours, and be of no use to anyone," the nun proclaims, slamming her fist on the table.

Although no longer assigned to community medicine, I still spend my day off, which is only once every other week, helping Sister Nora. It's not much, but it's something, and I feel better for making the effort. I've come to know many of the women living in the area extending out from the docks by name and am able to do nearly everything the experienced nun can do. Any struggles I had with abortion as a moral question, which weren't many to begin with, have evaporated because I believe motherhood should be a choice and no woman should ever be forced to bear a child. I firmly believe the Catholic Church which, admittedly does a lot of good in the world, is entirely wrong on this and on their anti-birth control policy. Even the nuns, understanding the effects these policies, made by men, have on women, ignore the institutional church on these issues.

"The Church can't have it both ways," Sister Michael Joan bellows one evening after aiding a mother of eight not to become a mother of nine.

"Forbidding women access to birth control forces them into either having abortions or becoming baby machines in service to the pope, who wants more Catholics because more Catholics mean more money for the Church… and that's just not right," the wise nun declares, kicking the door jamb for emphasis. I can't help smiling.

Six months later, right on schedule, Sister Immaculata affixes a nurse's cap to my head and places the pin signifying I am now truly and officially a nurse on my uniform, then congratulates me on graduating first in my class. I was shocked when, a few days ago, she announced I'd achieved a nearly perfect score on the national nursing exam, which turned out to be the highest score registered for the exam this year. In front of everyone assembled for the ceremony, including current students, other graduates, parents and relatives, and much of the hospital's medical staff, the head of the nursing education program asks me about my plans going forward.

"I have been offered a position in the community nursing program and will be working in the barrios," I whisper, struggling to keep my composure. Sister Immaculata shakes my hand, says she is very proud of me, knows I will be an excellent nurse worthy of the title and will bring honor both to the profession, and the nursing school that trained me.

"We have never had a student score as high as you did on the national exam, Nurse Rose. I am aware you have many choices for employment and, speaking personally, I am very pleased you are willing to remain at Divine Providence caring for the poorest among us – the destitute and suffering who need us most, and are the most difficult to reach. You are doing God's work on earth and there is no greater calling than accepting the obligation to make the world a better place." Her declaration sounds remarkably like the Jewish mandate Tikkun Olam – to repair the world, and for the very first time since I arrived three years ago, I truly believe that doing whatever I had to do, including lying about my name, my age and my religion, to become a nurse wasn't wrong. If I hadn't taken that risk, there would be one less nurse able respond to the desperation surrounding us.

As Sister Immaculata finishes speaking, my sister stands up, clapping, and soon others, including many of my classmates, join in. Not given to revealing my emotions, I am surprised to find tears running down my face. I wish my mother had lived to see this day and that my father had come for the ceremony. At the last minute, Edna wrote that he wasn't well enough to make the trip.

On my last night in the student dorm, after the celebrations are over and many of my classmates, including Callie, have already left, I am alone with my thoughts as I pack up a three-year accumulation of books, notes and other odds and ends. I can't help feeling that for a daughter of German Jewish immigrants, who didn't speak English until she was five years old, I've done okay – better than okay. Despite viewing the lies I had to tell to get what I wanted as justified, I remain haunted by the reality of having to deny my heritage and religious tradition to do it. I am ashamed that I'm not brave enough to be who I really am and feel I have betrayed myself in order to have the life I want, bristling at the reality that making my dreams come true requires me to pretend to be someone I am not. I can't help wondering whether this newly achieved nursing degree belongs to Rachael Rosenblum or to Charlotte Rose – and whether either one deserves it? One is too cowardly to step forward and be who she is, and the other is perfectly content pretending to be someone she isn't, hoping no one discovers the truth.

Chapter Seventeen
פרק שבע עשרה

Berkeley, California
Early fall, 1971

You come from good blood... strong and brave.

"You're right – this is a phenomenal story," I tell Adrian. Smiling, I hand him his hand-written translation of my mother's account of her experience in nursing school to place in the box of files we are sharing until I have copies made for each of us.

"Believe it or not, it gets even more remarkable. You're a lucky woman, Natalie. Sooner or later, you're going to realize you have some damned good blood running through your veins." Never having pondered things like genetic inheritances, family traits, or the origins of personal characteristics until recently, I'm not sure how to respond to his remark.

"I thought this was the last diary or notebook entry, but it turns out there's one more," Adrian continues. He gives me several more hand-written sheets of paper while I'm sitting at the kitchen table smearing marmalade on my toast.

"Thanks," I smile, then ask if he wants coffee as I pour some for myself.

"I'm running a little late. I have a meeting tonight so not sure when I'll be back," he says, gathering several things into his book bag.

"You've been gone at night a lot recently. What are you up to?" I tease.

"That's a question that requires a longer answer than I have time for right now but is something I've been wanting to talk with you about. We need to make time soon."

"Now that this translation project is nearly finished are you breaking up with me?"

"God no – I'd marry you tomorrow if you'd agree to it, which I know you won't," he answers, rummaging through a thick stack of papers in his bag.

"Then what is it?"

"Politics, in the broad sense... specifically the anti-war movement."

"Then go in peace, if there is any to be had, and call me tonight." After kissing me goodbye, he stops near the door and turns around to face me.

"This translation is a good read, Natalie. It reveals a lot about who your mother was, and there's not much question she was very talented and very far ahead of her time. If you read it from that perspective, I can't see any way you won't feel much better about everything. She might not have been a great wife or mother, but she was one hell of a courageous woman, and that's something to be very proud of."

"I hope you're right," I whisper, mostly to myself.

A few minutes later, still in my bathrobe, I refill my coffee cup and pick up the sheets of paper covered in Adrian's handwriting, walk out onto the fire escape, move one of the chairs slightly to the left to catch the morning sun, and begin reading. A dark-eyed junco lands on the railing, watching intently as I submerge myself in the riveting narrative.

Chapter Eighteen
פרק שמונה עשרה

Los Angeles
1936-1939

And so, dear Christians, beware of the Jews...

"I'm so, so proud of you! We'll drink champagne cocktails to mark the occasion," my sister gushes. She has invited me to lunch to celebrate my graduation. I truly can't remember the last time I let my hair hang loose, or wore a nice dress, gloves, and a hat. The thought of owning clothes that look almost fashionable is uncomfortable... a betrayal of my last three years of hard work and deep commitment to easing the plight of the suffering poor. The thought of drinking champagne in some fancy restaurant only makes it worse.

Two hours and two champagne cocktails later, over a decadent chocolate dessert, my sister announces Mick wants to try for another baby. Holding my fork in mid-air, I stare at her for a full minute before putting the bite I was about to take back down on my plate.

"I realize this is none of my business, Sally, but I really don't think you should do that," I scowl.

"Because my bleeding caused the other baby to die?" my sister asks, choking back tears bubbling up in her worried eyes.

"There's no way to know whether the bleeding caused the baby to die, but it nearly caused you to die. What you need to remember is that it was a really close call that could've gone either way." For no particular reason, other than we just don't, my sister and I rarely discuss personal concerns, and spoke very little about the details surrounding the death of my niece. The direction this awkward conversation has taken surprises me and from the look on her face, is a shock to her as well.

"I bleed a lot every month, and it goes on a while. After what happened to you, it has occurred to me we could have some kind of familial bleeding problem. If we do, it makes another pregnancy very dangerous for you… one you might not survive," I explain.

"What would you do if you were me?" my sister asks.

"I don't know, Sally. I've never really thought about having children."

"Mick took losing the baby very badly… said he's always wanted a big family, and thought that was one thing we agreed on. I don't recall ever discussing it with him, but after what happened, I'm really afraid."

"Sometimes fear is protective, Sally… a signal to pay attention. Any woman who went through what you did would be terrified of another pregnancy. Having a baby is dangerous, even for healthy women in the best of circumstances. A lot can go wrong." What I don't give voice to is my fear of losing my sister, who is my only real family since my father remarried and shifted all his attention to his new wife.

"Mick wants what he wants. He isn't patient about me refusing him. Sooner or later, he's going to start looking elsewhere," my sister laments, making no effort to hide the tears dripping off her chin. I exhale a deep sigh at the awkwardness of this free-flowing emotion in a public setting where everyone can see it unfolding, and hand my sister a tissue.

"I often hear women express their fears about not giving in to their husbands causing them to leave, but I never expected to hear it from my own sister," I bristle.

"A man who threatens to leave his wife when she won't let him have his way with her isn't worth keeping around, Sally. If that's the game Mick's playing, help the selfish bastard pack his suitcase and show him the door. You won't be losing anything."

Six months later, Sally is pregnant and terrified. I postpone moving into the two-room apartment above the dispensary in the barrios, where I have taken the job as a community nurse, so I can stay with Sally and Mick until the baby comes. When I explain this to Sister Mathilde, who sits at the right hand of Sister Nora, and is widely regarded as the fearless community rule enforcer, she doesn't take the news well.

"I need you living here to take night call and protect the dispensary, which is much less likely to be broken into if someone is living in the building. And, I need the rent," the nun, who could have been a prize fighter in another life, grumbles, after imploring the Holy Mother of God to step up and solve this problem. Following a lengthy back and forth, she agrees to delay my occupancy if I agree to pay half of what I would owe if I were living there, which isn't much, but the apartment isn't much, either.

"Aren't you worried the hospital will notice the loss of rent?" I ask.

"I'm more worried about some chronic drunk with the hangover from hell breaking in and helping himself to the pain meds. The missing rent's less of a problem. If I hadn't figured out how to cook the books, we'd have folded a long time ago," Sister Mathilde huffs, adjusting her wimple. I resolve to practice imitating her tough demeanor.

Surprising everyone, Emily Rachael appears several weeks sooner than expected. She is a small baby, and her arrival is perilous for both mother and child. I remain at the hospital, sleeping on a cot in my sister's room until both she and my niece are stable. When the time comes to send them home, the doctor issues a strongly worded warning against any more pregnancies. I watch Mick's face as the doctor outlines birth control options and readily grasp my sister's persistent fears about refusing her husband. *He'll wander in no time*, I tell myself.

"How reliable are the vaginal suppositories or douches?" Sally asks me a few days later.

"Better than nothing, but I wouldn't call them reliable. The surest preventative, other than avoiding sex altogether, is a diaphragm or condom, and a condom only works when a man is willing to use one, and a lot of men aren't." I don't add that I've already had this conversation with my brother-in-law, and it did not go well. On the other hand, there is a remote chance that nearly losing his wife in childbirth twice scared some sense into him.

My enchanting niece, who shares a tiny bedroom with me, requires most of my attention. Being so small, she requires feeding every two hours, and I take the night feedings so Sally can get as much healing rest as possible. During this quiet time I realize how little patience I have with Mick either as a husband or a father. Yet, despite his faults, which, in my opinion, are many, my sister persists in loving him. Ultimately, I conclude he must've been a rebound choice after divorcing Edwin, which may have been much harder on her than I realized.

"Who cares if Mick takes off, Sally – you and I can raise Emily just fine on our own. You won't have to do it alone, and if he makes unreasonable demands on you, you're better off without him," I reassure my sister whenever the subject of avoiding another pregnancy comes up, which is often. The conversation always ends with my sister in tears and my resolve to never get married further strengthened.

Emily is a beautiful baby who, despite the problems associated with her early arrival, is thriving. Sally is happy being a mother but is already saying she wants to go back to teaching which, I'm beginning to suspect, is her way of avoiding a problem she can't deal with, since having a full-time job working with children all day is a perfect excuse not to have any more of her own. Meanwhile, Sister Mathilde, who is frustrated by the ongoing vandalism in the neighborhood, is pressuring me to move into the apartment sooner rather than later.

Although I'm not sure why I think it is a good idea, I decide to use the graduation money my father sent to buy a used car, and convince Mick to help me learn to drive it. The main thing I learn from my first lesson is that I don't like driving and have made a big mistake. It takes a dogged determination to stick with it until I finally manage to pass the driving portion of the licensing examination. I am looking forward to moving into the apartment above the dispensary, which means that some days I can walk wherever I need to go and don't need to drive at all.

The conditions in the barrios, which were terrible to begin with, continue to worsen right before my eyes. Rotting garbage piles up, attracting more and larger rats, screeching stray cats and aggressive, starving dogs. Hungry people without jobs wander aimlessly, willing to work any amount of time for any amount of money, if they can find someone willing, or able, to hire them, which is isn't often. Each day brings more violence to neighborhoods that, even before the catastrophic economic collapse, were prone to every imaginable crime desperate men, and women, for that matter, are driven to commit.

"At least I am helping the poor people trapped in these circumstances as much as I can. It's not nearly enough, but it's something, and what we spent three years of our lives learning how to do," I tell Callie one Sunday afternoon when we both have a day off and arrange to meet for lunch. My former roommate is working in Riverside's new, well staffed community hospital, far removed from the suffering masses inhabiting Los Angeles' putrid inner-city, which now stretches all the way south to the Long Beach oil fields.

"Even though it is sad, frustrating, and hard, this is the only work that makes sense to me. I may not save many lives, but I might save some and relieve at least a little of the suffering of those facing life with no one but me to respond to their pain and anguish. If we can't help those who are victimized by problems they didn't cause and can't fix, then I don't see much point in life," I say, engaged in a stream of consciousness conversation with myself as my former roommate enjoys a cheeseburger dripping meaty juice. A few minutes earlier, she told me her biggest nursing challenge last week was teaching a private duty nurse how to change surgical dressings for a brother and sister who drank too much at a party and wrecked their family convertible, banging themselves up badly enough to require hospitalization. My response was to suggest her time might be better spent working among the migrant workers toiling in the agriculture industry surrounding Riverside who have no access to medical care and are often sick, infected or injured. After accusing me of not respecting the work she does, she leaves the café in tears. I don't regret my words, but I do regret what is probably the end of our friendship. Neither of us could've gotten through nursing school without the other, but that bond has slowly unraveled as we've come to realize we no longer have anything in common to bind us together.

As time passes it seems to me that I'm treating more men than previously – mostly for skin ulcers, respiratory illnesses, injuries resulting from accidents and fights, and venereal disease. These cases are add-ons to my regular patients, most of whom are the women these men have impregnated, abandoned, infected, or beat up. It doesn't help that my current working conditions include a chronic supply shortage, not enough hours in the day, and many more patients who need me than I can possibly care for.

Complaining about this to Sister Mathilde one afternoon, the nun explains that the current migration began in the wake of the catastrophic dust storms decimating Midwestern farming and people continue coming to California looking for work, without any guarantee they'll find it. Slamming a white-knuckled fist on the table, she admits she finds it impossible to understand the mind of a God that inflicts such suffering.

"People get the crazy idea that California is the land of milk and honey, with rainbows emerging from pots of gold on street corners in downtown Los Angeles. When they finally get here, they discover there isn't any milk or honey, and not a rainbow in sight, because it hardly ever rains. Instead, all they find is more of what they left behind, only now they're strangers in a strange land, face to face with a huge ocean and nowhere left to go. Everything they own is piled on top of a barely running truck and they're sick with Lord knows what. We're taught to take it on faith that God knows what he's doing, but frankly, even I could do a better job running the world," Sister Mathilde pontificates, shaking her head and throwing her hands in the air.

"It takes time to travel from person to person, and if even a few of the people could come to us, instead of us going to them, we could help more of them," I tell my immediate supervisor, pouring her a paper cup of lukewarm Coca-Cola as we sit in the back room of her dispensary.

"I couldn't agree more, Charlotte, but the last I heard, renting space cost money, and we don't even have enough for band-aids and aspirin. More floor space is out of the question – unless, of course, that pot of gold suddenly appears, and so far, after more years here than I can remember, I've seen absolutely no evidence that's going to happen."

"What about asking Mr. Fleming next door whether we can use space there. We wouldn't need much, and in return, it would bring more people into his variety store," I suggest.

"It would bring in more people to steal from him, and I doubt he'll greet that possibility with much enthusiasm, especially since he's letting us run a tab for supplies that we never fully pay off," Sister Mathilde answers.

I decide to approach Mr. Fleming anyway, and find he is somewhat sympathetic to my idea, but not enough to offer me free space. Instead, he suggests he might be able to persuade his vendors to donate first-aid items like bandages and ointments, if that will help, which, of course, it will.

"The other thing we need is a safe place for women to get away from the abusive men they get involved with," I tell Sister Mathilde a few days later, while reporting on my meeting with Mr. Fleming.

"We treat their wounds and then they go back to their abuser because their only other choice is the street. If they had a safe place to stay, even for a few days, it would give them a chance to consider other options."

"This is a wonderful idea, Charlotte, but it's totally unrealistic. After doing this work since before you were born, my experience is most of the women eventually go back to their abuser, regardless of their other options which, generally speaking, are few to none in any case. I've given up trying to understand this, and so should you. Our only choice is to accept that these women are trapped in horrible situations and not make them feel worse than they already do about making what we, and they both know is another bad decision that, in the face of no alternatives, it isn't a decision at all. When they show up bruised and battered again, we love them for exactly who they are, and above all, not judge them for living a life they have absolutely no control over."

"You know as well as I do that not judging the woman who makes these choices is damned near impossible, Sister. Forgive my language, but it's the truth… and there comes a time when all this accepting, loving and not judging becomes permission to keep on doing the same thing and not try to change."

"Judgments are God's job, not ours, Charlotte. You would do well to remember that," the nun says, finishing her Coke, then slam-dunking the crunched-up paper cup into the trash can twenty feet away and walking out the door.

"Nice shot, Sister," I call after her.

After the discussion with my immediate superior that went nowhere, I continue on as before, losing sleep over at least three or four patients each week. At the end of one unusually difficult day spent I drag myself up the stairs to my apartment sometime after nine o'clock and find a note pinned to the door.

Your sister called and said to call her right away. Use the downstairs phone – Sr. M. I hurry downstairs and unlock the dispensary door. Without turning on the light, which would alert the neighborhood that I have a key, I fumble my way to the office and dial Sally's phone number. She picks up on the second ring.

"Edna called this morning. Papa died," she says. Taken completely by surprise, I don't respond.

"She said he had been fine until a few days ago and she did not expect him to die. She assured me she would've let us know if she realized how sick he was. His will says he wants to be buried in Elyria and Edna doesn't want to take him there… said it's up to us to honor his final wishes. Otherwise, she'll bury him in Bakersfield."

"You mean I'll have to do it, since it will be next to impossible for you to leave teaching, or Emily, long enough to make the trip," I sigh.

"Edna did say that since he was a railroad employee, the railroad will pay for transporting him and that, in preparation, she already arranged to have him embalmed. Still, if you're going to take him to Ohio, you can't wait forever," my sister says.

"I can't remember the last time I saw him…"

"I haven't seen him since I told him I'd married again and introduced him to Mick. I did write to him about Emily, and he and Edna sent a beautiful blanket and baby sweater – and a nice card. But they never came to see his only grandchild, or invited me to bring her there," Sally continues, with a catch in her voice.

"Did you ever tell him about the first baby?" I ask.

"I doubt it. I was too distraught, so unless you told him, he probably never knew about her."

"We both could've tried harder, Sally, but I was never sure how much he cared one way or another," I admit.

"I don't know either, but I do think we should do what he wanted and take him to Ohio – and I can understand why Edna doesn't want to do it.

Current wife accompanying her recently deceased husband on a very long train trip just so he can be buried next to his first wife can't be a pleasant idea for her."

"Do you think he wants to be buried in Ohio because Mama is buried there," I ask.

"Why else would he want to be buried there?"

"I have no idea. Actually, there are a lot of things about Papa I have no idea about, including where he buried Mama. Regardless, if that's what he wants, I'll do it. It'll take me a day to arrange to be gone from here but go ahead and let Edna know I'll leave here Friday morning and ask her to have him waiting at the train station."

"Edna also said we have inherited money. She isn't sure how much but thinks it might be a fair amount. She sounded a little put out about it."

"It's the Depression – it can't be much," I remind my sister.

"According to Edna, he's been investing in government bonds for years. The way she explained it, those plus his railroad stock, which is one of the few stocks that survived the crash, have added up. It sounded like it might be enough for us to buy a little house of our own instead of renting this one, which is water down the drain every month. I'm sure it's equally divided and you can expect the same amount."

"I love my job and am happy where I am, living in the neighborhood where I am working. It saves time and I know more about what's going on. I have no idea what I'd do with money I don't need and couldn't enjoy when I live and work among people who have none." My sister doesn't respond.

Two days later, I claim my father's body in Bakersfield and see it safely placed on the train we both will take east to Cleveland. Off and on, over the next fifty-two hours, I wish my sister was with me, partly as a traveling companion and partly because, much to my surprise, I'm looking forward to going back to Elyria. My memories of that time are mostly good ones.

After finding my way to Agudath Achim Cemetery in Elyria, Ohio and seeing my father safely committed to the ground, I re-board the train, this time going west toward California. Satisfied that I respected my father's final wishes, as the train rolls across the Great Plains I revisit the hour I spent in the Elyria cemetery again and again, thinking about the headstones surrounding his. I doubt they mark actual burial sites of people related to me, including my mother, but can't think of any other reason they'd be there or that my father would want to be among them.

Up on my return, a heavy, dark melancholy envelopes my life in a cloudy, gray haze that the perpetual California sunshine fails to penetrate. My sister is the only person left in the world to care about me in the unbreakable way shared blood creates. Every other member of my family is either dead or half a world away from Los Angeles, and we are entirely unknown to each other, except by name.

Eventually, Sally calls to check on the trip. I fill her in on what I assume are other family markers I discovered at the cemetery, which she doesn't express any curiosity about. She's even less interested in the scenery between Los Angeles and Cleveland.

"When I changed trains in Kansas City all people talked about are the terrible dust storms. I didn't see any myself, but I did see some of the devastation – it's pretty awful," I tell my sister, who interrupts my flatland geography lesson to fill me in on our inheritance.

"Edna is upset about the money – says she needs it more than we do, but the lawyer told her there's nothing she can do about it. She said to expect to hear from him any day, then hung up on me and I haven't heard from her since," Sally reports.

"I don't expect she'll keep in touch, and I don't feel any compulsion to keep in touch with her," my sister proclaims. When I don't disagree, we chat a few more minutes, until Emily begins fussing in the background.

"I'll call you when I hear from the lawyer," Sally says, signing off.

A few days later, after a particularly difficult day pushing against my dark mood, Sister Mathilde brings me a request from the county sheriff.

"We're being asked to go to an encampment on the edge of the city populated with people who have migrated to California from the Dust Bowl states and are suffering from a chronic intestinal problem. He thinks it's caused by overcrowding and poor sanitation, but there's also an outbreak of what sounds like measles. He apologized for asking us to go into such abominable conditions, but says the people are desperate and he doesn't know who else to turn to. I explained I can't drive so didn't know how I could go out there, then remembered you have a car and said I'd get back to him."

"It doesn't sound like I have much choice, Sister."

"I hoped you'd see it that way, Charlotte. I'll tell him you'll be there day after tomorrow. On another matter, Sister Immaculata agreed to send us more student nurses, who came while you were gone. Only two of the first five returned the second day. They are afraid of the neighborhood and don't like the men saying impolite things to them. I made it very clear I am not sympathetic to either concern," she huffs.

Hearing this, I don't bother suppressing a smile. I am well-aware the neighborhood is dangerous, especially for women, but rely on my relationships with the people who know me and my close association with the nuns to keep me relatively safe. My experience so far has been that those we work among rarely attack anyone who is sincerely trying to help them.

"I'm sorry I wasn't here to reassure them, Sister. I don't think anyone would bother them too much, since they are obviously affiliated with us, but they are too young and inexperienced to know this."

"You are never afraid?" Sister Mathilde questions.

"I can't say never, but rarely. My Spanish is improving, and some of the babies I helped deliver a year ago are beginning to walk now, so I stop in to do well-baby checks on them, which the mothers appreciate. They know I'll treat their men also, if there is a problem. This keeps me from being a complete stranger among them."

"How are the babies you're following?" Sister asks.

"Most are growing, but they're not robust or thriving, and some just aren't right. Those are the saddest cases – they need so much, and there is so little, in practical terms, I can do for them," I stop just short of admitting I dispense birth control whenever possible and occasionally fix a problem pregnancy, which I'm sure Sister Mathilde knows, or at least suspects, and looks the other way. Her next sentence confirms this.

"Mr. Fleming is helping us to acquire more supplies, and I have a miscellaneous items budget to help mothers not to become mothers too often. If you run out of what you need, let me know," she mentions, feigning casualness as she busies herself sorting bandages. Her nervousness is only revealed as she slips into what sounds like a faintly German accent. I have long suspected she might be a native German speaker, but we've never asked each other anything about our backgrounds, despite one of us accidentally slipping a German word into the conversation when we're under duress.

Occasionally, I've sensed Sister Mathilde longs to talk about things other than our work which, despite her gruff manner, she obviously loves. She has, in an off-handed way, alluded to the threats Germans face in America, but not knowing whether the nun is actually pro-German, or anti-Jewish, which is common among Catholics, I avoid the temptation to engage in personally revealing conversations. This changes when telling Sister Mathilde about the money I have inherited and my desire to use it to set up a women's clinic and shelter.

"Forgive me for asking, Nurse Rose, but where, exactly, did this money come from? The nation is in severe economic distress, and it seems to me any possibilities for inheriting money are quite unlikely," the nun points out.

"As you know, my father died recently. It turns out he left my sister and me money."

"How did your father accumulate enough money to leave an inheritance? He must've been engaged in something illegal – rum running or organized crime."

"He worked for the Union Pacific Railroad, Sister."

"Doing what? It sounds to me like he owned it…"

"He was a civil engineer who designed routes… at least I think that's what he did. I never thought to ask him."

"You are a very, very fortunate woman, Charlotte. You have never known, and will never know, the suffering we see every day. Those who are born as lucky as you are owe something in return. I hope you realize this – and live your life accordingly." *If you knew the truth about me, born lucky isn't a phrase you'd automatically apply to my life,* I think.

"I wouldn't be standing here talking to you about using the money to establish a walk-in clinic to treat and shelter abused women if I wasn't very grateful for what you refer to as being born lucky, Sister. I hope you realize that," I shoot back. Casting her eyes downward, the nun is silent, but I see a slight smile break out of one corner of her down-turned mouth.

"If you can see patients in a walk-in clinic even one day per week, it will be possible to see more patients in the barrios and free me to go to the encampments one day per week. As you know, we are as desperately needed there as we are here," I continue.

"I'm not sure I agree with you about the need, Nurse Rose. The women in the encampments take care of childbirth and most other things among themselves. They don't readily accept medical care."

"Childbirth is the only thing that occasionally goes well, Sister, but only occasionally. Dysentery, respiratory illnesses, and skin infections I've only read about in books are rampant because contagious people are living in overcrowded filth, with nothing more than folk remedies to treat whatever ails them. They slap mustard plasters on everything from dog bites to head injuries. But without gardens to grow what they need, they can't concoct grandma's magical, miraculous or mysterious tinctures to treat whatever ails them at the moment, things are getting worse. I never thought I'd say the barrios are better than anyplace, but they're not nearly as bad as the encampments – and less dangerous, which is hard to believe."

"For better or worse, and I think we both agree, it's mostly worse, the barrios are fairly stable. People know each other and there's some security in that. Folks here know who the bad actors are and deal with them, and we do see a policeman wandering around occasionally. There's no consistent police presence in the camps and they're all strangers competing for the same jobs. It's everyone for themselves, making it much easier to get into knife fights, steal from each other, and ignore what's going on around you," Sister Mathilde says, then falls silent. After a few minutes doodling on the corner of the newspaper while trying to think of an argument against the clinic, the wise, all-knowing nun finally agrees to speak with Sister Nora.

"By the way, Sister – either call me Charlotte or Nurse Rose, but don't flip back and forth, depending upon your mood or the point you're trying to make. We're colleagues—and equals." For the second time in as many days, small smile cracks through the nun's carefully cultivated façade intended to reveal nothing of what she is thinking.

On my first day off in nearly a month, I visit my sister, who arranged for Mrs. Broderick, the neighbor who cares for Emily while she is teaching, to come on Saturday so we can have an entire afternoon to ourselves. We begin with a matinee at a downtown movie theater which, according to his wife, Mick wouldn't be caught dead doing.

"I heard *Top Hat* with Fred Astaire and Ginger Rogers is really good," Sally says while we are waiting for Mrs. Broderick to arrive. An hour later, our excitement over the movie quickly evaporates when the newsreel comes on, featuring an incident referred to as Kristallnacht, showing German Nazis torching synagogues, vandalizing Jewish homes, schools and businesses, and murdering hundreds of Jews. Bile rises in my throat as I watch live images of the incident, and I take several deep breaths to keep from throwing up. Haunted by the news report, which plays endlessly in my mind, I find my sister's ability to relax and enjoy the movie, despite what we've just seen, upsetting. After the movie ends, we walk the half block from the theater to Grandma Maude's, a little café known for its homemade pastries and hand-churned ice cream.

"Didn't that newsreel upset you?" I ask, after sitting down at the small table near the window and ordering an assortment of Grandma's rich, buttery treats to share.

"I didn't like it, but there's nothing I can personally do about it, and what's happening in Germany will never happen here," Sally insists, biting into a flaky, apricot-filled pastry covered in powdered sugar that reminds us both of the hamantaschen our neighbor in Elyria made for Purim.

"I'm not so sure. I've heard rumors about some terrible things happening in here in the U. S. regarding Nazis and persecution of Jews."

"Nazis in America? Honestly, Charlotte, that's impossible," my sister insists, dabbing powdered sugar off her mouth.

"It would seem so, but if the rumors are even half true, all bets are off in terms of Germans and Jews, especially Jews, being safe anywhere, even here."

"Are you still sending money to Aunt Irina?" Sally asks.

"I am, but secretly."

"How do you keep it a secret?"

"I never send it from the same post office twice, always use a fake name and return address, and told Irina not to write back because I don't want to answer questions about receiving letters from Germany since Germans are so unpopular in America right now."

"I wrote to Irina when Papa died, but also said not to send letters back because I didn't want to have to explain them to Mick. He's never met a negative opinion he didn't like and I'm sure that includes the Germans… and the Jews."

"How can you stay married to him if you think he hates Germans and Jews?"

It's easy. We don't talk about it," my sister smiles deviously.

"With all this secrecy, Irina must think life in America isn't so great after all – and she wouldn't be wrong," I frown, taking a drink of my strong black coffee liberally diluted with cream.

"I don't know what you mean, Charlotte. I don't think it's so bad." *You have no idea*, I think to myself. I want to confide in my sister about the rumors of pro-Nazi activity throughout California led by something called the German Bund that has recently begun actively recruiting in the barrios, but it's clear she doesn't want to hear it. Yet, something I can't define is compelling me to pay attention and prepare myself to fight back.

I manage to set my concerns aside for the rest of the afternoon, but later that evening, back in my apartment, The newsreel images continue to haunt me, bringing to mind an incident I observed several weeks ago in a park on the edge of the barrios. What the small crowd was saying, and what I saw, were horrifying. Men carrying red, white and black Nazi swastika flags were marching in goosestep chanting "the Jews won't control us." Giving the Nazi salute they shouted "Heil Hitler" again and again. Speakers incited the crowd, urging people to sign up to help pro-German efforts in Los Angeles. They made it sound as if the intention is for Germany first to conquer, then to rule the world, and that people should join in now. Otherwise, they risked their hesitation being interpreted as unsympathetic to the cause, which is eliminating Jews and creating the perfect Aryan race. I found the message deeply frightening, not just for what it says, but because so many people seem to agree with it.

Not long after seeing the newsreel, a woman who calls herself Hannah appears at the walk-in clinic, explaining that she has some knowledge of medicine and offering to volunteer. Desperate for any help we can get, Sister Mathilde and I ask few questions before accepting her offer, and within days are very impressed with her efficiency. Used to people whose English is less that perfect, we ignore her limits with the language.

Late one afternoon a few weeks later, I overhear her whispering to her husband in German when he comes to escort her home on the streetcar, which occurs each day she comes to us. They are a handsome couple, both slender, with dark hair, sad, fearful eyes and the quiet demeanor of gentle souls who keep to themselves and are determined to be invisible. Hannah works hard, dresses plainly, says little and is so capable we are soon depending on her to keep inventory straight, take care of the minimal bookkeeping we bother with, and help with anything else we ask of her. We are flooded with patients, and the more Hannah is able to do, the more time Sister Mathilde and I have to administer much needed direct patient care. Nevertheless, with my suspicions heightened after the rally. I'm not sure how much we should trust her, nor do I have any idea how to figure this out. Finally, at the end of a particularly busy day, I invite her to sit down and share a cup of tea.

"Perhaps I misunderstood, but I thought I overheard you speaking German the other day," I begin, leaking the German accent I'm normally careful to mask. Suddenly pale and obviously frightened at being discovered, Hannah fearfully admits she is a native German speaker. After a great deal of encouragement and reassurance, she reluctantly reveals she is a trained nurse, which accounts for her remarkable efficiency in the dispensary. Her husband, Chaim, is a rabbi, and they escaped Nazi Germany through Shanghai two years ago, eventually landing on the West Coast of California. A learned man, Chaim has a job cataloging books at the Los Angeles public library and she is hoping to parlay her experience with us into a paying job, perhaps in private duty nursing, which doesn't require a license. I compliment her bravery, determination, and abilities,

RED ANEMONES

then suggest we have tea together more often.

The next week, she brings a tin of mouthwatering homemade pfeffernüsse, which she places near the tea canister. Slowly, we grow more trusting of each other, then begin worrying together over the growing anti-Jewish sentiment overtaking Los Angeles. Without outwardly admitting I am also a Jew, I make it clear where my sympathies lay and that I fret greatly over the growing ugliness in the world, even here in America.

One Friday, she stays later than usual, asking to speak privately with me.

"There is an underground Nazi resistance movement in Los Angeles that relies on eyes and ears in the community for information. You are German-fluent, Charlotte, and you could help enormously to fight the anti-Jewish, pro-Nazi effort," she says, eyes wider than I have ever seen them. Several seconds pass before I respond.

"I really would like to help, Hannah, but I am not likely to overhear very much. People living in both the encampments and the barrios are barely surviving; they don't have time to get caught up in political movements."

"This is not entirely true. You've heard about the German Bund?" she asks. I nod, explaining I've heard it mentioned but know little about it.

"It is a German-American pro-Nazi organization with many members. They are recruiting in the barrios and encampments, promising that if the men sign up, they'll have paying jobs after the war ends. It is very a clever idea," Hannah explains. I admit having heard rumors about this but am surprised they are true and have no idea how I can help combat the problem.

"There are ways, and I can help you. You infiltrate the group – pretend to be pro-Nazi, then report what you hear to a Boyle Heights phone number I give you. I'll go with you the first few times, until you are comfortable," she implores, adding that anything I discover, no matter how insignificant it might seem, is potentially useful. I ask her how long she has been doing this.

"Almost a year. With great anguish and sorrow, my husband cut his forelocks and shaved his beard so he could join in the resistance effort, and he attends the Bund as an infiltrator. We have no children, so all we have is each other. I could not allow him to assume risks I am not willing to take myself. I go to rallies and keep my ears open. It's not difficult. For you it would be especially easy – and safe because you are a nurse with a medical bag in case there is trouble. No one will question you. The hard part is finding a way to make the phone call to repeat what you've heard as soon as possible. You can use the dispensary phone, but not too often." I ask if she has been using our phone for this purpose, and she nods slightly, looking at the floor.

"It's all right, Hannah, I'm glad you're doing this. Really, I am."

"Will Sister Mathilde be as glad if she finds out?"

"We'll cross that bridge when we come to it." Hearing this answer Hannah looks puzzled, and I realize she doesn't understand how a bridge fits into our conversation. I repeat that we won't worry about what Sister Mathilde thinks unless we have to, and if it comes to that, we'll figure something out.

Shortly after my conversation with Hannah, whooping cough breaks out in the barrios and, at the same time, an outbreak of typhus occurs in the largest encampment. It is only by the grace of God that neither Sister Mathilde nor I get sick, but tending to those who are very ill causes me to put what Hannah has told me entirely out of my mind until late on a Tuesday afternoon several weeks later, when she informs me that a large pro-Nazi rally is scheduled in a park on the edge of the barrios in four days and asks me to go.

"I'll meet you there. We won't know each other but I will stand next to you, and we can exchange casual comments. Bring your medical bag and come as a nurse. No one will ask questions because it makes you important," she instructs. Deciding I risk no one but myself if I do arouse suspicion, I tell Sister Mathilde I have an errand to run and ask her to cover the Saturday morning dispensary hours for me.

After arriving at the park and finding it crowed with enthusiastic pro-Nazi supporters, it takes me half an hour to find the place where Hannah promised to meet. The rally is already in progress and a large crowd has gathered around an open pavilion. The speakers, shouting pro-Nazi propaganda, are clearly recruiting for the Bund, which is what I expected, but seeing hundreds of people so captivated by what these men are saying is a shock. It's a hot day and the frenzy brought on by the fiery rhetoric and dramatic displays of German nationalism fires up the boisterous crowd, which quickly becomes unruly when anti-German bystanders start shouting at the demonstrators to get the hell out of their neighborhood and go back where they came from. Eventually, the police start swinging clubs and yelling at everyone, causing Hannah to quickly disappear. Caught between wanting to tend to the bruised and battered and leaving before anyone recognizes me, I'm riveted to the unfolding chaos, and do not hear my name called. Sister Mathilde, escorted by the police, grabs at my arm, motioning me to follow her.

"We'll talk about what in the name of God and all that is holy you're doing here later. Right now, just keep your head down and follow me," she growls, dragging me by my sleeve as she head-butts her way toward the edge of the growing crowd. This is when I notice she's carrying a medical bag.

"Don't just stand there – help me out," the nun barks, walking over to a picnic table. Before I can ask what she is doing here, she explains that the police showed up at the dispensary asking her for assistance rendering first aid.

The first man the police bring to me is wearing a swastika arm band and bleeding profusely from a head wound caused by a large, well-aimed rock. Not wanting him to see my face and risk being recognized later, I begin walking away as fast as I can, admonishing myself for getting into something so obviously sinister without thinking it through more carefully. Sister Mathilde yells at me to come back, then drags me aside and forcefully reminds me we are nurses, and our job is to treat the injured, regardless of who they are or whether we agree with their politics.

"March back there and bandage that Nazi, Nurse Rose," she growls with an anger in her eyes I've never seen before, struggling to stop herself from slapping some sense into me. Taking a deep breath, I do as I am told, doing my best to avoid looking directly at the man, then moving on to the next casualty as fast as I can.

Several hours later, without speaking further to Sister Mathilde, I unlock my apartment door, then walk directly into the tiny bathroom, and vomit. Once my stomach settles, I make a cup of tea and begin asking myself whether the nun I work so closely with is anti-German, pro-German, or a Nazi sympathizer. Perhaps she is a faithful follower of that Catholic priest – Father Coughlin, from Detroit who spews antisemitic hate across the nation on the radio every Sunday morning. I don't think she is, but it's hard not to wonder just how far her vow to love all of God's people extends?

The next morning, Sister Mathilde is waiting for me when I open the dispensary door.

"I'd like to speak with you," she says, motioning me to follow her into the back room where the supplies are kept. Although the morning is not warm, sweat trickles down my back.

"It's time we are honest with each other," the nun says, sitting down at the small corner table used mostly for junk, and inviting me to do the same.

"I don't know what your real name is, but it's not Charlotte Rose. My guess is that you are a native German speaker, and considering how intelligent and disciplined you are, my intuition is that you are both a German and a Jew," she begins.

"How do you know this, Sister?"

"Before I was Sister Mathilde, I was Kathleen Mary McMurrough, and before that, I was Kasia Moskopt, from a Polish shtetl only one kilometer from the German border. My parents escaped the pogroms, eventually ending up among the shanty Irish in south Boston when I was not yet three years old. I received a new name, and my family discarded Yiddish and German to adopt an Irish identity, claiming we were from some small village on the Scotch-Irish border with a unique dialect all its own, which explained our strange accent. They sent me to Catholic school and on Fridays, instead of eating fish and getting down on our knees to say 'the family that prays together stays together' weekly rosary, we closed the shades and celebrated Shabbat. They left teaching me how to live as a fraud the other six days of the week up to the nuns, who must've suspected something and kindly looked the other way. They never questioned my desire to enter religious life and never challenged who I claimed to be."

"I don't know what to say, Sister," I finally offer, stunned by her confession.

"I don't expect you to say anything. I just want you to realize I know a German Jew when I see one, and I don't care."

"Now that you are self-proclaimed Christian – no need to care," I remark.

"You are wrong. I am forever a Jew – and never became officially Catholic. I was familiar enough with the religion and rituals that fortunately, when I was admitted to my order, the superior never asked for proof of a Catholic baptism. If she had, I was fully prepared to forge documents." I feel my eyes go wide. "Like you, I wanted to be a nurse. Unlike you, my parents couldn't afford to pay for my education. My only possibility for fulfilling my dream was to take the veil – embrace religious life and enter the convent. I was intellectually qualified for the nursing orders and was accepted without too many questions being asked."

"But you gave up so much..." I counter.

"I didn't give up nearly as much as I gained, Charlotte, or whatever your name is. Above all else, I wanted to help others and knew being a nurse was the best way for me to accomplish this. Nothing else mattered.

Not even the young man I loved deeply and was engaged to marry mattered as much as my desire to be a nurse." I nod at the nun's soul-baring confession while remaining silent.

"Christians have one perspective on God, and I have another one. In the end, who cares? Certainly not me. Maybe Jesus was the son of God and maybe he wasn't. Nobody knows, and how important is it, when His message is a good one? What matters is being a good nurse, and I'm sure you understand this just as much as I do. We treat the hellaciously evil, sinful among us just as we treat everyone else – and perhaps our willingness to fight malicious intent with kindness is the small spark that transforms an immoral, hateful person into a gentler, god-fearing one. Maybe your kindness toward that wannabe Nazi whose head you so reluctantly bandaged will cause him to rethink his politics. Who knows? I certainly don't. All I know for certain is the world doesn't need any more angry, hateful people – it has plenty already. I relieve suffering where I see it and leave the rest to a force much more powerful than anything I possess. I recommend that you do the same." Finished with what she came to say, Sister Mathilde turns to leave.

"What happened to the family left behind when your parents emigrated?"

"I don't know. Any remaining in Poland are not likely to survive the Third Reich. I pray for them every day." I detect a huskiness in the nun's voice as she says this.

"And the young man you were engaged to?" I ask, still speaking to her back. She doesn't turn around.

"He visits me once or twice a year. In between, we write to each other."

"He never married?"

"No, he never did," the nun says evenly, continuing her exit.

"He must've really loved you... still love you, Sister," I whisper. She gives no sign she has heard me. Instead, she leaves me sitting in the supply room staring at the floor, awash in the realization that I am not as alone in the world as I thought – that there are others who, like me, twisted and manipulated themselves into someone they were not, and did it for the right reasons.

A few days later, I tell Hannah I will do what I can to pass along information concerning anti-Jewish or Pro-Nazi activities I overhear. She scribbles a telephone number in Boyle Heights on a piece of scrap paper.

"Memorize this and destroy it. Don't call from the same telephone twice. When someone answers ask for Maida, if the response is she is out for the afternoon but please leave a message, you say what you have heard, disguised…"

"Disguised how?" I interrupt.

"If something is going to happen, give as much information as you can, saying something like 'Tell her I will meet her for coffee next Thursday at our favorite restaurant near the park on La Cienega Boulevard. It might be crowded so try to arrive before 10.' This signals something is planned for Thursday morning at the park on La Cienega and likely involves a crowd. If the response is that she is out of town for several days, then say you will call back later and hang up. Tell me if that happens. It means there is a problem."

I make my first phone call ten days later, after I overhear a rumor at the encampment about the Bund recruiting men to do odd jobs. Anyone interested is told to show up on Monday mornings at a specific address in east Los Angeles county. My message is that a large company in east Los Angeles has several job openings, and anyone interested can go to an address on San Sebastian Boulevard on Monday mornings. Although very nervous, I find making that phone call deeply satisfying, and look forward to another opportunity to do it again.

Weeks pass and Sister Mathilde never brings up the rally again. She doesn't ask why I was there or pass further judgment on my unprofessional reaction to the pseudo-Nazi Brownshirt expecting to receive first aid for an injury resulting from his commitment to promoting an insane, cruel and murderous cause. Insofar as I can determine, things between the stern, compassionate nun and I have not changed appreciably, although now she doesn't ask where I am going when I say I need to run an errand or check on a patient on a day when I am scheduled to be doing something else. We perform our nursing duties companionably and effectively, occasionally making small talk about nothing in particular, until the afternoon Mr. Fleming comes to the dispensary just as we are closing up for the day.

"Do what do we own the pleasure?" Sister Mathilde asks warily. He says he's heard the building next door is for sale and suggests it might be a good place for the clinic and women's respite care facility we've been talking about.

"The owner is a builder who probably needs to unload it because he's paying taxes on dead space. Money isn't growing on trees these days, and he might agree to a sales deal that includes remodeling it into what you need," Mr. Fleming says, handing me a folded paper with the name and phone number. Sister Mathilde explains that Sister Nora hasn't given her okay on the idea because she's yet to discuss it with her, but instructs me to go ahead and make the call anyway.

"A little inquiry can't hurt, and if she doesn't have to put up any money, I can't see any reason for her to object too much. We certainly don't want someone else to snap it up and start a bootlegging operation or some other illegal activity that would bring the police around too often and complicate things for us. Sometimes it's better to request forgiveness than to ask permission," the nun winks. When I wonder aloud how more police in the area would complicate our work, Sister Mathilde, standing behind Mr. Fleming, vigorously shakes her head, frowning and putting her finger to her lips. Suddenly, what she is implying dawns on me, and I nod slightly, silently agreeing that the police don't need to become aware of everything we are doing.

Less than a week later, the building owner, an eye-catching man with an exceptionally kind face, agrees to give me a tour of the narrow, two-story, wood and stucco structure. Tall, and moving with the grace of a healthy, well-trained athlete, Paul Barlow introduces himself and asks me to call him Paul. I don't respond, nor do I invite him to call me Charlotte.

"Like I mentioned, the place is in pretty bad shape. I don't want you to have high expectations and then be disappointed," he says, unlocking the door then slowly and carefully guiding me through the building's upper floor. He wasn't exaggerating when he described the jumbled state of disrepair the building has fallen into and readily admits it needs extensive work before it would inhabitable. Every wall is leaking windows and crumbling plaster decorated with generous amounts of graffiti and other evidence of squatters, but the floors don't creak too badly, and he is honest about pointing out the less obvious structural problems. As we continue walking and talking, I begin wishing I hadn't worn my uniform to meet with him. *At least I removed my cap and combed through my hair*, I comfort myself.

"There's no question bringing it up to code would involve a lot of work and expense, but if it's half-way suitable for your purposes and you're even slightly interested in buying it, a deal that includes basic remodeling isn't out of the question," the exceptionally handsome building owner smiles, looking directly at me.

"It's never been properly wired, and the plumbing was an afterthought, but those aren't difficult problems to remedy if you're already renovating, and of course anybody who buys it is going to do that," he continues. I explain that I have some general ideas about how we could use the space, which is larger than I anticipated, but will have to give it more thought before we can talk details.

"Take all the time you need. If someone else shows a serious interest, I'll let you know. I promise not to sell it out from under you," Paul assures me, offering another pleasant smile. His straight, white teeth reflect lifetime access to good nutrition and routine dental care – something I never see among the patients I care for. What teeth they have, if they have any at all, are rotting in their mouths, emitting the foul odor that is a constant reminder for me to be on the look-out for the health problems chronically infected teeth invite.

We finish the tour on the ground floor with rooms at each corner, separated by a central hallway leading to what might've been a kitchen at the back. I ask what the building was originally used for.

"It was vacant when I bought it from the city for a song, so I'm not sure, but my guess is most recently, it was a flop house and soup kitchen, which unfortunately this area still needs. That's not a business I want to get into, although it's certainly something I support. It would please me to see the building put to such good use."

"A flop house or a soup kitchen, or both together, are all possibilities, but not exactly what I envision," I admit.

"When I bought the building, I thought the neighborhood was poised to go on the upswing and was planning to make the upper floor into three or four small apartments, with my office downstairs, but the economic recovery after the stock market crash has been much slower than I anticipated, and all bets are off. I don't know when things will turn around and can't see carrying it indefinitely if I can sell it. I don't need to make money on the deal, but I would like to break even – although if the building is going to be used in some way that helps the poor folks living in the barrios, I'd be willing to take a loss, if that would help."

"I can assure you that it will be put to good use in the interests of helping the people in the area. Sister Mathilde and I have daydreamed about several possibilities, but haven't made any formal proposal to the hospital, which will have the final say... unless we decide to just go ahead on our own. That would be a little trickier financially and operationally but isn't out of the question."

"Indirectly, my profit will come from being out from under the tax burden, so I'll eagerly entertain any thoughts you come up with. Paying taxes on unused property is like betting money on a longshot racehorse – you're pretty much guaranteed to lose," he chuckles. As he is explaining this, Paul fails to duck through a sagging doorway, hitting his head. The hard bump prompts a generous outburst of impolite language that continues as blood drips down his face. I pull a handkerchief from my pocket and hold it to his head.

"Head wounds bleed profusely, and this one definitely needs stitches," I tell him, sweeping his dark, softly curly hair away from his face and blotting at the cut.

"Come back to the dispensary with me and I'll stitch you up – unless you'd rather go to the hospital emergency room. In that case, I'll bandage it well enough to contain the bleeding until you get there."

"You know how to sew people up?" Paul asks, sheepishly tacking on an apology for his outburst of colorful language.

"I've heard worse, believe me," I smile, adding that I've had plenty of experience stitching up various kinds of wounds and am pretty good at it.

"This is a clean cut – it won't be complicated. But the black eye you're going to have will be a doozie that will take two or three weeks to completely disappear. The scar will eventually become a thin white line no one but you will notice."

"Then stitch away, Nurse Rose. I don't have any plans for the next couple weeks anyway," Paul grimaces.

"In that case, please follow me," I tell him, hoping my sudden nervousness isn't obvious as I lead him into the supply room behind the dispensary. After seating him beside the table, I prepare an ice bag, instructing him to hold it on his head while I locate the fine suture threads best for head wounds.

Paul Barlow is a cooperative patient and less than an hour later, the wound is neatly closed, bandaged and throbbing. Trying not to look directly into his warm, hazel-blue eyes, I explain it would be best if he takes it easy for a day or two, keeps his head elevated when he sleeps, and stays close to an ice bag, which will help with the swelling and inevitable headache. I ask whether he has had a recent tetanus shot.

"I'm not sure. Why?"

"That wound could've been caused by a rusty nail sticking out of the door frame and could cause problems if you're not vaccinated. We keep some tetanus vaccine here in the clinic and if you're willing, roll up your sleeve and I'll give you a shot, just to be on the safe side." In response, he offers a muscular, nicely tanned upper arm, which I clean with alcohol and very carefully inject.

"The arm might get a little sore, and you'll need to come back in a week so I can remove the stitches, but if you happen to be anywhere nearby tomorrow, I'd like to change the bandage and have a look just to be sure there's no infection and it's healing like it should. Not absolutely necessary, but advisable." I instruct, busying myself straightening up my supply tray.

"I'll do that, if you'll agree to dinner afterwards, assuming you aren't embarrassed to be seen with me. By then I'll probably have a shiner only a prizefighter could be proud of."

"I don't date patients, Mr. Barlow," I answer, reverting to formality to hide my continuing nervousness.

"I'm an accidental patient, Nurse Rose. Surely you can make an exception under these circumstances. By the way, do you mind if I call you Charlotte?"

"I'll have to think about it." I smile, knowing he is the only thing I'll think about for the rest of the day.

"Think about which – dinner or calling you Charlotte?"

"Both."

The next afternoon I return to the dispensary, dust-covered and exhausted, after an entire day at the encampment which is even more crowded than the last time I was there, which was only five days ago. Opening the door, I see Paul Barlow charming Sister Mathilde into believing his explanation for why he is there. Staring at him as though he's Jesus Christ, Sister offhandedly asks me how my day went.

"People keep coming, and most of them are sick, injured – or both. With no money, no job prospects and everything they own packed into a four-wheel vehicle with bald tires and a barely running engine, they are so defeated they can barely speak… and I can't blame them. A rattletrap carrying three generations of a family spilling off the back end is an invitation to mishaps ranging from dangerous to outright fatal. I have no idea how many are killed because the driver is going too fast and can't avoid a pothole or round a curve, sending some poor soul flying into the air at breakneck speed. The load shifts, crushing someone, or propelling the truck off the road, splintering wood and turning cooking utensils into deadly flying missiles. By the time I see them, their wounds are infected, their broken bones are permanently crooked, they're weak from lack of food and contaminated water, and there's very little I can do about any of it," I explode in frustration.

"The barrios are no better – just different," Sister reminds me.

"Every baby born there means another person crammed into a small amount of space, which breeds disease and violence. More people add up to more health problems and for every person I treat, there are ten more I can't do anything for. The only thing keeping most of them alive are nearby churches that have opened soup kitchens and then allow those with nowhere else to go to sleep in the worship space," Sister Mathilde adds, before apologizing to Paul Barlow for complaining about the privilege of doing God's work among the downtrodden and desperate, even if it is difficult and demoralizing. Pausing for a moment, she admits she has no idea how a merciful God tolerates masses of suffering humanity when, in her mind, it is totally unnecessary. Apologizing again for her outburst, she walks out, leaving Paul and I alone.

Since I had not agreed to dinner, I did not expect him to stop by today and am surprised, dismayed, and pleased to find him here. Wishing I'd had time to clean myself up before seeing him again, I take a deep breath and motion him to follow me through the side door into the back room, saying I'll return in a minute. I race upstairs to my apartment, wash my face, comb my hair and look for an apron to cover the dirt and other stains of various origin lingering on my uniform.

After examining my sutures and pronouncing his head healing nicely, I re-bandage Paul's wound, adding that I've seen worse black eyes, but not very often. He responds by asking about dinner.

"I've had a very long day and I'm just too tired," I answer honestly.

"That's what I thought you might say, so I brought cookies. If you have coffee, we can sit here and enjoy a late afternoon snack. You probably didn't eat lunch and could use one," he grins, holding up a brown paper bag stamped with a label from a bakery I've never heard of. *I could look at you across any table, anytime,* I think, turning toward the hotplate and fumbling with the coffee can.

"You look like you're about to drop. Why don't you sit down, and I'll make the coffee," Paul suggests after putting several gigantic cookies on a paper napkin in the middle of the table. I'm too exhausted to object, and am hoping Sister Mathilde doesn't return and feel compelled to ask about a scenario I'm not prepared to explain.

Chapter Nineteen
פרק תשע עשרה

Berkeley
Early fall, 1971

Keeping secrets about yourself is hiding from yourself.

I read Adrian's translation of my mother's diary twice, very slowly, trying to discern the person behind the descriptions of her life as a nurse, and how she met my father. It seems clear that she loved him... maybe not as much as he loved her, but she did love him. This is reassuring since there's no question in my mind how he felt – still feels – about her.

The issue in this translation that grabs my attention most is my mother's reference to anti-German and pro-Nazi activities in Los Angeles. This is something I want to learn more about, and the obvious person to help me is Rabbi Werner. As good luck would have it, all it takes is a quick phone call and he invites me to his office two days from now.

In the meantime, the unanswered questions about the Swiss bank account continue to nag at me. I confess this to Adrian while we are sitting on the fire escape watching the sunset and sharing a beer.

"You know the foreign bank account I discovered my mother was paying into after the war, up until she died?" I begin.

"I remember you mentioning it."

"I can't let it go. I keep wondering what it's all about? Do you have any thoughts?" He takes my hand into his lap before answering.

"Thoughts – yes. Proof – no. A war is a very emotionally intense experience, Natalie. This was especially true in wartime Europe – bullets and bombs were flying and nowhere was safe. People did a lot of things that under ordinary circumstances would never occur to them, and perhaps later, horrified them... things they'd never want those who loved them to know about. They were surrounded by imminent danger and impending doom, and no one knew whether they'd survive, or even be alive in five minutes. From what I've read, a lot of soldiers believed that one way or another, they'd die before the war ended. Living with that pervasive, gut-level fear can't help but rearrange someone's psyche in ways they never, in their wildest dreams, imagined."

"Go on," I say. He tightens his grasp on my right hand.

"One possibility is that she fell in love with an injured soldier or partisan who was never going to fully recover, and knowing she would eventually return to the U.S., wanted to ensure his care going forward. It's also possible she had relatives who somehow survived the war. If that was true, they would've been displaced persons left with nothing, and she could've been helping them get resettled. Maybe the money was going to a Jewish relief organization aiding camp survivors. She wouldn't necessarily have wanted that known, either."

"Aunt Sally is most likely to know these answers – or at least be able to reasonably speculate. But asking her is inviting an emotional firestorm I can't manage right now," I admit, falling silent.

"What's your best guess," I finally ask, not at all sure I want the answer. Staring out the window, Adrian doesn't reply right away.

"I don't have one. There are many reasons to maintain a trust in a country known for its iron-clad ability to protect financial secrets. My advice is not to pursue this for now. Other than the pressure of your own curiosity, there's no hurry about trying to find answers," he assures me.

"I think she had a love child and left it there. It's the only thing that makes sense to me."

"That's pretty far-fetched, Natalie. Mother's don't abandon their children."

"It's not that far-fetched, Adrian. She abandoned me."

"She left you intending to return. That's very different."

"Maybe, but it's a difference without a distinction, at least in my mind."

"Perhaps… but it's impossible to verify and speculating about it is going down a road leading to nowhere. There's not much point in setting out on that kind of journey."

"What other reason would there be to set up a foreign trust and fund it for a very long time? Something, or someone, had to matter a great to her."

"People do a lot of things that don't make sense to anyone but themselves. I wouldn't get too caught up in that assumption if I were you."

"If you were facing this situation, wouldn't you be thinking the same thing?"

"Honestly, I doubt it. Curious, maybe, but not enough to get tied in knots over it, when the chances of finding out the truth are basically zero. If your mother wanted you to know about the trust, she'd have either told you or made it easy for you to find out, and she did neither."

"She had to know I'd find out eventually."

"Not necessarily. Nothing really suggests she was planning on dying, so she probably wasn't thinking about that possibility. It could be a time-limited trust and she figured it would expire before she died, and you would never find out about it. My advice is to respect her wishes that the details remain secret and drop it. If you're meant to know more, the answers will find you."

Chapter Twenty
פרק עשרים

San Francisco
Fall, 1942

War demands sacrifice, gives suffering in return and only ends when the enemy decides to love its children more than it hates its foes.

Five weeks ago, after nine months gripped by a knot of fear I am still unable to untangle, I gave birth to the most beautiful baby I have ever seen. Paul and I had talked little about having children and I hadn't wanted to get pregnant – it just happened, forcing me to face very mixed feelings about impending motherhood and the tortured, uncertain world I would be bringing a child into. I delayed telling Paul for as long as possible, and when that conversation finally occurred, he was far more excited about the prospect of a child than I was.

I love being a nurse. Working in the barrios, and even in the encampments is deeply fulfilling in ways nothing else is. I had no plans to give any of this up, but upon learning the pregnancy I'd gone to great lengths to hide, Sister Mathilde, who had already broken hospital rules by allowing me to keep my job after marrying Paul, insisted I take a leave of absence. I balked at the idea, but she argued, correctly, that my job was neither a safe nor healthy environment for a pregnant woman.

"I desperately need you here, Charlotte, and I promise you can return as soon as you are ready, but in the meantime, I cannot, in good conscience, allow you to continue," she told me, clearing her throat several times.

Paul saw the situation differently and believed this was the opportunity he had been waiting for to implement his plan to move to San Francisco, where he had opened a second, much larger office. He had been wanting to do this for a while, but knew I loved my job and did not want to leave it. Our compromise had been that he commuted between Los Angeles and San Francisco and, on the nights he was gone, I stayed in my austere apartment above the dispensary instead of remaining in his charming bungalow overlooking the ocean. We both knew our current arrangement would be impossible with a child, and feeling trapped by circumstances I had no control over, I became an angry, sullen wife to a very loving, patient husband.

More and more, I wish Paul didn't love me so much. Rather than reassuring me, his untiring devotion induces mind-numbing guilt. I love my wonderful husband very much, but from the beginning I knew that being a wife was never going to be enough for me. The pregnancy he was so much more excited about than I was, forced me to face the uncomfortable truth that he deserves more love than I have to give, and marrying him was very selfish.

My fear of bleeding to death during childbirth was very real. I spent little time preparing to be a mother because I wasn't convinced I would survive to become one. I resented the changes pregnancy forced upon my body and refused to think about the burden of responsibility a totally dependent human being imposed on a mother. I had no grasp of impending motherhood and little sense of a relationship with the child I was carrying next to my heart. It was as though pregnancy and motherhood happened to other women, not to me. I never wondered whether I was going to have a son or a daughter, who my child would look like, whether it would be a happy baby or a difficult one, or what to name it.

I extracted a promise from my sister that if I died and the baby survived, she would raise it. After this tearful conversation, she took more than a passing interest in my pregnancy, and sometimes I felt she was preparing to claim my child regardless of whether I lived or died. Despite all this, I now have a baby daughter. From the beginning, her six lbs. stretched over nearly twenty-two inches endowed her with a subtle grace of movement and engagement with others. She has her father's hazel blue eyes, and from the moment she opened them, stared at him with an intensity that bonded them at once. His love seems to be enough for her because when I hold her she stiffens in my arms and refuses to look at me.

My surprise at having survived childbirth, although barely, and only because there was blood readily available, is present in my thoughts every waking moment. Off and on, I search for a deeper meaning in what I know was a near-death experience, but so far have failed to discern what it might be. To better rebuild my strength, I was encouraged not to nurse the baby, and she took to the bottle at once, preferring to receive it either from her father or her aunt. My sister brought Emily and traveled up from Los Angeles to oversee my convalescence, even though this wasn't necessary because Paul hired a wonderfully competent baby nurse to help us through the early days. It evolved that the nurse attended to my needs and my sister took over my baby's care.

Now, weeks later, the nurse has taken another case, my sister has returned to her own life and I am alone with my daughter. I suspect my child, named Natalie after my mother, senses my reluctance to take on the responsibilities she rightly demands of me. I'm still not convinced I'll be good at any of this, but despite my persistent misgivings, I hope she also senses that I love her deeply. Sometimes, when I look at her, I cry – with joy that we are both alive and with fear for her future in a conflicted, war-torn world I'm not sure how to live in, much less how to raise a child in. My darkest moments allow the question of whether my decision to continue with the pregnancy was a selfish mistake to creep into my consciousness.

Meanwhile, the horrors overtaking Europe and the South Pacific upset me more and more each day. Barely an hour goes by that I am not thinking about the human tragedy this war has wrought. Although he says little, I know Paul is heavily involved in the war effort. His company is building desperately needed military facilities up and down the entire Pacific Coast in an intensified effort to stop the Japanese, who are currently winning the war in the Pacific. I am jealous of his involvement, which we both know is vitally important and hate living so comfortably when I could be helping fight against a murderous madman with unrestrained power no one seems able to contain. Hitler has targeted my people, the Jews, for extinction, and if he succeeds, my baby daughter might not survive into adulthood. Even if the Third Reich falls, I am not so naïve as to believe the hate its leaders have spewed will not live on long after them. Either way, the world my child faces is a dangerous and frightening one, and I am doing absolutely nothing to make it safer for her. This, more than anything, contributes to feeling like I am a failure as a mother and a worthy human being.

Natalie is generally content, allowing me to spend long periods of time sitting in the overstuffed chair beside our large living room window, staring out into the street, watching the occasional car drive by while waiting for a signal that she wants something from me. She asks very little, leaving me many empty hours to fill.

I know I am an exceptional nurse, vowed to relieve suffering where I find it, and not putting my skills to use in a world succumbing to violent, deadly chaos is, to me, an act of pure selfishness. Little by little, as I stand idly by while the world explodes into a battle of good versus evil, a crushing guilt overtakes me. The pressure to fight back has grown so powerful I'm not sure how much longer I can keep pushing against it.

When a letter from my Aunt Irina arrives, I delay opening it, knowing it can only be more bad news. She thanks me for the money I sent, then describes the family struggles and Nazi atrocities against the German Jews in frightful detail. To punctuate the horror, she sends me my uncle's tattered, yellow Juden Magen David, which he ripped from the coat he was wearing when the Gestapo arrested him.

After reading the letter twice, I call my sister. The phone rings a long time before she finally answers.

"What took you so long? I almost hung up," I begin.

"Since Mick went overseas, I dread hearing the phone ring. I'm always sure it's bad news. Besides, I hate talking to a black box and would get rid of the damned thing except for the possibility Mick might call sometime, although that's wishful thinking. I doubt they have telephones in North Africa, and he's probably too busy with the war..." Sally's voice trails off. In the background I can hear Emily telling her imaginary playmates, Ingrid and Joe, to stop acting silly and eat their lunch before it gets cold.

"A letter came from Irina. Levi and Avram were both arrested. She sent Levi's star, so I'll have something to know him by in case he never comes back. She is now living with one of her daughters, and says food is sparse and she doesn't know what to expect next." As I am telling my sister this, I cradle my baby in my arm, balancing the telephone on my shoulder while holding her bottle. She's not a ravenous eater, instead sucking slowly and rhythmically, stopping occasionally to take a deep breath and open her eyes for a moment. While she grasps her father's fingers tightly, sleeps contentedly in his arms, gazes lovingly into his eyes when awake, and snuggles with her aunt, a brief glance is as much as she's willing to give me.

"Are you still sending money?" Sally asks.

"Yes... are you?"

"As much as I can. Mick's combat pay doesn't go far, and my salary got cut because of tax money needed to support the war – not that there's much public money coming into my district to support schools to begin with. I'm lucky I didn't lose my job," my sister sighs.

"Sally, I want to go... to help."

"Go where? Help how? You just had a baby, Charlotte. Forget going anywhere. You're needed at home now."

"Go to the war zone. I can help treat the wounded – civilians and American and Allied soldiers in Red Cross field hospitals. We have family in danger, Sally. I might be able to help them. The International Red Cross desperately needs nurses to help treat both combat and civilian casualties wherever they are fighting. There's plenty I could do…"

"For God's sake, Charlotte, you've flirted with insane ideas before, but this one tops them all. This is not the time to get all heroic and go fight a war. You're a wife and mother – your obligations are to your husband and daughter. Home is where you're needed most – not getting involved in a fight with some far-off country run by a lunatic hell-bent on destroying everyone who isn't a blue-eyed blond."

"It's much more complicated than that, Sally, and you know it. Both of us have lived our lives denying our Jewish heritage, and gained a great deal as a result, including choices we never would've had otherwise. Now the Jews are facing grave danger brought about by a political ideology many people have bought into and are perfectly willing to act on. For them, murdering Jews is no problem. Jews everywhere are obligated to step up to save our people from annihilation in all ways possible. There is something useful I can do to help, and nothing is stopping me, really. We sold out on our heritage once, Sally. We need to make amends by fighting for our collective survival now – not just as human beings, but as a culture, a religion… and to preserve our history and our bloodlines. This mass slaughter is threatening all of that."

"Seriously, Charlotte? You can't possibly believe you, as one person, can do anything about any of this?"

"Actually, I do believe that, Sally. Paul's rarely home and will get along fine without me. Natalie barely looks at me and will never notice I'm gone. She'll be perfectly happy with you caring for her – certainly more so than if I was doing it when what I really want is to be somewhere else."

"You want me to care for Natalie? You can't possibly be serious."

"It's what you promised to do – remember?"

"Yes, but only if you died, and thank God you didn't. You're alive and healthy."

"Alive, healthy, and miserable. A good nurse goes where she is needed, and I am needed in the war effort, not sitting safely at home in America, taking care of a baby who doesn't even like me."

"You're talking nonsense, Charlotte. Home taking care of a beautiful daughter you damned near died giving birth to is exactly where you're supposed to be. You're a mother now and need to get your priorities straight – and you have no way to tell whether Natalie likes you or not. She's a baby. All that matters to her is a full stomach and a dry diaper. The rest comes later. Think about how you took to Emily when she was born – you were great with her."

"That was different, Sally. I was taking care of you because you were too weak to care for yourself and Emily was a helpless infant. You both needed me. It was a temporary situation and Emily wasn't my responsibility, she was yours. I knew eventually I'd return to my own life. Natalie is a lifetime responsibility I've never been sure I was capable of taking on. I told you that when I was pregnant."

"And I told you you'd get over it…"

"Unfortunately, I can't, Sally."

"You do know you're sounding like a selfish, self-centered bitch… right?" My sister asks me in the coldest voice I've ever heard her use.

"You won't support my decision to join the International Red Cross as a nurse even though, if you did support it, you would be doing something to help save our people who happened to be Jews who are being mass-murdered."

"Of course I don't support your decision. The Jews have been saving themselves for five thousand years without my help – or yours. You need to get over yourself and start acting like a mother, Charlotte. Nothing else matters nearly as much as that." I assure my sister it has been nice talking to her and, with a click, end our conversation.

Three weeks later, I tell Paul I love him, and Natalie, with all my heart, but the call to fight off the German genocide against the Jews is so strong I am helpless to resist.

"I owe it to our daughter to fight the evil in the world we have brought her into," I tell my husband, explaining that I have signed on to the International Red Cross Nursing Corps. Other than promising to return at war's end I offer no further explanation. To my great surprise, he doesn't ask for one.

"I won't pretend to understand this, Charlotte, but if this is what you really want to do, I can't stop you. Just don't leave here assuming that when you return things will be same as they were when you left, because they won't be," my husband warns as all emotion leaves his face.

I expected greater resistance involving at least an argument, and perhaps even a scene. Because Paul surrenders to my desire to leave so easily, I am reluctant to ask him to explain what he means by things not being the same when I return. Instead, I remind him Sally promised to care for Natalie if anything happened to me, and feel sure she will step up now if he asks her to. He nods and walks out of the room. A moment later he returns. Looking at me with an anguished sadness I've only ever seen on the face of a man I had just informed about his beloved wife's death, my husband says he hopes I know what I am doing and will be mindful of the dangers.

"Take care of yourself, Charlotte," he cautions, quietly closing the door behind him. We don't speak again before I leave.

The next afternoon I say a brief goodbye to my daughter, who is sleeping soundly and never stirs at the sound of my voice or the feel of my kiss on her forehead. I don't know whether this is the bravest thing I have ever done, or the most cowardly, whether I am running away from something I fear or running toward a voice calling to me. But I do know it is something I have to do.

Chapter Twenty-one
פרק עשרים ואחת

Europe
1942-1946

War is organized murder conceived by power-hungry, pathological personalities. There are no winners.

I officially enlisted in the International Red Cross Nursing Corps three days before Christmas which has always been, for me, a meaningless holiday. The Red Cross field office in downtown San Francisco was short-staffed and short-tempered, and asked very few questions. I indicated I am unmarried and unencumbered by other family responsibilities, and my nursing credential spoke for itself, so I was accepted with no questions asked and told to report in twenty-four hours. Just like the other times I've lied to get what I want, I justified my actions by believing I was doing it for the right reasons.

After receiving the necessary vaccinations and general indoctrination into the Red Cross I am on my way to London to attend a one-month orientation on treating war wounded – a duty of care Red Cross nurses assume for both civilian and military casualties. Beginning the day after my arrival, we spend twelve hours a day in a large, dreary hospital six blocks from the East End docks, an area of the city that has sustained heavy damage from the relentless German blitzkrieg.

I am both surprised and disappointed to discover the International Red Cross is neutral regarding the war. Its mission is to provide humanitarian aid, treat the wounded on both sides of the conflict, and stay out of the politics. To my way of thinking, neutrality implies agreement, or at least a lack of disagreement with, in this case, murdering Jews. It takes me nearly two weeks to decide I have not made a terrible mistake and instead, can use the organization to achieve my goal of saving my extended family from Hitler's genocide, then abandon it as soon as it is no longer useful to my purposes. *Signing on to the Red Cross is not conscription into the military; I can leave whenever I wish*, I remind myself several times a day.

It soon becomes obvious my original intention to go directly to Germany in search of Irina is dangerously unrealistic. Every Red Cross official I speak with strongly discourages me.

"Asking after the Jews draws unwanted attention to you and to them. It's too risky. You could be talking to Gestapo informants and not know it. Better to wait until the war is over before trying to find your family," Maizie Travers, a young British nursing officer explains when I reveal my desire to go to Germany.

"And if they don't survive?"

"It's just a chance you'll have to take… same chance we're all taking, dearie. After the bloody krauts shot my husband down over the channel, I sent my boy… only child, he is, on an orphan train out of London nearly a year ago… get him to safety outta the blitz. I pray every day I'll see him again, but ain't no guarantees in this life we're living," she sighs, not quite dry-eyed.

"No point in crying over this. Wastes the energy I need to help fight this bloody war and I ain't no good to nobody wallowing in misery. I strongly recommend you do the same. There'll be plenty of time for tears when it's over," Maizie adds, handing me directions to the nearest bomb shelter.

"Best you step lively any time you hear a siren and always bring an aid kit so you can to help however you can," she instructs, returning to her paperwork.

Two days later, the sirens go off, and in my hurry to get to the shelter, I forget my first aid supplies. After the all-clear sounds, I do what I can to help. Rescue workers search frantically for survivors in the rubble, while I tear clothing and shoelaces off the dead to use as makeshift bandages and tourniquets for those who are still alive enough they might have a chance. This is what I came to do, I remind myself as I tie a rag around a bloody stump that was once an air raid warden's leg.

The next day Maizie Traver's desk is empty. When several days pass and she doesn't return, I ask after her during our lunch break

"Guess you didn't hear… killed in the last bombing raid. Building fell on her trying to save a baby. Real shame – right good nurse, our Maizie… and now her boy, poor little fella, don't have no mother or father coming for him when this is all over. Bloody Germans – I'd kill'em barehanded sooner than look at 'em," an older nurse sitting across from me says. I feel my face go pale at this news, which has the added effect of telling me that

I could die in this war which, until this moment, I had not seriously considered.

"You all right, dearie – you look a little peaked," the seasoned nurse asks.

Following orientation, my assignment, under the direction of a Canadian medical officer, is to teach less experienced nurses how to care for wounds and manage outbreaks of infectious diseases, which I gained considerable experience with in both the barrios and encampments. The Red Cross rules of war dictate that medical care is administered to wounded and captured prisoners of war and civilians caught in the crossfire, as well as to combat soldiers, and I volunteer for a field hospital assignment where front-line care is desperately needed. Without revealing that I'm fluent in German, I stress that this would be the best use of my nursing skills.

After seeming to ignore my request for several weeks, late one afternoon I receive a message to report to the main office to meet with an administrative nurse, one of several who cautioned me against trying to locate and assist my family in Germany. After briefly exchanging pleasantries, she says she understands that I am interested in a field hospital assignment, and one has become available, if I am still willing.

"The war is escalating, and the battles are becoming more intense, although it's hard to imagine how they could be any worse. This is a very dangerous assignment, and you need to be absolutely sure you understand the risks. Once you arrive, there is no going back," the stern, middle-aged nurse tells me. I assure her I am fully prepared to accept the dangers involved in field hospital work. Closing the folder she has been tightly gripping, she says she'll pass this information along and be back in touch.

Meanwhile, the blitz continues with frightening frequency. I can no longer remember what a good night's sleep feels like, which leaves me perpetually exhausted. Night after night, I'm either awakened by a symphony of sirens or unable to fall asleep because I'm anxiously waiting for them to go off. The people I have come to know best are those I see regularly in the tube station underneath the next block, which is our designated bomb shelter. One older woman, a grandmother of six, sacrifices her flour, sugar, and butter rations to make tiny cookies for the children.

"If Jesus can multiply five loaves and two fishes into enough food to feed five thousand, I can stretch my rations into a few biscuits," the emaciated, yet lively woman winks when I ask her how she manages to always bring a box of homemade treats.

Britain's King George VI has remained in London despite the danger. Often accompanied by his wife, the beloved king frequently tours London's hardest hit East End neighborhoods. The young Crown Princess Elizabeth joins the British army as a mechanic and ambulance driver. The British Prime Minister, a bulldog of a man with a voice to match, gives regular pep talks over the wireless, trying to keep spirits up as this small island nation unites to fight for its survival.

"I don't always agree with Winston, but I always feel better after listening to him," one of the older nurses in our dorm remarks following one of Mr. Churchill's cheerleader speeches. I can't help deeply admiring the unity, dogged determination and resolve to win this war that seems to come so naturally to the Brits, despite the overwhelming odds against them. When I mention this late one evening while sharing a corner of the shelter with a young mother I'm proudly told that "serving king and country is who we are. It never occurred to us not to fight back."

Shortly after my meeting with the administrative nurse, I receive a field hospital assignment in occupied France, near the German border. I'm warned the conditions are primitive, medical supplies are scarce, and the French have not lived up to their promise to keep field hospital facilities secure.

"Don't have much patience with the French myself," my immediate supervisor tells me when informing me of my new assignment.

"Lazy cowards, they are. Good for nothing bastards went belly-up to Hitler without firing a shot and now that evil monster's got the French secure in his pocket and is more powerful than ever. You tell me how that's helping win this war?" she huffs, handing me instructions for a three-day information session I'm to attend before leaving. The schedule includes a one-hour lecture on "What to Expect in France" presented by a British army officer who makes no effort to hide his distaste for the French generally and the Vichy government in particular.

"Rather than suffer a sure defeat, France quickly surrendered to Germany, allowing German occupation troops to overtake the country, then creating a puppet government under Marshal Phillippe Pétain, a French World War I hero. However, not every French citizen agrees with this decision. Some are actively resisting, but you must be cautious about who you trust – some resisters are quite possibly double agents... selling information to both the Germans and the Allies," our instructor repeatedly emphasizes.

"There is active resistance to French-German cooperation spearheaded by a government-in-exile led by French General Charles de Galle and headquartered right here in London," he tells us, adding that this is an underground movement, out of public view, and he doesn't know anything more about it.

The evening before my departure, I ask a French physician assigned to the training hospital when I have spent the last two months what he thinks about the situation in his home country. Just past midnight, over a cup of strong, lukewarm tea, Dr. Jacques Bernard says that some French favor the Vichy government, others vehemently oppose it, and most don't care.

"Those who find the Vichy government's "policy of least resistance" morally repugnant have formed an effective underground resistance movement that engages in guerrilla warfare... mostly blowing up roads, tunnels, bridges, and troop trains, and assassinating German officers whenever possible," he says, adding that the effort is backed by a wide support network of locals throughout the country who hide partisans on the run, forge documents and help the resistance in the thousands of little ways that keep it alive.

"This is a loosely organized effort of small partisan cells capable of inflicting a remarkable amount of damage, making the German occupation much less effective as a military stronghold than it might otherwise be. I am proud of my countrymen who are doing this. They restore my belief in France a little bit; otherwise, I could never forgive my country for bowing down to Hitler," the earnest young physician says, stretching over the table to kiss both my cheeks, wishing me good luck and Godspeed. Three hours later, as I am packing to leave, my supervisor delivers my travel documents.

"Just do your job, attracting as little attention to yourself as possible. Then be patient, the rest will come," she whispers, squeezing my hand and bidding me safe travels.

An agreement between the Red Cross and the French-German high command allows Red Cross nurses to enter France as replacements for those who leave for whatever reason. On this trip six of us are traveling from London, first by ship across the English Channel to Marseilles and then across France by train, eventually reaching our destinations. One nurse stays in Marseilles, three go on to Paris, another takes a bus to Normandy, and I travel on toward Strasbourg. After several hours sitting on a bench behind the train station in Villy-la-Ferté, growing increasingly anxious about whether I am in the right place, a Red Cross supply truck finally shows up.

"Sorry to make you wait... weren't sure what day you was coming," is all the gruff driver says in barely understandable English while loading my small suitcase into the truck. As we bounce along deeply rutted roads, he explains that Field Hospital Six is approximately thirty kilometers north, just west of the Maginot Line and not far from the main rail route to and from Paris. He does not reveal that this location makes the hospital a highly desirable bombing target, information I discovered while reading through my travel instructions.

Perhaps foolishly, I am far more exhilarated than fearful. While I remain torn between pride at my small attempt to fight against the evil threatening the world and deep shame over leaving my husband and infant daughter to do it, the satisfaction of answering the call I heard from deep in my heart far outweighs my guilt. There is no question in my mind that this is exactly where I am supposed to be, doing exactly what I am supposed to be doing.

The hospital complex is a canvas tent and concrete fortified encampment hidden in a densely forested area so quiet I can hear falling snow hit the ground. In late January, the trees are bare, the skies are perpetually gray, and the ground is a sloppy mix of dirty slush, slightly frozen, slippery mud and putrid liquid runoff. The driver drops me at a small wooden building resembling a garden shed. Inside, a medic issues me a helmet, several pairs of poorly fitting fatigues with a red cross sewn on the sleeve, boots, woolen socks, and a jacket, then directs me to Tent C, where the nurses are housed. I explain that it's colder than I expected and I'm not sure my clothing will be warm enough.

"There's a box by the door with odd bits of clothing other nurses left behind. You might find a sweater in there. Choose any empty cot but be quiet about it; the night shift nurses are sleeping," the young man instructs, adding that I'll find pillows and blankets in the footlocker under the cot.

"Hope you stay longer than the last one. She weren't none too brave and hightailed it outta here after the first bombing raid," he calls after me in a fragmented combination of French and English.

Later that evening, sitting around the kerosene stove heating the tent, I learn that currently the staff includes four doctors, several French and German medics, and only twelve nurses – five Swiss, four French, two from the Canadian Red Cross, and myself. Over the next days I discover that four of the Swiss and one of the Canadian Red Cross nurses are battle-tested veterans of the Great War and unbothered by the regular bombings and frequent artillery bombardments that hound us. They never complain about there being too few of us, about the exhaustively long hours caring for seven wards of patients either heroically clinging to life or fighting a losing battle with death, and never mention the other gruesome hardships most ordinary human beings find unacceptable.

"This is luxury. The trenches – they were the real pits… operating rooms were mud up to our knees," the oldest Swiss nurse tells me.

The French nurses are giggly and less interested in caring for the sick and wounded than in fraternizing with the soldiers, which is against the rules they obviously have no intention of obeying. The Swiss nurses are serious, not particularly friendly and stay to themselves, which is fine with me – the less my life is probed, the less I'm forced to lie. If asked, I'll admit to being from the United States, but we are so busy, and so tired the rest of the time, that no one bothers with many personal questions. Our conversations are mostly confined to complaining about the weather, the war, and our unrelenting weariness. A damp cold permeates everything and any memories of ever feeling warm and dry have disappeared. Sleep does not come easily and is never restful. Many nights I pass the dark hours counting stars through the slit I tore in the canvas tent seam next to my cot to offset the likely possibility our kerosene heater is faulty. I generally doze for a while, then wake with a start, sometimes disoriented, while cold air plummets my face.

Nearly all our casualties are a consequence of the bombing raids or skirmishes between Germans soldiers who believe they have a right to be in France, and French opposition soldiers and civilians who disagree. When they can get past the German Luftwaffe and ground-based anti-aircraft fire, the Allies bomb the rail lines, convoy routes, supply depots and other targets intended to cripple German troop movements. These attacks, always without warning, bring an influx of both civilian and military casualties. The combination of wounded and those seriously ill from various diseases unique to wartime keeps our ninety-seven-bed hospital spilling over with patients. Sometimes we are so crowded we are forced to use spare sleeping cots for patient beds.

France's notoriously bad water accounts for the high number of typhoid, cholera, and jaundice cases we treat. The most severely jaundiced soldiers, so orange they resemble pumpkins, are often at greater risk of dying than the wounded. Adding to the difficulties, at one time or another, all of the staff have been leveled by dysentery. Despite all this, we remain focused on patching up less seriously ill and wounded soldiers sufficiently to return them to combat duty as quickly as possible and moving everyone else to other hospitals as soon as they are stable enough to survive transport. Although rarely spoken about, everyone assumes that, sooner or later, the Allies will invade France and do ground battle with the German occupation troops. Because of our location, we will be dealing with heavy casualties from structural damage across a wide area. In the meantime, we exist day by day in an atmosphere of waiting for the next bomb to drop.

Despite receiving regular deliveries, we never have enough supplies, seriously impeding our responsibility to care for the sick and wounded, regardless of their national origin. Because the Germans and French co-exist, this is not generally a problem, but when a civilian, who may, or may not, be a resistance fighter, shows up, keeping them safely away from the Germans, who are arrogant and suspicious of everyone, becomes one of our bigger challenges. Unfortunately, it is not unusual for a civilian patient thought to be recovering to suddenly die, and the staff are in general agreement that the Germans are the culprits in these unexplained deaths. The medical staff privately admits that when handing out medications and changing dressings it is nearly impossible to treat all patients equally and not give preferential treatment to the non-Germans. Often I give a full dose of pain medication to a wounded yet grateful resistance fighter and let the arrogant German officer suffer. Other times, I change the Nazi's bandages less often or forget to give him the penicillin prescribed to fight off infection.

The first patients I am entirely responsible for turn out to be German soldiers severely injured when the French underground blew up a troop train traveling from Paris to Strasbourg. It requires intense mental discipline to stay focused on my role as a nurse whose obligation is to relieve suffering wherever I find it. Fighting against my strongest impulse, which is to turn my back on these Nazis and let them die, is extremely difficult. As we hear more and more stories of terrible atrocities Nazi soldiers are committing against Jews and other civilians I give in to this temptation more and more, soon realizing I truly don't care whether a Nazi under my care dies, because his death might save a Jew or other innocent person caught in Hitler's cross-hairs.

These passive actions console me that at least I am doing something to fight back and assuage my frustration at being unable to elicit useful information from wounded Germans that could be used against the Third Reich. It is surprising what comes out of the mouth of a man in agony. Most would readily agree to shoot their wife, their mother, or their girlfriend in exchange for a dose of morphine and quickly respond to comforting words forthcoming in their native language. It's not hard to figure out which phrases elicit the most articulate responses, and I quickly become skilled at saying the right thing. Yet after several months, I've not learned anything that seems valuable enough to pass along to the partisans populating the French underground resistance efforts, who I make a special point to care for.

Things begin to change not long after we receive word that the long-awaited Allied invasion has finally occurred and American, British, and Canadian combat troops have landed at Normandy. As the soldiers advance inland, the fighting in the air and on land is fierce and bloody. Several of the less experienced nurses become uneasy being so close to battlefield action. They don't complain but are sullen and silent – speaking only when spoken to. The French nurses, on the other hand, come and go at will, and generally cannot be relied upon to be available when needed, leaving us chronically and severely short-handed, overworked, exhausted, and resentful. For my part, I try to ignore what is happening around me, and focus on my immediate task.

"I don't mean to complain, but we are in their country, in harm's way, treating their soldiers. The least the French nurses could do is show up and help us out. I don't know about you, but I got no use for these here today, gone tomorrow, disappear whenever they feel like it floozies who have no bloody right to call themselves nurses," a young British nurse who arrived a year after I did, mutters angrily one evening as four of us are preparing for bed after a twenty-hour shift.

I assure her I agree but see no point in wasting energy being angry when it takes everything I have just to stay awake. The others nod, collapsing on their cots, too tired to discuss it further.

As soon as the Allied invasion begins, my main responsibility shifts to surgical nursing in the battlefield triage facility, a concrete bunker about fifty yards of deep, slippery mud from the nurses' tents and mess hall. Our job is first assessing the severity of the injuries and send as many as are able to survive the trip to larger hospitals outside the combat zone. The remaining casualties are the most severely wounded in need of immediate, life-saving emergency surgeries performed under less-than-ideal conditions. Nearly half die, either in the operating theatre or soon after, frequently from loss of blood. Others survive surgery only to succumb to infections we are unable to control in a non-sterile environment. We don't have enough of anything and improvise on bandages, use less than the required amounts of disinfectant, and cut the prescribed doses of medication in half, or in thirds, attempting to stretch them further. Patients who survive in spite of our woefully inadequate care are the exceptionally strong, unusually lucky ones.

Most often, I assist Dr. Karl-Josef Meister, our chief surgeon, who is also an officer in the German Army Medical Corps and a superbly talented orthopedic surgeon able to efficiently amputate crushed limbs, repair bullet holes in most bones, and realign compound fractures, even of the skull. Because there is only one other surgeon, a Swiss-trained generalist who prefers assisting over doing an actual surgery himself, Dr. Meister is frequently called upon to repair wounds he claims he is not qualified to treat. Yet, his skilled hands produce small, precise stitches that hold firm and, absent infection, heal without complications. His smile, which is rare in this atmosphere of unnecessary suffering brought about by a brutal war many Germans seem to disagree with, if their wounded soldiers are to be believed, lights up his otherwise somber face.

It has not escaped my notice that I am assigned to the chief surgeon far more than the other nurses. After a particularly long, difficult surgery involving the amputation of two legs and one arm on a patient crushed under a tank, I question this.

"You are correct, Nurse Rose. Whenever possible, I specifically request you as my nurse assistant." Seeing my surprise, he continues, pulling his blood-stained surgical robe off at the same time he focuses his dark brown eyes on my weary, sweat-stained face. Wearing my surgical cap, with my mask hanging off one ear, I am too tired to care that I look frightfully bad in the presence of an effortlessly handsome man.

"You point out when I am about to make a mistake, which saves me from making one. Knowing I can rely upon you to help me when my focus grows weak, and my tired eyes fail me, makes my job much easier. I trust your courage to say what you think," he explains, walking away.

"You don't make many mistakes," I respond to the back of his head. He stops and turns to face me.

"I am only human, Nurse Rose, and humans make mistakes. It seems I don't make quite as many when I have you working with me."

If asked, I would be unable to justify my sense that Dr. Meister is a Jew. Ever the committed healer, in the time I have been working alongside him subtle signs that his heart is not with the German cause appear, especially under duress. Sometimes it is the mutterings under his breath during surgeries carried out in spite of episodic bombing raids that rattle what's left of our windows, causing the lights to blink and sway wildly, and raining debris down onto the blanket we now routinely stretch across a makeshift frame barrier between the patient and the ceiling. Other times, for no discernible reason, he singles out a partisan among the steady stream of incoming casualties with injuries ranging from minor to fatal and spends extra time with him. I have never heard him mention Hitler by name or make any attempt to defend the Third Reich.

Late one night, weeks after the invasion, and following a particularly harrowing twenty-two hours of surgeries, Dr. Meister asks me to join him in his tent.

"We need to review the current cases and determine which patients can be transferred, which are likely to die in the next twenty-four hours, and which linger on the bridge between life and death and could go in either direction," he says.

Taking a deep breath, I tell him I will join him after checking on the patients. What I am really saying is I need an hour to wash my face, refasten my hair, and regain my composure after being invited to be alone with the gentle, somber surgeon whose graceful hands perform miracles that continually amaze me.

"Please, sit down, Nurse Rose," Doctor Meister smiles when I enter his tent through the flap he has left loose, despite the chilly air outside.

"May I offer you a beer? I think we both could use one," he says, opening a box in the corner. After handing me the beer he asks whether I mind if he fastens the flap to maximize the pitiful outflow of warm air from his kerosene heater. I shrug, then toss my head back for a long draw on the cold beer, hoping the surge of alcohol will quiet my nervousness and slow my racing heart in the presence of a man I find very attractive.

"I have a small cheese also, if you wish," he offers. I decline, not bothering to ask how he obtains these rare luxuries and why he is willing to share them.

"Am I correct you are an American?" he begins.

"Why do you think that?" I ask, straining not to reveal alarm at the question.

"Your teeth. They are straight and healthy, which is rare among Europeans. Adequate dental care is nearly non-existent, especially since the war began."

"Your teeth look fine," I point out.

"I spent six months in New York on a surgery fellowship and allowed students in the hospital's dental program to practice on me. We both gained from the experience."

I'd never thought about my teeth giving me away when trying to pass myself off as German and am not sure what can be done to offset what is apparently a dead give-away regarding my identity.

"All our patients are still alive?" he asks minutes later, after realizing I'm not going to answer his question.

"At the moment, yes, but none are ready to be moved, so I hope we don't get more soon. The last bombing doubled us up and we are extremely overcrowded."

"If we have to, we will make room. There is no choice."

"No, I suppose not," I admit, taking another drink of my beer which, though strong and bitter, is surprisingly soothing.

"Why are you here, really, Nurse Rose? Red Cross nurses are volunteers, and America only entered this war when there was no other choice. Nothing is forcing you into an active war zone." Dr. Meister asks, again fixing his tired, liquid brown eyes on my own. Wary of trusting the kindness I see in his face, I am too exhausted for anything but the truth, yet remain silent.

"Silence tells its own story, Nurse Rose," he prods. When I still don't answer him, he speaks again.

"You seem trustworthy and honest. Perhaps I should chance telling you why I am here, and then you will become more comfortable talking with me," the kindly doctor with a gentle bedside manner says, then pauses. I wait for him to continue.

"I am a deserter from Hitler's army. With every breath in me, I detest the Third Reich and have no use for that evil fool calling himself our fuehrer. He is orchestrating a bloodbath that is destroying Europe," he explains, his voice rising. I put my finger to my lips, warning him to speak quietly.

"I'm sorry, but I don't understand. Shouldn't you have fled somewhere other than occupied France? You'll be shot if discovered," I finally whisper, as he hands me a second beer.

"My options for escape were limited. As you have no doubt figured out, French medical personnel are so scarce as to be a rarity, so they are desperate and accept anybody. No one bothered to ask for my credentials. For all they know, I am a veterinarian trained to only treat animals and am masquerading as a physician capable of treating humans. Even if this were true, I doubt the French would care, as long as at least some of my patients survived."

"It does seem the French are desperate," I admit.

"My family are – were – Jews from Hanover. I received medical training first in Berlin, later in London, and became a competent surgeon. As Hitler expanded his efforts, medical personnel were in great demand, and I was conscripted into the choice between serving the Reich or going to Auschwitz-Birkenau where I would be forced to perform medical experiments. I agreed to serve on the condition my family receive safe passage out of Germany. Otherwise, I said I would refuse, and we would go to Auschwitz together."

"Wasn't that taking a terrible risk? What if the Nazis didn't agree?"

"It was a calculated risk. I had something they wanted badly enough I thought bargaining for my family's safety was worth the gamble. I was led to believe we had an agreement, but after reporting for duty I never heard anything further. I knew trusting the Nazis was stupid, but I was desperate, and don't regret trying."

"You've never heard anything at all?"

"Nothing. I made inquiries, but only infrequently, so as not to let on that I was suspicious. My wife is a very strong woman, and my son is healthy and plus five years – old enough to survive. My daughter is now barely past one year old, and my younger brother is disabled – for them survival would be much more difficult, as it would be for my elderly mother, who is unwell. A clandestine escape route would be impossible. Certified travel is their only hope, and this is what I was promised. If this did not occur, Auschwitz, or somewhere similar, is the only other possibility. My father had already been sent to Dachau, and his release was also guaranteed, but he was probably already dead by then. Otherwise, he would've managed to get word to me somehow." Involuntarily, I suck in my breath. Doctor Meister stares at the floor for several seconds before continuing.

"Once I concluded I had been taken for a fool, I hated the Reich even more. One night I rode out of the military hospital near Munich in an ambulance with a patient and never returned. I made my way to Strasbourg intending to cross into France, but while I was waiting for forged travel documents France surrendered and the Vichy government was too disorganized and confused to ask questions. I walked straight through the checkpoint without stopping"

"Your family?"

"There is no way to know. It is irrational to hope but sometimes I can't help myself. Sadly, those moments are becoming fewer and fewer, and I am forced to accept that G-d has abandoned us."

"You were observant Jews?"

"Somewhat. More importantly, we were proud, educated Jews... and proud Germans who lived comfortably and safely among other Germans. I was slow to believe the evil emerging around us was gaining a foothold and thought that as soon as the people figured out what was happening, it would blow over. It is very difficult to accept having been so badly mistaken." He stops speaking to take a long drink from his beer.

"My understanding is that not all Germans support the Third Reich…"

"Perhaps not, but they oppose at their own peril, and I cannot know this from personal experience," he interrupts. We sit in silence for some time before our conversation continues.

"Now that you've heard my story, what is your excuse for wallowing in this miserable existence?" he asks again, looking directly at me. I'm sure he knows that by listening to his confession I will feel compelled to answer him.

"You guessed correctly. I am American, but both my parents were originally from Hildesheim, and their families, if any are still alive, remain there. I know some by name and through letters, but not personally. The Gestapo arrested my mother's brother and nephew – my uncle and cousin – and perhaps others I don't know about, but I hope to find out. If they survive the war, I plan to do what I can to help them recover. I could not, in good conscience, accept a safe, comfortable existence in America when others, whose blood I share, are suffering at the hands of an evil monster who must be stopped. I can't really explain it any more clearly than that. I just felt compelled to come, because I believed I could be of some use… no other reason."

"You are a Jew?" he asks.

"Not a very good one, but it is in my blood, yes." I feel my face grow warm at this admission, which I've not made since childhood.

"Do you know the risk you take being here?"

"I don't think about it." I answer truthfully, as a sudden exhaustion overtakes me after two beers and more than twenty-four hours without sleep. Wanting this conversation to go no further, I say we both need rest, and I must leave.

"Promise me we can talk more," he says, his eyes begging for understanding as he reaches for my hand.

"Why have you chanced telling me all this? There is great risk in anyone knowing your situation. Secrecy is your only safety," I whisper.

"Everyone I have ever cared about is gone – forever, most likely. In these circumstances, safety no longer matters because I have nothing left to lose. This unfortunate reality allows me great freedom."

"Perhaps it feels that way now, but I'm not sure how realistic it is, and I don't have the intellectual energy for a philosophical debate at this moment."

"I don't want to die of loneliness, and too often I come very close. Please promise me we can talk again," the kind surgeon implores, still holding my hand.

"I promise…" Then, barely able to stand up, I start to sway as I move forward, not releasing his hand.

"You are too tired to go all the way to your tent. I have a spare cot. Stay here," he says, gently guiding me toward a pile of blankets in the far corner of the small tent. About to pass out from fatigue, I don't argue. He places a flat pillow under my head and pulls a heavy woolen blanket over the length of my body. From the corner of my eye, I see him turn down the heater and stretch out on the cot opposite mine.

I'm not sure how much time passes before rhythmic snoring wakes me up. I see a glimpse of dawn's early light beneath the tent. Throwing back the cover and swinging my feet over the side of the cot, a blast of cold air greets me, causing me to gasp.

"What is it," the exhausted doctor suddenly alert. Then he sees me and smiles.

"I'm sorry I woke you, Dr. Meister," I offer, hoping no one suddenly appears, looking for the doctor and finds me in his tent. The wind howls outside, our breath is visible, and our fingers are numb, reminding me of childhood winters in Elyria.

"Since you have just slept in my tent, I think you should call me Karl, and I will, with your permission, call you Charlotte. We will save the formality for when we are on duty," he says, half smiling. Under other circumstances, if I were not so cold and so concerned about being discovered in a compromising situation, I would surrender to Karl Meister's irresistibly warm demeanor with a genuine smile. Instead, I check the area outside carefully, leave his tent and walk directly to the hospital. *If anyone sees me, I'll say I was concerned about a patient and came for the doctor,* I tell myself.

After an extended period of ferocious fighting, resulting in horrific injuries and too many deaths we could have prevented under better conditions, there is finally a lull. The consensus is both sides have retreated to regroup, then will go at it again, with reinforcements, and we should use this time to catch our breath.

Meanwhile, I have noticed that we are treating more civilians, most likely a result of intensified French underground resistance efforts. The partisans, working in small cells, are successfully blowing things up and shooting people on a regular basis, whenever and wherever they see an opportunity, planned or otherwise, and civilians are often collateral damage. Everyone suspects everyone else of collaborating with the German occupation forces, and no one trusts anyone. The pervasive distrust makes steady resistance more difficult in some ways; in other ways, clever partisans have figured out how to use widespread suspicion and German paranoia to their advantage.

More than three weeks pass before Karl and I have another opportunity to talk in other than professional circumstances. When the opportunity finally presents itself, it causes an unsettling flutter in my stomach.

"Are you still glad you left America or are you now convinced it was the worst mistake of your life?" Karl asks me, handing over a beer and motioning me to sit down next to him on his cot.

"It never occurs to me that coming here was a mistake. But surely you must wonder for yourself, not having heard anything from your family."

"Of course, I wonder. It's possible that by agreeing to serve the Reich I saved my family, but it is also possible that by disappearing, I signed their death warrant. I have no way to know," he frowns, taking a long drink of cloudy beer. I ask him how he gets the beer and fresh cheese he routinely offers me.

"A local peasant farmer supplies me with home brews and aged cheese in appreciation for coming to his house and safely delivering his wife of a healthy baby when unexpected complications arose and she was close to death," he answers. While this explanation seems plausible, I suspect there is more to the arrangement.

"Each passing hour forces me to accept I was betrayed, and everyone is most likely dead. I have no way to obtain information, but even if there was, the possibility for real answers is questionable. Still, a sliver of hope that the stronger ones – my wife and son – survived stays with me. Foolish though I know it is, I cannot help myself."

"It's never foolish to hope, Karl. As a physician, surely you know this. Otherwise, there would be no point to the work we do."

"Of course you are right, and my love for my wife will endure this uncertainty for as long as necessary. If there is any possibility of survival, she will find it. But if I knew, with absolute certainty, they were all dead, of course I would do things differently."

"Differently how?"

"I cannot answer that question. Already, I have endangered you by giving you details about my life that could ultimately bring you great harm. I was wrong to take you into my confidence, but the release was so great I could not stop myself. Nevertheless, I misspoke, and beg you forgive me, then forget everything I said."

"I can't do that, Karl. Like you, I detest the Reich, and hate treating German soldiers, who are fighting for an evil cause. But as a nurse, this is what I am obligated to do. I assume this same commitment is true for you."

"Better you don't assume anything about me, Charlotte. I am fractured and unhealed. Too much about me is unpredictable and unknowable, even to myself." Lacking a comeback, I remain silent.

"I think there are more reasons for your being here... ones you have not revealed," he says a few moments later, looking tenderly into my eyes. After swallowing a large gulp of the nearly frozen beer which shoots a sharp pain across my eyebrows, I confess my desire to join the underground resistance if the opportunity presents itself.

"You would do that?"

"It has been my intention all along. I just haven't figured out how to do it."

"What would you say if I told you I have connections?"

"I'd kiss you and promise to love you forever," I tease, feeling my face grow warm in the glow of the single light bulb hanging above us.

"Then for that reason alone, I will tell you," Karl smiles broadly. He runs his fingers through his hair, so dark it nearly matches the weary circles beneath his eyes. I realize I do not look much better, but foolishly hope he finds my own smile slightly attractive. He says he will invite me to follow him into his tent one of the times we find ourselves in the mess hall together and explain more then. Hearing this, I frown.

"If we speak openly, no one will become suspicious, and the French never care about a man and a woman together. They like sex and assume everyone else does, too. At most, they will be momentarily envious, which as concerns you is definitely possible," he chuckles, watching me blush bright pink.

"I will approach openly and ask you to check on that day's surgery patients, then come to my tent to review the patient orders for those ready to be moved. No one will question this."

"If you say so, but I'm not sure I agree that no one will notice," I reply, doubtful of his plan, but feeling a vague excitement take hold. When I open the flap to leave, snow is falling hard, blowing in circles around the tent as the orange glow from distant rocket fire flashes across the sky. In any other circumstances, it would be a beautiful sight to behold

Days later, as predicted, the fighting resumes with even greater intensity. The official word is that the German army prevails, but the casualties tell a different story. Wounded German soldiers freely admit the Allies are driving them backwards, behind the Maginot Line, and if the opportunity presents itself, they will desert. Many believe going on the run is far preferable to following the orders of panicked German generals obeying a mentally deranged leader who is losing a war they don't agree with, yet are forced to fight.

"Deserters get the firing squad, which would be no worse than the punishment for losing, but they'd have to catch me first," are utterances I hear repeated often.

Meanwhile, I am so consumed with caring for severely wounded soldiers and badly injured civilians that, if asked, I would not know what day of the week it is or instantly identify the month. Hours, days, and weeks all run together and I deal with the immediate problem in front of me, then fall into my cot any chance I get, nearly dead with exhaustion. I am not sure how much time passes before Karl presents another opportunity to meet in his tent.

"Still no word about your family?" I ask, shivering through a thick sweater as the wind howls outside.

"I have made myself very difficult to find. If any word about them got to me, it would mean I am in imminent danger."

"I'm so sorry, Karl. This is terribly difficult, and I wish there was something I could do to help," I say, reaching to hug him, then quickly drawing back. He moves toward me, pulling me into him.

"Your existence is enough comfort to me, Charlotte… more than enough," he whispers. Before I can respond, mortar fire explodes in the distance.

"We only have a few moments, and what I have to say is important. There is a possibility of going to Berlin to join an active resistance cell there. It is one with many contacts, and it would be very dangerous. They would want you to work as a nurse in the German state hospital treating wounded Nazis and occasionally making an unfortunate mistake. You are clever enough to know how to do that without being caught."

"This is a crazy idea, Karl. Red Cross nurses aren't serving the Reich directly."

"We will forge papers for you. Your German is that of a native speaker, and Germany is desperate. No one will look too closely."

"And my teeth won't give me away?" I ask, half teasing.

"Not as long as you don't smile, which I strongly advise against," he answers evenly, willing me to take his advice seriously.

"The Germans have nothing to smile about, so this should not be difficult," he adds.

"How did you find out about this?" I ask, my heart suddenly gaining speed like a runaway horse on a racetrack to nowhere.

"Ambulance drivers know what is going on and those in sympathy with the Allies pass on information. The one who got me out has sent word."

"And these drivers are trustworthy?"

"So far, I have no reason to doubt them. It is in their best interests to see the Reich fall as soon as possible so this war will end and they will be out of constant danger." Karl's face betrays annoyance at my questions. Taking a deep breath, he sits down on the bed and reaches for a cigarette.

"Why are you asking? Do you not trust me?" he asks, his hand shaking slightly as he lights the cigarette.

"Of course I trust you, but I am new at this resistance game and have yet to become skilled in the nuances that make it work. I am completely dependent upon you for all these things. You must try to understand that this is a very uncomfortable position to be in."

"Yes, I suppose it is," he finally agrees, after two more draws on his cigarette.

"And you? Where do you fit into this plan?" I ask, still warming myself by the flimsy kerosene heater.

"For the time being, I stay here and maintain contact with the Partisans. Going back to Germany is too risky for me, even with forged papers. The Germans are growing more paranoid each day. They see everyone as a potential spy or informant passing them false information. My nervousness is too great; it would betray me."

"I want to keep assisting you, Karl... we do this together, or not at all."

"We are doing it together."

"I don't see it that way."

"How you see it doesn't matter. It is not in my control. The contact in Berlin decides what happens next. In my possession are three sets of forged documents. In France I am Karl-Josef Meister; in Germany I am now Klaus-Adolph Messner, in reality, I am Yosef David Meyerhoff... and most days I am so exhausted it is difficult to remember who I am. If it is considered safe for me to return to Germany, I will return. Otherwise, I remain in France, where my usefulness is limited to the local resistance, which something slightly more than nothing. Other decisions are not mine to make."

"How are you useful to the resistance?"

"I go to the wounded when I can... steal medicine and supplies to give to them, pass along information if I hear anything that might be useful... and sometimes a patient who is a partisan target fails to survive." Although

I have been suspicious for a while, this is the first time I have heard our chief surgeon frankly admit his role in the French underground.

"Would we be in the same German resistance cell?"

"It will be possible we occasionally cross paths. It is best we are unaware of what the other is doing. Personal feelings are dangerous and only complicate things. Successful acts of resistance are all that matter – nothing else. Otherwise, mistakes happen."

"I would rather remain with you," I say, unbidden tears filling my eyes.

"I have been both wishing you would want that, Charlotte, and hoping you would agree to go to Berlin and help end this human horror," Karl says, looking directly at me as he rises from his cot. The conversation and the intensity surrounding us these past weeks suddenly draws us into a deep, lingering embrace. Neither of us retreats nor apologizes.

"Our commitment to stop Hitler's madness and overthrow the Third Reich supersedes everything – especially our desire to be together. Surely you know this," Karl says, clearing his throat and carefully avoiding my eyes.

"I know it's what I signed on for, although I had no idea what to expect when I did it," I answer, leaning into his chest, my arms tight around his waist.

"This is not a natural situation we are in. We may die at any moment and falsely believe this gives permission to do things we would never do otherwise... things we could come to regret."

"It is impossible for me to imagine regretting anything where you are concerned," I whisper, still holding him tight as I struggle to control the intensity of what I am feeling.

"You say this now, Charlotte, but we are fighting a war, not living in the realities of ordinary, day-by-day life where lasting attachments form and ordinary existence makes the rules. Both of us have other lives we will one day return to."

"How can you say that when your family may all be dead?" I ask, instantly regretting the question.

"I just know that is how it will be. I will remain in Germany to help rebuild my homeland and you will return to America, where you belong. Regardless of our feelings for each other, there are no other possibilities."

"You speak of a future that may never come," I point out, refusing to let go of his hand, which he has slipped warmly into mine.

"And you think too much. We must rest while we can. When it becomes possible for you to leave, I will give you further instructions. At this moment, the challenge is that it is snowing hard, and you face a long walk back to your tent. Tonight, you should remain here, where it is warmer," Karl tells me, turning off the only light illuminating the space surrounding us.

The French underground's resistance to the German occupation becomes more sophisticated as the Allied efforts to defeat the German army intensify dramatically in the coming months. Something is always exploding, either because of an air attack or due to local sabotage, making sleep nearly impossible. I lay awake staring at the top of the tent, waiting for the artillery barrage I know is coming, the next bomb to explode, and the next plane to be shot out of the air. In between, my mind wanders back to my husband and daughter. That I wish to be here rather than in California with them induces a guilt that would cripple me if I allowed it. My only defense is to shut those thoughts down as soon as they arise, and with practice, I've become quite good at doing that.

As the Allies advance and it becomes more apparent that Germany will fall, efforts to hasten the demise of the Third Reich intensify, causing more casualties and bringing Karl and me together more often. It's very doubtful anyone cares that one of the doctors is sleeping with one of the nurses; more likely, everyone is under too much stress to notice. No instructions about moving on to Berlin are forthcoming, and we continue feeding any information we can draw out of wounded German soldiers, which isn't much, to the ambulance drivers, who pass it on. Every so often, we are contacted about a severely injured resistance fighter hiding in a barn or a safe house and occasionally I accompany Karl on these dangerous mercy missions. We can never be certain we aren't walking into a trap and never know whether the wounded patient we do as much for as we possibly can, ultimately lives or dies.

Late on dangerously bright moon-lit night, as we are preparing for another mercy trip, this one about twelve kilometers from the hospital unit, Karl gives me a gun.

"What am I supposed to do with this?" I ask, astonished.

"Keep it in case you need it, what else?" He frowns as he continues packing supplies.

"I don't know how to use a gun. I've never even touched one before," I say, staring at the shiny gun-metal gray pistol in my hand.

"It's not that difficult. You aim and pull the trigger. Even if you miss, the shooting itself will frighten the person you point it at."

"Or make them very angry and they will grab it away to use on me," I snap back, with growing unease.

"Come here, I'll show you how to load it," he continues, producing a handful of bullets he places in a chamber.

"Where did you get this?"

"Off a German casualty I was, unfortunately, unable to save. His pockets were full of ammunition, and I discovered the gun strapped to the leg I had just amputated. You need to keep it with you. It might come in handy." he says, removing the bullets and handing the weapon back to me. Not knowing what else to do, I place the gun, and the box of ammunition, in my rucksack alongside bandages and disinfectant.

"I take it you have your own gun, which is why you're giving me this one?"

"Of course."

"And you are bring it with you now?"

"It would be very foolish not to…"

Moments later, we leave the compound to care for a pregnant resistance fighter hidden in a hayloft, suffering acute distress. The man on the run with her begged for help from the local farmer in whose barn they are hiding. The farmer, who is also Karl's beer supplier, appeared at the field hospital under the guise of making a delivery and informed Karl of the situation.

"How often do you do this?" I ask as we are huddled under blankets in the back of a donkey cart filled with straw.

"Do what?"

"These errands of mercy."

"As often as I'm asked and am able to respond…"

"Are you still supplying the partisans with medical supplies…"

"Sometimes…"

"And information…"

"Patients under anesthesia tend to be silent, so I don't hear much that is useful. Mostly they go to sleep and wake up invoking their mothers and girlfriends. Sometimes they threaten Hitler and occasionally, they call for someone they refer to as the Holy Mother of God. At first, I thought this was a code for something, but the chaplain explained that Catholics believe God had a mother who was a very holy woman."

We ride the rest of the way in silence, eventually arriving at a dilapidated farm where we find a thin, pale young woman, perhaps still a teenager, hiding in the hayloft. According to the man with her, she has been in labor for two days. She is exhausted, frightened and bleeding heavily, and we quickly determine her baby is dead. To save her, Karl must remove her uterus. He tells me to give her as much whiskey as she will take, then hold my hand over her mouth to muffle her screams, because nothing stops the sound from traveling across the flat terrain, alerting German patrols something is amiss. Mercifully, as he begins to make an incision, she passes out.

When he is finished, Karl instructs the young man presumed to be her lover about how to care for her, then decides we should remain with her for a few hours. Dawn is breaking as we depart in the same donkey cart we arrived in, this time hidden beneath blankets, squeezed among empty beer crates and half-filled milk cans. If a German patrol stops him, the farmer will claim he is delivering milk, which is a plausible excuse for being on the road at such an early hour. Skilled in the ways of the black market, he trades the beer he brews and the sour, unpasteurized milk he uses to make cheese for gun powder, which he supplies to the partisans for manufacturing explosives.

"Do you think she will live?" I whisper as we bounce along the snow-covered, potholed road, against a ferocious wind out of the north that whips at the blanket covering us.

"Only if she is very strong and very lucky. We did all we could, but the odds are not in her favor," Karl replies, sounding defeated.

"People should not have sex in wartime – it only complicates things," he adds.

"Perhaps not, but living with the constant threat of death strengthens the urge to create life. That desire becomes very strong – nearly impossible to resist. As a physician, you must know that."

"Of course I do. But the consequences of giving in to this urge are sometimes severe... self-defeating. And bringing a child into this cruel and inhumane world to replace those who have died is a selfish act. Often, I think the dead are better off than those of us forced to deal with the remains of this mass carnage; other times I believe saving a German soldier is the best punishment I can inflict because he will be forced to live with the murderous hate and cruel conditions he helped create every hour of the rest of his life. But most often, I view the fatally wounded as the lucky ones."

This is obviously not the time to tell him I suspect I am pregnant, I think as I listen to him. Suffering the same chronic, low-grade nausea that everyone else living in this war zone suffers, I cannot be sure. Coupled with a pervasive exhaustion that prevents making love very often, it has not been difficult to both deny and mask the possibility.

Weeks later, as my nausea is receding to a less active state, Germany surrenders, and the war in Europe is over. At first, no one believes that after all the bloodshed, death, and destruction, the Allies are victorious, and when this reality finally sinks in, we are too exhausted to celebrate.

Many of the nurses, myself included, burst into tears as we realize none of us has any idea how to leave behind the moment-by-moment intensity that has defined every hour of our lives more than two years. None of us can begin to imagine re-entering the dull and boring world of ordinary living. We can never forget what we have seen and endured, and no one who has not been here with us can begin to grasp all the ways being immersed a dangerous, unpredictable, life-and-death war zone for more than two years has changed us. Our loved ones at home have not seen what we have seen, heard what we have heard, or been so frightened for so long it's impossible to remember what it feels like to not be on emotional high alert, even when we are sleeping. Although we will scatter far, unlikely to ever see each other again, we've trusted each other, leaned into each other, and worked well together. The realization that all this is coming to an end settles into a deep loneliness I know my life at home in California can never relieve. And I am not the only one among us struggling to figure out our next steps.

"I stopped writing to my Ronnie months ago. Injured on the farm, he was declared unfit for duty, so I said I'd go instead. He claimed war's men's work and women don't have no business being involved in it. Every letter, he wouldn't let me forget that and all he wrote about was chicken feed and how his mother's flour ration didn't stretch to making pie crust… made out that was a big hardship they were suffering," one of the Canadian nurses exclaims, referring to the fiancé she left behind when she volunteered for overseas duty.

"After patching up poor blokes who'll never walk again, see again, or be right in the head ever again, how can I ever give a rat's arse about chicken feed or pie crust. Truth is, we don't have nothing to say to each other no more. Better he finds a wife who wants to be cooking his meals and raising his babies – and that just ain't me," she shrugs, continuing to stuff her rucksack.

The two older Swiss nurses, fluent in German and skilled in the art of neutrality say they're thinking about helping with recovery efforts. Expecting there will be a nursing shortage, they believe signing on with a hospital in what's left of any of the larger European cities outside France, perhaps Munich or Berlin, will be welcome. The younger Swiss nurse says she plans to enter the convent, if she can find an order that will accept her.

"How can you still believe in God after all we've seen?" the Canadian nurse, about her age, asks.

"I can't, and this is my great sorrow. God was always very important in my life, and He is lost to me now. I hope solitude and prayer will reacquaint us… bring us back together, because I miss Him very, very much." When no one comments on a lament sounding like the young nurse is actually in love with God, we continue our sorting and packing in silence. Thankfully, no one asks about my plans, because at this moment, I have none.

It turns out that first on the Allies' post-war agenda is liberating the forty-four thousand concentration camps throughout war-torn Europe, including the one thousand death camps the Germans established. Still not having revealed my pregnancy, which I am sure Karl does not suspect, I decide to leave Red Cross nursing and follow him back to Germany, where he plans to help care for the survivors of Hitler's attempt at mass human extermination. Thankfully, he doesn't question my decision, because it would be difficult to explain before I'm ready to tell him about the baby.

Three months later, after a very long day caring for emaciated camp survivors at a rehabilitation clinic in Bad Nauheim, I suddenly pass out in the corridor. Soon after, the nurse who has been attending to my care informs Karl I am very anemic, and in need of bed rest for the duration of my pregnancy. Seeing his face, she asks him why he looks so surprised.

"You are a doctor – you did not notice this about your wife?" she scolds.

"She's not my wife – and no, I did not notice."

"She did not tell you?"

"No, she didn't. We have been working long hours and not seeing each other often. There has been no time for discussing such an important topic," he explains, talking across the bed where an intravenous blood drip prevents me from getting up and walking away from this conversation. Instead, I close my eyes. Finally, the nurse asks whether I need anything. After shaking my head no, she leaves.

"Why didn't you tell me?" Karl asks, with greater tenderness than I have any right to expect under the circumstances.

"I didn't know how to begin the conversation," I reply weakly.

"Since you are now confined to your bed, there will be plenty of time for conversation," he answers, briefly squeezing my hand, then leaving. A few hours later, after receiving a second unit of blood I believe concentration camp survivors deserve much more than I do, the doctor treating me recommends two more days in the hospital to be sure I don't start bleeding again. I had expected this would occur... almost hoped for it, because I am deeply conflicted about a baby – even a baby of a man I love more than I ever thought myself capable of. The complications this child brings to my life are too overwhelming for me to think about. The doctor treating me picks up on my ambivalence.

"You have survived a horrible war to bring new life into our broken world. You should be profoundly grateful. Nazi atrocities ruined thousands of women for the rest of lives – robbed them of the God-given privilege of motherhood. You did not suffer this fate. You should be humbled by this precious opportunity to return thanks for your good fortune," he scolds.

"I am not a camp survivor. I am – was – a Red Cross nurse. I was never in danger of experiencing Nazi atrocities," I point out.

"You do not think that if the Germans would have captured you, they would not have done unspeakable things to you – a beautiful young woman caring for the enemy wounded? They would have raped you until you wished only for death. They would have carved up your face... impregnated you then cut off your breasts so your infant would starve... left you naked and bleeding by the side of the road. I know this because I have seen these atrocities with my own eyes," the doctor continues, until I put my hands over my ears and beg him to stop.

Later, when I repeat pieces of this conversation to Karl, he tells me what the doctor claims is true. Kissing my cheek, he says he will return in two days to bring me to our flat on the top floor of an old house near the city park klinik where, weather permitting, patients are taken for a daily outing of fresh air and the healing warmth of the sun, when it chooses to appear. It seems that in this devastated, post-war world, even the sun struggles to shine.

"You are under no obligation, Karl," I protest.

"You are both right and wrong about that," he answers, smiling only slightly.

Three weeks later, weeks sooner than expected, I deliver a baby boy. He is not a robust infant, but his will to live is strong. I'm unsure how many blood transfusions I required, but it is nearly three weeks before I am strong enough to leave the maternity klinik. In the meantime, the baby is sent to a makeshift facility in Frankfurt, run by Catholic nuns who specialize in caring for sick infants and children.

Immediately after Germany surrendered, the nuns created this facility to treat child victims of the Allied bombing raids as well as the few children who survived the camps. Seeing a need, they quickly expanded to include a small maternity home for pregnant women with nowhere to go. Although the facility is poorly equipped to care for a frail newborn, the nuns never turn a vulnerable child away. Karl accompanies our son, Josef Mikael, in the ambulance to St. Elizabeth Kinderklinik, occupying what's left of a small, squat building in central Frankfurt.

Another three weeks pass before I am well enough to meet my pale, scrawny son for the first time. He has his father's dark hair and narrow face but barely moves as he lays in a crude oxygen and warming chamber the sisters hastily configured from supplies scavenged from the defeated German army. It is better than nothing for small babies struggling to survive, but not by much. His tiny chest slowly rises and falls. The nursing sister assigned to his care tells me he has yet to open his eyes, so she does not know what color they are.

"Most babies start out life with blue eyes, but only the lucky ones get to keep them," she says in an obvious reference to the Nazi preference for fair-haired, blue-eyed Aryan characteristics. Our son's frailty rendered a traditional circumcision out of the question, so the kind nun has no way to know she is caring for the child of two Jews.

As we are returning to Bad Nauheim after several hours beside our son's incubator, able only to stroke him, Karl tells me a name has appeared on one of the concentration camp survivor lists that gives him reason to believe his wife may be alive.

"In four days, I am traveling to Munich to find out if it is her," he announces.

"Please understand that I love you and our son, Charlotte, but if I find my wife in Munich, I will remain with her. If she is not there, I will try to learn all that I can about what happened to her, and to the others, then determine what I will do next. It's possible I will return to my work here and continue to wait, but there is no way to know that at this moment. Until there is absolute proof of death, I am unable to give up hope." Hearing this, I slowly exhale the breath I am holding, and remain silent. Anything I would try to say would be wrong.

"I don't expect you to like this, but I can't help wishing you are not too angry with me," the father of my son pleads, his sad eyes avoiding my own. I claim to understand, because I have no choice… and no right to expect anything different from him. He has never lied about his situation or led me to believe a future together is guaranteed. Even so, I know that if he returns to his wife and I never see him again, I will never fully recover from the pain of loving and then losing him.

Our son, who we registered as Josef Mikael Meyer, a name that seems bigger than he is, remains in the hospital, under the sisters' loving care. He continues to struggle, but somehow manages to hang on, which those caring for him view as hopeful. I return to work in Bad Nauheim's rehabilitation clinic and travel to visit my son as often as I can get away for more than a few hours. When two months pass with no word from Karl, I assume he has reunited with his wife and will not return to me, forcing my thoughts to wander in the direction of my own future. Bringing my son to America and returning to my former life as Paul's wife and Natalie's mother is out of the question, but so is remaining in Germany raising a sickly child by myself. I have been unable to confirm that any of my family in Hildesheim survived the war, and am forced to accept that if I remain in Germany, I will do so alone… and I do not believe I am capable of taking on such a monumental challenge.

One afternoon, while I am in the hospital nursery coaxing Josef to take his bottle, an older nun whose only job is spending endless hours holding the weakest babies, encouraging them to live, sits down beside me.

"Your little one is trying hard. His progress is slow, but his determination is strong. He may always be weaker than most, but God willing, he will be well enough to live a life of many years," she smiles. Then she asks about his father.

"He has not been to visit here in a long while. Is he not coming back?" she asks me.

"I don't think so," I reply, feeling tears burn behind my eyes.

"He sends money for the child regularly. It is not a generous amount, but he is faithful in his obligation to his son. This shows he cares… it's possible he may return someday," the nun tells me. The news that Karl is sending money for his son's care is a welcome surprise, but after so much time without word from him, I know better than to interpret it as a sign of hope for any future with him.

"What are your plans?" the old nun asks, taking my frail infant from me and placing him back into the warming chamber with only a light bulb to provide heat.

"I have none," I admit, explaining that the family I was hoping to find does not appear to have survived.

"In the beginning I checked the survivor lists nearly every day. Enough time has now passed, I have given up expecting to find them and only check every week or two," I tell the kindly nun, who nods her understanding.

"You also check the death lists?" she asks.

"Nothing there, either. At least not so far…"

"Unfortunately, those lists may never be complete," she says, patting my hand. We sit in companionable silence for several minutes, watching Josef settle into sleep.

"Since you are a nurse, may I suggest you join with us here at St. Elizabeth. You will be close to your son as he continues gaining strength and the arrangement will allow you time to decide the best future for you both."

"I have no place to live near here," I point out.

"The hospital has a small nurses residence in nearby Bockheim. The building is war damaged, but habitable. We can provide you a room there."

I agree to think about it.

Days later, I relinquish our comfortable apartment in Bad Nauheim. The kindly landlord agrees to store Karl's things in case he returns. I bring only my clothes and a few books with me to my new living arrangement, leaving all other evidence of Karl's and my life together behind.

My new apartment is a small corner room containing a bed, rust-stained sink, a small wardrobe on the second floor of an unheated building that is missing several ground-floor windows and a front door. The bathroom down the hall, containing a toilet and a cracked bath tub, is shared with four other nurses. A kitchen, a working refrigerator and a large population of roaches occupy a corner of the ground floor, which also houses an older man missing one eye, likely a war casualty, who serves as the building caretaker. Three feral cats wandering freely about the building are the only means for controlling the rats and mice. Most of the time the toilet flushes, the electricity works and unheated water flows from the faucet in my room. We are cautioned about using kerosene heaters, considered a fire hazard, although it is hard to imagine how a fire could damage the building any more than it already is. The accommodation, barely more than a leaking roof over my head, is only a slight improvement over my field hospital tent and not a place I could bring my infant son if he ever gains enough strength to leave his protected environment to live with me.

I soon realize I don't like pediatric nursing. The frustration of seeing innocent children suffer and, despite the heroic efforts by those caring for them are still unable to recover, wears on me. With adults it is very different, because they have lived at least some life. A child has yet to live any life. Not being able to promise a safe, happy future to an orphaned, innocent child I often find myself becoming deeply attached to is crushing – and very different from how I felt when I left my infant daughter. I knew that no matter what happened to me, there were others to love her, and her future was secure. These children have nothing to look forward to and no one to care for them.

As months pass, Josef Mikael's growth and development are painfully slow. He gains weight a few grams at a time and remains pitifully small for his age. Rarely smiling and content to remain in his crib, at six months old, he lacks curiosity and remains remarkably oblivious to the world around him. Floppy when held, he makes little effort to roll over or to sit up and I am not sure he recognizes me when I come to him. The nurse assigned to his care pushes his crib closer to the window, hoping the moving trees and birds outside will stimulate him to pay attention to something. His only consistent reaction is to raise his arms to be picked up when he sees me come to his crib each evening, but he makes the same gesture to Sister and rarely sustains eye contact with either of us for very long. The day my constant smiling, cooing, and slight tickling finally brings on an audible laugh is a major milestone that surprises me so much I don't at first believe it. The consensus among the nuns and doctors overseeing my son's care is that he will likely require special attention for the rest of his life, however long that becomes.

"His muscle tone is weak, but he moves his arms and legs and we know he can hear and see, so how much he will progress is an open question. This is a problem in his brain, which is a perplexing organ we understand very little about," the doctor explains.

"He could live a normal lifespan in years, but he will be unlikely to ever fully care for himself. You should plan for this eventuality," Sister Marguerite, the kindly nun who has befriended us from the beginning, tells me one evening, as I am rocking my baby son to sleep.

"If the Reich had prevailed, he would be euthanized. But now, God willing, he will live always as a loving child consoling his lonely, distraught mother," she says, in a sincere attempt to comfort me. She has no way to know I have a husband and a daughter in America I had intended to return to after the war ended and now may never see again.

Over the past months I have become deeply attached to my forever fragile, vulnerable son, each day loving him more. I no longer view returning to America as a possibility unless I bring Josef with me. I could claim he is a war casualty I adopted after his mother's death, but maintaining this hoax would be difficult because I am named as his mother on his birth certificate and this document is required to obtain a passport and travel documents. The bigger risk is the possibility that sooner or later

Paul or my sister would become suspicious, especially if Josef began to resemble me.

Weeks go by with no solution, until late one evening as I am leaving the hospital and meet a man about to enter. We both stop and stare at each other.

"I never expected to see you again," I stutter, looking directly at Karl, who appears to have aged dramatically since I last saw him a few months ago.

"Nor did I – expect to see you again," he admits.

"What brings you here?" I ask.

"To check on our son. I am aware he is still in care, with enduring difficulties. I did not know you had stayed in Germany with him. I thought it certain you left him with the nuns and returned to America."

"I thought I might do that, too, but days passed, and I didn't. Now I find I can't leave him," I admit. Hearing this, Karl sighs deeply.

"My wife – she survived. Perhaps after so much time you guessed this," he begins. I nod.

"Our children did not survive, and as a virile young woman, Mengle, the Nazi angel of death, performed experiments on her that make it impossible to bear more children... and thus for me to have more children. She agrees that we should raise Josef Mikael, and rejoices in another opportunity to be a mother. I have come to claim him. Finding that you are still here obviously complicates this plan."

"Your wife, after all she has been through, is willing to raise a child you had with another woman?" I ask my son's father, wondering whether this is his idea or hers.

"She understands the effects of war – knows things happen that would never happen otherwise. She does not resent you, or me, for what developed between us, and is able to love our son as her own. So yes, she is willing to raise the child I had with another woman."

"He is a needy child, Karl. He will never be normal. A good life for him is not guaranteed, and caring for him will be costly."

"I suspected as much from the beginning, and we willingly receive this responsibility as a gift to us both. We will figure it out... if you agree not to stand in our way and are willing to let us have him, that is." Karl's voice pleads, his eyes looking directly into mine. I remain silent, taking in the war-weary face of a man I've loved like no other and, after tonight, will most certainly never see again. The yellow gaslight behind me shines on us both, making it impossible to disappear, or to hide from each other.

"Unless you plan to forgo life in America to raise a disabled child alone here in Germany, which I don't believe you want to do, this is the best solution for you and for Josef. He would be with his father and a mother who loves him as her own, and you will be back in your home country where you belong."

"I love him, too, Karl... more than I have words for."

"I'm sure you do, but can you take him back to your life in America?"

"Perhaps..."

"Somehow, I doubt that, Charlotte. I know he is not your first child, which allows me to assume there are important things about your life you have chosen not to reveal. You have forbidden me from knowing you except on your terms. In all things that truly matter between a man and a woman, you are a stranger to me."

"How do you know he is not my first child?"

"I am a doctor... I suspected as much when we made love and it was confirmed when you developed problems at our son's birth. I don't know what happened to your other child, but if it survived and you abandoned it to someone else to raise, I am unable to believe you would choose to raise our forever dependent son. I returned here certain you had left Josef in the care of the nuns and gone on your way. I am surprised to find you have remained." A hornet could not have stung worse than Karl's words. He is right that I chose a far-off war over being a mother, and I can't expect him, as someone whose children were murderously stolen from him, to ever understand this. Time stands still as I struggle to form a response.

"You are right that you can give him a better home than I am able to do... a home with two parents who love him, and each other, is far preferable to having one lonely mother who, so far, has failed in her ability to care for any child. I will arrange to help with the financial burden of his care, whatever that turns out to be. Please assure your wife that I am deeply grateful for her goodness and loving generosity, and if either of you are inclined, please remind my son I loved him deeply and only surrendered him because I knew in my heart it was in his best interests." Karl nods.

"I hope you realize your wife is a much better woman than I can ever be. I am comforted knowing that because she loves you, she will love our son as her own. With her, he will thrive as a much happier child than he could ever be with me," I admit. Hearing this, Karl reaches into his pocket and draws out a slip of official-looking paper.

"This is the information for a secret account in a Swiss bank. My family sheltered assets there before the war officially began and the Nazis stole everything from us. When I left for Munich, I instructed the bank to send a certain amount to the sisters each month to support Josef's care. I will inform the bank to distribute whatever amount you need to ease your return to America and take up your life again."

"I don't need money, Karl. That is the one thing, perhaps the only thing, I will always have enough of. I will use this bank to set up a trust account for our son's care, for as long as he lives. The money will be yours to be used however you wish to assure his needs are adequately met."

Without saying more, I walk away from the hospital entrance. Returning to my room as quickly as possible, I pack my clothes and, despite the late hour, go directly to the Hauptbahnhof in central Frankfurt. I secure a ticket for the next train leaving here without regard for the destination. The huge piece of my emotional life I allowed to escape into Karl's arms more than three years ago, and then gave over to our son, is tightly locked away in the trunk I am leaving behind.

Chapter Twenty-two
פרק עשרים ושתיים

Berkeley
Fall, 1971

Find yourself and you find your freedom.

Adrian's final translations raise even more questions I find impossible to let rest in peace. Yet, nearly a week passes before I bring myself to do as he has suggests and contact Rabbi Werner. Finally, late on a Friday morning, I call him.

"I hear upset in your voice, Natalie. You must come today. I am waiting for you," he says when I ask if he has time to see me.

On the one-hour walk to the rabbi's office, I stop at the corner kiosk to select a bouquet of flowers as my offering for his kindness. It is a pleasant day, and I take my time, marveling at how, in a few short months, my life has turned completely inside out. I could have a half-brother or half-sister I have little hope of ever knowing. My cousin Emily, her two children, and I might be the only ones left to carry forth a German bloodline that Hitler would have permanently eradicated if my grandmother had not made the decision to come to America earlier in the century. I'm not sure how to respond to this inheritance, bestowed on me by a mother I never really knew and will never understand. Yet, the obligation to respond in some meaningful way sits heavy on my heart. The only thing I am truly certain of is that no matter what the answers to the questions occupying so much rent-free space in my head reveal, they will be better than having no answers at all.

"Ah, Natalie, come in… please. I am honored you are entrusting your troubles to me. Keeping them bundled up inside yourself corrodes the soul," Rabbi Werner smiles when I knock lightly then peek around his office door. Perhaps it is my imagination, or just the light through the window at this time of day, but even with his oxygen hooked onto his face, his color is a little duskier than the last time I saw him. He now has a window air conditioner, which improves the effect of the pipe smoke polluting his office, giving the flowers a chance to smile at him for at least a day or two before wilting from smoke inhalation.

"You are too kind to such an old man. I hope you saved a few for Adrian," he says, not making much effort to hide his pleasure at receiving a half dozen big, bright yellow sunflowers. He motions me to the chair in front of his desk, then apologizes for not coming around to sit beside me.

"Today is a day when I need more oxygen, and this tube I'm tethered to doesn't stretch very far," he scowls. Once we are finally settled, he asks for details on what brought me to him. I explain that Adrian finished translating the last of my mother's fragmented diary entries and I have questions I hope he can help me with. Assuring me he is honored to try, he adjusts his oxygen dial, then repositions the yarmulke constantly doing battle with his slightly deranged hair.

"There is a reason Einstein never wore one of these," he mumbles, then says to pay him no mind and instead describe what brought me to him on this lovely afternoon.

"I hardly know where to begin. There is so much to try to digest, and all I'm trying to do is understand the mysterious woman who claimed to be my mother – so to speak," I complain.

"Begin anywhere – at the beginning, in the middle, or with what is bothering you the most. The important thing is to begin somewhere and see where it takes you," the rabbi wisely counsels.

"My mother refers to a German organization known as the Bund as an active pro-Nazi organization in Los Angeles, and implies she participated in spying on them. I have no idea what to make of this."

"It is sadly true that there was a German-led, pro-Nazi movement across America in the 1930's as Hitler's evil was raping and pillaging Europe. President Roosevelt, may his memory be for a blessing, was nervous about this but limited in his ability to do anything about it. The president was a good and decent man who was very friendly with Jews – had several in his cabinet. But not everyone believed more Jews in America was a good idea. Many made no secret about thinking it was a very bad idea."

"Limited how?"

"Congress set immigration quotas, tying Roosevelt's hands in terms of admitting Jews as refugees. Most Jews believed he wished to do all that he possibly could do to help, but allowing more Jews into the country would have been a huge political risk for him." I admit I don't understand any of this.

"It was complicated, liebling. No one really believed Jews were being murdered across Europe, and certainly not in the numbers claimed. Government officials Roosevelt depended upon for information told him the mass genocide reports were rumors and exaggerations – nothing more. The much greater concern was figuring out what to do about the threats posed by an increasingly militaristic Germany on the move, led by a rabid fascist." Becoming more agitated, the gentle rabbi stops for a breath before continuing.

"A Polish resistance fighter, Jan Karski, came to America to plead the cause of the Jews. He met with several high-ranking government officials, including Roosevelt and United States Supreme Court Justice Felix Frankfurter, who was not the first Jew to serve on the high court. Frankfurter's foolish response was that he was not calling Karski a liar, but he didn't believe him either, claiming there was a difference between those two concepts. The honorable Justice was a brilliant legal mind and very skilled at splitting hairs, and a very poor excuse for a Jew. His response was shameful, and his memory is not, for me, a blessing," Rabbi Werner exclaims, taking as deep a breath as he is able.

"Most officials had no qualms about refusing entry to ships bringing Jewish refugees seeking asylum in the United States, and thousands were turned back. Basically, America was sentencing them to death." The distress of relating this brings on a heavy coughing episode that causes the old rabbi to stop speaking, unable to catch his breath. I go into the hallway in search of water. Without looking up, his secretary hands me a cup and points to the drinking fountain down the hall. I return with the water, then sit with my hands in my lap, quietly waiting while he drinks it, then rests until his color improves, to the extent it ever does. After thanking me for rescuing him, he continues.

"American citizens were trying to regain their economic footing after the crash of '29. Most weren't' paying much attention to what many believed was merely an altercation between small, neighboring countries a large ocean away and best worked out among themselves without American interference. What was happening to the Jews just wasn't that important in the broader context of the unrest, which always risks civilian casualties. All this occurring in the shadow of lingering dislike – often intense dislike – of Germans that gained a foothold after World War I just made it easier to ignore the Jewish problem… pretend it wasn't happening. Roosevelt did what he could, but it wasn't nearly enough. Many Jews who could've been saved weren't."

"But why pick on the Jews, Rabbi? They weren't doing anything."

"Not everyone would agree with that assumption. Many believed Jews controlled the banking industry, and in a country suffering a deep economic depression that included hundreds of bank failures, blaming the Jews gave them a needed scapegoat that made intellectual sense. German-Americans, driven by fear, felt a strong need to prove their loyalty and patriotism. One naturally easy way to do this was to get organized, then turn on the Jews. This is how the Bund began right after WWI, led by Fritz Julius Kuhn, a bad man who appointed himself the American Fuehrer and convinced other Germans that villainizing the Jews proved they were loyal Americans. Eventually, he developed such strong Nazi sympathies he was deported. But he was not the only Nazi sympathizer. You've heard of Charles Lindbergh? He was a outspoken, powerful antisemite. So was Henry Ford, the Catholic Priest Father Charles Coughlin, and even the pope. It is a very long list. In reality, then and now, more people hate Jews than there are Jews in existence."

"I'm not a student of history, but it seems to me the Jews are the first ones to get blamed for everything. It's as though the world despises us for sport," I note.

"We are despised because we keep surviving, for five thousand years, so far. This is a very strong argument for the belief we really are God's chosen people. By comparison, other religions are here today – gone tomorrow… lasting maybe a few hundred years. They can't claim fifty centuries of unbroken history, which is our strength and their weakness. These newer religions, unsupported by thousands of years of culture and tradition, are the product of men's minds and manipulations of the core beliefs Moses handed down from G-d to the Jews. They tend to forget two things: Jesus, the Christ Christians follow, was a Jew, and the common thread binding us together is we are all Abrahamic religions. We all worship the same G-d; we each just do it a little differently. This is only a problem for those who make it one."

"So, this hatred of Jews is an issue of religious insecurity" I comment.

"Perhaps that is one way to look at it. But Jewish reality includes fighting for our survival, which we've gotten quite good at, because we've had so much practice," Rabbi Werner chuckles, adding that whenever any group becomes too good at something, it invites jealousy from weaker groups, and trouble always follows.

"Judaism is a lived religion – we stay alive by arguing about everything. Some ultra-orthodox spend their entire lives doing nothing except debating the Torah… a little excessive, but how they spend their time is their business. It's the perfect life for those who love to argue and don't mind living off the dole. Two Jews have three opinions on the same thing, three Jews have six opinions, maybe more, depending… I think you get the idea," the wizened rabbi smiles, shaking his head and again adjusting his yarmulke.

"Besides Torah, we have Midrash and Talmud – interpretations of Torah, and one interpretation is maybe as good as the next one – who knows? I certainly don't. But I do know it is this debate that keeps us alive – paying attention – re-interpreting and applying ancient wisdom in the context of modern time, unless you're Hasid, but they are a different conversation. My point is Christians do not discuss. They live by biblical dogma, which is like cement – inflexible and crumbles eventually. They follow men who claim to know the mind of G-d, ignoring the reality that the mind of G-d is unknowable. Christians think everyone is a sinner and must do penance. Jews atone for their sins once a year during High Holy Days and then get on with life, celebrating every chance we get – at least once a week."

"Based upon what you describe, I'm surprised more people aren't drawn to Judaism," I offer.

"They probably would be, if it didn't include being labeled a Jew," Rabbi Werner wheezes.

"What happened in Los Angeles in the 1930's?" I ask, returning to the questions I came seeking answers to. As he begins speaking, Rabbi Werner has another, more frightening attack of coughing that causes me to again dash into the hallway for water.

"Should we call someone?" I motion to his secretary, panicked.

"No – this happens all the time. He'll drink some water then unhook his oxygen to smoke his pipe and settle his nerves. That old Jew is indestructible," she says, not bothering to look up from her typewriter. I hurry back to his office, hand the choking rabbi more water, then watch him do exactly as his secretary predicted.

"If the pipe bothers you, open the window," he says.

"I think you're supposed to keep it closed when the air conditioning is running; otherwise you're letting in too much hot air," I point out.

"Every time I speak, too much hot air escapes," he mumbles.

"Getting back to Los Angeles…" I restart after the rabbi's breathing settles into a pattern of occasional wheezing and intermittent gasps.

"Both Nazis and Fascists were active across Los Angeles, and they were taking orders directly from Hitler and Goebbels, whose quest to conquer the world included taking over the United States. They convinced a couple, Norman and Winona Stephens, to purchase fifty acres above Pacific Palisades, near La Crescenta, to build Hitler a western White House, perfectly situated midway between Berlin and their Japanese allies headquartered in Tokyo. They spent millions building a totally self-sustaining compound that included more than twenty bedrooms, a swimming pool and meeting space. They hired experts to train their sympathizers in marksmanship, urban warfare, and hand-to-hand combat – even formed storm trooper units that held regular paramilitary training exercises. It was extremely well organized. Members wore brown shirts and swastika armbands, attracting armies of brothers in hate – the KKK, Nazi supporters known as Silver Shirts, and other like-minded organizations claiming to be patriotic: the American Nationalist Party, the Christian-American Guard, and the National Protective Order of Gentiles."

"And nobody did anything about it?"

"I didn't say that. Jews haven't survived all this time by ignoring threats to our existence. A Jewish lawyer originally from Wisconsin named Leon Lewis began investigating anti-Semitic hate groups, and recruited fellow WWI veterans, and their wives, to go undercover and join every Nazi and Fascist group in Los Angeles. A brilliant strategy, if you think about it. Your mother was probably among these. It would make sense that she would be very valuable to them because she was a fluent German speaker so would be able to report on conversations in German not meant to be overheard... about things like overthrowing the American government and killing every Jewish man, woman, and child."

"Wow..." is all I can think of to say as Rabbi Werner takes another break to puff on his pipe, further irritating his rattling lungs.

"Lewis understood hate has no national boundaries and made this an American issue instead of merely a Jewish one. Some of his operatives were Christians who regarded the Nazi problem as a moral and patriotic concern, not a religious one, and set about gathering evidence of illegal activities in these groups that they could turn over to the government for prosecution. They were quite surprised to discover the government was either indifferent or actively supporting the Nazi efforts. I think I have information about this somewhere," Rabbi Werner says, rising from his chair and unhooking the inactivated oxygen tube dangling from his neck. He reaches to the bookcase behind his desk, then motions to me to pull a box off the shelf and hand it to him. He rummages through its contents for several minutes before he finds what he is looking for.

"This is a copy of a memo from the Los Angeles Chief of Police,

James Edgar 'Two-Gun' Davis to Leon Lewis after Lewis informed Davis of a Nazi plan to take over control of armories in San Diego and San Francisco, infiltrate Los Angeles's local government and carry through with a plan for mass execution of Jews." He hands me a yellowed piece of paper. Reading through it, it is obvious Chief Davis admired Hitler and supported the Nazi cause.

Germans could not compete economically with the Jews in Germany and had been forced to take the action they did, the police chief wrote, adding that the greatest danger the city faced was not from Nazis but from communists living in the heavily Jewish neighborhood of Boyle Heights. Davis strongly believed every communist was a Jew, every Jew was a communist, and neither could possibly be a patriotic American. Both Jews and accused communists faced double jeopardy.

"My mother mentions Boyle Heights in one of her diaries," I say.

"It is important to understand that Lewis' organization was small – no more than twenty-four or twenty-five people. But they were persistent, and it paid off. They penetrated these groups and foiled their plots and became a remarkably clever and effective underground resistance effort."

"For example?" I ask.

"The Bund planned to murder famous Jewish actors – Eddie Cantor, Charlie Chaplin, James Cagney, Samuel Goldwyn, Al Jolson... Such a Kol Nidre Jolson sang. It breaks your heart, that voice of blessed memory. I have a recording here someplace," Rabbi Werner says, returning to the box. Eventually he hands me a 78-rpm record and a tape reel.

"Take these with you and listen to them. You will never hear anything more beautiful. Jolson takes up residence in your soul and you will never let him leave," he instructs, tears in his eyes. I start to say I don't have anything to play them on, then decide to just figure it out, and promise I'll take good care of these treasures. Assured I grasp his affection for Al Jolson, Rabbi Werner continues.

"The Nazis were going to make like Capone and drive through Boyle Heights gunning down Jews with machine guns. They planned to masquerade as bug exterminators and fumigate Jewish homes with cyanide while across town other Nazis were blowing up military installations and stealing ammunition. These plans failed because Lewis' spies had infiltrated the hate groups and foiled them."

"How?" I ask, by now completely captivated by this story.

"They were clever... found ways to turn the Nazis against each other – a tried-and-true method for defeating an enemy. They spread rumors that the Bund and Silver Shirt organizations had been infiltrated by government informants and inside leakers who, for a price, would sing like canaries, leading to arrests and imprisonment. No one could be trusted, paranoia overtook the leadership, and the organization destroyed itself from within. A simple strategy that works every time…" he smiles proudly.

"Without ever firing a gun, Lewis' little group defeated its enemies, and when Congress finally declared war on Germany, the U.S. government decided to listen to Lewis – widely regarded as the most dangerous Jew in Los Angeles – and undertake its own surveillance. Lewis and his little group became government operatives and continued as informants for the remainder of the war. They refused to allow their homeland to be governed by hate and their actions are the greatest example of how, when government fails to take action against violent extremists, citizens must step up and claim their destiny – not allow someone who does not have their best interests at heart to define it for them. Based upon what you tell me, your mother was similar, Natalie. You should be very proud – she was a very brave woman." Hearing this, tears spill down my cheeks.

"What you must realize is the personal cost a willingness to take a stand against the face of evil extracts from a person. It is a matter of life or death, and your mother chose a life that honored the Talmud mandate telling us we are not bound to complete the work of fixing our broken world, but neither are we free to abandon or ignore it. Your mother did not ignore the evil she saw enveloping the world, she stepped up to do what she could to stop it. It is a great inheritance she has left you, and with it comes an even greater responsibility."

"Thrust upon me by someone I never really knew," I whisper, followed by a deep sigh.

"You may not have known her in life, but you are coming to know her in death… and with this knowledge comes choices you must make."

"I don't understand what you are telling me," I exclaim.

"A great legacy has passed to you, coming from a tradition previously unknown to you. You must first decide whether to accept this bequest and then, if you do accept it, decide how you will live it out, and at what cost. These are not small matters you are facing."

"I don't even know how to think about this, Rabbi Werner. All I know is whatever I decide will upset someone – maybe me, maybe my aunt, maybe my cousin, who is like a sister to me, maybe even my father, although I doubt that. A lot of people, including me, could end up being very distraught. In fact, my aunt, whom I love dearly, is already deeply troubled by this, and I don't know how to handle that."

"Your mother lived her life in denial of who she was, and it was a living death. She was never able to be herself; instead, she existed in constant fear of being found out. Unimaginable, the pain she suffered, without relief. It was a life of constant vigilance, with no space for happiness. Where is the joy in her? It is nowhere, and she would not want to pass that vacant, empty life lived in terror of being discovered as a fraud on to you. Instead, she left enough clues for you to insure you discover who you really are. This is a great gift she has willed to you... one she could not give to you in life."

"I don't think she gave much thought to what she wanted for me..."

"Have mercy and compassion, Natalie. You will never know what your mother suffered, and as her child you should not be expected to understand. But as an adult, you can forgive her and respect her memory. Honor her for the woman she was brave enough to be and forgive her everything else. Most important of all, forgive her failures as your mother. She did the best she could under the circumstances she faced."

"I'm sorry to challenge you, Rabbi, but you have no way to know how hard she did or didn't try to be a mother," I bristle.

"Whether they fail or succeed, all mothers try very hard; they can't help themselves. It is in a mother's blood to love and care for her child. I have never known a situation that was otherwise, and I have known many, many mothers. I meet another one every time one of my students receives a bad grade."

"I still don't know how to think about this. I have no idea where I fit into this story. All I know is I don't want to repeat my mother's life. I want to be authentically me and not pretend to be anybody else. The problem is I'm no longer sure who the authentic me is..." Giving voice to these thoughts, which have been floating in my head for months, brings on a flood of tears. Taking a deep breath, I stop speaking. Rabbi Werner waits until I am calmer before continuing.

"You have inherited big questions, and you cannot force the answers. You must allow clarity to reveal itself in its own time. Waiting can be quite uncomfortable, but if you want the true answers, you have no choice except to trust that they will appear when you are ready to receive them. Otherwise, in the end, you have nothing."

"And in the meantime?"

"In the meantime, you carry on... never abandoning the search but never pushing it further or faster than it is willing to go. Push too hard and you will make mistakes... potentially big mistakes that are difficult to undo. The important thing to remember is that everything comes at a cost – gaining something often means letting go of something else. Not always, of course, but more often than not."

"OK – I see where this is heading. I must determine precisely what the cost of embracing the life that is my birthright is, and then decide whether I want to pay it, which isn't news to me. I'd already figured out that much."

"Then you have clarified the central question surrounding your future."

"I have?"

"The question facing you is whether you are truly willing to pay the cost living your most authentic life will extract from you? Now, you must follow your heart in search of the answer, no matter how long it takes or where the search leads you. A difficult journey is guaranteed, but the intentional life, while the most rewarding, is rarely easy." Seeing that the old rabbi growing tired, I thank him for his time and insights and prepare to take my leave.

"You are in my thoughts and prayers, liebling… as the daughter I never had. Always remember this," he reassures me.

"I already have a wonderful father, but if I ever need another one, you're first on my list," I reply, grasping both his hands in both of mine. We are each tearful. As I am walking out the door, he calls me back.

"Think about having a Yahrzeit for your mother. It will help you put her to rest peacefully," Rabbi Werner says, plowing through the mess of papers on his desk.

"I don't know what that is," I answer.

"It is the ceremony one year after death – to set the permanent marker. It is the final goodbye for this lifetime. I have the prayers here somewhere…" he says, continuing to search. Finally, he hands me a tattered prayer book.

"This one has the English and the Hebrew. Read through the Yahrzeit prayers, and let them speak to you," the rabbi says, in full rabbi mode. Taking the book, I thank him and promise to think about what he has suggested.

"Don't think, Natalie. Just do it. The results may surprise you."

Later that evening, I thumb through the prayer book, which reads like a volume of poetry. I am intensely studying the Yahrzeit when Adrian walks through the door. I don't look up as he sits down beside me, and asks about the book that has so thoroughly captured my attention. I tell him that Rabbi Werner has suggested a ceremony at my mother's gravesite as a way to put her, and everything else, to rest, and has given me the proper prayers.

"He's right, Natalie. Prayer and ritual go a long way toward letting go in peace and love. My suggestion is you do it," Adrian says, reaching for my hand.

"I really wish my dad, and my aunt would also be there. And afterwards, I would like to go to Germany again... explore the country with new eyes and pay my respects at one or two of the death camps. Would you be willing to come with me? I'm not sure this is something I can do alone."

"Of course I'll come with you. I couldn't sleep or eat for days after visiting Auschwitz and I don't have any family members who may have died there. I can't begin to imagine what visiting must be like for those who may have lost loved ones there. I wouldn't want you to go alone," he assures me, squeezing my hand.

"I'm also thinking about going on to Israel. Have you ever thought about returning?"

"Every so often it crosses my mind. You are aware that things are a little politically volatile there right now?"

"When aren't they? It seems to me Israel is destined to be engaged in an eternal struggle for the right to exist, so there's probably no right time to go."

"The red anemones will be blooming... carpeting the western Negev and Dvira Forest of the southern Judean foothills. It's something you need to see."

"Why?"

"They symbolize protection from harm... resiliency... embracing the changes that lead to new beginnings... hope and life's fleeting nature. Some say the red anemone also symbolizes love and passion. To me, seeing them was a glimpse of the promise of life at its very best. It took my breath away," Adrian explains, not bothering to shield the dreamy, far-off look in his eyes.

"I'll discuss the Yahrzeit idea with my dad over tomorrow night's weekly dinner," I whisper, not wanting to break into the reflective silence surrounding him.

My father quickly agrees with Rabbi Werner and Adrian that a final ceremony for my mother is a good idea but isn't sure my aunt will think so. We spend several minutes discussing who should ask her. I suggest it should be him, because she listens to him, and trusts that any idea he has is a good one. My dad insists that because I'm her favorite niece, I should extend the invitation, and he'll back me up.

"I'm not her favorite niece – I'm her only niece," I remind him.

"That's not the point," he smiles. Then he asks whether I plan on trying to find out more about the mysterious trust in the Swiss bank.

"I've decided to leave that alone for now. Apparently, privacy is Switzerland's official state religion, and it would be easier to get information from the Kremlin than from a Swiss banker, so there's not much point in trying." My dad nods his agreement – or his approval. I'm not sure which.

Later that evening, I phone my aunt. She answers on the fourth ring, slightly out of breath. I ask her if she has time to talk and she says she'll call me back in a few minutes.

"I'm at dad's," I remind her. Half an hour later, the phone rings.

"Sorry I couldn't talk before. For reasons known only to him, Mick went grocery shopping, and the entire car was full of crap nobody in their right mind would even consider eating. I had to sort through it before letting him bring anything into the house," my aunt explains. She continues venting her frustration with her husband until she suddenly remembers that I called her earlier and asks me what I want to discuss.

"I've decided I want to go back to Cleveland on the anniversary of my mother's death and have a brief burial service... bless the headstones, and so on. Dad and my friend Adrian have both agreed to come, and I'm hoping you'll come, too."

"Are you talking about a Yahrzeit?" my aunt whispers. A little surprised at hearing her say a Hebrew word, let alone knowing what it means, I acknowledge that's exactly what I'm talking about.

"I don't see how I can do that, Natalie. How could I explain it to Mick?"

"Just say we're having a small graveside service for Charlotte, and you want to be there. You don't need to go into details."

"No, I suppose not. But what about Emily?"

"Same thing. I doubt either of them will ask any questions." My aunt falls silent.

"Am I right in assuming this means you've decided to live as a Jew?" she finally asks.

"Yes... that is what I've decided, Aunt Sally, and I hope you'll come to terms with it, because it's something I have to do."

"You don't have to do it, Natalie. You're deciding to do it."

"We have family members who died in Hitler's death camps. I can't turn my back on that reality. I feel compelled to honor their memory."

"They were distant relatives… no one either of us knew personally. I'm not sure how obligated we are to their memory."

"We are their surviving bloodline, Aunt Sally. Without them, there would be no us. That's a huge obligation." Hearing this, my aunt is so quiet I can hear her breathing through the telephone.

"Here's the thing, Aunt Sally… as I see it, denying my Jewish bloodline is denying those who came before me and disrespecting those Hitler exterminated for no other reason than being Jews. They were plain, ordinary people, living plain, ordinary lives until, all of a sudden, some warp-minded, evil politician decided they didn't deserve to live. I'm the last surviving member of the family willing to honor our Jewish heritage, and I can't turn my back on that responsibility and still live with myself. I desperately wish you to be on this journey with me, but you're the only one who can make that wish come true." Still no response.

"You can come to Cleveland with Dad and barely be gone 24 hours. It would be your chance to meet Adrian…"

"I've been wondering about that. Paul has nice things to say about him," my aunt says, finally rejoining the conversation.

"So that's a yes?"

"I need to think about it, Natalie. I'll let you know," my aunt answers, then, after a pause, says she needs to hang up because she hears Mick coming in from the garage.

"I think she'll do it," I say, smiling.

"That was a nice touch, throwing in Adrian. There isn't an army in the world capable of holding her back from an opportunity to meet your next husband," my dad chuckles.

Chapter Twenty-three
פרק עשרים ושלושה

Auschwitz, Germany
January 1972

What's stopping you? Start repairing the broken world today.

Adrian and I arrive at Auschwitz early on a cold, gloomy Saturday morning. The camp is enveloped in fog so thick it liquefies into a fine mist. Perhaps it is my imagination, but it seems as though the faint smell of smoke and flecks of ash permeate the air.

Descending from the train, my chest knots as I come face to face with a place where the mass extermination of more than one million innocents occurred, in a massacre that began before I was born and continued without cease for the first, nearly four years of my life. But more than tied in knots, I feel honored to pay my respects to extended family members I only know as victims of Hitler's murderous Third Reich, not as living, breathing human beings.

One of these was Avram Weiss, victim number 77320 on the list the International Red Cross compiled. He was the son of my grandmother's brother, making him my mother's first cousin, and my first cousin, once removed. He died here, as did two other family members. Another one succumbed in Dachau; and three more were either gassed or starved to death in Buchenwald. These are the ones I am aware of; others are not yet, and may never be, accounted for. They are people with whom I share a bloodline, yet I will only know them through the horror of their history. I'll never know whether they were musicians, writers, professors, merchants, dressmakers, or something else. Were they tall, short, dark or light haired, brown or blue eyed, funny, serious, intellectual, or frivolous and silly? What they enjoyed, what they didn't like, their politics or how they lived their lives as Jews before the Third Reich imposed its reign of terror on them will remain a mystery. What I do know is that if I am ever to fully understand myself, I must find a way to recognize and appreciate them. I am aware that this is destined to be a long and sometimes very difficult journey, but I have no thoughts of abandoning it.

Less than forty-eight hours ago, my father, my mother's sister, and I were standing together in Agudath Achim Cemetery in Elyria, Ohio where my mother's remains had been laid to rest one year ago. I assume my grandparents are also buried there, and the other markers are tributes to my great grandparents. Our purpose was to honor the Yahrzeit tradition of unveiling the grave marker a year following the death. Technically this wasn't necessary since those markers had been in place for a long time, but a Star of David was added to all of the headstones and the date of Charlotte's death was added to hers. More important, to me, was honoring their lives and deaths in the Jewish tradition we were all born into.

In addition to my aunt and me, a rabbi and a minyan that included my dad and Adrian were present. As a gesture of respect for a family by marriage he only found out about a year ago, yet has often remarked that he wished he had known, my dad wore the tattered yarmulke I found among my mother's possessions. Adrian wore the yarmulke he brought back from an extended spiritual retreat spent working and living on an Israeli kibbutz. The rabbi led us in the Mourner's Kaddish and other prayers, first in Hebrew, followed by English, and then uncovered the headstones. Because none of us had anything to add, the ceremony took less than fifteen minutes.

Unlike the day a year previously, when my dad and I stood under thick, dark clouds, facing a bitter wind off Lake Erie as we buried my mother, on this day the lake was calm, puffy white clouds danced across the winter blue sky above us, and the temperature was slightly above freezing. Later that afternoon we all said goodbye at Cleveland International Airport where Adrian and I boarded a plane for Frankfurt, Germany and my dad and my Aunt Sally returned to California.

Walking away from the Auschwitz train platform we follow the railroad tracks that once held cattle cars jammed with Jews who had been deported to this death camp. Soon we are face to face with an iron archway forming the words "Arbeit Mach Frei" – *Work Makes You Free*. Those words, at the entrance to a labor camp where political prisoners were forced to manufacture supplies and equipment to enable the Third Reich's expansive war machine that was imprisoning, then gassing them, shooting them, or hanging them, is a horrible irony.

RED ANEMONES

"Working here only makes you free because it makes you dead," I whisper to Adrian as, hand-in-hand, we walk silently forward. The entrance to the Auschwitz extermination camp complex is guarded by a rusted railroad gate, currently in the upward position and beyond which are long rows of low brick buildings. The entire area is surrounded by once-electrified barbed wire sharpened to either instantly electrocute or tear away the flesh of anyone who made contact with it. A fine film of ice forms beneath my feet as the mist meets the stone walkways. Ahead of me a small, stooped man with tufts of white hair springing sideways from the tattered yarmulke fastened to the back of his head is shuffling along. A threadbare, off-white prayer shawl stripped in black hangs over his shoulders as he walks gingerly, using a cane for balance. Letting go of Adrian's hand, I catch up to the old man to offer him my arm. He takes it, without looking at me, and we walk in silence until we come to the first barracks. He stops, nods, and rolls up his sleeve to show me five numbers, 49792, tattooed on his forearm.

"You are a survivor," I say in English. Somehow understanding me, he nods, then guides me toward the ovens, where he pauses to recite Mourner's Kaddish, the Jewish prayer for the dead I had recited at my family's grave a few short hours ago, in Hebrew. I motion for Adrian to join us. If the man decides to talk, we'll need a translator. A few minutes later, he begins speaking.

"This entire area is a cemetery. Maybe one million Jews are buried here—it is impossible to know for certain how many," Adrian translates, as the old man sweeps his arms across the barren killing fields. I see a deep scar down one side of his face, permanently closing his right eye. His nose and jaw have both been broken and poorly set, several fingers are missing, and one leg drags.

"May we walk further with you?" Adrian translates for me. The old man nods, saying nothing.

"My name is Natalie, and this is Adrian," I say. Again, Adrian translates and again the man nods.

We walk, slowly and quietly, for nearly an hour, his arm clinging tightly to mine. Occasionally, he stops and gestures at something he wants us to see – gallows, straw on wooden planks where prisoners slept, a photograph on a wall. He isn't compelled to explain anything; instead, he just wants us to truly see what our eyes are looking at… bear witness to the tragedy that defined his life, and there are no words to adequately explain.

"Perhaps this is his way of telling us who he is, and how he wants us to know him," I whisper to Adrian.

"I have family who died here. I did not know them, but I wish I had…" I offer.

"You are alive – you know them," the old man reassures, then leaving me in silence to reflect on this possibility.

"Tell me their names," he asks. I offer those that come immediately to mind, adding that as far as I know, they all lived in or near Hildesheim.

More silence ensues as we continue wandering for another half hour. With so much history written on this old man's face, I have many questions I would like to ask him, but sense that he prefers being alone with his thoughts and would not welcome the intrusion. Quietly, step by step, the three of us walking together takes on a sacred holiness I don't want to interrupt. Instead, I offer him my arm again and with my left hand gently grasp his twisted, fragile fingers.

"Is this your first time coming back here?" I ask.

"I come every week. In good weather sometimes more, but at least once every week," he answers, neither encouraging nor discouraging further questions.

"You didn't relocate to Israel after the war ended?"

"I lost my wife, my children, my brothers, my sisters, my parents – all together the bones and ashes of thirty members of my family are scattered here… not buried in decent, proper graves, but thrown like dead animals into huge holes the ground. Their lives ended here, and my life ended here. There is no reason for me to leave. Abandoning them is abandoning what's left of myself, and I don't know how to do that. Visiting and remembering keeps me alive, but for what purpose is unknown to me," he explains. Unaccustomed to such devotion to grief, which flies in the face of the American mandate to "grieve and move on". The certainty of his resolve is so humbling it embarrasses me into silence.

"Perhaps I survived to bear witness to this evil crime against all of humanity. I do not know, but there is no other reason my life continues when six million other lives did not. Why me to go on living and not my children, or their mother – or any of the others? I ask myself this question every day, and every day there is no answer. I live in the crosscurrent of my memories, saying Kaddish every day, coming here to bear witness to what happened to my family as often as I can, and being grateful to be a Jew who can celebrate Shabbat every Friday. The rabbi told me living on to remember our ancestors, whose memories are the most important blessings in our lives, is our revenge against the evil that rained down on us. I am faithful to those memories but my guilt at being alive when so many died is the sack of rocks I carry with me everywhere I go."

"Isn't remembering difficult?" I ask.

"Forgetting is difficult – impossible, and it should be. Remembering is continuing to love them, and it has never occurred to me to stop doing that. Life is hard and believing its purpose is to be happy is chasing a silly dream. The purpose of life is to be useful, honorable, and compassionate toward others, then maybe a little happiness finds you. Seeking happiness for itself is a selfish waste of precious time that could be put to better use. For me, remembering this terrible tragedy is the most useful I, as an old man, can be. It is not enough, but it is what I can do. Pursuing a life that forgets is to die as if Hitler executed me himself, and I cannot allow him that satisfaction..." the man says, laying bare the soul of who he is with quiet conviction.

"I guess we Americans got it wrong when we settled on a constitution that insists we are entitled to pursue happiness," I whisper to myself, aware that what the old man is saying resonates with something deep inside me pushing to be heard... some small voice that wants to tell me something. Hearing me mumble, the man looks at me with his remaining eye, then at Adrian, and frowns.

"He wants to know if you disagree?" Adrian says.

"Tell him I agree – very strongly agree."

"Good. Otherwise, we have nothing to talk about," the man remarks after Adrian translates my words.

The three of us walk on in comfortable silence, covering a considerable distance. I am surprised the man can walk so far, but he carries on without complaint. He leads us around the area, pointing out more ovens and mass graves, and the ruins of what the Nazi's tried to destroy to hide lingering evidence of their atrocities. We stop frequently to recite Mourner's Kaddish. In fractured Hebrew, I join in, repeating the prayer for the dead again and again... for those in my family who died here and in other death camps and live on in me. Soon the sun begins to set on what I am coming to believe is the most important day of my life.

"It is getting late. You came by train?" he asks. I nod.

"Where will you go?" I ask.

"Onto the bus for two hours, to a Jewish family in Bedzin who took me in after the liberation. They gave me a new family... show me deep kindness and care for me as their own opa, had he survived. I read to the children, take them to the park, prepare the boys for Bar Mitzvah, help keep our traditions alive for them to be proud of. I live two lives – one in mourning and one in celebration and gratitude. This is the biggest slap in

Hitler's ugly face. He thought he could destroy us, but instead, he made us stronger. We show the world he was not only evil, he was also a very, very stupid man to think he could destroy the Jews. We can mourn and celebrate at the same time… we know the secret to an indestructible life."

"Thank you for allowing me to walk with you. I will never forget what happened here, or forget today, or forget you," I say, attempting to swallow the lump forming in my throat.

"This is all I ask – that someone else also remembers. Forgotten history is destined to repeat itself and another wholesale slaughter of Jews is not an impossibility." The old man bows slightly toward me as he turns to walk in the opposite direction of the train station. I start to call after him to ask his name, then think better of it. If he wanted me to know, he would have told me. A moment later, he turns around.

"You belong to the innocents who died. Honor them as a good Jew, by using your life to repair the brokenness you find in the world. Tikkun Olam is your inherited obligation to those who were not granted the full life you have been given. Do not waste it – use it for good… to triumph over unspeakable, incomprehensible evil… to prove Hitler wrong," he commands. He walks a few more steps then stops again.

"We were Jacob and Hedvig Weiss, coming originally from Hanover." Hearing this, I stand perfectly still and begin shivering. Adrian puts his arm around me, hugging me close.

"It's a common Jewish surname, Natalie. There's no way to know for sure…"

It Takes a Village
זה דורש כפר

Originally, my inspiration for writing this book was my newly-discovered Jewish great-grandmother. However, before I could write a word of her story, I had to convince myself to embark on an adventure into a world that, while it is my heritage, is one I knew almost nothing about in ways that would be useful for credible storytelling. It turned out I loved every minute of the following nearly two years I devoted to learning about Judaism's culture, traditions, and widely varying spiritual approaches to life from both original and secondary sources.

As every Jew knows, it is impossible to learn everything there is to know about Judaism in one lifetime and my effort was a tiny dip into the bucket holding five thousand years of Jewish history that took on an intensity that rivaled writing another doctoral dissertation. Ultimately, my biggest takeaway is that there are nearly sixteen million Jews in the world, nearly sixteen million different ways to be Jewish and at least sixteen million Jewish opinions on everything!

While my great-grandmother motivated me to write this story, my inspiration came from the six million Holocaust victims whose memories I am personally committed to preserving in all ways possible. Simply thinking about distant extended family members I have reason to believe perished in the Holocaust provided great encouragement. I don't know anything about any of them, other than they lived and then, because of a murderous Third Reich that overtook their homeland, died far too soon. I don't know whether there were any musicians, scholars, scientists, lawyers or merchants among them, or whether they were a simple collection of ordinary people, with a few shady characters thrown in to make the family more interesting… and it doesn't matter. Each person who died in the Shoah was a human being whose right to live a full life was violently stolen from them, and they deserve to be acknowledged for having once existed on earth. This book is my way of paying my respects to them all, no matter who they were. We may not be closely related by blood, but we are brothers and sisters bound together by our common Jewish heritage and five-thousand-year-old rituals and traditions.

Although I strongly suspect but cannot, with absolute certainty, claim to be directly descended from the victims of the most heinous crimes humankind can visit upon itself, the "Never Again" concept is real to me, and I strongly believe that evil prevails when good people remain silent… that when injustice threatens, there can be no sidelines and no silent observers who just stand idly by. This book is my way of not remaining silent and not standing idly by.

I am deeply grateful to Arolsen Archives #everynamecounts for allowing me to join the team of volunteers who are recording the names of the 17.5 million victims and survivors of Germany's darkest hours under a fascist regime driven by unwavering national socialism. The act of writing these names into perpetuity introduced me to real people who led real lives of deep suffering not of their own making. They became my imaginary friends and an army of muses who gave this story a life of its own and pushed me to keep going whenever my writing hit a brick wall.

As always, deep gratitude to my award-winning writer husband, who is the world's best proofreader as well as my most trusted critic. I am also deeply grateful to the Jewish Book Council for pushing against the growing antisemitism in the publishing industry, for their commitment to Jewish storytelling, and for their generosity in offering the resources and connections to ensure this happens. They bring Tikkun Olam to life by repairing the world one story at a time.

About the Author
אודות המחבר

A writer's only purpose is to keep civilization from destroying itself.

A native Californian, **Paula Dáil** is an emerita research professor of social welfare and public policy and award-winning author. Widely published in the social sciences, she has also been recognized for her non-fiction and fiction writing, both under own name and her pen name, Avery Michael. She is the recipient of first or second place Readers' Favorite, Readers' Choice, Independent Publisher, Bookfest and Literary Titan awards, two non-fiction book-of-the-year awards, a Booklist Starred Review and several other five-star reviews, including Goodreads, The Book Commentary, and Independent Book Review. She holds a PhD from the University of Wisconsin-Madison and lives with her husband and dog in the Great Lakes region of the Upper Midwest. *Red Anemones* is her tenth book.

For more, visit www.paula-dail.com; Facebook.com/paula.dail.73; Facebook.com/paula.dail.books.

www.historiumpress.com